ORNAMENTATION
AND IMPROVISATION
IN MOZART

Frederick Neumann

Ornamentation and Improvisation in Mozart

Princeton University Press

1986

To Mozart,
this modest token of gratitude

Contents

Preface

A previous book of mine, *Ornamentation in Baroque and Post-Baroque Music*, aimed mainly at freeing the "small," symbol-indicated ornaments from the rigid rules that modern scholarship had imposed on them. As a sequel to this endeavor, Part I of the present study attempts to extend a comparable liberalization to Mozart's small ornaments by offering evidence that this master's *Vorschlag*, slide, trill, turn, and arpeggio had a wider range of freedom and flexibility than is usually believed to be the case. Since a good deal of documentation in the earlier volume is pertinent to the present one I often refer to the former to avoid having to repeat such material *in extenso*.

Part II, under the heading "Improvisation," addresses the problem of pitches that the performer was expected to add to Mozart's text. Such additions, which today are more often prepared than improvised, range widely from single notes to lengthy cadenzas. The purpose here is to explore where such additions are necessary, where optional, where improper, and to offer guidelines for their desirable form and design.

In the course of my research I examined over 250 of Mozart's autographs (not counting those of fragments), either the originals, or facsimile prints, photostats, xerox copies, or microfilms. Included were many of the priceless manuscripts (owned by the Staatsbibliothek Berlin) that, sequestered since the end of World War II at the Biblioteka Jagiellonska in Krakow, were only very recently made available to research in the form of microfilms.

Many of the music examples in the book are based on autographs, which for reasons to be presently given, are almost always the primary source for Mozart. Where autographs did not survive or were not accessible to me, I had to have recourse to what seemed the next best sources. Among first editions those by André in Offenbach stand out for their reliability (as attested to by those works for which autographs survive), whereas those by Viennese and Parisian publishers are more questionable. The *NMA*, with its analytical prefaces and probing *Kritische Berichte* (which are, alas, slow in appearing) offered an indispensable supplement, incomplete as it is at the time of writing. Once in a while I had to use the old *W.A.M.*, which varies greatly in dependability, with some volumes remarkably trustworthy, others far less so.

In the music examples, notation and clefs were modernized; thus, for example, single 16th- or 32nd-notes that Mozart wrote ♪ and ♪ were transcribed as ♪ and ♪ respectively. When Mozart failed to mark the obligatory slur between a *Vorschlag*-type ornament and its parent note, because he took the linkage for granted, the slurs were filled in without comment.

For the sake of simplicity and readability I speak of "piano sonatas" or "piano concertos" in full awareness that Mozart's principal keyboard instrument was the fortepiano. For the same reason "violin sonata" stands for the more accurate "violin-(forte)piano sonata." English translations are mine unless otherwise indicated.

Source materials are usually gathered together; easily spotted, they can be omitted by readers more concerned with practical suggestions than their historical background.

Readers may find some discrepancies between the way the various numbers of an opera are indicated in the music examples and the way they are listed in their own editions. Such discrepancies stem from the different ways in which various editions number those pieces that Mozart wrote for a later performance of a work. Thus, for example, Donna Elvira's aria "Mi tradì quell' alma ingrata," written for the Vienna performance of 1788, is 21b in *NMA* and *W.A.M.*, 23 in the sixth edition of Köchel, 8c in Einstein's Eulenburg score (which, in accord with Mozart's own practice, restarts the numbering with Act II.) Here I tried, whenever possible, to follow the numbering of the *NMA*.

Another difficulty refers to the measure numbers for arias that are preceded by an accompanied recitative. Some editions number both sections without interruption, others restart the aria with measure 1. Here the numbers restart.

Chapter 12 on the recitative presents yet another problem of identification. Practically all secco recitatives occur *between* numbers; hence in that specific chapter, the arabic numerals often refer to scenes, not numbers (and are so marked).

The readers' indulgence is solicited for the inconvenience of any adjustment they may have to make in locating a particular example.

Acknowledgments

The work on this book stretched out for many years and, understandably, involved much travel and considerable expense. Without the generous support of various foundations it would have been physically impossible to undertake this project. Hence, my first thanks have to go to these benefactors: the National Endowment for the Humanities for a fellowship; the John Simon Guggenheim Memorial Foundation for a (second) fellowship; the American Council of Learned Societies for a (fourth) grant-in-aid; the American Philosophical Society for a (second) grant-in-aid; the University of Richmond, before my retirement, for a final research grant.

I am greatly indebted to my colleagues George Buelow and Alfred Mann who have read a few chapters and given me, along with splendid advice, great encouragement. Dr. Wolfgang Rehm and Dr. Wolfgang Plath, both from the Mozart Institute, have been most generous in lending me xeroxes and microfilms of autographs that would not have otherwise been accessible to me, notably those of the large collection of "Cracow" autographs mentioned in the Preface. Both Dr. Rehm and Dr. Plath have also kindly shared with me their expertise on various matters concerning this study. I am deeply grateful for their helpfulness. Professor Marius Flothuis and my good friend Eva Badura-Skoda have both obliged me by giving informative answers to various enquiries. I am also greatly indebted to my editor, Barbara Westergaard, for her invaluable help with idiom and style, and for the extraordinary care with which she detected countless lapses and inconsistencies. Barbara Anderson has earned my gratitude for having prepared the index with painstaking devotion and expert precision.

In the various libraries I have been helped by so many that I find it hard to single out individuals. I have to content myself with expressing collective thanks to the staffs of the Music Division of the Library of Congress; the Music Division of the New York Public Library; the Pierpont Morgan Library; the Bibliothèque Nationale; the British Library; the Deutsche Staatsbibliothek, East Berlin; the Staatsbibliothek Preussischer Kulturbesitz, West Berlin; the Österreichische Nationalbibliothek; the Gesellschaft der Musikfreunde, Vienna; the Internationale Stiftung Mozarteum and the Mozart Institute in Salzburg. I do have to mention Bonlyn G. Hall, music librarian of the University of Richmond, who over the years has been unfailingly helpful in securing needed materials for me.

Finally a word of thanks to my wife, Margaretta, for her patience and for her determination in overcoming my resistance to acquiring a word processor (which considerably speeded up the proceedings). She taught me that age should be no deterrent to moving profitably with the times.

List of Abbreviations

aut.	autograph
Badura-Skoda	Eva Badura-Skoda and Paul Badura-Skoda, *Interpreting Mozart on the Keyboard,* trans. Leo Black, London, 1962.
BN	Bibliothèque Nationale
GMF	Archives of the Gesellschaft der Musikfreunde, Vienna
K 00 (00)	*Köchel Verzeichnis,* 6th ed. (numbers of 1st ed. in parentheses), Wiesbaden, 1965
MGG	*Die Musik in Geschichte und Gegenwart,* 16 vols., ed. Friedrich Blume, Kassel, 1949–1979
MJb	*Mozart Jahrbuch*
NMA	*Neue Mozart Ausgabe,* Kassel, 1955–
ÖNB	Österreichische Nationalbibliothek
Ornamentation	Frederick Neumann, *Ornamentation in Baroque and Post-Baroque Music,* Princeton, 1978
W.A.M.	*W.A. Mozarts Werke,* Gesamtausgabe, Leipzig, 1876–1905

PART I
THE ORNAMENTS

Introduction

———◆•◆———

Not long ago most scholars were certain that they had all the answers about Mozart's symbolized ornaments, and even today many still cling to this belief. Their answers are derived from two simple rules: all ornaments start on the beat, and trills have to start with the upper note. These rules have been applied to all 18th-century composers and to a number of 19th-century ones; hence Mozart was only one among many. The practice was based on several old theorists who conveyed these principles mainly through ornament tables, but the book that most profoundly influenced modern thought on 18th-century ornamentation, including Mozart's, was C.P.E. Bach's famous treatise in which he proclaimed the two rules both verbally and graphically.

Having written before at some length about proper and improper research procedures in the field of historical performance,[1] I shall be very brief on these matters and only add a few remarks that concern Mozart's usage.

We must not belittle the importance of historical documents on performance, but we must keep them in proper perspective; that is, we have to be aware of their usually high degree of abstraction, aware also of the fact that ornaments lend themselves to regulation less than perhaps any other musical matter. In this connection the modern French organist and scholar Antoine Geoffroy-Dechaume used a felicitous expression that could well serve as the motto to this whole first part: "It is sufficient," he wrote, "to be aware of the great variety of execution of which each grace is susceptible to realize *the inanity of ornament tables* [l'inanité des tables], which offer only a single transcription for each grace and one, to boot, that is mostly only a pattern without musical merit."[2]

What is bad and dangerous about ornament tables is not the individual model, which is often written by eminent musicians and which gives us a *general* idea of the ornament's design, but the way in which modern scholars and musicians apply its design with unmerciful literalness to each and every occurrence of its symbol. It is, briefly, the fatal blunder of mistaking the abstract for the concrete, the general for the specific, not realizing that the abstract idea has to be in each case adapted to the requirements of the concrete individual situation. Bad enough in itself, the blunder is magnified by the scholars' cherished belief in a "common practice" that justifies the automatic transfer of any theoretical statement, be it a rule or an ornament table, to any composer of the same century.

Such a "common practice" is a chimera for *any* period. At a given time we find certain conventions of performance, but they never cover every detail, and vary from one country, region, or school to another, from one composer to the next. Hence to "apply" a rule from a treatise to another master's music, let alone to that of a unique genius, is a dangerous procedure, comparable to a surgical transplant

---

[1]"The Use of Baroque Treatises on Musical Performance," *Music & Letters,* vol. 48 (1967), pp. 315–324; "External Evidence and Uneven Notes," *Musical Quarterly,* vol. 52 (1966), pp. 448– 464; both reprinted in *Essays in Performance Practice,* chs. 1 and 5 respectively; *Ornamentation,* ch. 3.

[2]"L'appoggiature ancienne," p. 91.

of a vital organ that can succeed only on condition of full compatibility and superb surgical skill—a condition, needless to say, that is difficult to achieve.

A transfer of rules from C.P.E. Bach to Mozart's music does not pass the test of compatibility. The child Mozart had close rapport with Johann Christian Bach, but the aesthetic of Philipp Emanuel was alien to him. Some scholars turn for answers to Leopold Mozart, but though he was Wolfgang's first and almost his only personal teacher, relying on him is not without danger either. Not only did Wolfgang receive brief guidance from, for example, Padre Martini, he also vastly extended his father's instruction by hearing and studying the music of other masters. From his earliest childhood he absorbed the immensely rich and varied musical experiences to which he was exposed during his foreign travels in childhood and adolescence. Whole libraries have been written trying to explore and dissect the reflections of these influences on the evolution of his style. Thus it would be simplistic to think that Leopold's book could provide us with ready answers to the many questions we have to ask. We must not disparage Leopold's principles, but the greater danger is to overrate the father as a source because the son's genius took such early flight that he emancipated himself from paternal tutelage far sooner musically than personally.

To minimize the danger while increasing the usefulness of old theorists we must look at a wide spectrum of treatises, not just the usual famous two or three. In so doing we get a revealing picture of agreements and disagreements that mirror diversified practices. Their variety alone should free us from monolithic orthodoxy and will do so even more effectively if we take care not to mistake the abstract for the concrete. I therefore generally start the discussion of each individual ornament with a survey of theoretical sources that could conceivably have some relevance.

Whatever weight we may ascribe to the theorists, we have to resort to *musical* evidence to get a direct bearing on Mozart's usage. If such evidence can be reasonably established, it bypasses the problems of both compatibility and abstractness by pointing to a specific spot in his music. This spot is then likely to shed light on analogous ones.

We can derive *external* evidence from Mozart's exceptionally clear autograph notation, which often provides performance clues and besides represents in almost all cases the definitive text. By contrast, nonautograph evidence can be misleading, and first editions in particular, even those published in Mozart's lifetime, can be deceptive. When they vary from the autograph, as they frequently do, we have no right to assume that the changes were prepared or authorized by Mozart. We do know that one or another student, like Josephine Ammerhauer, did some proofreading for him, but as I was told by Alexander Weinmann, the foremost authority on Viennese publishers of the classical era, and coeditor of the sixth edition of the Köchel catalogue, we have no evidence that, with the exception of the six quartets dedicated to Haydn, Mozart ever proofread any of his own printed works. Publishing houses like Torricella, Artaria, or Hoffmeister had editors who were composers and who often took the liberty of arbitrarily changing the text to their liking. Thus when we find discrepancies between autograph and first edition, only a very careful stylistic analysis can suggest, though hardly ever prove, that the changes originated with Mozart.

We can gather important information from *internal* evidence that is based on musical logic (or just plain musical common sense) in the light of what Mozart's letters reveal about his ideas on performance. In these letters we find a pervasive stress on musicianship, expression, and taste—*"gusto"* as he calls it—as final arbiter in matters of execution.[3] This means that ornamentation too in all its aspects is governed not by rules but by the higher imperative of taste, expression, musical sense. It further means that we have the right to resort to our musical judgment—refined, let it be hoped, by a thorough grounding in Mozart's style—to decide what makes the best sense in a particular circumstance. The alternative is to go strictly by the book and be victimized by the "inanity of ornament tables" or by the inanity of other similar items lifted with uncritical reverence from old texts.

Skeptics may say that what we conceive of as musical sense might not agree with Mozart's concepts. There is no way to disprove such an argument. But we have good reason to assume that no fundamental change has occurred in the aesthetics of performance; that what Mozart called *gusto* will still be artistically compelling today and that we would be as moved and enchanted by Mozart's playing as were Clementi, Dittersdorf, and other eminent contemporaries. In particular nothing that Mozart himself reveals about his artistic ideas appears dated today. We are therefore on fairly firm ground in assuming the basic identity of an informed, cultivated taste of today with the one Mozart expected to encounter in his audiences. Also, since there is no conceivable way in which we can discover all the details of Mozart's intentions, it seems preferable to meet the challenges of his music with a musical rather than an archival approach.

On the basis of these considerations I shall, in addition to making use of whatever facts are known, draw on musical sense as a means to explore plausible solutions to Mozart performance problems in the field of ornamentation. I say 'plausible' solutions, because in matters of historical performance there are very few definite answers—beginning with the very concept of what constitutes historical performance.

Concerning ornaments, there are cases where the answer is reasonably clear, many others where we can aim only at approximations. Hence in this first part I suggest solutions on a scale that ranges from near certainty to wider options, where alternatives of roughly equal merit are available. The book tries to guide without issuing marching orders; in the end performers cannot escape the responsibility of their own artistic judgment.

[3]The French had long before stressed this point, and whenever they proclaimed rules, they explicitly or implicitly subjected them to the veto power of the *goût*. Among Germans, Mattheson was the most eloquent spokesman for the primacy of the ear over any rule.

1 The *Vorschlag*: Types, Terms, Symbols, Sources

———◆———

TYPES AND TERMS

For want of a satisfactory alternative, the German word *Vorschlag* (plural *Vorschläge*) will be used as a generic term for any single ornamental pitch that precedes its principal note, is slurred to it, and in vocal music, shares with it the same syllable. The specific term "appoggiatura" will stand for those *Vorschläge* that fall on the beat, "grace note" for those that precede the beat. Normally an appoggiatura is emphasized, a grace note unaccented.

Since appoggiaturas vary in length, most theorists distinguish a "long" and a "short" type (Badura-Skoda, pp. 70–71). "Long" and "short" are of course relative terms, and their dividing line is accordingly vague. Nevertheless the differentiation is useful because length adds a new dimension to the character of the grace. A very brief and strongly accented appoggiatura will make a rhythmic impact but hardly a harmonic or expressive one. Also, "long" does not have to be mathematically defined.[1] An appoggiatura that takes only a relatively small part of the principal note can still be "long" when it is amenable to expressive nuance or the creation of a perceptible harmonic effect. If not capable of such effects it is "short." It is in this reasonably well circumscribed sense that I shall use these terms.

SYMBOLS AND THEIR RATIONALE

Why did Mozart, along with all of his contemporaries and many masters of the next generation, use symbols, when with no more, and often with less, trouble he could have indicated his intentions with regular notes? For the grace note the symbol is an obvious convenience that cuts through the notational complexities of compound ties, rests, or dots and for that reason is used to the present day; hence the question centers on the appoggiatura. Here the answer seems to have several components. One of these may be the different treatment in expression and dynamics that an appoggiatura calls for, such as the type of emphasis it ought to receive. Tartini may have been the first to point to the difference in execution between a symbolized long appoggiatura and a corresponding pitch written out in regular notes. The former, he says, should replace a metrical accent by starting gently, then swelling and tapering the grace (see *Ornamentation,* pp. 174–175). Whatever the application of this principle might be for Mozart, the symbol generally invites greater dynamic and rhythmic flexibility than would a regular note. By contrast, a short appoggiatura is likely to summon a stronger accent than that called for by its metrical position alone. Leopold Mozart gave another answer to justify the symbol: it indicates, he says, that an ornament is already in place and

[1] L. Mozart calls an appoggiatura "long" that takes one half the value of the principal note, however short the latter.

serves as a warning to an unmusical performer not to add another *Vorschlag* on top of the one indicated.[2] Wolfgang often uses the symbol as a notational convenience. Whereas he very often writes in regular notes a 1:3 rhythmic ratio such as ♪♩ he hardly ever writes out a greater short-long disparity where he would have had to use one or more ties such as . To avoid such complication, he resorts to the symbol as illustrated in Ex. 1.1 from the C minor Mass.[3]

Ex. 1.1. K 417a (427) Gloria

Less certain is the role of the reasons occasionally given that the symbols served either to clarify the harmony by pointing up the dissonance, or to camouflage impurities of voice leading. True, we find symbols more frequently for dissonances, but they do occur on consonances too; true, too, that the symbols are often written for pitches that would not pass muster with Palestrina, (but would with Monteverdi), and many that are written for dissonances are prepared in full conformance with the rules of strict counterpoint. It seems that a major factor was the inertia of notational habits that continued to assert themselves after their original raison d'être had ceased to exist. More will be said on this matter in connection with the formulas and .

THE THEORISTS ON THE APPOGGIATURA

In turning to theoretical documents I shall be very brief in dealing with the appoggiatura, both long and short, for here we find large areas of agreement among the writers. I shall have to go into greater detail for the grace note, which is controversial and receives from the theorists a far less unified and at times ambiguous treatment.

Concerning the *long appoggiatura,* Tartini speaks of the *appoggiatura lunga ossia sostenuta* and gives the since much repeated rule that such an appoggiatura takes one half of a binary, two-thirds of a ternary note (see *Ornamentation,* pp. 174–175). He limits the use of this type of grace to slow expressive pieces, to heavy beats, and to rhythmic contexts where the principal note is longer than the ones that follow, such as . Geminiani allows the long appoggiatura more than half the length of any note (see *Ornamentation,* pp. 173–174).

For the long appoggiatura many German theorists after mid-century follow Tartini's rule about the binary and ternary notes, among them Quantz, C.P.E. Bach, L. Mozart, Marpurg, Agricola, Löhlein, Petri, Milchmeyer, Kalkbrenner, Lasser, Müller, Koch, Türk, and a number of others. Some theorists, for example

---

[2] *Versuch einer gründlichen Violinschule,* 1756 ed., ch. 9, par. 3.

[3] For other illustrations see Exx. 2.7a, 3.4, 3.12a and b, and many more.

Galeazzi, assign the appoggiatura before a ternary note only one-third of the latter's value; others, like Clementi, offer both alternatives.

C.P.E. Bach, Quantz, and L. Mozart, the three pre-eminent mid-century theorists present another long appoggiatura pattern, not mentioned by Tartini, Geminiani, or any Frenchman. In it the appoggiatura, which could be called "overlong," takes the whole value of the principal note if the latter is followed by either a tie or a rest: [musical notation]

C.P.E. Bach contrasts the long "variable" *(veränderlich) Vorschlag* with the short "invariable" *(unveränderlich)* species. The latter's appoggiatura character is established by its being struck on the beat and being accented. Marpurg, Agricola, and Türk follow Bach in this distinction and so do many other German theorists, notably the clavier players. It is interesting that Tartini, Quantz, and L. Mozart, writing about melody instruments, are silent on the issue of the short appoggiatura. They limit themselves to describing the long appoggiatura and the grace note. Pleyel, a Haydn student, translates [musical notation] into [musical notation] and so does Cardon in circa 1786.[4]

THE GRACE NOTE

In Mozart's vocal music the appoggiatura in its long form predominates decisively. It is primarily in his instrumental music that the grace note plays a large role; here the incidence of appoggiatura and grace note is roughly comparable. Under the spell of C.P.E. Bach, many scholars, editors, and performers still consider the grace note to be illegitimate for Mozart. To counter this point of view it will be helpful to show what other old theorists had to say on this subject. Before reporting their opinions some clarifications need to be made.

The short-appoggiatura–grace-note contrast is not as clear-cut as one might assume. The difference between the two types of *Vorschläge* is more than a simple matter of prebeat or onbeat placement; it is, as briefly mentioned before, also a matter of dynamics. Normally the grace note is weaker, the appoggiatura stronger than their respective principal notes. Hence when C.P.E. Bach and many of his followers insist on the precise onbeat start of the *Vorschlag* they logically stipulate that the *Vorschlag* ought to be stressed. The very point of onbeat execution is the greater prominence achieved by the placement into the metric-rhythmic highlight of a strong beat. The accentuation of the beat being the usual procedure, we perceive a distinctly accented *Vorschlag* as an appoggiatura even if, for whatever reason, it should fall ever so slightly before or after the exact mathematical point of the beat. If, on the other hand, the accent falls clearly on the principal note and the *Vorschlag* is rendered fast and soft, we perceive the latter as a grace note even if the *Vorschlag* happens to coincide with the beat. On the strength of these considerations, a theorist, speaking of short *Vorschläge*, who stipulates that the accent should fall on the principal note and the *Vorschlag* be treated "lightly" or "fleetingly" or "flatteringly" gives the classical description of the grace note as perceived by the ear, even if the same theorist requires by word, implication, or illustration, that the *Vorschlag* fall on the beat.

By spontaneous musical impulse an accent seeks the beat, and the soft

[4]Ignaz Pleyel, *Klavierschule*, p. 6; Jean-Guillain Cardon, *Le rudiment de la musique*, p. 44.

antecedent to an accent seeks the rhythmic shade before the beat.[5] Exceptions to the spontaneous functional relationship of accent and beat occur often in ensembles through unintended imprecision or, in solo playing, in an occasional rubato intent, as agogic inflections. The latter can have the charm of the unexpected but would turn into an insufferable mannerism when repeated routinely. The result would be a mechanical pattern, standardized like a prefabricated fixture with no trace of the freedom that is part of the rubato's essence. True, C.P.E. Bach prescribes such an unnatural dynamic pattern for the *Anschlag* (a kind of two-note *Vorschlag* whose pitches straddle that of the principal note), and a few later theorists call for the same reverse pattern for the short *Vorschlag*. Most prominent among the latter are Koch and Türk who thereby, probably unwittingly, promote the grace note. (The Badura-Skodas are mistaken in reporting that L. Mozart also asks for the unaccented downbeat rendition of the short *Vorschlag*. He never mentions the downbeat in this connection, and all his explanations point to prebeat meaning.)

Apart from the sense of affectation emanating from a routinely applied reverse dynamic pattern, it is for a simple reason highly improbable that anybody, including the authors themselves, followed this prescription with any degree of consistency. Such reverse dynamics are feasible only in a slow tempo, before single, long principal notes. The faster the tempo, the less feasible they become. We never find Mozart, nor presumably any other classical master, combining his frequently spelled-out "Lombard" rhythm ♪♫ ♪♫ with reverse dynamics ♫, not
p f
even in slow tempos. The very point of the Lombard rhythm is the snap effect produced by the accentuation of the short note. If, instead of accenting the short note we deemphasize it while keeping it on the beat, the resulting pattern becomes unidiomatic in a fast tempo, and indeed, impracticable for *any* medium.[6] Without an inordinate effort, it is simply too unnatural to be maintained for any length of time. We can thus safely assume that a directive for reverse dynamics will, in the vast majority of cases, result in grace-note rendition.

Fortunately, a number of editors of the *NMA* have taken the theoretically innovative step of suggesting grace notes in many cases that would be frowned upon by many modern scholars, but where artists, following their musical instinct have used them for a long time and keep using them because nothing else makes musical sense. Also, the Badura-Skodas in their fine book make a case for using grace notes, though a more limited one than I believe to be in order. Thus the sanction given to the grace note by a number of eminent Mozart scholars greatly facilitates my task in staking out the large role this *Vorschlag* type ought to play in Mozart's music. It does not, however, relieve me from taking a thorough look at the question. Not only is the *NMA* inconsistent, unavoidably so in view of the multitude of editors, but often the editors do not make any performance suggestions, and when they do, they often understate the role of the grace note.

[5]This musico-psychological phenomenon must not be confused with an intended syncopation where an accent conflicts with the metrical pulse. For a syncopation to be perceived as such, a time span must elapse that is distinct enough not to be taken for an accident or a slight agogic shift.

[6]Readers are invited to test this proposition by clapping a fast beat and trying to sing, perhaps to the syllables *ta-rà*, a simple melodic pattern in Lombard rhythm with reversed dynamics. With practice and great effort they may succeed a few times, but it won't take many claps before either the dynamics disappear, or the *rà* starts coinciding with the beat. Made with instruments, such an experiment will yield the same results.

In *Ornamentation* I presented a wide assortment of theoretical and musical evidence about anticipated ornamentation in general, and grace notes in particular—evidence that reached well into the period of Mozart's life. As before, I shall limit myself to brief résumés of the theorists discussed in that study, referring the reader to the book's more detailed discussions and adding new material mainly from the latter part of the century.

Very enlightening is Tartini's discussion of the appoggiatura *di passaggio,* which is both described and illustrated as a grace note. Whereas, as reported before, he limits its counterpart, the appoggiatura *lunga* to a rather narrow range of uses, he assigns a wide scope to the grace note which, he says, can be used in all styles and all tempos. Very significant, because so very logical, is his prescription to use it in any context of *even* notes, be it in slow or fast tempo, because a genuine appoggiatura would interfere with the intended evenness of rhythm (see *Ornamentation,* pp. 174–176).

Padre Martini, Mozart's mentor during his youthful Italian ventures, used grace notes extensively, and so did other Italian masters of the period (see *Ornamentation,* 167–170).

Quantz, speaking of *durchgehende* (i.e. passing) as contrasted to *anschlagende* (i.e. onbeat) *Vorschläge* gives a number of contexts in which the former, genuine grace notes, are to be applied. Of special interest, but by no means limited to them, are the *tierces coulées* (the filling in of descending thirds), *Vorschläge* preceding a written-out appoggiatura, and interestingly, the pattern of ♪♪♪ ♪♪♪ (*Ornamentation,* pp. 90–91, 190–191).

Even Marpurg, who after 1755 follows C.P.E. Bach quite faithfully, introduces a special symbol ♪, a small note with an inverted flag to signify grace notes. (*Ornamentation,* p. 187).

L. Mozart adopted Quantz's term *durchgehende Vorschlag* for the grace note and assigns it a wide range including many cases of improvisatory use where no symbol appears in the notation. For the symbols, he points to grace-note character in part explicitly with attendant illustration, in part by implication when he speaks of very short *Vorschläge* whose accent falls on the principal note, not on the *Vorschlag.* The grace-note implication is reinforced by contexts that overlap with those of the explicitly illustrated ones. The contention of modern writers, among them Beyschlag and the Badura-Skodas, that L. Mozart intended the *Vorschlag* to be placed on the beat, as mentioned above, finds no substantiation in Leopold's text. (*Ornamentation,* p. 193).

Löhlein, in 1767, spells out grace-note use in text and illustration. (*Ornamentation,* pp. 195–196).

Türk, who is often more rigid than C.P.E. Bach himself, contradicts for the short *Vorschlag* C.P.E.'s requirement of an accent and suggests instead that it be played with reverse dynamics "flatteringly," which happens to be, hardly by accident, the term that Quantz used for his grace notes (*Ornamentation,* pp. 198–199). In contrast to L. Mozart, Türk reaffirms onbeat placement.

C.P.E. Bach had already complained that anticipated and other interbeat ornaments, which he tried to outlaw, were nevertheless "eminently fashionable" (*Ornamentation,* pp. 40, 184). Later in the century we get a similar report from his follower, J.C.F. Rellstab, about the widespread practice of anticipation which he, too, condemns. He shows, as given in Ex. 1.2, how the written version of Ex. *a* "is usually played" *(b)* and how it ought to be played *(c)*.[7] This only proves again that musical impulses will rebel against unnatural restrictions.

Ex. 1.2. Rellstab

Many theorists who follow C.P.E. Bach for many principles, nevertheless part company with him when it comes to his prohibition of all kinds of *Nachschläge*. And under the guise of *Nachschläge* some theorists not only introduce interbeat ornaments prohibited by Bach, but occasionally even write them as grace notes.

Some theorists not covered in *Ornamentation,* to whom I turn now, are of later date but still presumably of interest, because certain practices linger and because there is often a time lag between the observation and report of a practice.

Although many theorists of the German-speaking realm limit themselves—in some cases well into the 19th century—to presenting the various forms of the appoggiatura with little or no deviation from C.P.E. Bach's designs, there are some who, in addition, spell out the grace-note alternative. Significant is the testimony of a treatise written by J.C. Bach and F. Ricci for the Naples Conservatory. In it the authors say that *Vorschläge* and other ornaments consisting of more than one note that are written as small notes, take their value either from the preceding or the following note.[8]

Reichardt gives the usual rules for the long appoggiatura, then adds: "There are also very short *Vorschläge* attached to notes that do not seem to lose anything of their value [ohne dass diese etwas von ihrer Geltung zu verlieren scheinen]; one writes them generally with two or three flags."[9] Example 1.3 shows his illustration. Only unaccented brevity, in other words de facto grace notes, can give the impression he describes.

Ex. 1.3. Reichardt

Very important is the documentation of Milchmeyer in 1798 because his principles make such eminently good sense.[10] He does not indicate the length of the *Vorschlag* by its denomination: the length he says depends on the expression, but he does use longer denominations for the long appoggiaturas and three- or

[7]Johann Carl Friedrich Rellstab, *Anleitung für Clavierspieler,* Berlin [1790], as cited by Walter Georgii, *Die Verzierungen in der Musik: Theorie und Praxis.*

[8]Johann Christian Bach and F. Pasquale Ricci, *Méthode . . . pour le forte-piano ou clavecin* p. 5. "La valeur des *Petites-Notes,* qu'on appelle autrement Port-de-voix, ou Notes-de-Goût, soit en montant, soit en descendant, ne se compte pas dans la mesure, mais se prend sur la durée de la Note qui les précède, ou de celle qui les suit."

[9]Johann Friedrich Reichardt, *Über die Pflichten des Ripien-Violinisten,* p. 41.

[10]Johann Peter Milchmeyer, *Die wahre Art das Pianoforte zu spielen,* pp. 37–38.

four-flagged *Vorschläge* for the grace notes. He describes the latter as very short *Vorschläge* that are "rendered as if they still belonged to the preceding measure" ("als wenn sie noch zu dem vorhergehenden Takt gehörten"). His illustrations, of which Ex. 1.4 gives a few specimens, show anticipation explicitly by juxtaposing notation and execution. Thus we see that he favors the grace-note style before groups of three notes in the ternary meter of Ex. *a*, before repeated notes *(b)*, even notes *(c)*, fast notes *(d)*, triplets *(e)*, and leaps *(f)*. It so happens that all of these illustrations also fall into Tartini's category of *Vorschläge* before even notes that call for anticipation.

Ex. 1.4. Milchmeyer

The very specificity of Milchmeyer's illustrations can be assumed to shed light on similar contexts presented by other theorists who ask for extreme shortness and fail to mention accentuation, yet still pay tribute to the downbeat principle by saying that what such *Vorschläge* take away from the principal note is either "very little" or "can hardly be perceived" or other formulations to that effect. In such cases the *Vorschläge* will be eye appoggiaturas but ear grace notes (to use an old simile used in connection with forbidden parallels).

A case in point is A. E. Müller in his flute treatise from the turn of the century.[11] Interesting is his more complete list of contexts and his illustrations, shown in part in Ex. 1.5, which even use a symbol for the grace note, which, for a North German at that time was presumably new, in contrast to Mozart's South German manner of indicating a single 32nd-note with a crossed-out 16th. Müller's categories, as illustrated, are: *a* at the start of a piece or phrase; *b* before repeated notes; *c* before disjunct pitches; *d* on upward leaps; *e* before notes of even value; *f* before dotted notes in fast tempo; *g* before syncopations; *h* before staccato notes; *i* before groups of two notes; *j* before groups of three (even) notes; *k* before triplets; *l* before groups of six (even) notes.

This fine listing of contexts for the very short *Vorschlag* also coincides with many instances in which the editors of the *NMA* suggest grace-note execution. They include cases in which the logic of rhythm—as formulated by Tartini in its

———————

[11]August Eberhard Müller, *Elementarbuch für Flötenspieler*, pp. 23–25.

Ex. 1.5. Müller

basic form—or the logic of articulation militates against onbeat rendition. In syncopation an onbeat *Vorschlag* would blunt the sharp contour of this characteristic design, and a staccato would lose its sharpness, that is its essence, by an accented *Vorschlag*. We see here and in parallel cases in the implied onbeat rules (the taking away, however little, from the following note) perhaps the psycho-sociological phenomenon of resistance to innovation vis-à-vis famous treatises. For those theorists who show the downbeat in illustrations there may have been an additional factor in the hesitation to trespass in an abstract paradigm beyond the limit of its nominal value; since in the *abstract* the space before or after a given model is a musical no man's land that may or may not allow the intrusion of any foreign note values. This fact, I believe, explains why we find many verbal explanations of the grace note and similar anticipations, but rarely with the explicitness of Milchmeyer's paradigms, or of Quantz's, L. Mozart's, and Tartini's examples. (There must have been at least one more theorist who was equally explicit, as we shall presently see when Türk criticizes two writers of such, in his eyes heretical, views, and identifies only Milchmeyer.)

Koch, the eminent theorist, suggests by the term "ungenuine" ("uneigentliche") *Vorschläge* that the very short species belongs to a different class altogether. Elsewhere he refers to this type as *Vorschläge* of "undetermined duration" ("von unbestimmter Dauer") because they are "slurred so fast to the principal note that the latter seems to lose nothing of its value."[12] Their accent, he stresses, falls on the principal note, not on the *Vorschlag*, and they occur, he adds, mostly in gay movements. He illustrates their use before leaps, repeated notes, and tied notes.

[12]Heinrich Christoph Koch, *Musikalisches Lexikon*, cols. 1725–1726. The term "uneigentliche Vorschläge" appears in the *Journal der Tonkunst*, pp. 185–187 ("... weil sie so geschwinde an die Hauptnote geschleift werden, dass es scheint, als würde derselben dadurch nicht das Geringste von ihrem Werthe entzogen. . . .").

He shows onbeat start, but in the fast tempo of the "gay movements" idiom will assert itself as usual for such reverse dynamics, in the form of grace notes.

The grace-note implication is at least as clear in J. F. Schubert's substantial vocal treatise of 1804. After giving, like most other theorists, the usual rules for the long appoggiatura, he postulates that the short ones have to be very short and can be used "anywhere."[13] He neither specifies nor implies their rhythmic design and gives contexts that parallel those of Milchmeyer and Müller: before notes of equal values, before staccato notes, triplets, and leaps. An illustration of the last in Ex. 1.6 clarifies the grace-note intent, since the only way of making sense out of this awkward setting without destroying the intended melodic climax on *Gott* is to sing the *Vorschläge* as grace notes. Schubert also gives (p. 55) an interesting listing of configurations, including the formula , that are ambiguous and can accommodate, according to the performer's judgment, either an appoggiatura or a grace note).

Hö-   re   Gott

Ex. 1.6. J. F. Schubert

Giuseppe Cajani describes as an "appoggiatura" *only* the anticipated *Vorschlag*, taking one-half the value of the *preceding* note (clearly having in mind a short preceding note.)[14]

Gervasoni in 1800 illustrates all *Vorschläge* on the beat but in the text offers the alternative of doing the short *Vorschlag* in the time of either the preceding or the following note according to the "just expression."[15] This explanation can serve as an object lesson for the skepticism we have to bring to the interpretation of downbeat illustrations.

J. J. Klein, in 1783, says nothing about the rhythmic disposition when he asks that the short *Vorschlag*, indicated by a much shorter denomination than that of the principal note, be rendered very fast. We also find the same treatment—great shortness without specified rhythm—in Knecht (1803).[16]

Bisch, a German musician living in France, writes in 1802 that for the *Vorschlag* the voice only touches the grace and glides lightly from the little note onto the principal one.[17]

Even though, as mentioned before, Türk had in his 1789 edition of his *Klavierschule* given a de facto endorsement to the grace note by his reverse dynamics for the short *Vorschlag*, even in the 1802 edition he keeps insisting on its downbeat execution. He strenuously objects to two recent authors (of whom only one is later identified as Milchmeyer) who ask for clear prebeat style not only for *Vorschläge* but for other ornaments as well. To rebut them, Türk cites passages

---

[13]Johann Friedrich Schubert, *Neue Singe-Schule,* pp. 53–54.

[14]Giuseppe Cajani, *Nuovi elementi di musica . . .,* p. 8. "Abbenchè [l'appoggiatura] non sia affatto calcolata in valore nelli parti della battuta in cui si trova è nonostante considerata ordinarimente per la metà della notta che *precede*" (italics mine).

[15]Carlo Gervasoni, *La scuola della musica,* vol. 1, p. 184: ". . . si appoggiano queste a quella nota della misura, presso la quale sono collocate, e nell'

esprimerle viene presa la loro brevissima durata, o da una parte della nota anteriore ovvero da quella posteriore sopra la quale cadano, seconda la richiede la giusta espressione."

[16]Johann Joseph Klein, *Versuch eines Lehrbuchs der praktischen Musik,* p. 44; Justin Heinrich Knecht, *Allgemeiner musikalischer Katechismus . . .,* p. 57.

[17]Jean Bisch, *Explication des principes élémentaires de musique,* p. 68.

from Mozart and Haydn, given here in Ex. 1.7, where the preceding note is so short that it would not have time to spare for an anticipated *Vorschlag*.[18]

a. (Mozart)   *b.*   *c.* (Haydn)
Allegro   Adagio

Ex. 1.7. Türk

The argument has several weaknesses. In Ex. *a* there is sufficient time; in *b* onbeat execution makes both technical and musical sense in that the broken octave passage is continued into the next measure. Besides it is clearly one of the cases where Mozart uses a symbol for a short appoggiatura to simplify the notation (by avoiding a tie under the slur). In Haydn's example the adagio tempo might provide sufficient time for the furtive grace note, but even if it did not, a slight rhythmic adjustment of the two 64th-notes, or a slight delay of the downbeat, could easily accommodate an intended grace note. Türk shows his pedantry by not taking into account the need for music to breathe and not be shackled by a mechanical beat. But be this as it may, and granted that there are a few instances where lack of time suggests or requires onbeat rendition of an ornament, what does it prove for the countless instances where there is no such lack? In the overwhelming number of cases where an onbeat rendition of any ornament is called for, the reason is musical and not mechanical. And it is rather naive to turn the exceptional cases where the mechanics alone dictate a certain execution into a general principle. In connection with the trill and the arpeggio we shall encounter other equally spurious arguments by Türk made in his zeal to defend a dogma.

THE FOREGOING documentation and discussion should answer the question about the legitimacy of the grace note. I passed in review theorists who explicitly called for this ornament (among them Tartini, Quantz, L. Mozart, Milchmeyer, J. C. Bach and Ricci, Gervasoni, Cajani), some who implied its use by stressing the great shortness and lightness of the grace (among them Koch and Reichardt), some who admitted its use by not specifying any rhythmic design and thus leaving the option open (among them J. F. Schubert and J. J. Klein), and some who often unwittingly promoted the grace note by asking for the reverse dynamics of the short *Vorschlag* (among them Müller and Türk). And when authors like C.P.E. Bach and Rellstab report the widespread practice of ornamental anticipation in defiance of their own rules, this only proves the ineffectiveness of rules that run counter to spontaneous idiomatic and musical impulse. Even Türk's polemics reveal by the strained nature of their arguments the weakness of his orthodox stand. Great creative artists are never concerned with rules, only with artistry and good taste, Mozart's *gusto*. With *gusto* as my yardstick, assisted by musical common sense, gratifyingly used in many instances by the editors of the *NMA*, I shall, when the time comes, set out to explore the contexts that favor the use of grace notes in Mozart.

[18]Daniel Gottlob Türk, *Klavierschule* . . , 1802 ed., p. 255.

The Vocal Appoggiatura

The Long Species

The denominations of Mozart's *Vorschlag* symbols are a very important but far from infallible guide to their interpretation. Half-note symbols are very rare and seem to disappear after 1778; dotted notes never occur; for his mature works quarter-notes are the longest denomination and quite reliably stand for a long appoggiatura that can range in length from about an 8th-note to a dotted quarter-note. The 8th-note symbol is ambiguous: it can reach quarter-note length or be much shorter, and once in a while it can stand for a grace note. Sixteenth- and 32nd-note denominations are almost always short, approximating their nominal value, and are often grace notes. Musical evidence shows that Mozart did not follow the standard formulas for the long appoggiatura, nor, with exceptions so rare that they can be disregarded, those for the "overlong" models before ties or rests.

In his vocal works Mozart often writes the symbol for the singer, using a regular note for a doubling instrument, and never the other way around. Frequent juxtapositions of this kind give us important insights into the desired interpretation. Though singers, by virtue of their idiom, are not bound to strict coordination with an attending instrumental line, deviations have to remain within a rather narrow range and thus do not detract from the value of such passages as sources of authoritative information. We have already seen one such case in Ex. 1.1: though shown to illustrate an orthographic habit of Mozart's it offers at the same time a specimen of nonconformance with the half of a binary note rule. In Ex. 2.1 from *Figaro* we see the first appoggiatura follow this rule for *short* (up to about a quarter-note) values, while the second appoggiatura is one of a multitude of cases that shows noncompliance with the two-thirds of a ternary note rule.

Ex. 2.1. K 492, IV, Finale

A further small sampling, which could be endlessly multiplied, will give additional specimens showing that Mozart did not, or at best only in very rare cases involving short note values, follow the two-thirds rule for ternary notes. In Ex. 2.2*a* from *Don Giovanni* (in an aria composed for the Vienna performance) we see two such cases. In *b* from *Die Entführung* it is also clear that the appoggiatura can be shorter, but hardly longer than a quarter-note. For shorter values we find the same evidence in *c* from the same opera, in *d* and *e* from *Die Zauberflöte*.

a. K 527, II, 21b

b. K 384, III, 17

c. Ibid., 20

d. K 620, I, Finale

e. Ibid., II, Finale

Ex. 2.2.

Surprisingly we find much evidence against the application of the rule even in the works of his earliest youth, which may suggest that his father, who endorsed these rules, was probably lax in following them himself. For just one illustration from *La finta semplice,* Ex. 2.3 shows that the violin *Vorschläge* in spite of their 8th-note denomination cannot have 8th-note meaning without badly clashing with the voice; they must be very short.

Ex. 2.3. K 46a (51), II, 12

By contrast I have not found a single spot where the musical evidence of an accompanying voice would indicate that Mozart was abiding by the two-thirds rule for *Vorschläge* preceding dotted notes. Now lack of evidence does not mean Mozart never used the pattern. But it does impress on us the need for extreme caution: we should consider such a solution only in exceptional cases when diction, context, and denomination combine to favor it. Thus in Ex. 2.4*a* from the aria "Resta oh cara" the *NMA* suggestion seems doubtful and a shorter execution in keeping with the 8th-note denomination preferable. Yet even favorable denomination must not always be taken literally. There are a number of cases where reasons of diction, of affect, of musical considerations contradict notation. In Ex. *b* from the "Tuba mirum" from the Requiem the autograph shows clearly quarter-note denominations for the appoggiatura, whereas in all parallel spots Mozart wrote 8th-notes. Also Süssmeyer's accompaniment in this passage admits only 8th-note meaning.

Ex. 2.4.

The nearly identical passage of Ex. 2.5*a* from *Così fan tutte* may be a similar case in which the quarter-note appoggiaturas, especially the second one on the short syllable *rav-* would make for better diction as approximate 8th-notes. In Ex. *b* from *Die Zauberflöte* the *NMA* gives the interpretation of *c* to honor the *Vorschlag* denomination, but since the rest suggests a breathing spot for the singer, the rendition of *d* seems more likely.

Ex. 2.5.

The denomination seems deceptive also in Ex. 2.6*a* from the Belmonte-Constanze duet in the third act of *Die Entführung*. In the andante tempo an approximate 16th-note duration for the appoggiatura is suggested by both the violin accompaniment and the analogous chromatic ascending 16th-notes on *mit* and *ster-(ben)*. We also find occasional inconsistencies, attributable no doubt to the great speed with which Mozart wrote down more or less mechanically what he had already securely fixed in his mind. In Ex. *b* from the first aria of the Queen of the Night, the appoggiatura that should have approximately 8th-note meaning is written in the same manner for the unison oboe, but as a quarter-note for the unison first violins.

Ex. 2.6.

Although we must not become captives of the denominations, we should deviate from them only for good cause. In Ex. 2.7 from *Idomeneo* the words of the High Priest, "the jaws [of the sea monster] always soiled with blood," do not favor the *NMA*'s suggestion of a quarter-note on *san-(gue)* nor of an 8th-note on *lor-(de)*, which creates too gentle an effect for the horror of the vision. Brief appoggiaturas on both of these syllables, reflecting the tremor of the voice would seem more fitting. For reasons of harmony, too, the first appoggiatura has to end before the bass changes on the second beat.

Ex. 2.7. K 366, III, 23

The following examples show that Mozart did not follow the "overlong" practice of extending the appoggiatura for the whole length of the principal note when the latter is followed by a tie or a rest. For the tie, Ex. 2. 8*a* from the C minor Mass shows approximate 8th- and not half-note value for the rising appoggiatura, and Ex. *b* from the *Freimaurerkantate* quarter- and not half-note meaning. For the note followed by a rest, Mozart's nonobservance is illustrated in a passage from the same cantata in Ex. *c,* and in two spots from *Figaro:* from the Countess's "Porgi amor" in Ex. *d,* and Susanna's second-act aria in Ex. *e.*

Ex. 2.8.

c. Ibid.

d. K 492, II, 10

e. Ibid., 12

Ex. 2.8 *cont.*

The "overlong" rules must have been widely followed in Germany, but not, so it seems, by Mozart. In contrast to the innumerable cases where musical evidence contradicts their use, I found only two passages, namely Ex. 2.9*a* from *Don Giovanni* and *b* from *Der Schauspieldirektor,* that would apply to a rest, and none that would apply to a tie.

That a widely practiced performance manner, taught by, among others, his father, should have touched the son was to be expected. What is surprising is that it touched him so lightly. He adopts it so rarely that it must qualify as an exception. Perhaps this manner was going out of fashion; perhaps the stronger leaning of Mozart's orthography toward Italian ways where these patterns were apparently not known accounts for this trait. At any rate it is advisable to refrain from applying these models to Mozart.

The striking fact that several rules proclaimed in a wide consensus of important German treatises of the second half of the 18th century applied to Mozart not at all or at best only in marginal cases, speaks louder than any theoretical disquisition about the need for extreme hesitation in using rules from any treatise, including that of his father, unless we can verify them for a specific case with convincing musical reasons.

Ex. 2.9.

Yet many editors, writers, and performers often apply those rules automatically with dubious musical results. A good illustration is "Das Veilchen"; Ex. 2.10a shows Mozart's setting of the poem's first two lines, b its interpretation by Rudolf Steglich,[1] c that by Ernst August Ballin in the *NMA* edition of Mozart's songs. As can be seen, both follow the two-thirds rule for dotted notes. Steglich, moreover, adds extra dynamic and rhythmic emphasis to the appoggiaturas before the plain, undotted 8th-notes.

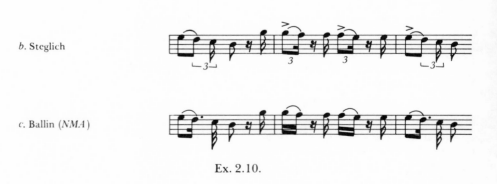

Ex. 2.10.

[1]Rudolf Steglich, "Das Auszierungswesen in der Musik W. A. Mozarts," pp. 208–220.

Both these interpreters have done what we must not do: mechanically applied a rule without considering the meaning of the words, affect, and diction, which are always paramount in Mozart's vocal music. If we pay attention, as we must, to these factors, we realize that the *Vorschläge* reflect the tender feelings evoked by the thought of a small, delicate flower that craves love. This alone is reason enough to make all the *Vorschläge* gentle and unobtrusive. Looking further at word meaning and diction, the word *Wiese* (meadow) is in no need of emphasis: "A violet stood in the meadow" is a simple matter-of-fact statement. *Wiese* would call for emphasis only if a meadow were an unexpected locale for a violet; *gebückt in sich und unbekannt* (stooped and unknown) is a simple, touching portrayal of shyness and insignificance. Hence the *Vorschläge* on *gebückt* and *sich* (the latter a simple reflexive pronoun!) must not be accented, and with this proviso it is immaterial whether they are sung on the beat, between beats, or before the beat. The *Vorschläge* on *unbekannt* (*un-* is a short, and in this context, barely accented syllable) and on *Wiese* should shun the spotlight and be only lightly touched, "flatteringly" (in Quantz's term), and briefly. It is hardly a coincidence that in the catalogue of his works Mozart wrote all these *Vorschläge* as 16th-notes!

Related is the case of Ex. 2.11*a* from Blondchen's lesson to Osmin on how to win the favor of girls through tenderness and flattery. The *Vorschlag* on *Schmeicheln* (flattery) in a gentle, ingratiating melody should be only lightly, caressingly touched. Any accentuation would not only contradict the expression but make for clumsy diction. In the rendition of a sensitive singer the *Vorschlag* here will have the character of a grace note even if, after the long anticipated consonant cluster *Schm*, the vowel sound should happen to fall on the beat. A few measures later in Ex. *b* the syllables *dass* and *we-(nig)* with *Vorschläge* written as 8th-notes fit spontaneously the appoggiatura style, but with approximate 16th-, not 8th-note length.

a.

b.

Ex. 2.11. K 384, II, 8

Singers have to be given a measure of rhythmic latitude to enable them to respond to the combined demands of textual meaning, affect, and diction.

In Ex. 2.12 from Tamino's "Bildnis" aria the vocal line has no instrumental shadow to offer guidance. The first appoggiatura on *neu-(er)* should have about the 16th-note length of its denomination. Three measures later the appoggiatura on the same word, whether by intention or carelessness, is written as an 8th-note.

The intensification inherent in the repeat on a higher pitch level would, independently of denomination, entitle the singer to lengthen the appoggiatura at his discretion beyond a 16th-note value, though an 8th-note would make for awkward diction by an unnatural extension of the *o* sound of the diphtong *eu* (pronounced oy).

Ex. 2.12. K 620, I, 3

For the same reason of vocal flexibility we must not assume, as briefly noted before, that when the voice is supported or attended by an instrument there has to be *exact* rhythmic-melodic coordination between the two. Small deviations are not at all bothersome, and presumably one of the reasons Mozart often wrote the symbol for the voice and a regular note for the shadowing instrument was to give the singer a measure of latitude called for by the vocal impulse and the nature of ornaments. We find a number of spots of unison or octave doubling between voice and instruments where Mozart, like other composers who knew how to write for the voice, differentiates rhythmically in order to give the voice, in deference to its idiomatic needs, a line that is rounder than that for the instruments. The matter is, I believe, of sufficient interest to merit a brief digression, especially since such rhythmic discrepancies have often been mistaken for an oversight that needed to be corrected. Characteristic for such treatment is, in Leporello's "Madamina," the three times repeated phrase to the words *vuol d'inverno la grassotta, vuol d'estate la magrotta,* with double dotting for the doubling violins, single dotting for the voice. For other examples see the start of Don Ottavio's "Il mio tesoro," Don Giovanni's "Metà di voi," m. 24 on the words *gran mantello,* Pedrillo's Serenade ("Romanze") in the third act of *Die Entführung.* We find similar examples even in works of Mozart's earliest youth. Yet some editors find these innocuous rhythmic clashes untidy and expurgate them by assimilation. Thus, for example, in the second finale of *Die Zauberflöte* the three boys stopping Pamina from suicide sing in a milder rhythm than the doubling woodwinds:

In *W.A.M.* the voices were assimilated without comment. In the *NMA* the same assimilation is given as an editorial suggestion. Mozart's vocal setting, as usual, makes for perfect prosody by giving due prominence to *glück-,* but not to the short, unaccented *-che,* and by not contracting the important syllable *Un-* nor the word *halt,* while the sharper orchestral rhythm adds urgency to the plea. See also *Mitridate,* I, 3, m. 78, where the *NMA* suggests assimilation through rhythmic sharpening of Arbate's "L'odio nel cor fremate"; *Figaro,* II, Finale, mm. 188–190; C minor Mass, "Qui tollis," mm. 47–49.

Melodic assimilation is even less justified in a spot the Badura-Skodas singled out, obviously as a model to follow in similar circumstances. They write that Figaro in his aria "Non più andrai" should sing what is shown in Ex. 2.13*a* as in *b,* resolving the quarter-note on *-ro-* into a turn to match the violins (Badura-Skoda, p. 90). The suggestion is not a happy one. First, Mozart from his earliest youth often let instruments that attend a vocal line wind around it with richer melismas in keeping with the idiomatic nature of both media, and a principle of assimilation would lead to massive incongruities. Second, in this particular case, such figuration would be out of style for Figaro, whose part is throughout devoid of ornamental melismas—as is Susanna's—in contrast to the sophistication of the Count and Countess with their occasional coloraturas.

Ex. 2.13.

Neither can I agree with the Badura-Skodas' idea that in Ex. 2.14 from the first Terzetto in *Così fan tutte* the two voices should follow the oboes and bassoons and accordingly change the pitch repetition on *spada* into an appoggiatura leaping down a seventh (Badura-Skoda, pp. 89–90). *Fuori la spada!* (Out with the sword!) is a challenge whose belligerent tone is ideally realized in the repetition on *spada* and in the dotting of the preceding beat. Assimilation to the appoggiatura leap of the woodwinds would fatally soften the martial sound of *spa-da:* the passage has to be sung as written. The woodwind appoggiatura with exquisite subtlety gives a smiling hint to the listener not to take the heroics too seriously; similarly the provocative dotted note is softened in the instruments in both rhythm and articulation. I shall have more to say about the power of pitch repetition in the chapter on the recitative (Chapter 12).

Ex. 2.14. K 588, I, 1

A further argument against such assimilation is that Mozart characteristic-ally uses the downward leaping appoggiatura to express a feeling of warmth, tenderness, vulnerability, and related emotions, as shown in Ex. 2.15. In Ex. *a* from Tamino's aria, the *NMA* makes the sensible suggestion to render the appoggiatura, written as an 8th-note, with the length of a 16th. In the larghetto tempo the approximate 16th is long enough to convey the nuance of feeling inherent in the word. The downward leaping appoggiaturas of Exx. *b* and *c* from the duet "Là ci darem la mano" from *Don Giovanni* and from Belmonte's aria in *Die Entführung* are best sung in keeping with the denominations: Zerlina's and Belmonte's as 16ths, Don Giovanni's as an 8th-note. All of these are "long" appoggiaturas according to my working terminology in that they are capable of carrying an emotional tone. They cannot enrich the harmony since a dissonance would have to be resolved stepwise; they belong to the harmony of the principal note and always repeat the preceding pitch.

a. K 620, I, 3

b. K 527, I, 7

c. K 384, I, 4

Ex. 2.15.

Often, but less often than in instrumental music, Mozart writes out in regular notes stepwise falling appoggiaturas as shown in Exx. 2.16*a-c* from *Figaro*. For further illustrations see Exx. 13.2 and 13.3.

a. K 492, II, 10

b. Ibid., I, 6

c. Ibid., III, 16

Ex. 2.16.

Long appoggiaturas from below have a stronger flavor and therefore occur less frequently, Mozart usually writes them out, as shown in Exx. 2.17*a* from *Don Giovanni* and *b* and *c* from *Figaro;* he rarely indicates them by symbol. See also Ex. 13.6.

a. K 527, I, Finale

b. K 492, III, 19

Ex. 2.17.

THE SHORT SPECIES

The "short" appoggiatura, in my working terminology one that is not long enough to carry an expressive nuance or to make a noticeable harmonic impact, will instead tend to add an element of rhythmic or dramatic animation. The borderline with the long species will be unavoidably fluid, as will be that with the grace note (discussed in Chapter 4). Such gray areas of ambiguity are congenital to ornaments and must not deter us from trying to establish with reasonable likelihood when a *Vorschlag* belongs to one or the other category.

Clearest are cases where, in vocal music, diction calls for accentuation, and the meaning of the words for great brevity. The magnificent aria "Ah t'invola" offers a fine illustration which is given in Ex. 2.18*a*. The word *barbaro* with articulation fitting the poignancy of the passage, calls a whiplash appoggiatura. It is no accident that the appoggiatura is written as a 16th- before a whole note, whereas a few measures later (Ex. *b*) we find the long appoggiatura on *Dio* written with a quarter-note. The same duality of notation recurs on the return of the passage. In Ex. *c* from *Zaide* the words "skipping she looks for a way to flee" combined with the nimbly tripping staccato notes of the violins call for great lightness and shortness of the appoggiaturas. These must be no longer than 16th-notes lest they collide with the offbeat violins. In Ex. *d* from the Missa solemnis the violin figure strongly suggests 16th-note meaning for the appoggiatura on *De-(us)*, which is fittingly notated as such. In the adagio tempo, this may lie on the border between short and long appoggiaturas. In Ex. *e* from the "Agnus Dei" of the same work the vertical dash over the single principal note, *D*, in the violins has accentual in addition to staccato meaning, hence favors unaccented brevity for the *Vorschlag*, tantamount to a grace note for the violins, while the vocal grace on an accented syllable is likely to lean to short appoggiatura style. Similar is the case of Ex. *f* from *La finta giardiniera* where the *fp* markings for the violins refer to the principal note (as any accentual markings do with Mozart) and move the *Vorschlag* as grace note before the beat. But the violence of the words "I would like to tear out your heart" calls for their strong accentuation and hence for sharply clipped appoggiaturas. Again the comparison with the later spot of Ex. *g* in the same aria where on *sospirar* (to sigh) 8th-note *Vorschläge* signify long appoggiaturas is revealing.

Ex. 2.18.

d. K 337 Sanctus

e. K 337 Agnus Dei

f. K 196, II, 13

g.

Ex. 2.18 *cont.*

    Very interesting are Exx. 2.19*a* and *b* from the *Credo* Mass. For either *Vorschlag* the accented syllable on the downbeat calls for appoggiatura treatment, while the violins, with their unornamented sudden forte 8th-note (in unison with the vocal principal note) create both times an acciaccatura that needs to be resolved quickly; hence the appoggiatura has to be very brief, as is also suggested by the notation. The sudden brief forte in the violins would make no sense, in *b* still less than in *a*, if the appoggiatura were to have 8th-note value.

Ex. 2.19. K 257 Gloria

SUMMING UP we can say that vocal *Vorschläge*, notably those preceding an accented syllable carry the presumption of appoggiatura meaning. In slow or moderate tempos, as well as in cantabile passages in a lively tempo, they will tend to be of the "long" species but will rarely exceed the value of a quarter note. Appoggiaturas before dotted notes will rarely exceed one-third of the latter's value. The "overlong" species, which takes the full value of the principal note, can be safely disregarded in Mozart interpretation. Downward leaping appoggiaturas need not be long in value but will tend to be "long" in character according to my working terminology. Where the meaning of the words calls for brevity or brusqueness and the denomination is small, that is a quarter or less of the value of the principal note, the case is strong for a "short" appoggiatura. Cases where even the vocal *Vorschlag* is more likely to assume grace-note character are discussed in Chapter 4.

The Instrumental Appoggiatura

THE LONG SPECIES

For instruments the *Vorschlag* follows different lines, a fact due partly to different idiomatic demands, partly to the loss of guidance that diction and textual meaning can provide. Parallel, though, are some of the principles governing the length of the appoggiaturas, notably the nonobservance of both the two-thirds of a ternary note rule and the "overlong" pattern before ties or rests. Affect is still an important factor but has to be guessed instead of being revealed by the words. Also there are differences in notation. Long instrumental appoggiaturas are much more frequently written out in regular notes than they are for the voice, as we have seen before in a number of unisons or near-unisons between vocal and instrumental lines. In orchestral writing such explicitness was a necessary precaution when appoggiaturas of undetermined length were involved, but the practice also influenced soloistic and chamber music. This is presumably the reason why, notably in the works of Mozart's last 10-12 years, we find in instrumental works few *Vorschlag* denominations of a quarter-note or longer. Half-note symbols are rare at any time in Mozart's career and, as said before, seem to disappear after 1778. For that year, though, we still have such specimens for appoggiaturas preceding trills, probably with a literal meaning and with interesting harmonic implications. In the Violin Sonata in G major we see in Ex. 3.1*a* the half-note symbol where the *Vorschlag* is dissonant with the bass whereas four measures later the trill preparation is consonant and written out in regular notes. This is no accident: the same pattern is repeated in the piano in mm. 15 and 19, and again in the recapitulation (written out in the autograph),[1] in mm. 123 and 129, 131 and 135, in the same notational pattern and same harmonic context. We find an analogous passage with the same harmonic link: symbol on dissonance, regular note on consonance, in the Rondo of the Flute and Harp Concerto as shown in Ex. 3.1*b;* the pattern is repeated twice more. These examples seem to reveal one of

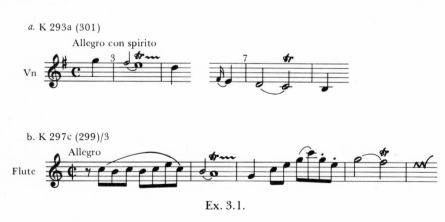

a. K 293a (301)

b. K 297c (299)/3

Ex. 3.1.

[1]In cases of an exact repeat of a passage Mozart often refers the copyist to a "dal segno" indicating the number of measures to be filled in.

the roots of the symbol convention, but we must beware of generalizing. Mozart was not consistent, and many are the cases in which he used *Vorschlag* symbols with appoggiatura meaning on consonances.

Quarter-note symbols will again always stand for a—mostly long—appoggiatura, and the presumption will usually be for approximate quarter-note value. In one of its rare uses in a late chamber music work, the String Quartet in D of 1789, the quarter-note shown in Ex. 3.2 (which recurs in the same theme in the first violin in m. 78 and again in the cello in m. 188) may have been so written because it was *not* meant to be played as an exact quarter-note. As such it sounds somewhat square against the quarter-note movement in the other instruments and loses its flavor as appoggiatura. Rendered slightly shorter, say, as a dotted 8th-note with an extra touch of warmth, it adds the kind of flexibility and plasticity to the theme that is a valuable attribute of an ornament.

Ex. 3.2.

In the E minor Violin Sonata (of 1778) the quarter-note symbol is flanked in the same theme by an 8th- and a 16th-note appoggiatura, shown in Ex. 3.3*a.* The mixture is definitely purposive, since it recurs eight times in the exact same pattern. The length of the 8th- and the quarter-note—the latter with a slight emphasis—should correspond roughly to their value; the 16th-*Vorschlag,* however, need not be as short as its denomination, but should be perhaps one-third the length of a quarter-note to avoid the effect of a snap in this gentle theme.

In Ex. *b* the fermata suggests a slight retard, and the length of the appoggiatura should fit into the pattern of the slowing pace.

Ex. 3.3.

The 8th-note denomination offers more problems. For orchestra and chorus it was most likely intended to be taken literally to avoid ensemble problems. In Ex. 3.4 from the C major Piano Concerto, the 8th-note appoggiatura is doubled in m. 18 by the oboe, three measures later by flute, oboe, and bassoon, and in later parallel spots by other instruments. Eighth-note meaning here is also logical for melodic reasons as a continuation of the descending line of 8th-notes. It is one of the cases of the symbol's use as notational convenience as pointed out above in connection with Ex. 1.1.

K 467/2

Ex. 3.4.

For soloists or chamber music players the symbol allows the possibility of slight variations in length. An interesting document shows Mozart's flexibility regarding the denominations. In the autograph of the String Quartet in D K 575, the first theme, in its many appearances, is always notated as shown in Ex. 3.5a. In the autograph "Index [Verzeichnüss] of all my works" Mozart wrote, almost certainly from memory, the *incipit* as shown in Ex. *b*. In the third measure he made a mistake. Probably he wrote a half-note instead of a whole note for the first violin, but with all notes stemmed upward, it is barely possible that the quarter-note a″ was not a symbol but a regular note, in which case he forgot to dot the half-note. In either case we have a discrepancy with the original notation with longer values for the appoggiaturas, which in turn confirms the idea that we need not feel confined by the symbols' denominations. In this particular case the solution suggested by the *NMA* follows the value of the symbols, but it seems to me that more flexibility is desirable. I would suggest dwelling a little longer on the first, rather strongly affective appoggiatura, whereas the second and third *Vorschläge* have more the nature of passing notes with a linking function of *tierces coulées* that does not call for emphasis. One of several possibilities is shown in Ex. *c*, which in turn can always be varied slightly within the same general character.

a. K 575/1

Vn I

b.

c. perhaps

Ex. 3.5.

A similar rhythmic modulation can be brought to bear on the spot of Ex. 3.6a from the String Quartet in B flat (of 1789) where the appoggiatura need not be played the same way for all repetitions of the theme and can range somewhere between ♩♪♪ and ♪♩♪ . In Ex. b from the Violin Concerto in A, the second appoggiatura could be played a little shorter than the first one. In Ex. c from the Violin Concerto in D (No. 4) the symbolized appoggiatura could be made a little shorter than an 8th, say ♪♩ , or ♩. , to set off to greater advantage the expressive nuance of the written-out ascending appoggiatura in the next measure.

Ex. 3.6.

Apart from the rhythmic nuance, the difference between symbol and regular note is not always a greater emphasis; the symbol can also provide a touch of tenderness that the regular note would not evoke. In Ex. 3.7a from the Violin Sonata in F K 374e (377), the appoggiaturas seem to call for a gentle nuance rather than an accent, and even in the Presto movement of Ex. b from the Piano Sonata in A minor, the appoggiaturas of circa 8th-note length should be played gently, "flatteringly," not with brisk accents.

Ex. 3.7.

There are pitfalls both in relying too literally on the denomination and in deviating too widely. In his youth, however, Mozart was less circumspect about denominations than he became in his maturity, and we find in early works quite a few 16th-note *Vorschläge* in circumstances that point to 8th-note meaning. In Ex. 3.8 from *La Betulia liberata* of 1771, the violins are at first written as given in Ex. 3.8*a* with 16th-note *Vorschläge*. The second of these is, in the unison horns, written as a regular 8th-note. This is not necessarily conclusive, since the horn writing is idiomatic and a small clash would be innocuous. More revealing is a later parallel spot (Ex. *b*) where the appoggiatura is written out in the violins as an 8th-note.

Such use raises the question whether in the *Little* G minor Symphony of 1773 the *Vorschläge* of Ex. *c* may not have been intended as 8th-notes.

Ex. 3.8.

On the other hand, the *NMA* goes too far in suggesting quarter-note meaning for the 16th-note *Vorschläge* in Ex. 3.9 from the Serenade in D of 1774. Since Mozart usually writes out long *rising* appoggiaturas, the *Vorschlag* on F sharp in Ex. *a* could hardly have been longer than an 8th-note and was most likely even shorter than that. In the later passage of Ex. *b* the *Vorschlag* before a weak beat in a syncopationlike phrase has to be short, presumably unaccented, bordering on a grace note. The suggested quarter-note value seems inappropriate.

Ex. 3.9.

Vorschläge leaping downward by a sixth or more usually have, like their vocal counterparts, an affective coloring and therefore tend to be appoggiaturas. They always start from the pitch of the preceding note, are, in other words, prepared (a couple of rare exceptions for grace notes are shown later), and seem to occur only in soloistic situations. They should be long enough to convey their affective message with a caressing inflection and usually need not be longer: in a slow tempo an approximate 16th-note length will usually do, in a fast tempo an approximate 8th-note length. As with many soloistic appoggiaturas that are not doubled by another voice, it will as a rule be preferable not to render them in exact metrical units since the resulting sense of rubato will radiate greater warmth. In Ex. 3.10*a* from the String Quartet in D K 575, and Ex. *b* from the late Violin Sonata in A K 526, both in an andante frame, a length of slightly more than a 16th, when accompanied by a gentle emphasis of the bow, will be more eloquent than a straight 8th-note. In the Andante of the G major Piano Concerto the appoggiatura in Ex. *c* seems an elegant continuation of the preceding notes and a fairly precise 16th value therefore justified. In the slow tempo of Ex. *d* from the Adagio in E for Violin, the appoggiatura could be a little shorter than a 16th.

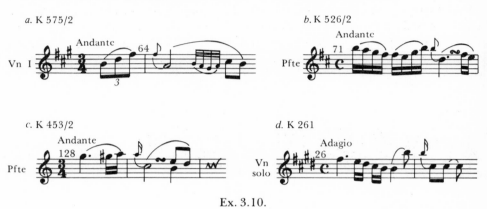

Ex. 3.10.

Upward leaping instrumental *Vorschläge,* for reasons to be discussed later, tend to be grace notes, but once in a while, context, supported by denomination, will suggest appoggiatura treatment. Example 3.11 from the String Quartet in E flat offers an illustration in a leisurely allegro non troppo. The *NMA* suggests here quarter-note length with the obvious intention of providing an echo of the two preceding written-out leaps of a fourth. Such an intention would be hard to guess, given the 8th-note denomination; also such an echo is musically not justified, indeed unwelcome. A third repetition of the leap formula would be redundant whereas a rhythmic variant in combination with the sudden dynamic change offers a delightful modification. The duration of an 8th-note or shorter would be advisable.

Ex. 3.11.

THE SHORT SPECIES

The short instrumental appoggiatura is difficult to isolate. There are many contexts that call for a short *Vorschlag,* but lacking the guidance of diction, it can be difficult to decide between accentuating the *Vorschlag* or the principal note.

Occasionally we find spots where the context favors onbeat placement, as in Ex. 3.12a from the Violin-Viola Duo in G. Here the upward leaping *Vorschlag* is a direct continuation of the foregoing passage, hence will most naturally fall on the beat without any distinct accent. The violinist can give the long note the needed prominence by a gentle swelling and tapering of the sound. Similarly in Ex. *b* from the C minor Fantasy, the *Vorschlag* grows organically out of the preceding passage and should most likely have 32nd-note meaning.[2] The Badura-Skodas suggest an onbeat 32nd while placing the accent on the main note to let it sound through. The pianistic need to prevent the sound from dying out, as well as the need to clarify the reentry of the theme, can justify this solution, preferably done without too great a contrast in dynamics. Another possibility that defies notational spelling could derive from the purely ornamental *Eingang* character of the passage that need not and ought not to be nailed down with metrical precision: when playing the passage poco rubato, the left-hand entry can be delayed by a 32nd—the time it takes the right hand to sound the *Vorschlag* ostensibly *on*, de facto *before* the beat of the bass.

a. K 423/2   *b.* K 475

Ex. 3.12.

Problematic and much debated are the *Vorschläge* in the first movement of the A minor Piano Sonata. In Ex. 3.13a, giving the beginning of the piece, undiscriminatingly equal treatment seems out of place. Several reasons suggest grace-note treatment for the opening *Vorschlag*. An appoggiatura on the downbeat start of a piece—or even a phrase—is generally inappropriate and rejected by all theorists who address the issue. In this particular case an appoggiatura would weaken the martial vigor of the first measure's rhythmic design. The only other option would be an *acciaccatura:* the simultaneous striking of both notes and quick release of the *Vorschlag*. Mozart who frequently wrote out appoggiaturas long and short (the latter as Lombard snaps) never to my knowledge started the downbeat of a piece with either kind of appoggiatura, let alone one from below. The Badura-Skodas who agree with the grace-note interpretation point out that before the recapitulation the *Vorschlag* on D sharp is written out in the form of an anacrusic 16th-note (Ex. *b*). They justly say that the addition of the original D sharp *Vorschlag* by several editors "seems a crude misunderstanding of Mozart's abbreviation: Da Capo 8 mesur" (pp. 84–85).

A better case for a sharp, brief appoggiatura could be made for m. 2 where such an appoggiatura is prepared and does not interfere with an incisive rhythmic design, in which case the *Vorschlag* in m. 4 might, for variety's sake, be ever so slightly lengthened to, say, a triplet eighth: ♪♩. As a probably better alternative, the *Vorschlag* in m. 2 may again be done in anticipation, the one in m. 4 as a short

---

[2]The autograph is lost. The first edition by Artaria with its usual quota of laxness has an 8th-note value for the *Vorschlag*. The 32nd-value of the *NMA* is more logical, and as the Badura-Skodas point out, is based on the edition by Rudorff, who had consulted a copy with autograph additions that has since disappeared.

snappy appoggiatura. In m. 9 (Ex. *c*) the return of the theme should duplicate the start. But the written-out 8th-note appoggiatura in measure 10 is *not* an illustration for m. 2, because the theme, as so often in a repeat, is varied, and this lengthened appoggiatura is a distinct part of an ornamentally softened version which leads, with a modulation, to a momentarily calmer episode.

Ex. 3.13.

The Badura-Skodas postulate short appoggiaturas for the D major Rondo K 485. For reasons discussed in greater detail in Chapter 5, I believe this piece is better served by grace notes. Though there is no reason not to vary the rhythmic pattern here and there, in so doing I would always avoid accentuation since the resulting snap effect seems out of keeping with the ingratiating gentleness of the theme. Playing the *Vorschläge* throughout as Lombard snaps (as written out without comment in *W.A.M.*) results in a rigidity and the very impression of "a purely mechanical beat" that the two distinguished authors want to avoid (Badura-Skoda, p. 83).

For the passage from the Violin Sonata in B flat shown in Ex. 3.14*a*, the Badura-Skodas give the significant information that Mozart first wrote the *Vorschläge* as 8th-notes, but later changed them (in darker ink) to 16ths—a further indication of the importance Mozart attached to the denomination of little notes. On the basis of this change, the Badura-Skodas propose rendering all three *Vorschläge* as either 𝄢 or 𝄢, hence as accented appoggiaturas. There is, however, no need to play all three in the same manner. Given the very slow tempo, there are many possible solutions. (The *NMA* makes no suggestion here.) The first *Vorschlag*, on the strongest beat, might be done approximately as a 16th, or slightly longer, with expressive-dynamic emphasis; the second somewhat shorter and less emphasized; the third short, approximately as a 32nd, and unaccented. The proposed expressive decrease takes into account that the measure precedes a turn on a rising melodic line which calls for intensification. The appoggiatura at the start of m. 7 has a longer denomination, is prepared, and forms a strong dissonance, hence should be longer again, maybe as an approximate 16th—which in the given tempo is rather long. For a rough sketch of the proposed rendition of this phrase see Ex. *b*. Other solutions will be as good or better. All three *Vorschläge* of m. 6 could have been meant to be brief and unaccented to provide a foil for the following enhancement of m. 8 with its written-out ornamented version in forte (Ex. *c*).[3]

Ex. 3.14.

By advocating short appoggiatura treatment in such *tierces coulées* contexts (including such spots as the second movement of the Two-Piano Concerto, m. 67) the Badura-Skodas refer not only to C.P.E. Bach and L. Mozart, but also to Wolfgang's fondness for the "Scotch snap" rhythm: ♪♩ . Neither rationale is convincing. I need not repeat that there is no justification for "applying" C.P.E. Bach to Mozart. But the reference to his father is also mistaken. Though Leopold is not an infallible guide to his son's practices, it is of some significance that Leopold saw *tierces coulées* as the prime context for grace-note use (see *Ornamentation*, p. 193). There is no denying Wolfgang's fondness for the "Scotch snap" which he wrote out in specific notation throughout his career. The point is that he *wrote it out*, and though this fact does not preclude the occasional Lombard meaning of *Vorschlag* notes, it certainly does not *prove* such a meaning[4]. The argument is greatly if not fatally weakened by the fact that I am not aware of a single instance in

[3]The turn symbols in m. 8 are written in the autograph *between* the notes, not on top of the first 32nds, as given in the *NMA*. Presumably their meaning is: [music example]. In m. 5 the *NMA* editorial forte marking under the half-note B flat is probably mistaken. It seems to have been prompted by Mozart's piano in m. 9 for the violin which was necessary to establish the contrast with the simultaneous forte for the piano.

[4]The written-out Lombard snap is so frequent that I shall list here at random only a few of its characteristic occurrences: Piano Concerto in A K 385P (414)/1, m. 2; *Così fan tutte,* I, Finale, mm. 429ff.; G minor String Quintet/1, mm. 43ff.; *Haffner* Symphony, Minuet, mm. 6–7; Clarinet Trio, Finale, viola in G minor section; String Quintet in D K 593/2, m. 97; Piano Sonata in E flat K 189g (282), Menuetto II, mm. 17–20; ibid., Finale, mm. 9, 11; Symphony in C K 189k (200)/2, m. 25; Piano Sonata in D K 205b (284)/2, mm. 57–58; Violin Concerto in A/1, mm. 64, 66; Violin Sonata in C K 296/1, mm. 27–29; Piano Variations K 300f (353), var. 1; *Don Giovanni,* I, Finale, mm. 129ff.; String Quartet in D K 499/1, mm. 65ff.; ibid,/4, m. 94; Wind Serenade in C minor, K 384a (388)/1, mm. 108–109.

which a written-out Lombard passage is notated in a parallel or analogous spot with *Vorschlag* symbols.

In Ex. 3.15*a* from the Four-Hand Sonata in B flat the gentleness of the adagio theme could easily suggest grace notes in the first measure. If these are played on the beat, one should at least refrain from accenting them. At the start of the third measure on the strong beat an appoggiatura would be more fitting, but not one of 8th-note length as suggested by the *NMA*. Rather, in deference to Mozart's autograph notation, the appoggiatura should be shorter. In Ex. *b* from the Symphony in C K 189k (200) the *Vorschlag* is consonant and should be brief.

Ex. 3.15.

For the frequent cadential formula like the one from the D minor Concerto shown in Ex. 3.16*a,* and presumably all similar ones, the Badura-Skodas (pp. 72–73) ask for a brief accented appoggiatura (Ex. *b*). Certainly this solution will often fit, but I doubt it is the only possibility. This is one of countless contexts in which we should free ourselves from the bondage of a rigid formula, especially since it occurs so often that alternative readings will bring welcome relief from complete predictability. The main alternatives would be to play it long as in *c,* or, more often, short and before the beat as in *d* (more about this in Chapter 6).

Ex. 3.16.

Summarizing briefly, the long species will, for instruments as well as for the voice, find a congenial climate in slow movements and in cantabile passages of livelier ones; it will be suggested by a combination of expression and *Vorschlag* denomination. Again, some of the standard textbook rules do not apply, such as the two-thirds design for ternary notes, or the "overlong" design before ties or rests. For binary notes, except where the denomination calls for it, the appoggiatura will hardly ever exceed the length of a quarter-note and in general reach that only in fairly fast tempos.

Whenever denomination and musical reasons combine to favor shorter *Vorschläge* it is, in the absence of any guidance from diction or its instrumental counterpart, a dominant mood, not easy to formulate general directives as to whether a short appoggiatura or a grace note would be the more fitting choice. We shall be in a better position to do so after examining the circumstances that favor grace-note use. For the time being I can only advance the tentative proposition that in an energetic setting with a sharp profile the appoggiatura is likely to be preferable and that when, after considering the pros and cons of both alternatives, we cannot arrive at a clear preference, it will probably not greatly matter how we decide. In such cases we can vary our choice and thereby add a refreshing element of spontaneity to the performance.

4

The Grace Note

Many elements combine to emancipate Mozart's *Vorschläge* from the grip of the downbeat dogma as proclaimed by a few influential old theorists and perpetuated by many modern scholars. Among these elements are the wide spectrum of 18th-century attitudes toward this ornament, as shown in Chapter 1; the awareness that rules from treatises, however famous, are fallible; the fact that a growing number of eminent Mozart scholars, among them many editors of the *NMA,* are sanctioning in theory a varying range of grace-note interpretations—something countless sensitive artists have instinctively been doing all along in their performances. We are therefore at liberty to explore without self-consciousness musical evidence and musical common sense to help us sort out the contexts in Mozart's music that favor the use of the grace note. This will be done under various headings that to a large degree overlap with Milchmeyer's explicit, and with Koch's and other eminent theorists' implicit grace-note use in certain musical situations. The main categories considered are: *Vorschläge before* written-out appoggiaturas, triplets, even binary notes, staccato notes, single notes, and repeated notes; *Vorschläge* rising a half-step; clues of diction, dynamics, rhythm, melody, expression, and notation; and *Vorschläge* leaping upward by a third or larger interval.

Vorschläge before Written-out Appoggiaturas

Quantz, as mentioned before, had wisely written that a *Vorschlag* that precedes a written-out appoggiatura should be played before the beat. He illustrated the principle as shown in Ex. 4.1. He has melodic-harmonic logic on his side, since the effect of a genuine appoggiatura that strikes on the beat with a dissonance would be drained of its harmonic substance if a second appoggiatura were to be placed on top of the first one. His solution makes such excellent musical sense—especially if the second one were to form a consonance with the bass—that it has the ring of timelessness. Theorists who will not permit the displacement of any ornament from the beat do so for reasons of doctrinaire conformity, not musical logic. The latter speaks so loudly that many editors of the *NMA* support the grace note in such contexts. Three such illustrations are given in Ex. 4.2: a representative sample from Mozart's childhood, Ex. *a* from the aria of c. 1765, "Conservati fedele"; one from his early maturity, Ex. *b* from the Violin Sonata in G of 1781; and one from his consummate maturity, Ex. *c* from the Clarinet Trio of 1786.

Ex. 4.1. Quantz

a. K 23

b. K 373a (379)

c. K 498/3

Ex. 4.2.

We are on reasonably safe ground in using the grace note whenever the appoggiatura character of the regular note is apparent from the harmony. We are on safer ground still when Mozart underlines that character by slurring the two notes. Further samples picked at random from the great multitude of occurrences are shown in Ex. 4.3. They are taken from the Violin Concerto in G *(a)*, the Violin Concerto in A *(b)*, the Piano Sonata in A minor *(c)*, the Missa solemnis *(d)*, the Piano Concerto in A K 385 p. (414) *(e)*, *Zaide* *(f)*, and the Adagio in B minor for Piano *(g)*. See also the Piano Sonatas in B flat K 189f (281)/1, m. 4; and in C, K 300h (330)/2, m. 24.

Ex. 4.3.

g. K 540

Ex. 4.3 *cont.*

VORSCHLÄGE BEFORE TRIPLETS

Musical logic suggests that a characteristic rhythm, that is, one that is integral to the thematic essence, not be disturbed by ornamental additions. Since rhythm is defined by the *starting* points of the notes involved, ornaments have to be rendered before the beat so as not to displace these starting points. One aspect of this principle was, as mentioned above, lucidly formulated by Tartini in his rule that *Vorschläge* before even notes must be anticipated in order not to compromise their intended evenness. Among various types of even notes, triplets, or their counterpart, groups of three notes in a ternary meter, probably have the greatest need to have their rhythmic integrity preserved. This explains why, as shown above, Milchmeyer, and, by implication, other theorists, such as Müller or Koch, singled out triplets as calling for grace note treatment of any inserted *Vorschlag*. There are so many cases where Mozart's triplets or even ternary notes favor anticipation that we are entitled to see it as the first interpretive choice, especially when, in a lively tempo, they are strung in a series of six or more notes. In case of doubt it will be well to test whether the grace can be omitted without noticeable loss to the musical thought. If it can be, then the purely decorative character of the *Vorschlag* should preclude any rhythmic obtrusiveness in its rendition. For Mozart, and presumably for other masters of the time, grace-note treatment is further supported by the fact that when *Vorschläge* come before triplets, the triplets are usually marked with dots or dashes, and, as will be discussed later in more detail, staccato articulation always favors anticipation in order not to blunt the intended sharpness of the principal note.

Again, the grace note has in many cases the editorial support of the *NMA,* starting with works from Mozart's earliest youth such as Ex. 4.4*a* from the Mass in C minor K 47a (139) of 1768 (or, not shown here, an almost identical passage from the Mass in C, K 66 of 1769, Gloria, m. 109); Exx. *b* and *c* from the Violin Sonatas in A K 293d (305) and D K 300l (306); for Ex. *d* from the Piano Concerto in F K 459 the editors (the Badura-Skodas) comment in the preface that to play the *Vorschläge* in this passage on the beat would not only be unelegant but would, in mm. 71–73, cause unwelcome friction between the left hand and the basses; Exx. *e* and *f* from the Piano Concertos K 450 and 595, both in B flat; *g* from the String Quartet in G; *h* from the second Finale of *Die Zauberflöte.*

For other cases of grace-note support from the *NMA* see also the Violin Sonatas in E flat K 374f (380)/3, m. 7, and in B flat K 454/3, m. 258; the String Quartet in B flat K 458/1, m. 53; the Variations on "La Bergère Célimène," K 374a (359), var. 4; the Piano Concerto in E flat K 449/3, m. 285.

A few other specimens that call for the same treatment are given in Ex. 4.5*a* from the Piano Sonata in D K 284c (311); *b* from the Violin Concerto No. 4 in D, *c*

Ex. 4.4.

from the Wedding Chorus in *Don Giovanni*. See also the *Salzburg* Symphony in D
K 133/4, mm. 32–33; the Four-Hand Sonata, K 497/3, m. 1, and numerous similar
passages.

Ex. 4.5.

VORSCHLÄGE BEFORE GROUPS OF EVEN BINARY NOTES

Similar considerations apply to even binary notes. Especially in a fairly fast tempo,
or its equivalent in smaller denominations, Tartinis rule will frequently turn out to
make excellent musical sense. We find again a number of such instances in which
the editors of the *NMA* convincingly suggest grace-note use. A random selection
of a few such cases with different denominations and articulations is given in Ex.
4.6. Among them are Exx. *a* and *b* from the Finale of the *Linz* Symphony; *c* from
the Piano Concerto in G K 453; *d* from the String Quintet in E flat; *e* from the
Violin Sonata in C K 293c (303); *f* from the Eight Piano Variations K 613; *g* from
the Violin Sonata in C K 296; *h* from the Sinfonia Concertante.

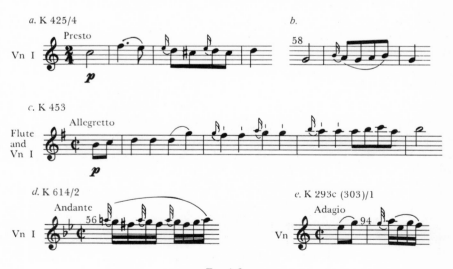

Ex. 4.6.

Ex. 4.6 *cont.*

For further *NMA* endorsements of such usage see also Nine Variations in C, K 315d (264), var. 4, mm. 19 and parallel spots; Aria for soprano K 368, start of recitative; Five Variations for Four Hands, K 501, var. 3, mm. 15–17; Violin Sonatas in G K 293a (301)/1, m. 53; in C K 296/3, m. 13; in F K 374e (377)/3, m. 23; Serenade in D K 213a (204)/3, m. 12.

Other passages include that shown in Ex. 4.7*a* from *Eine kleine Nachtmusik,* which is almost always heard with appoggiaturas of 16th or even 8th-note length. Yet anticipation is not only more graceful but provides a clearly intended contrast to its explicitly varied form of two measures later (Ex. *b*). At the start of the andante grazioso theme of the variations from the Violin-Viola Duet in B flat (Ex. *c*), the frequently heard repeated appoggiaturas seem to nail it to the ground. With grace notes it takes wings. In its sister piece, the Duo in G (Ex. *d*), we often hear the first theme deprived of its spirit and gaiety by three plodding appoggiaturas in m. 2. Again, grace notes are the obvious answer. In Ex. *e* from the start of the overture to *Die Entführung,* the autograph dashes over the quarter-notes could not accommodate appoggiaturas. The same autograph dashes (shown as dots in the *NMA*) in Ex. *f* from the E flat Symphony carry the same message. In Ex. *g* from the String Quartet in D *(Hoffmeister),* the evenness of the smooth 32nd motion extending over two whole measures should be safeguarded by anticipation of the *Vorschläge.* In Ex. *h* from the *Don Giovanni* overture the case for grace notes is strengthened by the appoggiatura character of the two F sharps. The same is true of the *Vorschläge* at the start of the Presto in the overture to *Così fan tutte.* In both instances the accent should fall on the first regular note. In Ex. *i* from the Sonata for Two Pianos the repeated pattern is an accompanying figure whose dynamically smooth evenness calls for grace notes since appoggiaturas would be both obtrusive and clumsy. The figure in this tender Andante spot is even smoother than the similar one of Ex. 4.6*g*, which was justly marked for grace-note use by the *NMA.* In the recitative and aria "Mia speranza" of Ex. *j* the figure, which recurs several times, calls for a grace note. Here the need for rhythmic integrity of the four even 32nd-notes is strengthened by their appearing at the start of a phrase after a rest. The phrase of Ex. *k* from the Wind Serenade in C minor is derived from the pervasive motive (Ex. *l*), the final fragment of the principal theme. Its half-step move after the downward leap of a diminished seventh forms part of the thematic essence, occurring repeatedly in its original sequence and in its inversions. A grace note with the accent on the principal note maintains the integrity of the half-step progression which an appoggiatura would impair.

The four-note formula of Ex. *j* occurs in many works and should always be treated in the same manner. See, for example, the Piano Sonata in E flat, K 189g (282)/1, m. 23; the Rondo from *Tito*, K 621/,II,19, m. 12; the start of the Recitative and Aria for soprano "Ma, que vi fece, o stelle," K 368.

a. K 525/1

b.

c. K 424/3

d. K 423/1   *e.* K 384, Overture

f. K 543/4

g. K 499/3

h. K 527, Overture

Ex. 4.7.

Ex. 4.7 *cont.*

VORSCHLÄGE BEFORE STACCATO NOTES

A *Vorschlag* before a staccato note will usually call for grace-note treatment. The need for grace notes is magnified when Mozart uses a dash symbol, which often implies accentuation as well as staccato articulation. An appoggiatura would at best blunt, and for short notes wipe out, the intended sharpness of articulation. For these reasons the *NMA* suggests grace notes for Ex. 4.8*a* from the early aria "Sol nascente" of 1767; for the end of the slow movement of the *Hunt* Quartet (Ex. *b*) where Mozart wrote "staccato" in all four parts; for Ex. *c* from the String Quartet in F K 590; and for many other similar spots.

Ex. 4.8.

For other cases of recommended grace-note use see Exx. 4.9*a* and *b* from the Piano Sonatas in D K 205b and C 189d (279); *c* and *d* from the Violin Concertos in G and A; *e* from the *Haffner* Serenade; *f* from the *Posthorn* Serenade; *g* from the *Missa solemnis*; *h* from the Symphony in G K 318.

Ex. 4.9.

Ex. 4.9 *cont.*

VORSCHLÄGE BEFORE SINGLE NOTES

Very closely related to notes with staccato markings are those that are short and followed by a rest. Their effect is usually indistinguishable from staccato notes; hence here, too, in most cases grace notes are the fitting solution.

In Ex. 4.10*a* from the Piano Concerto in B flat K 456 such a rendition is recommended by the *NMA*. The same treatment suggests itself for Exx. *b, c,* and *d* from the Violin Concertos Nos. 3, 4, and 5—in the last case the comparison with the written-out design shown in Ex. *e* is revealing of the contrasting intent—; Ex. *f* from the Piano Sonata in A; Ex. *g* from the Two-Piano Sonata for the three times repeated brief, wistful interjections (in a passage that recurs twice more) where the often heard rendition of the *Vorschläge* as 8th-notes destroys their delightful humor; Ex. *h* from the Violin Sonata in C K 293c (303).

Ex. 4.10.

b. K 216/3

c. K 218/3

d. K 219/3

f. K 300i (331)

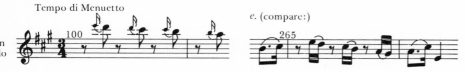

g. K 375a (488)/1

h. K 293c (303)/1

Ex. 4.10 *cont.*

VORSCHLÄGE BEFORE REPEATED NOTES

We often find two or more repeated notes, each of which is preceded by a *Vorschlag,* rising by a half-step and written as a 16th-note or shorter. One can rarely go wrong in treating them as grace notes. Appoggiaturas should be used in such a situation only for sufficient cause.

Grace notes should be used for Ex. 4.11*a* from the slow movement of the

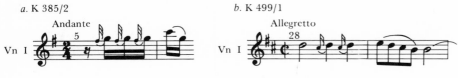

Ex. 4.11.

Ex. 4.11 *cont.*

Haffner Symphony (with slurs added of course); *b* from the *Hoffmeister* Quartet; *c* and *d* from the Violin Sonata in F K 374d (376); *e* and *f* from the String Quintet in E flat; *g* from the Piano Concerto (the last) in B flat. The *NMA* endorses grace notes for Exx. *b, c, e, f,* and *g.*

For analogous treatment see also the Piano Sonatas in B̈ flat K 189f (281)/2, mm. 17, 19, and in C K 300h (330)/2, m. 24; the Two-Piano Sonata, K 375a (448)/2, first ending; the Oboe Quartet, K 368b (370)/3, m. 162; the String Quartet in F, K 590/4, mm. 298–300 (second violin); the Horn Concerto in E flat, K 417/3, m. 73; the *Posthorn* Serenade, K 320/3, "Concertante," m. 1; the Violin Concerto in A K 219/3, m. 321.

Where such repeated notes were meant to be played with appoggiaturas, Mozart had to write them out for every note, as shown in Ex. 4.12*a* from the first Finale of *Don Giovanni,* where five times alternating flutes and violins mockingly comment on the Don's guile. Very revealing, too, is the contrast in Osmin's aria "Ha, wie will ich triumphieren" between the consistently written-out appoggiaturas in m. 4 and parallel spots (Ex. *b*), and the symbols in mm. 29 and 33 (Ex. *c*) on the words *[die Hälse] schnüren zu,* a graphic portrayal of snapping off the necks, where grace-note use is obvious.

Ex. 4.12.

VORSCHLÄGE RISING A HALF-STEP

A single *Vorschlag* rising a half-step and written as a 16th or shorter, will also create a strong presumption of grace-note nature. As pointed out before, Mozart writes out the great majority of his genuine rising appoggiaturas in regular notes. In the few instances in which he does use symbols as, for example, in Ex. 2.6*a* or 2.8*c*, he writes them with 8th-note values. We shall always find borderline cases, but by and large we are reasonably safe in using a grace note for a *Vorschlag* of 16th-note or shorter value that rises by a half-step.

The *cause célèbre* of the opening of the A minor Piano Sonata with its presumed grace-note solution was discussed earlier (see Ex. 3.13). If we consider Ex. 4.13*a* from the very early aria "Quaere superna" of 1770, the *Vorschlag* on a weak beat after a long ascending leap, is derived from the vocal idiom. The Italians called it *cercar della nota* (searching for the note), a stylized portamento that helped the singer locate the pitch securely and attractively and that was, like the vocal portamento, always anticipated. For other specimens see Ex. *b* from the characteristic bass figure in the second variation of the A major Piano Sonata; *c* from the Piano Sonata in B flat K 189f (281); *d* from the Oboe Quartet; *e* from the Piano Quartet in E flat.

Ex. 4.13.

CLUES OF DICTION AND DYNAMICS

As pointed out in Chapter 2, diction will, on an accented syllable, in most cases favor the appoggiatura. There are, however, exceptions for those Italian diphthongs whose first component is unaccented. Such is the case in Ex. 4.14*a* from *Così fan tutte* where on the word *diàvolo* the *Vorschlag* belongs clearly to the unaccented *di-*, the principal note to *à;* hence the *Vorschlag* has to be a grace note which in turn logically transfers to the parallel *co-da*. Very interesting is Ex. *b* from the aria "Voi avete un cor fedele" of 1775, where the twice repeated *vuò* requires the same interpretation which again transfers to *voi*, and to the violins as well. Here we find another confirmation in the *fp* or related symbol that applies to the principal note, not to the ornament. Similarly in Ex. *c* from *Don Giovanni* the accent on *è* in *diè* favors unaccented shortness for the *Vorschlag*. In Ex. *d* from *La finta giardiniera*, the combination of the unaccented syllable *hi-* and the violin figure with the 8th-note e″ preceding the d″ will prompt a sensitive singer to anticipate the *Vorschlag*.

Ex. 4.14.

Dynamics such as the *fp*'s in Ex. 4.14*b*, or *sf*, or a dash in a clearly accentual meaning (the sign > not being known at the time), or a sudden *f* in the middle of a phrase offer instrumental counterparts to the clues of diction. Such markings practically always refer to the principal note, not to any ornament that might precede it. Two out of a multitude of cases confirming the fact that the signs belong to the principal note are shown in Exx. 4.15*a* from the Symphony No. 25 in A, and *b* from the Divertimento in D K 167A (205). In the autographs the intended alignment of the *fp* with the principal note is clear, even if we take into account Mozart's habit of always writing dynamic markings slightly ahead of the note to which they belong. There is hardly ever any doubt about this relationship which, incidentally, seems to indicate that Mozart wrote the dynamic marks before he wrote the notes to which they refer. In our cases, as probably in most similar ones, the *fp* calls for grace-note use. Very similar in meaning and alignment is the case of Ex. *c* from the String Quartet in G K 387, where the *NMA* sensibly suggests the grace note before the sudden forte.

Ex. 4.15.

CLUES OF RHYTHM

The striking feature of *syncopation* is the cross accents that clash with the metrical pulse. In the vast majority of cases this characteristic profile forms part of the thematic essence and hence must not be blurred by the intrusion of onbeat ornaments that would usurp the accents destined for the principal notes. The presumption is therefore strong that a *Vorschlag* within a syncopated figure is to be anticipated. For illustrations see Ex. 4.16*a* from the Piano Sonata in E flat. Here the need for grace notes is underlined by both the insistent intensification of the three times repeated A flat, and by Mozart's clearly intended concomitant crescendo through the tied note, as shown in the autograph by the placement of the *f* sign. Of course, on the keyboard this crescendo can only be suggested, not realized; whereas a grace note can support the illusion, an appoggiatura would destroy it. In Ex. *b* from the Piano Sonata in D *(Dürnitz)* the syncopations are set against steady 16th-notes in the left hand. The intended interplay is again better served by grace-note treatment. We find the ascending counterpart to this figure in the A minor Sonata, K 300d (310)/2, m. 13, where grace-note leaning is made even more explicit by 32nd denominations. Example *c* from the Violin Concerto in A again favors grace notes for the same reasons.

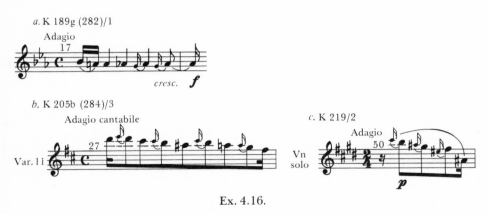

Ex. 4.16.

The rhythmic figure ♩. ♪♪ in 3/8, 6/8, and similar meters becomes the more striking the faster the tempo and could easily lose its intended edge were an appoggiatura to invade the downbeat. True, in a slow tempo, when the figure can be more songful than rhythmic, an appoggiatura can on occasion be needed as will presently be shown. But even at a slow pace, say in a siciliano-type passage, the rhythmic profile can be of sufficient thematic importance to warrant preserving its identity by placing a *Vorschlag* before the beat. Gratifyingly, we find recommendations in the *NMA* for grace-note use, as in Ex. 4.17a from the Violin Sonata in A K 293d (305); *b* from the String Quartet in B flat *(Hunt)*; *c* from the Finale of the String Quartet in D Minor K 417b (421) and *d* from its slow movement; *e* from the Oboe Quartet. See also var. 5 from the Six Variations for Violin and Piano, K 374b (360).

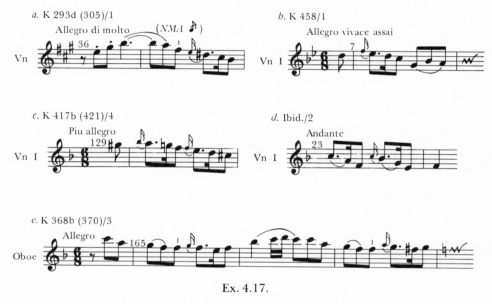

Ex. 4.17.

The simple dotted figure of ♩. ♪ (or ♩. ♪ in a slower tempo) invites similar considerations. When, as is usually the case, the piquancy inherent in the design is thematically prominent, the rhythmic design has a claim to being preserved by anticipation of the *Vorschlag* (or any other ornament). This principle applies with greater force when the two notes of the pair are not slurred, because the detached articulation sharpens the rhythmic contour and strengthens its claim to integrity. But even when they are slurred, an appoggiatura will often be out of place, especially when the dotted rhythm is continued, ♩. ♪ ♩. ♪ , thereby manifesting its thematic importance.

First let us look at cases where the *NMA* supports this point of view. Among them we find suggested grace notes in Ex. 4.18a from the Violin Sonata in C K 296; *b* and *c* from the Adagio of the String Quintet in D K 593, *b* in a shorter, *c* in a longer denomination. For Ex. *b* the grace note seems the logical answer; for Ex. *c* an appoggiatura of circa 16th-note length would be a reasonable alternative, here as well as in m. 32 for the viola; the note pair is not conceived as a self-contained rhythmic unit, because the 16th-note D is ornamental in nature, a *Nachschlag* that could be slightly shortened in value (a design that used to be called *anticipazione della nota*); *d* and *e* from the Serenade in D K 213a (204) in both the Allegro and the

Andante; and *f* from "Sancta Maria," where two factors strengthen the grace-note option: 1) the 32nd denomination of the *Vorschlag*, consistently repeated in mm. 36, 41, 42, and 45; and 2) the unornamented unison of the soprano part that would unnecessarily clash with an appoggiatura.

Observe that the *Vorschläge* in Ex. 4.18*a*, for which the *NMA* convincingly suggests anticipation, are written as 8th-notes—a further reminder of the need to keep an open mind about denominations.

For slurred notes see Ex. *g* from the Violin Sonata in G 373a (379); *h* and *i* for the repeated pattern from the Nine Variations for Piano, and the last Piano Concerto in B flat respectively.

Ex. 4.18.

In the Four-Hand Sonata in C K 521 the passage of Ex. 4.19*a* calls for a grace note, but later in the movement (Ex. *b*), with larger denominations for both the dotted-note group and the *Vorschlag*, the latter should probably be an appoggiatura of circa 16th-note length. In the excerpt of *c* from the late String Quartet in B flat the 8th-note *Vorschlag* suggests appoggiatura intention, but the *NMA* advice of 8th-note length and subsequent contraction of the dotted-note pair is not a likely solution. It happens to fit this particular place but not its two parallel spots: in the first, two measures later, a resulting rhythmic conflict with the second violin and viola is not logical; in the second, at m. 87, such an interpretation is even less appropriate, as it would collide with the turn in the cello. Approximate 16th-note length here too seems the best solution.

Other contexts in which grace-note use is probably always preferable are at the beginning of a phrase, and even in mid-phrase after a rest, as in Ex. *d* from *La Betulia liberata,* where the case against an appoggiatura is strengthened by the energy of the motive and its start in mid-beat.

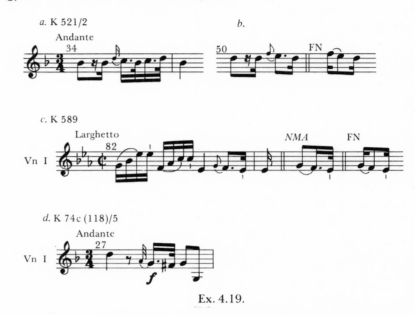

Ex. 4.19.

Another highly characteristic rhythmic figure following a *Vorschlag* is the anapest ⸭ ♪♪♪ ⸭ which is in a class by itself when, as is usually the case, its three regular notes are arranged in the melodic design of a mordent. In this form it amounts to a standard ornament occurring with great frequency in Mozart. For illustrations see Ex. 4.20*a* from the Piano Concerto in B flat K 450; *b* from the Count's recitative in the third act of *Figaro* (for both of these the *NMA* suggests grace notes); and *c* from the String Quintet in C. See also the *Haffner* Serenade K 248b (250)/6, mm. 91–107 where the figure is repeated 34 times in the second violins. A slur over the group is required and is understood, as befits a mordent, even if by oversight it was not notated.

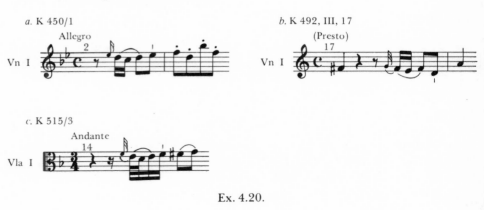

Ex. 4.20.

The main difference between the Mozartian mordent and what I have called in *Ornamentation* the "Italian mordent," Andante · Allegro ·, is that the latter often occurs *on* the beat and reinforces it, whereas Mozart's is typically placed *after* the beat. This beat is either taken up by a rest as in Exx. 4.20*a-c* or, more frequently, by a—usually staccato—8th-note (a 16th for shorter denominations) on the pitch of the first and third mordent note: ♪. In this form we find the snap effect of the mordent combined with the melodic shape of a turn. Example 4.21 shows just a few illustrations of this pattern from an overabundance of choice: Ex. 4.21*a* from the String Quartet in E flat K 421b (428); *b* from the Piano Quartet in G minor; *c* and *d* from different movements of the Piano Concerto in C K 467; *e* from the Piano Concerto in C minor; *f* from Don Giovanni's aria "Fin qu' han dal vino"; *g* from the Piano Trio in B flat; *h* from the Piano Sonata in A; *i* from the Clarinet Trio.

Ex. 4.21.

Almost all the editors of the *NMA* who made performance suggestions for this formula prefer a grace note for the *Vorschlag* and rightly so; it seems that only the Badura-Skodas differ on this point. In their book they show three possibilities for its execution, but prefer the triplet version: . As *NMA* editors of the Piano Concertos in G K 453, B flat 456, and F K 459 (vol. V/15/5) this is how they recommend rendering this formula on its frequent occurrence in these works. It is true that in a fast tempo the difference between the two designs can become indistinguishable, but *only* if one does not accent the first triplet note. The danger of such a principle is that it entices the player to do just that, in which case the rhythmic difference between the two styles becomes marked. This is the case in a fairly fast tempo and far more so in a slower one. Once the difference can be perceived it is difficult to justify turning a clearly intended binary figure into a ternary one, and in the process transforming a mordent into a turn. Though, as said before, the pitches are those of a turn, the articulation, as well as the implied rhythm and accentuation, is that of a mordent. For this reason I would in almost all instances consider it advisable to try to accent ever so slightly the principal note that follows the *Vorschlag,* and if speed makes that impracticable, at least to avoid any accentuation of the *Vorschlag* itself.

That such considerations are not pure hairsplitting sophistry can be seen in excerpts like that of Ex. 4.22*a* from *La Betulia liberata* where in a series of stripped down mordents the difference between binary and ternary execution would be very tangible; or in Ex. *b* from the Piano Concerto K 450 in B flat where the difference between anticipation and synchronization of the *Vorschlag* with the quarter-note B flat would be clearly distinguishable, and where, again, the *NMA* with good reason recommends anticipation.

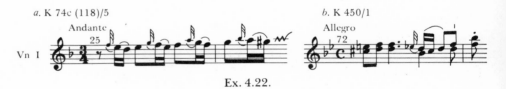

Ex. 4.22.

A still stronger case for this style can be made when we see how Mozart invariably wrote out a triplet when the pitches of the formula were *slurred* to the preceding note: . The slur encompassing the five notes of this design (the sixth note may or may not be slurred) is as essential to its character as a turn as the slur connecting the *Vorschlag* and the three notes of the anapest is to its character as a mordent. A few specimens of such written-out turns are given in Ex. 4.23 of which *a* and *b* are from two different movements of the String Quartet in E flat K 421b (428); *c* from the Violin Sonata in F K 374d (376); *d* from the *Coronation* Concerto in D; and *e* from the Piano Concerto K 503 in C.

Ex. 4.23.

b. Ibid./4

c. K 374d (376)/3

d. K 537/1

e. K 503/1

Ex. 4.23 *cont.*

This pattern is actually far more frequent aurally than visually, it being the standard resolution of the turn symbol when that symbol is placed between a dotted note and its companion: 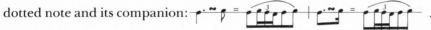 .

Interesting in this connection is a spot in the F major Rondo K 494 where we find a juxtaposition of the two styles, as shown in Ex. 4.24.[1] In m. 99 Mozart's autograph has no articulation markings: the mandatory slur for the three

a. K 494

b.

c.

d.

e.

f.

Ex. 4.24.

[1]For a facsimile of the autograph and a thorough analysis of the scholarly controversy surrounding this piece see Hans Neumann and Carl Schachter, "The Two Versions of Mozart's Rondo K.494."

mordent pitches is missing as is the equally mandatory one from appoggiatura to resolution in m. 102. The first 8th-note B♭′ in m. 99 is the end of a long preceding phrase and is therefore detached from the mordent figure, which starts the new phrase with a measure-long unaccompanied anacrusis whose pitch repetitions imply detached articulation. The written-out turn in m. 101 forms under the legato bow a gentle contrast with the perky anacrusis. The contrast in notation conforms to the usual pattern for a legato turn and a detached mordent and hence is not an oversight. Nor does it permit the conclusion that the two formulas are rhythmically equivalent.

In this piece we find a few more spots with legato turns, for example in mm. 43, 49, 93, and 124 (Exx. *b-d*). Yet we also have two exceptions from the usual pattern in mm. 17 and 38 (Ex. *e*) where Mozart has a staccato first note followed not by a mordent but by a triplet. They are, it seems, rare exceptions to Mozart's usual orthographic habit.

CLUES OF MELODY

Whenever an appoggiatura would obscure rather than embellish the underlying melody, we should substitute a grace note, since a melody has a right to its basic integrity. Situations of this kind are more frequent in fast tempos where the melody notes do not have enough time to be clearly perceived, and more generally, when the melody has a strikingly characteristic profile. A fine illustration is shown in Ex. 4.25*a* from the Finale of the *Haffner* Symphony, as written in the autograph (but misrepresented in a number of well-known editions). The chromatic line rising through 14 steps would be not only obscured but obliterated by onbeat treatment of the *Vorschläge*. Grace notes are imperative here. Though less fast, the melody of Ex. *b* from the Piano Quartet in E flat K 493 would be noticeably altered by appoggiaturas. The solution here too is grace notes which, as pointed out before, are in general the most likely reading for rising *Vorschläge* written with symbols of 16th-note or shorter value.[2]

Interesting on several counts is the passage of Ex. *c* from the Symphony No. 30 in D of 1774. Here we have the unusual case of a series of downward leaping *Vorschläge* that repeat the same pitch in a quasi organ point, while the melody of the principal notes ascends chromatically. Musically the moving line has to have precedence over the static one, the melody over the organ point: the *Vorschläge*

a. K 385/4

Ex. 4.25.

[2]No autograph survives. In the first edition of Artaria the denominations of the *Vorschläge* are inconsistent: some are printed as 32nds, some as 16ths. The first *Vorschlag* in this example is given as a″ which almost certainly is a misprint for b″.

b. K 493/3

* *Vorschläge* according to *NMA.* They are inconsistent
in Artaria, but never printed as 32nds.

c. K 186b (202)/1

Ex. 4.25 *cont.*

have to be grace notes. This conclusion is further supported by the notational
contrast of the *Vorschlag* series with the first measure of the example where
appoggiatura-type leaps are spelled out in regular notes.

CLUES OF EXPRESSION

The start of the solo in the Violin Concerto No. 4 in D, given in Ex. 4.26*a* has the
bold, military character of a bugle call. A snappy, anticipated *Vorschlag* adds to its
provocative resoluteness, whereas an appoggiatura (generally out of place at the
beginning of a phrase) would detract from it. The first solo in the Violin Concerto
in G (Ex. *b*) starts with a theme of a similarly aggressive, martial vein, then softens
in mm. 40 and 41 in a contrast underlined by the *fp* accents of the orchestra on the
downbeats of mm. 38 and 39, and the gentle, soft throbbing of the strings in mm.
40 and 41. The contrast in the solo is best brought out by playing the *Vorschlag* in
m. 39 as a grace note with a clear accent on the principal note, in contrast with the
written-out appoggiaturas in mm. 40 and 41. The scintillating gaiety of the Violin
Sonata in A K 293d (305) (Ex. *c*) calls for grace notes throughout (these have the
backing of the *NMA*). A closely related mood would make grace notes seem
preferable in the excerpt of Ex. *d* from the Finale of the Fourth Violin Concerto.

a. K 218/1

b. K 216/1

Ex. 4.26.

c. K 293d (305)/1

d. K 218/3

e. K 300i (331)/1

f. K 497/3

Ex. 4.26 *cont.*

They add to the phrase a sparkle that is dimmed by the usual appoggiatura style. The jolly, lighthearted tone of the sixth variation of the Piano Sonata in A (Ex. *e*) reinforces the clues of even notes and pitch repetition in suggesting grace notes. The affinity of prepared downward leaping *Vorschläge* to expressive appoggiaturas has been discussed in Chapters 2 and 3. Clearly such affinity can assert itself only in an appropriate mood. By contrast, in a sprightly, brilliant movement such as the Finale of the Four-Hand Sonata in F (Ex. *f*) all the *Vorschläge* ought to be grace notes since they alone can do justice to the prevailing spirit of the piece.

CLUES OF NOTATION

As we have seen on several occasions, the notational clues are important but far from unequivocal. Above all we must beware of the often proclaimed rule that Mozart's *Vorschläge* have the value of their denomination. This rule is misleading if for no other reason than that it wrongly implies that all *Vorschläge* are appoggiaturas. Nor can we follow a principle like the one formulated by Walter Senn in the preface to *NMA*/IV/12/5 to the effect that *Vorschläge* of half the value of the principal note are long (i.e. appoggiaturas) and those of less than half the value are short (presumably meaning grace notes). The first part of the principle will often work for quarter-note symbols before half-notes, for 8th- before quarter-notes. But for the smaller denominations of 16th and 32nd symbols it does not work, as we have seen in numerous examples where grace notes are the more likely solution. The reverse is true of the second part of the principle about *Vorschläge* of less than half the value of the principal notes. For the mature Mozart it will often fit for denominations of a 16th or shorter, but it will often mislead for the longer ones: thus a 16th before a quarter-note or a longer value, a 32nd before an 8th or longer, is likely to be short, and often a grace note. But an 8th before a half- or whole note is just as likely to be a (long) appoggiatura. Denomination must always be considered, though not in isolation but in reference to the musical environment: length of the principal note, tempo, the prevailing expression, diction, articulation, rhythm, melody, dynamics, and any other musical element that can affect the environment.

In his early years, Mozart was often casual in choosing the value of his *Vorschlag* symbols. Often he wrote 16th-note values with probable 8th-note meaning as suggested, for example, in Ex. 4.27 from a tenor aria of 1766. (Note in this excerpt the rhythmic discrepancy in the second beat of the first measure with its greater sharpness for the instruments than the voice. It is an interesting document of Mozart's awareness, at age 10, of the divergent idiomatic traits of the two media.) A similar case from *La Betulia liberata* was shown in Exx. 3.8*a* and *b*.

Ex. 4.27.

With maturity Mozart became more circumspect about his *Vorschlag* notation, but never fully consistent. We have seen how he used different values in a unison passage (Ex. 2.6*b*) or different values for parallel spots with no detectable motive for a variant (Ex. 2.4*b*). Similarly, in the Adagio of the Triple Piano Concerto, the 8th-note *Vorschläge* in mm. 5 and 6 become 16ths in mm. 29 and 30 with no likelihood of a different intention. That for reasons of diction the 8th-note *Vorschläge* in "Das Veilchen" had to be shorter was shown above (and confirmed by Mozart's use of 16th notes in the catalogue of his works). In other cases voice leading suggests or requires a deviation from the *Vorschlag* values. In Ex. 4.28*a* from the Piano Concerto in E flat (*Jeunehomme*) quarter-note duration would produce unacceptable octaves, the same situation repeating itself in mm. 240 and 244. In Ex. *b* from the Flute Quartet in D, 8th-note duration of the *Vorschlag* note would result in an unpleasant seventh–ninth sequence; hence the appoggiatura ought to be shorter than that. See also Ex. 4.18*a* for the presumable grace-note meaning of its *Vorschläge* in 8th-notes.

Ex. 4.28.

Notational clues achieve notable eloquence when we find consistency in differentiation: that is, where different values appear in exact analogy in either simultaneous parts or parallel spots. A few illustrations should suffice. In Ex. 4.29*a* from the early Symphony in F K 130, the contrast between the Lombard rhythm of the first measure and the symbol in the second one is maintained in all repeats of the phrase as well as in its imitation in the second violins. It points to grace-note intention. In Ex. *b* from the Flute and Harp Concerto the consistent 8th-note values in the first theme (with probable 8th-note meaning) are contrasted with the equally consistent 16th-note values in the theme of the harp (mm. 58ff. and parallel spots), suggesting great shortness of the *Vorschläge* which could come before or on the beat. In Ex. *c* from the Divertimento in D of 1776 the pattern of difference between the two 8th-notes and the one 16th-note is identical in the given oboe part and the simultaneous first and second violin parts written out in the autograph an octave and a tenth below. The difference was clearly intentional and would seem to call for two long appoggiaturas framing a short, probably anticipated, *Vorschlag*. Very interesting is Ex. *d* from the Piano Sonata in F where we find the 16th symbol in m. 73, a written-out appoggiatura on the same pitch in m. 75. The pattern is immediately repeated an octave higher with identical notation, then twice more in the recapitulation in another key. Here a long appoggiatura would make little sense and even a short one would be redundant; a grace note would make the best musical sense by leaving intact the sequential pattern of the two groups of two measures each, as well as the thematic threefold repeat of the quarter-note. Similar considerations apply to Ex. *e* from the Piano Sonata in C K 300h (330), where we find in the autograph a notational contrast between the 32nd symbols and the written-out appoggiatura on the same pitch on the second beat. Again, an appoggiatura on the first beat would be redundant, whereas a grace note provides a satisfying foil for the intensification of the second beat. A comparison with the analogous passage three measures later is revealing: the *Vorschlag* symbol is replaced by a written-out appoggiatura, and the intensification for the second part of the phrase achieved by its ornamental enrichment. Thus the whole phrase, on its repeat, is raised to a higher expressive level. That the notation was premeditated becomes clear when Mozart in the autograph spells out the whole passage in the exact same way on its later return, without resorting to his frequent labor-saving device of referring copyist or printer to the previous passage. In Ex. *f* from the String Quintet in B flat, the unfailing consistency with which the two-measure motive is notated calls for shortness of the 16th-note *Vorschlag*, not for its 8th-note interpretation, as suggested by the *NMA*. Closely related is Ex. *g* from the Violin Concerto in A, where of three successive sequential *Vorschläge* the second and third are written out as long appoggiaturas, the first (though the only consonant one of the three) as a 16th-note symbol. Again the difference in notation is clearly intentional, and the first *Vorschlag* is to be played very short, on or before the beat. In Ex. *h* from the Violin Sonata in B flat K454, the different values for the symbols make excellent musical sense: the 16th for the grace note of the upward leap, the 8th for an expressive appoggiatura before the dotted half-note.

For other cases of systematic differentiation see Exx. 3.3*a* from the Violin Sonata in E minor K 300c (304) and 3.5*a* from the String Quartet in D, K 575.

Generally, we find many more instances in which a *Vorschlag* is rendered shorter than its denomination than the opposite. This, as pointed out, does not necessarily apply to Mozart's youthful years, but after circa 1776–1778 a 16th-note symbol before a quarter-note or longer will rarely stand for an appoggiatura of roughly 8th-note length, let alone for one of quarter-note length. Thus in Ex. 4.30*a* from the third-act march in *Idomeneo*, the *Vorschläge* have to be very short, first, because they are written as 16th- before half-notes, and second, because they are consonances before dissonances. For these two reasons the *NMA* suggestion of

Ex. 4.29.

quarter-note value is infelicitous. It is well-nigh inconceivable that Mozart in 1780 would have written an intended quarter-note appoggiatura with a 16th symbol and just as improbable that orchestra violinists would have so interpreted the notation. We find, even for lesser disparities, much musical evidence that shortness was intended. In Ex. 4.30*b* from the Missa brevis in F the *Vorschlag,* though unquestionably an appoggiatura, has to be short, since an 8th-note would clash intolerably with the alto. Similarly in Ex. *c* from the Church Sonata in G, 8th-note values in mm. 10 and 11 would result in similar motion to a unison. In the Serenade

Ex. 4.30.

in D of 1775 the recurring pattern of Ex. *d* is consistently written with a 32nd symbol which the *NMA* with good reason transcribes as a grace note. In Ex. *e* from the Trio of the *Haffner* Symphony the grace-note nature of the 16th symbol in the violins is supported by the unison oboe parts which have staccato dashes in mm. 2 and 6. In Ex. *f* from the Piano Concerto in E flat (*Jeunehomme*) the 16th-note *Vorschlag* before the quarter-note should be short; whether it is played on or before the beat is immaterial. The *Vorschläge* in the excerpt of Ex. *g* from the Violin Concerto in A have to be short and sprightly lest they dim its humor.

The greater the disparity between the value of the symbol and that of the principal note, the more the scales are weighted toward grace-note intention. In Ex. 4.31*a* from the Two-Piano Sonata, the consistent 32nd-symbols before the half-notes that form an organ point and are reinforced by the unornamented octaves in the left hand should be played in anticipation. In this way they serve to illuminate and add graceful touches of life to the organ point, but to obtrude on the unison of the bass with an accented appoggiatura would be musically improper and disturbing. In Ex. *b* from the G minor symphony K 550, the 32nds before quarter-notes call for anticipation. For the second *Vorschlag* that leaps upward on a weak beat such rendition would be mandatory regardless of denomination. In Ex. *c* from the String Quartet in F K 590, I would also suggest grace notes rather than the short appoggiaturas proposed by the *NMA*. Not only would the tender alternation of the same two pitches (of which the first D should receive a gentle emphasis) be diluted by being preempted by the appoggiaturas in the preceding two measures, but also, in the transformation of the motive in mm. 15–19, the powerful chromatic ascent of the second violin and viola would be weakened by appoggiatura treatment of the *Vorschläge* since the line G-A♭-A-B♭ would be obscured by the prominence of the appoggiatura sequence A♭-B♭-B♭-B♭.

a. K 375a (448)/1

b. K 550/2

c. K 590/3 Trio

Ex. 4.31.

The importance of notation for *Vorschlag* interpretation has come up in many references scattered throughout these first chapters. The point of this section has been to sum up briefly with a number of illustrations both the importance we have to attach to it and the care with which we must evaluate its often clear but sometimes blurred signals.

UPWARD LEAPS

The downward leaping appoggiaturas that carry a strong affective coloring, illustrated in Exx. 2.15 and 3.10, are always prepared by the same pitch. In a moderate tempo Mozart usually wrote their symbols as 8th-notes or longer, in a slow tempo often as 16ths, but hardly ever as shorter values. In clear contrast to these vocal or voice-inspired appoggiaturas are a multitude of instrumentally conceived upward leaping *Vorschläge* which are typically unprepared, indeed occur often at the beginning of a phrase or following a rest. Written, regardless of tempo, mostly as 16th- or shorter notes, these *Vorschläge* are prime candidates for grace-note treatment.

Some of these *Vorschläge* simply have the function of smoothing the voice leading, hence play the subservient role of lubricants and should be as unobtrusive as possible. Illustrations of this type are given in Exx. 4.32*a* from the String Quartet in D *(Hoffmeister)*; *b* from the String Quartet in B flat K 589; and *c* from the String Quartet in F K 590, where the leaping *Vorschlag* in the second violin, and an octave below in the viola, prepares the unisons with the first violin and the cello which are written without *Vorschläge*. In all three cases the *NMA* suggests grace notes as the only sensible solution.

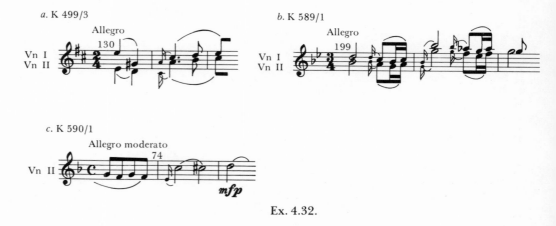

Ex. 4.32.

Another kind of upward leaping *Vorschlag* probably has a vocal origin in the stylized portamento with which many singers approach a high note by gently gliding into it, hitting the desired pitch on the beat. Such a portamento is always anticipated. The upward leaping instrumental *Vorschläge* have a similar function, serving as a brief prefix which by its very inconspicuousness in the rhythmic shade allows the principal note to cast a brighter light. In spite of their presumably vocal origin these *Vorschläge* have been thoroughly naturalized by keyboard and many melody instruments. Here they are closely related to the arpeggio and indeed represent a kind of semiarpeggio, which is an additional explanation of why they leap upward far more readily than downward.[3]

The most characteristic of these *Vorschläge* is the leap of an octave, because it lies so naturally in the hand of a pianist, a violinist, or a viola player. First, a few illustrations for the piano from a lavish supply. Ex. 4.33*a* gives the start of the solo from the C minor Piano Concerto. Comparing the two phrases from mm. 108–111, the Badura-Skodas justly point out that mm. 110 and 111 are "obviously a varied intensification of the [preceding] two bars." The 16th-note *Vorschlag* of bar 108 "has broadened out and become an expressive quaver anacrusis to bar 3 [i.e. bar 110]." They see in this notation a proof for the anticipation of the symbolized *Vorschlag*. They also point to the spot of Ex. *b* in the D minor Concerto with its written-out prebeat *Vorschlag* to show that Mozart himself often played *Vorschläge* as anticipations (Badura-Skoda, p. 84). It is a regrettable commentary on our rule-bound mentality that such proofs need to be adduced to justify the only approach that makes musical sense. If *Vorschläge* like these are, as often happens, accented on the beat, they subvert their very function of illuminating the high principal note; instead they cast a shadow on it by usurping the light of the downbeat. Such an interpretation can be explained only by the performer's trust

Ex. 4.33.

[3]Such prebeat *Vorschläge* were written with symbols for the same reason that prevails today: to avoid complex fractionalization of the preceding beat.

in musicological wisdom. Unfortunately such trust is often misplaced, and the upshot can range from an annoying affectation to tasteless aberration.

In Ex. 4.33c from the Piano Sonata in C K 189d (279), the accentual implication of the staccato dashes necessitates grace-note character for the *Vorschläge*. Even without support from staccato dots or dashes the same rendition is indicated in all cases of such leaps, as in Exx. *d* from the Piano Concerto in D minor and *e* from the Piano Sonata in D K 284c (311).

For octave leaps by melody instruments we have even more decisive proof. Walter Senn, in his *NMA* edition of the *Posthorn* Serenade, points to a spot where octave leaps for the flute are written the first two times with symbols, then a few measures later in an exactly parallel spot spelled out in anticipation, as shown in Ex. 4.34*a*. For samples of similar octave leaps for the violin, to be done in anticipation, see Ex. *b* from the Violin Concerto in B flat; *c* from the Concerto in G; and *d* from the Violin-Viola Duo in G.

Ex. 4.34.

Obviously, a specific musical situation can call for exceptions. In the same Violin-Viola Duo the sequence of broken octaves, shown in Ex. 3.12*a*, encourages placing the *Vorschlag* before the dotted half-note on the beat. The preceding greater metrical emphasis on the lower notes here gives musical sense to the slightly accented onbeat treatment of the leap.

For upward leaps smaller than an octave we have an excellent illustration of the portamento type in Ex. 4.35 from the Violin Concerto in A. A fine singer would not execute such a leap in a tender passage of an adagio without a gentle portamento slide. The delicately touched anticipated *Vorschlag* (played on the E string) followed by a discreet small slide is the violinistic answer to this challenge.[4]

Ex. 4.35.

For most other leaps smaller than an octave, the arpeggio implication will be stronger still, because the interval suggests a harmony that supports the top melody note. Most commonly, the principal notes are the carriers of the melody, as we can clearly see in Ex. 4.36*a* from the Piano Sonata in F K 189e (280), where the melody line is Bb-A-G, in stepwise descent, and not E-F-E; or in Ex. *b* from the Fantasy in C minor, where the melody clearly picks up the initial D before starting its stepwise descent, or in *c* from the Piano Sonata in B flat K 315c (333), where the rising melody F-G-A-Bb would be illogically disturbed by appoggiatura treatment of the *Vorschlag*. In Ex. *d* from the Sinfonia concertante even this isolated part reveals what emerges with full force from the whole score, that the *Vorschläge* represent an inner harmony part that has no claim to displace the melody of the principal notes from their metrical prominence.

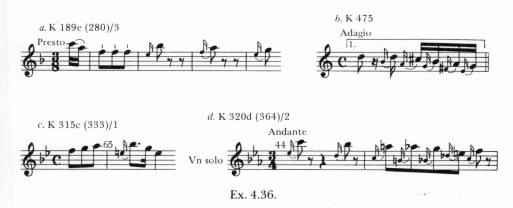

Ex. 4.36.

The need for caution in the appoggiatura interpretation of upward leaping *Vorschläge* is further pointed up by the numerous passages where Mozart wrote out the onbeat Lombard rhythm to ensure a design that would not have been understood had he used the symbol instead. A few characteristic specimens are shown in Ex. 4.37*a* from the Trio of the String Quartet in D minor K 417b (421),

---

[4]The expressive glissando on strings that, a generation or two ago, was probably overused, has recently fallen into disrepute. In their studied avoidance of glissandi many modern violin virtuosi seem to be looking to the piano rather than the voice as their interpretive ideal. Certainly, heavy, sensuous portamenti are out of place in Mozart, and equally objectionable are obtrusive, smear-like slides that are due to defective technique and not to artistic intent. But the occasional tender touch of a tasteful, discreet portamento is too lovely a vocal effect to be banished from the palette of violinistic coloring.

b from the Finale of the Sinfonia concertante; *c* from the G minor Symphony K 550. In all three cases, as in all similar ones, the explicit onbeat notation is maintained with complete consistency.

Ex. 4.37.

We find an interesting juxtaposition of notational contrasts in the Flute concerto in G, as shown in Ex. 4.38*a*. In m. 60 we see the solo flute take up the melodic thread and the rhythmic pattern of broken thirds in 16th-notes from the tutti violins; ten measures later the analogous passage in the violins is followed by an ascending passage for the flute, this time written with *Vorschlag* symbols. The difference in notation derives neither from negligence nor accident. The first passage of m. 60 leads to brilliant virtuoso figurations, the second one in m. 70, which, unlike the preceding one, does not continue the melodic thread, leads to a contrasting, wistful theme. The intentional nature of the difference in notation is confirmed in the recapitulation, where in a parallel spot the identical juxtaposition

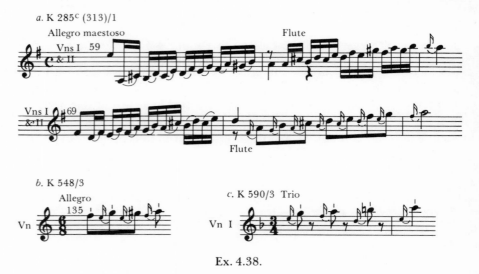

Ex. 4.38.

recurs in a different key. Clearly, Mozart intended a different execution, and the logical way to bring out the melodic ascent to the high A is grace-note rendition. For a similar passage in the Piano Trio in C, as given in Ex. *b,* the *NMA* suggests grace notes, whose case is further strengthened by the staccato dashes. Another combination of clues of melody and articulation prompted the *NMA* to recommend grace notes for Ex. *c* from the String Quartet in F K 590.

There are many more spots where the *NMA* supports grace notes for upward leaping *Vorschläge.* In the volume of the piano variations alone the reader will find a multitude of convincing suggestions for grace-note use in such situations. The recommendations of the editor, Kurt von Fischer, are throughout eminently sensible. Among others, see Twelve Variations in C, K 189a (179), var. 11, mm. 31, 43–45; Twelve Variations in E flat K 299a (354), var. 12, mm. 14 and 19; Twelve Variations in E flat K 300f (353), var. 7, upbeat, m. 2 and several others; Twelve Variations in B flat, K 500, var, 11, m. 6, var. 12, m. 42.

In summarizing it is reasonable to say that for upward leaping *Vorschläge* that are written as 16th or smaller values, the first choice should always be the grace note and that an onbeat, accented appoggiatura treatment should be considered only when rare, specific circumstances seem to warrant it.

THIS CHAPTER has had to be a long one because too many scholars, performers, editors, and teachers are still imbued with a belief in the downbeat dogma that burdens Mozart interpretation with a leaden rigidity and often outright unmusicality. I hope to have succeeded in showing, after the theoretical preliminaries of Chapter 1, that even in Mozart's vocal works, the grace note played an occasional role and that in his instrumental music it played a very large one. The picture is not complete yet. This chapter has attempted to pass in review those contexts that strongly favor grace-note use; the next one discusses further possibilities where, in the choice between one or the other type of *Vorschlag* design, the scales are not tipped decisively in either direction.

5   Ambiguities and Special Cases

There are, as I trust to have shown, many cases where the *Vorschlag* symbol can only mean an appoggiatura and others where it can only mean a grace note. Then there are cases that lean heavily toward one or the other solution, but there will always be some where it is difficult to express a distinct preference. Such uncertainty may be disconcerting to searchers for immaculate authenticity, but it gives the thinking musician a chance to change the style from one performance to the next, from one parallel spot to another, and even from one note to the next. We can be quite sure that Mozart's, or any other great master's, own renditions were not strictly identical when he performed the same piece. Such freedom of choice has always been open to soloists or chamber music players. For the modern orchestra the conductor can give directives, but in the orchestras of Mozart's time detailed rehearsal directives were much less likely and nothing seems to have ever been entered in the parts. We can only speculate that the resulting unavoidable differences in ornament execution were taken in stride by an audience not conditioned to our modern standards of ensemble precision.[1]

One of the most frequent cases of ambiguity is the cadential formula with a *Vorschlag* before the fifth of the dominant, usually, but not always, with a slur from the preceding note, as shown in Ex. 5.1 (see also Ex. 3.16). For this formula the *NMA* often suggests the grace note, often the appoggiatura, and the former, it would seem, more frequently. Both will be generally possible and it will be well to alternate their use. If one chooses the appoggiatura it will be advisable to minimize any accentuation in view of the formulaic character of the phrase and of the predominantly—soon to be explained—*Zwischenschlag* character of the grace.

Ex. 5.1.

Tierces coulées

Apart from this cadential pattern and a few other formulaic contexts, ambiguities are particularly frequent for *Vorschläge* connecting descending thirds. This pattern, often called *tierces coulées*, is so characteristic that it deserves to be singled out as a special case. I discuss cases that seem to lean to grace notes first, then those that are more likely candidates for appoggiaturas.

For the French, the *tierces coulées* usually implied unaccented interbeat rendition with the function of easing the downward flow of the melody. This

---

[1] We must also be aware that, thanks to a beneficent acoustical phenomenon, individual inaccuracies within an orchestral section have a way of cancelling each other out so that the total is better than the sum of its parts. Generally, though, the orchestral standards of technical proficiency must have been inferior to today's, as we can infer simply from the fact that in the German-speaking countries there existed no music schools before the 1830s!

grace-note solution is often the likeliest one for Mozart too, particularly in lively tempos and in pieces of a gay, cheerful character. Notation will often provide further clues when the *Vorschlag* values are one-fourth or less of the principal notes. Thus in Ex. 5.2*a* from the Violin Sonata in C K 296, grace notes are suggested by character, tempo, and notation. They are further supported when we contrast the passage, always written in the same manner, with the spot in Ex. *b* from the first movement with its written-out Lombard snaps (which recur in the parallel spots of mm. 77–78).

Ex. 5.2.

In the well-known, charming Piano Rondo in D, (briefly discussed in Chapter 3 after the Ex. 3.13), the *Vorschläge* of Ex. 5.3*a* are mostly heard as appoggiaturas, sometimes of 16th-, sometimes even of 8th-note length. But here too, French style *tierces coulées* seems to fit the character of the piece best, and here, too, we have notational evidence for this option: first, in the consistent 16th-note value of the *Vorschläge;* second, in the contrasting passage of mm. 53–56 (Ex. *b*) where the theme is transformed from coquettish gaiety to tender lyricism by being written out in flowing 8th-notes; third, in the passage of Ex. *c* where we find three times a clearly intended prepared appoggiatura, written as an 8th-note, juxtaposed with

Ex. 5.3.

the *tierces coulées* of the principal theme, which is here as throughout written with 16th-notes. Grace notes are strongly urged for the principal theme. Hans-Peter Schmitz concurs: in a personal letter he expressed his special annoyance with performers who use downbeat *Vorschläge* in this piece.

In Ex. 5.4*a* from the Violin Sonata in E minor, K 300c (304), the *tierces coulées* in an allegro alla breve tempo are probably meant to be done as grace notes, whereas the *Vorschlag* on F natural at the start of the next measure, being prepared and falling on the strong beat, is probably intended as a brief appoggiatura. The *NMA* suggestion of 8th-note appoggiaturas for the falling thirds is difficult to justify in view of character, tempo, and notation. The same grace-note treatment is likely for Ex. *b* from the Violin Sonata in D K 300l (306). Here in allegro con spirito tempo the intertwined dialogue of *tierces coulées* between piano and violin (repeated a few measures later) loses its light-footed playfulness if done on the beat. (The *NMA* makes no suggestion here.) In the slow movement of the same sonata (Ex. *c*) the grace-note nature of the *tierces coulées* (in shorter values) is clarified by the staccato dashes (not dots as in the *NMA*) over the principal notes. The same solution is then indicated for the previous passages, given in Ex. *d,* that have no staccato marks. The same option is likely and certainly musically justified in Exx. *e* and *f* from the Piano Sonatas in A minor and F major K 300k (332).

At the start of the Adagio in the Four-Hand Sonata in B flat (Ex. *g*), the *Vorschläge* of the first measure could be played as grace notes in contrast to the appoggiatura on the strong beat of m. 3 written in the autograph as an 8th-note. Its length, however, will be shorter than an 8th, in order to resolve before the left hand moves on. The *Vorschlag* in the seventh measure, though written as a 16th, is probably meant as a short appoggiatura in view of its being prepared and falling on the strong beat.

In a similar spot, albeit in a somewhat faster tempo, from the Serenade in D K 167a (185) (Ex. *h*), the *NMA* suggests grace notes for the solo violin. In the Symphony No. 34 in C (Ex. *i*) we find an interesting juxtaposition of *tierces coulées* written for both first and second violins as 16th *Vorschläge* that are preceded and followed by four measures each of Lombard rhythms. The notational contrast suggests grace notes for the symbols.

Often, when Mozart wanted either the greater energy or the sharper contour of appoggiatura-style *tierces coulées* he spelled them out, as in Exx. 5.5*a* from the Clarinet Trio; *b* from the Violin Sonata in C K 296; *c* from the *Hoffmeister* Quartet, and, in a different manner, but rhythmically analogous, *d* from the String Quartet in D K 575.

Nevertheless there are many instances where appoggiaturas rather than grace notes seem to be called for by the symbols. Such will usually be the case when the *Vorschläge* are more important to the melodic essence, and start their downward motion on the strong beat where they are more subject to the gravitational pull of the metrical accent. The line between them is often difficult to draw. We have seen before a few passages where such criteria apply, among them Ex. 3.5*a,* the beginning of the String Quartet in D K 575, where at least the first of the *tierces coulées* should be an expressive appoggiatura, or Ex. 3.14 from the Violin Sonata in B flat K 454. Generally, in a slow movement, or as in K 575, in a very lyrical, slow-moving melody, the *Vorschlag* is likely to carry greater melodic weight than in a gay and lively theme.

Ex. 5.4.

Ex. 5.5.

The decision is easier to make when Mozart writes 8th-notes for the *Vorschläge* as he does in Ex. 5.6*a* from the D minor Piano Concerto which might be played as in *b*. The vocal medium leans idiomatically toward the appoggiatura, and in Ex. *c* from *Der Schauspieldirektor* the violin accompaniment strongly supports long appoggiaturas, though, as often remarked, a shadowing instrumental voice need not be exactly coordinated. We see a lack of such coordination in Ex. *d* from *Die Entführung:* the violin part would seem to suggest short *Vorschläge,* but their denomination and the vocal idiom are more congenial to approximate 8th-note length. The resulting clashes with the violins, creating mild *acciaccatura*-like effects, are innocuous between voice and strings; they would create greater friction between two voices of the same medium. For similar *acciaccatura* effects between voice and instruments see among many others, Exx. 2.3 and 2.7.

The slower the actual sequence of notes, regardless of tempo marking or notation, the greater the scope for varying the interpretation. Passages in slow expressive settings are likely to lean to appoggiatura treatment: consider Exx. 5.7*a-c* from the Piano Sonatas in B flat, K 315c (333) and C K 300h (330); *d* from the Serenade for 13 Winds; *e* from the Violin Sonata in B flat K 317d (378). Here,

Ex. 5.6.

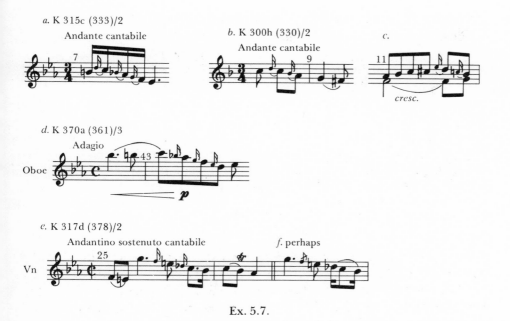

a. K 315c (333)/2
Andante cantabile

b. K 300h (330)/2
Andante cantabile

c.
cresc.

d. K 370a (361)/3
Adagio
Oboe
p

e. K 317d (378)/2
Andantino sostenuto cantabile   f. perhaps
Vn

Ex. 5.7.

as in many other passages from a slow movement, the soloist can introduce subtle
nuances, such as an effect of intensification by playing the first *Vorschlag* like a
grace note, the second as a 16th but unaccented appoggiatura, to lead to the
written-out 8th-note appoggiatura preparing the trill, as sketched in *f*. This is the
opposite of the declining nuance suggested in Ex. 3.14 from the later B flat Violin
Sonata. In each case such subtle manipulation of the *Vorschläge* adds to the phrase
a welcome measure of plasticity.

THE TURN FORMULA AND THE SCALE FORMULA

The rhythmic formula ♪♩♩ and its counterparts ♪ ♩ ♩ in fast, and ♪♩♩ in
slow, tempos form another special case.

Mozart, and presumably most of his contemporaries, used the pattern
predominantly in the two melodic designs of a turn ♪♩♩ and a descending
scale ♪♩♩ (hereafter the "turn formula" and the "scale formula"). Unknown to
the masters of the late baroque, both formulas are a product of the *galant* style. In
the second half of the century their use became ubiquitous and reached a climax in
the classical era with Mozart and Haydn.

We now routinely resolve both of these formulas into four equal notes in what I
shall call "equalization": ♪♩♩ = ♩♩♩♩ . So sure of this procedure are many editors
that they resolve the formulas into four regular notes, often omitting the
mandatory slur from *Vorschlag* to principal note, without troubling to indicate the
editorial nature of such transcription. Now equalization probably applies in most
cases for Mozart, but an area of ambiguity seems to remain. If equalization were
always intended the obvious question arises as to why Mozart and others over and
over again used an equivocal and more complex notation when they could have
indicated their intentions more simply in regular notes; the answer may be that at
first the *Vorschlag* was written as a symbol to clarify its nature as an ornament and
more specifically as a dissonant appoggiatura, but that constant use froze the

formulas into a stereotype, which came to be written routinely and without regard to its harmonic context. There are other problems. One is even somewhat of a mystery, namely the fact (which Wolfgang Plath has kindly brought to my attention) that in writing the formulas Mozart never put dots or dashes over the two short notes. Plath found a spot in the *Coronation* Mass where Mozart had at first written ♪ ♫ , then corrected it to ♫ . Though dots apparently never occurred in these formulas, slurs did and could either cover all four pitches or encompass them in a larger slur. The reason for this orthographic practice is not clear to me. But it does imply that the four notes involved must have been considered as a unit, and that, consequently, whatever applies to the *Vorschlag* within the two formulas does not necessarily apply to the same *Vorschlag* outside of these patterns. A further problem is the disagreements of contemporary theorists whom we need to consider now.

THE THEORISTS

Quantz, as mentioned in Chapter 1, writes that the little notes of Ex. 5.8*a* have to be played in the time of the preceding note and must *not* be played like Ex. *b* lest it sound "as if they had been written by regular notes."[2]

Ex. 5.8. Quantz

C.P.E. Bach, who rejects all anticipated ornaments, gives the scale formula of Ex. 5.9*a* as one of several specimens of the "invariable" *(unveränderlich)* appoggiatura which he defines as being so short that one can barely notice the loss of value to the following notes.[3] Agricola shows a scale formula in which, however, the *Vorschläge* preceding the 8th-notes are written as 32nds: ♪ ♫ . When he demands that, in accord with C.P.E. Bach, the *Vorschläge* must not be equalized, not even in fast tempos, but rendered as 32nd-notes, one could ascribe this solution to the different orthography (Ex. *b*); but for the smaller denominations the notation is the standard one (see Ex. *c*), and here, too, Agricola insists on the invariable, extremely short species that has the function of adding brilliance and sparkle ("den Brillant und Schimmer").[4]

Hiller writes in 1774 that Ex. 5.10*a* is to be sung as shown in *b*. In 1780 he deals at greater length with ornaments and confirms the use of the very short, invariable appoggiatura for both formulas in a lengthy passage, excerpted in Ex. *c*, which is intended to demonstrate the "obvious" use of the *Vorschläge* "solely for adding vivacity and brilliance."[5]

Petri, in 1782, as a byproduct of his discussion of "good" and "bad" (i.e. metrically strong and weak) notes, makes it clear that for both formulas the

[2]J.J. Quantz, *Versuch einer Anweisung, die Flöte traversiere zu spielen*, ch. 17, sec. 2, par. 20.

[3]C.P.E. Bach, *Versuch über die wahre Art das Clavier zu spielen*, pt. 1, ch. 2, sec. 2, par. 13 and Table 3, fig. 8.

[4]Johann Friedrich Agricola, *Anleitung zur Singkunst*, p. 60.

[5]Johann Adam Hiller, *Anweisung zum musikalisch-richtigen Gesange*, p. 166; *Anweisung zum musikalisch-zierlichen Gesange*, pp. 43–45.

Ex. 5.9.

Ex. 5.10. Hiller

Vorschläge should be short, presumably of grace-note character.[6] In binary meters,
he writes, the first, third, fifth, and seventh notes of equal values are always
stronger ("gut" abbr. "g"), the even-numbered ones weaker ("schlecht" abbr. "s").
He illustrates this principle in a musical sequence of which Ex. 5.11 gives revealing
excerpts. We see in Ex. *a* the four-note scale pattern in regular notes with their
alternating g's and s's according to their number. By contrast, in Exx. *b* and *c*,
which happen to present our two formulas, and are, significantly, shown as
illustrations of *unequal* length, the *Vorschlag* is ignored, the g and the number 1
placed under the principal note. This tabulation would make little sense if the
Vorschlag were a long appoggiatura which would relegate the principal note to the
secondary role of being metrically weak, hence *schlecht*. It makes the best sense if
the *Vorschlag* is a grace note.

Ex. 5.11. Petri (1782)

[6]Johann Samuel Petri, *Anleitung zur praktischen Musik*, 2nd. ed., pp. 160–161.

Very interesting are Türk's comments of 1789. He lists both formulas (Ex. 5.12a) among those cases where the *Vorschlag* is "mostly" short, as shown in Ex. *b*, and their shortness stipulated by "almost all music teachers." He considers such execution often valid in, for example, such contexts as Ex. *c*, where the formula occurs in isolation; or as in *d*, when several formulas follow each other in close succession. But he has reservations about the general application of this solution. Thus, when the figure (here the scale formula) grows out of a sequence of 16th-notes, as in Ex. *e* or *f*, Türk prefers equalization with an accent on the appoggiatura as shown in Ex. *g*, while admitting that, here too, the Lombard-style execution will be more frequently used. Thirteen years later, in the 1802 edition of his book, he does endorse equalization as a general principle which by then must have gained in acceptance.[7]

Ex. 5.12. Türk (1789)

In a clavier treatise by Dussek and Pleyel the values for the scale formula are equalized; the dynamic markings for both the symbolized and written-out version are somewhat puzzling, but are probably intended to show the long appoggiatura character of the *Vorschlag* with its usual emphasis (Ex. 5.13a).[8]

Milchmeyer, in his important treatise of 1797, does equalize the scale formula without dynamic indications (Ex. 5.13b), and is apparently one of the very few to do so.[9]

Ex. 5.13.

---

[7]Türk, *Klavierschule*, 1789 ed., pp. 222, 225–226; 1802 ed., p. 258.

[8]Ignaz Joseph Pleyel, *Klavierschule*, p. 6.

[9]Johann Peter Milchmeyer, *Die wahre Art*, p. 38.

The Thomas cantor Doles in 1794 specifically condemns equalization for the scale formula, albeit for a passage written with *Vorschläge* of shorter denomination, but Lasser does the same for standard notation.[10] Following C.P.E. Bach's lead, both of them stress that in this case the *Vorschlag* has to take "as little as possible" from the principal note.

These documents alone should suffice to call into question the absolute validity of equalization, even for Mozart.

MOZART'S USAGE

In Mozart's music the two patterns occur both with symbol and written out in equal values. Symbols are used far more frequently, particularly for the turn formula. What may be significant is that no matter which style of notation Mozart uses, he persists in that style with almost complete consistency whenever the melodic fragment occurs in simultaneous voices or returns in parallel spots.[11]

A rare, interesting disparity occurs in the Piano Concerto in G K 453. In its first movement, as the Badura-Skodas point out in their *NMA* edition of the work, flute and violins have in m. 20 a trill with a suffix (Ex. 5.14*a*), whereas in the parallel spot of m. 246 flute and violins have the turn formula (Ex. *b*). More intriguing still, in m. 98 violins and bassoons have the turn formula against the simultaneous trill in the solo piano (Ex. *c*). The Badura-Skodas assume that here the trill and the turn formula have the same meaning, implying—hazardously, I believe—that the trill should be executed as an equalized turn (Ex. *d*). It seems unlikely that Mozart used the trill symbol to achieve the result of Ex. *d*, but however trill and formula are rendered any resulting clash would be innocuous.

Ex. 5.14.

---

[10]Johann Friedrich Doles, "Anfangsgründe zum Singen"; Johann Baptist Lasser, *Vollständige Anleitung zur Singkunst*, pp. 121, 125.

[11]For a few typical examples of such uniformity see the symbolized scale figures in the Finale of the *Hunt* Quartet; the written-out scale figures in the Andante of the C major String Quintet, mm. 32, 34, 40, 42, 44, 100, 102; in the Andante of the E major Piano Trio, mm. 32, 34, 36, 38, 96–97, 99–101; or in 8th-notes, but Presto alla breve, in the Finale of the Violin Sonata in A K 526; the symbolized turn figure in the first movement of the *Hoffmeister* String Quartet, K 499, the written-out turn figure in the overture to *Die Zauberflöte*, or in the Minuet from the String Quartet in D K 575; a combination of written-out scale and turn figures in the Finale from the String Quartet in C K 465, mm. 70–82 and the later parallel spot.

Though equalization is almost universally accepted today, some scholars have voiced reservations. In his great work on musical ornamentation of 1893–1895, Dannreuther, a very sensitive musician, considers it possible, and certainly permissible, to play either formula with a grace note and an added trill on the principal note (which would, incidentally, resolve the discrepancy in the G major Concerto).[12]

Among modern writers Rudolf Steglich holds that in the Rondo of the Piano Sonata in B flat K 189f (281), 16 measures before the end Mozart wrote the scale formula in four 8th-notes, then crossed them out and replaced them by the symbolized version, as shown in Ex. 5.15.[13] This could have been striking proof of nonidentity, but at least in this form the statement is inaccurate. In the autograph there *is* a correction in that particular spot, but not in the clear-cut manner of Steglich's example. Mozart did not cross out the first half of the measure and rewrite neatly next to it, but made a correction on the spot. The graphic result is unclear and confusing. At least from the microfilm, which is never as revealing as the original, it is possible neither to detect the sequence of events, nor to establish unequivocally the intended final version.[14] It is very likely, though, that Mozart tried to change one style of notation into the other, which would suggest that he was sensitive to their difference.

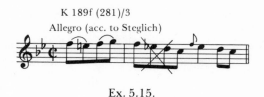

K 189f (281)/3
Allegro (acc. to Steglich)

Ex. 5.15.

Steglich considers equalization to be "totally wrong" ("grundfalsch") in a case like the excerpt from the Piano Sonata in B flat K 315c (333) of Ex. 5.16*a* which, he writes, ought to be played as in Ex. *b*. Steglich's solution for this particular example is questionable. The first note of a piece is an unlikely candidate for a long appoggiatura. Moreover, the four-note figure is a naturally unaccented anacrusis leading into the written-out appoggiatura on *c″* whose implied emphasis would be upstaged by an expressive stress on the starting note. Unaccented lightness of the *Vorschlag* note would seem a more fitting solution.

K 315c (333)/1
Steglich

Ex. 5.16.

We can find a better illustration for Steglich's idea in Ex. 5.17 from the second movement of the Violin Concerto No. 4 in D. Here we have two related scale

[12]Edward Dannreuther, *Musical Ornamentation*, vol. 2, pp. 96–97.

[13]Steglich, "Auszierungswesen," p. 202.

[14]A beam connecting all four notes is thick-ened, as if written over, from the second to the fourth note with no part of the beam deleted. What appears to be a rather large *Vorschlag* symbol is superimposed on the first note head.

figures, both on the third beat, each starting with a dissonant note, yet the first is written with a *Vorschlag* symbol, the second in regular notes. The same notational pattern recurs three times in parallel spots; hence it is reasonable to assume that, far from being an inconsistency of the scale-formula notation, it represents a case of consistency in differentiation—one, moreover, that makes excellent musical sense. Tempo, affect, and melodic climax combine here to favor an expressive intensification of the appoggiatura, perhaps as in Ex. *b*. To repeat this nuance in the next measure would be redundant, and, appropriately, the notation suggests an easy, fluid, unaccented upbeatlike lead into the following downbeat.

Ex. 5.17.

    Döbereiner argues that an appoggiatura is proper only on a dissonance.[15] Hence in a case like Ex. 5.18*a* from Leporello's "Madamina" where the *Vorschlag* symbol is consonant, the main note dissonant, the turn formula must not be equalized. In the common interpretation, he continues, "the long *Vorschläge* displace the dissonant principal notes, replace them and become thereby part of the harmony; while the principal notes are degraded to passing auxiliary notes." He suggests gentle and short grace notes here and in similar passages, such as the fourth measure of the Minuet (Ex. *b*), the Duet No. 2 in *Figaro* (Ex. *c*), and the oboe interjection in the Countess's aria "Dove sono" (Ex. *d*). His best case is Ex. *e* from the accompanied recitative preceding the Count's aria, No. 17. As far as I have been able to ascertain, Mozart's sforzandi and similar dynamic markings always seem to refer to the principal note, not to a symbolized grace. Had he wanted a strong accent on the first note of the turn figure, he would normally have had to write it out as a regular note in order for it to carry the sforzando mark. It is possible, though, that our two formulas are an exception if, as suggested above, they had in Mozart's usage frozen into so solid a stereotype as to neutralize the ornamental nature of the *Vorschlag* symbol.

    On the whole, Döbereiner's ideas are noteworthy for their denial of automatic equalization, and *theoretically* he has a point in linking appoggiaturas and dissonance, since the main function of the long appoggiatura is enrichment of the harmony. *Practically,* however, individual orchestra players, who do not see the score, cannot tell whether a note in their part is dissonant or consonant. More important, the priority of the dissonance is by no means a matter of course, since there is no absolute value to a dissonance that makes it per se preferable to a consonance. In a case like that of the oboe figure of Ex. 5.18*d*, its sorrowful tenderness is better served by gently passing through the dissonant pitch than by emphasizing it.

    Nonetheless, looking at a possible correlation between harmony and notation we find that for the symbolized turn formula the dissonances are in a clear majority. This fact, though, has more to do with the turn character of the pattern

[15]Christian Döbereiner, *Zur Renaissance alter Musik*, pp. 33–37.

a. (Döbereiner) K 527, I, 4

b. Ibid.   Finale

c. K 492, I, 2

d. Ibid., III, 19

c. Ibid., 17

Ex. 5.18.

than with an intended appoggiatura nature of the symbol: with its four-note ornamental design, which winds around the principal note, the first pitch will tend to be dissonant. This will be so in the frequent cases where the turn formula is applied to triadic melodic progressions such as in the adagio introduction to the *Prague* Symphony, mm. 17, 19, 21, and so on; in the theme of the Alla Turca Rondo; at the start of the last movement of the Two-Piano Sonata. Here and in analogous cases the main notes are consonant, the first turn notes dissonant. Yet the formulas are on weak beats where the winding embellishment ought not to obscure the melodic progression by a distinct accentuation of the first note in appoggiatura fashion. Then there are other cases where similar chains of turn formulas occur on strong beats and call for accentuation, such as the down-rushing passage in the first movement of the Two-Piano Concerto, K 316a (365), mm. 42–43.

For the scale pattern we find both dissonances and consonances with no clear preponderance of one or the other. Thus the harmony-notation relationship offers no confirmation of the clue that Döbereiner thought he had found and therefore no clear guide to execution. Yet the evidence of the theoretical sources is reason enough to make us explore the possibility that the ornamental nature inherent in the symbol may have on occasion allowed a certain latitude of rhythmic-dynamic design. The main variations to be considered are 1) evenly spaced notes with the first one emphasized beyond its normal metrical stress (which is probably what Pleyel had in mind); 2) in slow tempos, and mainly for the scale formula, a slight lengthening of the *Vorschlag* note (which is what Steglich had in mind); 3) the shortening of the appoggiatura in the sense of Hiller, Lasser, and Türk; 4) once in a while grace notes in the sense of Dannreuther, Döbereiner, and, presumably, Petri.

Certainly soloists can use their inherently greater freedom of execution to vary the rendition of the formulas in one of these ways when the musical context favors such adjustment. One hundred years ago Joachim offered two versions for the passage of Ex. 5.19*a* from the A major Violin Concerto in its "Turkish" section, as given in Exx. *b* and *c*. A generation later, Henri Marteau, who was a superb Mozart interpreter, suggested in his edition of the work playing grace notes the first time and equalizing in the repeat.

a. K 219/3

Ex. 5.19.

What is feasible for the soloist might not be for the orchestra. What I said before about the unavoidable imprecision of orchestral ornament renditions under 18th-century rehearsal and performance conditions, applies here too of course. In the particular case of our two formulas we have no reason to assume that the players automatically honored equalization when so many contemporary witnesses testified against it. We can only assume that the players did what came naturally to them as result of their training and musicianship, and of what the conductor may have told them. By and large no musical, theoretical, or technical reasons prevented either formula from having a variety of meaning in orchestral as well as in solo playing.

In most cases equalization is the indicated solution for Mozart. It is nevertheless likely, as shown in a few examples, that, here and there the ornamental origin of little notes will call for special treatment in one of the forms described above. The likeliest option will be a measure of dynamic or agogic emphasis due the first pitch in its character as appoggiatura, whereas Döbereiner's grace note will only rarely, if ever, be advisable.

The *Zwischenschlag*

A one-note grace is a *Zwischenschlag* when it is embedded in a slur that links it equally to the preceding and the following note.[1] The slur is usually written out but may, in vocal music, be implied by an uninterrupted vowel. By its balanced link to both the preceding and the following note the *Zwischenschlag* partakes of the character of both the *Vorschlag* and the *Nachschlag*. Since the *Nachschlag* is always brief, unaccented, and off the beat, and the *Vorschlag can* be brief, unaccented, and off the beat, we shall find that the alloy of both graces will tend to bring to the fore their common denominator of unaccented brevity in interbeat space. There are exceptions and doubtful cases, but the tendency is usually clear. Sometimes, provided there is no accent, the exact metrical placement can be irrelevant.

In *vocal music* diction can again provide guidance. By definition a *Zwischenschlag* falls in the middle of a syllable where accentuation in the vein of an appoggiatura will normally make no prosodic, hence no musical, sense. Looking, for example, at Ex. 6.1 from *Die Zauberflöte* we see that the *Zwischenschlag* in the middle of the colorless auxiliary verb *war* (was) can only be lightly touched without creating an unseemly bulge. In Ex. *b* from the same work, an accent on the syllable *Lie-* with its sharp *ee* sound would be signally incongruous. The same is true of Ex. *c* from the very early Mass in C *(Dominicusmesse)* of 1767. In Ex. *d* from the Missa solemnis an accentuation on the vowel *a* would be vocally less disturbing but would still be unjustified, and the same is the case in Ex. *e* from the Requiem. For Ex. *f* from the aria "Misera, dove son" the *NMA* sensibly suggests anticipation of the grace.

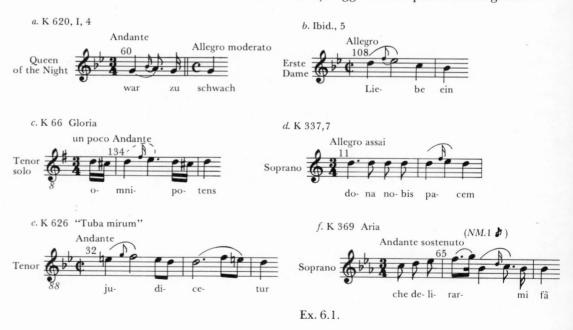

Ex. 6.1.

---

[1]The term *Zwischenschlag*, coined by L. Mozart, is ungainly in English, but, like *Vorschlag* or *Nachschlag*, seems to lack a fitting equivalent.

In most of the preceding cases and in many others to follow we find the *Zwischenschlag* in the melodic context of ♩·♪♩ where the grace is a stepwise inflection from above before a rising second on a weak beat, whereupon the melody typically falls back to the first pitch for the following strong beat.

There are spots in vocal music where an onbeat placement makes good musical sense, but in an easy, unaccented melodic flow rather than in the style of a Lombard snap, as a cambiata rather than as an appoggiatura. In these cases Mozart occasionally spells out the onbeat placement in regular notes in both vocal and instrumental music. See, for example, the second measure of Ex. 6.1*e*, the String Quartet K 575/4, m. 18, or the Piano Concerto in A K 488/3, m. 492. Thus we could well imagine that Ex. 6.2*a* from the Missa solemnis might have been written as in Ex. *b*, and Ex. *c* from the "Sancta Maria" as in *d* (though such an intent is unlikely in view of the 16th-note value of the symbol). Also, the likelihood of a different, presumably anticipated rendition is suggested by the interesting spot of Ex. *e* from *Zaide,* where an onbeat grace would cause unpleasant friction with the violins.

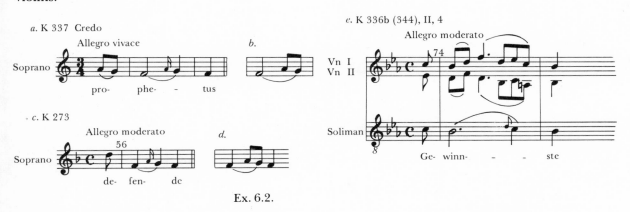

Ex. 6.2.

The case for anticipation is strengthened when the *Zwischenschlag* precedes a syncopation that is characteristic enough to warrant preserving its rhythmic integrity. For this reason, in Exx. 6.3*a* from *Così fan tutte, b* from *Die Entführung, c* from *Litaniae Lauretanae,* and *d* from the aria "Mia speranza," the graces are best done before the principal note. We have to be aware, though, that a solo singer needs a measure of rhythmic latitude for *any* ornament: we can rationalize a desirable solution but must not hamstring the vocal impulse.

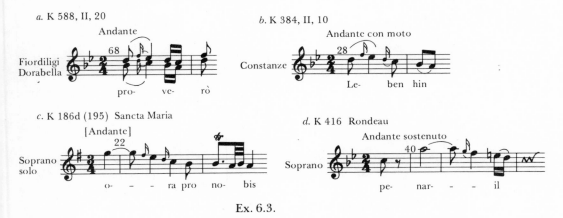

Ex. 6.3.

In instrumental music similar considerations prevail. Again, in most cases there will be no distinct accent. Whether the grace will tend toward anticipation, rhythmic ambiguity, or starting on the beat, will depend on the musical environment, notably the functional relationship of the parent notes, the tempo, expression, and dynamics. Here, too, we usually find the *Zwischenschlag* in the same melodic context as a falling insertion between two stepwise rising parent notes.

Mozart himself offers in the Piano Concerto in B flat K 450 a significant clue for anticipation of a *Zwischenschlag*. The second movement, an Andante in variation form, starts with the strings giving the first part of the theme. In the autograph, m. 7 reads for the first violins as in Ex. 6.4a. In mm. 9–16 the piano solo repeats, with gentle ornamentation, the eight-measure phrase. Now the corresponding m. 7 is written as in Ex. *b,* that is with spelled-out anticipation. In the following variation, m. 39 in the first violins reads as in Ex. *c* and the piano again as in *d*. This, I believe, is a strong indication that the *Zwischenschlag* of m. 7 was indeed intended to be anticipated and that Friedrich Blume, in his Eulenburg edition, was mistaken in forming the syncopation of Ex. *e* (without a hint of editorial intervention). Before Blume, *W.A.M.* had made an even more drastic revision by changing the slur and transforming the *Zwischenschlag* into an appoggiatura, as shown in Ex. *f.*

Ex. 6.4.

In view of the kinship of the anticipated *Zwischenschlag* with the grace note, certain contexts listed before as favoring the grace note will similarly suggest anticipation of the *Zwischenschlag*. As the reader may remember, these contexts included occurrence before characteristic rhythmic figures such as groups of even notes, especially triplets, and before short note values and their counterpart, staccato notes.

Thus a *Zwischenschlag* that precedes a thematically important rhythmic figure will best precede the beat. For illustration of the simple dotted note see Exx. 6.5a from the Piano Trio in G K 496; *b* from the *Idomeneo* ballet music (in both these spots anticipation is endorsed by the *NMA*); and *c* from the Piano Sonata in D K 284c (311). Later in the movement, however (Ex. *d*), the inserted turn may preempt all the interbeat space and ease the *Zwischenschlag* onto the beat.

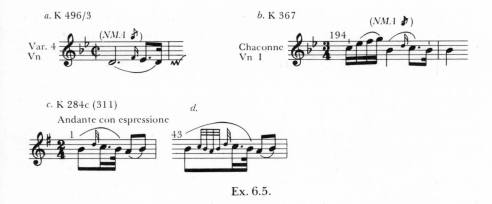

Ex. 6.5.

When several *Zwischenschläge* occur in succession within a setting of *even notes* they will generally tend to be anticipated, as in Ex. 6.6*a* from the Piano Sonata in E flat in the rather unusual form of upward leaping thirds; in Ex. *b* from the String Quintet in E flat K 614 (a borderline case with the *Vorschlag* and as such shown in Ex. 4.6*d*); and probably also in Ex. *c* from the Symphony in A K 186a (201). The case for anticipation is stronger still when *Zwischenschläge* occur within a string of triplets as in Ex. *d* from the Violin Sonata in B flat K 317d (378).

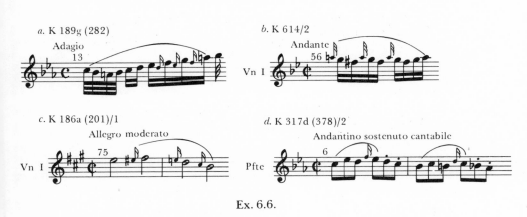

Ex. 6.6.

Then there are the frequent instances where, in analogy to the vocal illustrations of ex. 6.3, a *Zwischenschlag* before a syncopated note should get out of the latter's way.

As in the case with the grace note, a lively tempo and a spirit of gaiety and playfulness provide a favorable climate for anticipation. In Exx. 6.7*a* from the Two-Piano Concerto and *b* from the Violin Sonata in F K 374d (376) such a rendition is endorsed by the *NMA*. The passage of Ex. *c* from the Violin Concerto in A with its provocative resoluteness will also profit from anticipation rather than from the usually heard translation into two 8th-notes.

In analogy to a *Vorschlag* that precedes a written-out appoggiatura, a *Zwischenschlag* that precedes a nonharmonic note (such as a cambiata) is best done before the beat. Illustrations are Exx. 6.8*a* from the Sinfonia concertante; *b* from the Violin Sonata in F K 374e (277); *c,* the closely related figure from the opening scene of *Die Zauberflöte;* and *d* from *Idomeneo.* In these four cases anticipation is endorsed by the *NMA*.

Ex. 6.7.

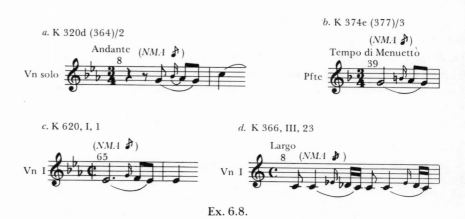

Ex. 6.8.

Dynamics can give occasional clues. In Ex. 6.9*a* from *Die Entführung* the crescendo to a sudden piano demands a gradual swelling in the course of which the 8th-note at the end of the measure ought to be louder than the preceding grace. The simplest and most natural way of achieving this result is by fast anticipation of the *Zwischenschlag* since the metrical weight implicit in an onbeat placement, be it ever so light, would hinder the gradual increase.

A passage from Gluck involving dynamics is interesting enough to be shown here. In the autograph of *Alceste* (at the BN) we find the notation of Ex. *b*. The sforzandi are clearly placed under the 8th-notes, but an orthographic detail we do not find in Mozart provides definite proof that the graces were to be anticipated: the second of these is neatly written in the form of a *Nachschlag,* slurred to its preceding note only.

Ex. 6.9.

Notation can provide some guidance. In Ex. 6.10*a* from the Quintet for Piano and Winds we find the grace within our standard melodic formula written with

32nd-note symbols (repeated in the parallel spot of m. 103), which certainly suggests great brevity and most likely anticipation. In Ex. *b* from the Piano Concerto in D minor the 8th-note denomination might favor onbeat style.

Ex. 6.10.

Often, in our standard melodic context, and especially when the *Zwischenschlag* is followed by a *single note* only, musical reasons do not speak loud enough to preclude either the prebeat or the onbeat alternative. Where both solutions seem equally satisfactory, performers can indulge their preferences and in the absence of a preference, vary their renditions. A few such ambiguous specimens are given in Exx. 6.11*a* from the Two-Piano Sonata; *b* from the Violin Sonata in F K 374e (377); *c* from *Die Entführung;* *d* from the Violin Sonata in A K 526; and *e* from the *Posthorn* Serenade. Whenever, especially in lively tempos, the solution makes as much sense as we have one of those cases mentioned before where the exact rhythmic disposition is of little importance. See also the closely related cases of Exx. 3.16 and 5.1 along with the accompanying comments.

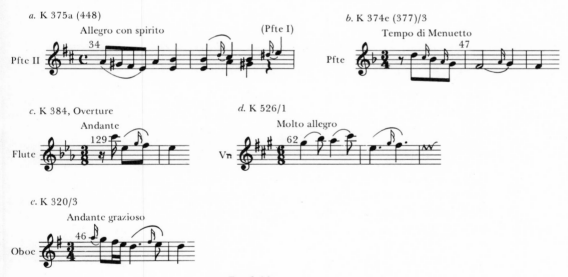

Ex. 6.11.

Occasionally we find cases where melodic line, metrical placement, and expression lean to appoggiatura character and therefore favor onbeat rendition. A good illustration is Ex. 6.12 from the Clarinet Quintet where moderate tempo, a sense of grace, tenderness, and warmth, and the occurrence on the strongest beat combine to elicit an appoggiaturalike interpretation, perhaps . The notation as *Zwischenschlag,* however, may not be authentic, since the autograph has not survived.

K 581 Trio I

Ex. 6.12.

IN SUMMING UP let us recall that the *Zwischenschlag* as a blend of *Vorschlag* and *Nach-schlag* combines characteristics of both graces and has to do so in a way that is compatible with either of them. Its *Nachschlag* component will usually prevent it from being accented and at the same time favor those strains of the *Vorschlag* that lean to anticipation: that is, those of the grace note rather than the appoggiatura.

In many cases anticipation is clearly indicated, as, for example, before nonharmonic notes or notes that have appoggiatura function, before staccato notes, and before triplets or other characteristic rhythmic figures (including often a series of even notes) that have a claim to integrity. There are other cases where, given the absence of accentuation, the exact metrical placement matters little and performers should follow their musical judgment. Finally there are the unfrequent occasions where in the guise of *Zwischenschläge* we encounter genuine, even long, appoggiaturas which should be treated accordingly. But by and large the first option will lie where *Nachschlag* and *Vorschlag* meet on common ground: unaccented brevity and anticipation.

In Mozart's usage, the slide is a *Vorschlag*-type ornament in that it belongs, and is slurred to, the following note as its parent and is detached from the preceding note. The slide consists of two or more pitches that lead into the parent note in stepwise motion, usually upward, occasionally downward. Most frequent is the two-pitch ascending type, and unless otherwise indicated this species is meant when speaking of the "slide" pure and simple. Related is the suffix of a trill when it leads to the upper neighbor note: ♪♪♪♪, but as *Nachschlag* belonging to the preceding note, it serves a different function.

Mozart wrote the symbol for the slide with little notes and, it seems, always in 32nd denominations: ♪♪ | ♪♪ | ♪♪♪. It is these symbols that we are concerned with here; slides written out in regular notes offer no problems of interpretation.

In the pre-Mozart era the slide occurred in three main forms: the Lombard ♪♪, the dactyle ♪♪, and the anapest ♪♪♪. In France the anapest was the overwhelming favorite; in Italy composers used all three forms, but the symbol ♪♪ usually stood for the anapest. In the Germany of Bach's time we find all three forms with preferences varying from one composer to the next. With the advent of the *galant* style and the spread of the onbeat principle for ornaments, German treatises usually transcribed the symbol in the Lombard style, while the first note of the dactyle (with a symbol of its own) gained in length. (For a detailed discussion see *Ornamentation*, Part IV.)

There are, though, some notable exceptions. J. C. Bach and Ricci, in their only illustration of the grace, show the slide symbol placed before the beat, as in Ex. 7.1*a*. Petri does so too in an illustration devoted primarily to the intermingling of *Vorschläge* and *Nachschläge* (Ex. *b*). Two pages later, speaking specifically of the slide *(Schleifer)*, Petri mentions its symbol of two little notes and says that like *Vorschlag* and *Nachschlag* it can be placed either before or after its principal note. In his illustration (Ex. *c*) only the first slide is definitely of the *Vorschlag* type; the others, written close to their preceding parents seem to be of the interbeat *Nachschlag* type. In the absence of any comment it is very unlikely that Petri intended the first of these slides, graphically indistinguishable from the others, to contrast as sharply to them as a Lombard type would to the *Nachschlag* types.[1]

a. J.C. Bach and Ricci   b. Petri

c.   d. Koch

Ex. 7.1.

[1] *Anleitung*, p. 153.

Koch, using the symbols of Ex. *d,* stipulates for the two- or three-note slide that the accent be placed on the principal note. This virtually forms an anapest since an accent seeks the beat.[2]

Mozart uses the Lombard type, always written in regular notes, fairly often and does so typically when he aims at rhythmic incisiveness, as shown in Exx. 7.2*a* from the overture to *Le nozze di Figaro; b* from the String Quartet in E flat K 421b (428); *c* from the Violin Sonata in E flat K 293b (302) (the motive is repeated 16 times); *d,* the descending species from the overture to *Der Schauspieldirektor; e* from *Don Giovanni.* For other random specimens of the same trenchant character see the Piano Concerto in F K 387a (413)/1, mm. 12–15; the Violin Concerto in G, K 216/1, mm. 29–33; *Die Entführung,* first act Terzett, mm. 26–39; the Missa [longa] K 246a (262), Credo, mm. 2–16.

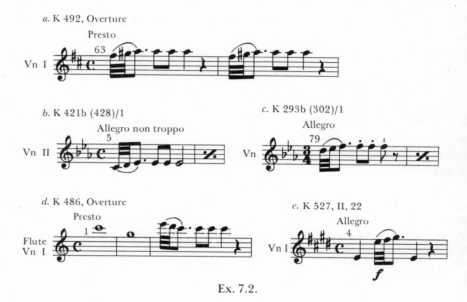

Ex. 7.2.

The written-out form of the Lombard slide is never replaced in analogous spots by symbols, and this alone suggests a difference in meaning. Yet there are some cases where a Lombard interpretation of the symbol makes good sense: before a note longer than a quarter, Mozart may have used the symbol to avoid the notational complications of a tie (as he did for the appoggiatura before long notes). He may have never, or at best very rarely, written ♩ and may have used ♩ instead. Such was perhaps the case in the first movement of the Serenade for 13 Winds, when the oboe motive of Ex. 7.3*a* is followed later in the codetta by the passage of Ex. *b* where the upward slide occurs simultaneously in oboes and basset horns, with a downward slide in the clarinets, against a martial rhythm in the horns. It is this rhythm that provides a favorable context for the Lombard style. (This, incidentally, is not an analogous spot to Ex. *a* to which it bears neither melodic nor rhythmic resemblance.)

There are, on the other hand, numerous indications that the symbolized slides were usually meant to be unaccented in Koch's sense. This would place them in the anapestic class, even if by a slight metric shift, whether due to inaccuracy in ensem-

———

[2]*Musikalisches Lexicon* s.v. "Vorschlag," cols. 1725–1726.

a. K 370a (361)/1

Ex. 7.3.

ble or to agogic flexibility in a soloistic situation, the first note should coincide with the beat.

Several considerations can help our decisions. One is dynamic markings. In the autograph of the String Quartet in D minor the sforzandi of Ex. 7.4a are clearly placed under the main note and unquestionably refer to it, not to the slide. This connection here and in almost all other similar cases is unmistakable in spite of Mozart's (above mentioned) notational habit of writing dynamic marks slightly ahead of the note to which they belong. The same link between dynamics and principal note is clear in Ex. *b* from the Serenade for Six Woodwinds K 375 (the autograph of which, contrary to the sixth edition of Köchel, had not been missing from the Berlin library) as well as in the same spot of Mozart's autograph transcription for eight woodwinds. In the second aria of the Queen of the Night musical necessity and external evidence reinforce each other. It is obvious that in Ex. *c* from the beginning of the aria, the slide in the basses serves to spotlight, not to obscure, the dramatic top pitch of the descending triad. The placement of the *for*[te] under the d′ provides graphic confirmation. At the end of the aria on the words *Hört, hört* the dramatic bass motive recurs, this time written out in regular notes (Ex. *d*). See also *Tito*, I, Finale, mm. 34, 36, 38, and *Idomeneo*, I, 1, Ilia's aria, mm. 23–27. Slides like these evoke the swing of a hammer, sword, or similar implement before it hits its target.[3]

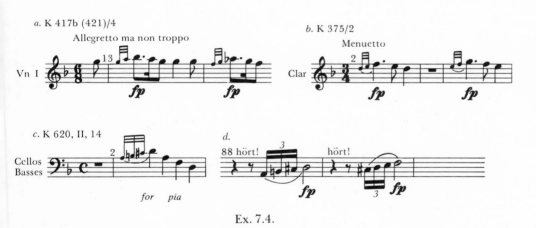

Ex. 7.4.

[3]A similar function of (four-note) slides in the scene of the furies from Gluck's *Orfeo* makes their anticipation a matter of course:

We find a similar spotlighting of the first note of a descending triad in the Finale of the *Posthorn* Serenade (see Ex. 7.5*a*) where onbeat rendition would disturb the melody and the rhythmic sparkle of the theme, especially on the third phrase with its three-note slide (Mozart, as usual, wrote the slides here as 32nds, not as 16ths as given in the *NMA*.) The same applies to the passage of Ex. *b* from *Don Giovanni* as confirmed in Ex. *c* where in a parallel spot the anticipation is spelled out.

Ex. 7.5.

In Ex. 7.6 from *Die Entführung* two factors combine to establish the need for anticipation. Near the end of No. 2 in the first act, Osmin's fury on the words *"Fort, eures Gleichen,* underlined by a sforzando in the orchestra, is made more emphatic by a group of simultaneous slides, both rising and falling, of two, three, and four notes. The message of the autograph, with its clear graphic alignment of the *sfp*

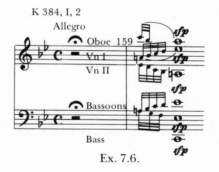

Ex. 7.6.

signs and their respective whole notes, is reinforced by the different number of notes involved in the slides: unless anticipated they would all arrive at different times on the principal note.

Rhythmic incisiveness and sharpness of thematic contour would be blunted by Lombard interpretation of such passages, as shown in Ex. 7.7*a* from the Violin Sonata in F K 374e (377) with its descending scale motive and an implied accent on its motoric propellant, the dotted quarter-note; in Ex. *b* from the Two-Piano Concerto with its signallike, quasi-military motive; in Ex. *c* from the C minor Piano Concerto where the thematic prominence of the parent notes is fully revealed in the martial variation of Ex. *d*.

The slide has a counterpart to its "hammerstroke" aspect in its role as stylized portamento for the expression of gentle affections. Derived from the vocal portamento, which by its nature is unaccented and anticipated, this type of slide will also lean toward the anapest. Its ancestry is unmistakable in cases like Ex. 7.8*a* from the first aria of the Queen of the Night with its sighlike expression of grief. In

Ex. 7.7.

Zerlina's aria "Vedrai carino" the slide of Ex. *b* is an inflection of tenderness that would be lost by accentuation. A similar affection of tender melancholy favors the anapest in Ex. *c* from the slow movement of the A major Piano Concerto K 488 where this solution has the advantage of maintaining the integrity of the siciliano rhythm. In Ex. *d* from the Sextet in *Don Giovanni* the slides in the violins picture Leporello's pitifully sobbing plea for mercy and are better anticipated; the B flat must have the emphasis as is obvious from the vocal part.

A staccato mark over the principal note invites the anapest lest the sharpness of articulation be blunted. Illustrations are Exx. 7.9*a* from the Oboe Quartet, *b* and *c* from *Tito*, *d* from the Divertimento in D (1776). In Ex. *e* from Basilio's aria in the fourth act of *Le nozze di Figaro*, the evenness of the thumping rhythm favors anticipation, which is corroborated in the third measure where the slide precedes staccato 8th-notes.

For other examples from *Le nozze di Figaro* that suggest the anapest see Figaro's fourth-act aria, mm. 1–3, and 5–7, where the sudden *fp*'s clearly belong to the principal notes. The same melodic figure, repeated 14 times in the fourth-act Finale, mm. 47–50, should be done in the like manner, and so should the slides in the chorus of Act III, No. 21, where the ingratiating tone of the piece favors the anapest over the angular Lombard.

Interesting is the case of Ex. 7.10*a* from Belmonte's aria at the beginning of *Die Entführung*. Here the two little notes are *not* a slide: they do not belong to the following note but, like a *Nachschlag*, to the preceding fermata as indicated graphically in the autograph by the slur to the preceding note and the dash placed in the text extending the syllable *mir*. They may have been meant as a transition from a brief cadenza that might have been inserted at the fermata. The two little notes, written in spite of their *Nachschlag* character after the bar line and on a new

Ex. 7.8.

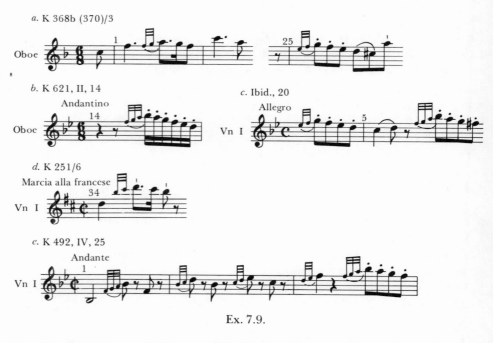

Ex. 7.9.

page in the autograph, have to displace the *die* from the beat because an accentuation of that word would cause faulty diction. Suggestions for their possible execution are offered in Exx. *b* and *c* without and with cadenza.

a. K 384, I, 1

Andante

Belmonte

zu- rück, gieb mir - - - - die Ruh zu- rück

b.

mir- - - - - die Ruh

c.

mir- - - - - - - - - - - die Ruh

Ex. 7.10.

Against the backdrop of the prebeat predominance of the symbolized slide in France and Italy (as documented in *Ornamentation*) the examples shown in this chapter along with numerous similar passages strongly suggest that in most cases Mozart's symbol of little 32nd-notes probably stood for the unaccented, hence primarily anticipated, type. A soloist can, of course, with a touch of rubato have the slide enter astride, on, or even after the beat: that is in the nature of ornamental freedom, provided one or the other of these designs does not harden into a mannerism. Certainly the Lombard style might occasionally be indicated or be a reasonable alternative. But for Mozart's symbolized slide it will by and large be advisable to give first consideration to the anapest.[4]

[4]The same is true of Beethoven where, for example, the slides in the slow movement of the Seventh Symphony ought to be anticipated, as should the famous three-note bass slides in the Funeral March of the *Eroica*. Not only does it make no harmonic sense to turn the first strong beats of this movement into 6/4 chords; here the slides have a function akin to the upbeat figures of the snare drums,   or   , in military marches and funeral music. Beethoven actually spells out in mm. 3–7 prebeat slides for the basses; then, in mm. 8–15 and several parallel spots, he has the whole string section play the anticipated drum rhythms. The identical rhythms are often given to other instruments, symbolizing gloom or death: they are used often and tellingly by Verdi in, for example, the "Miserere" of *Il trovatore* and appear pervasively in *Les vêpres siciliennes;* they are in the execution scene of Bellini's *Norma*, the Funeral March in Spontini's *La vestale*, and numerous other related passages.

8   The Trill: Theory

The trill is a complex ornament that can assume many shapes, most of which can be found tabulated in *Ornamentation*, pp. 241–243. Here I limit myself to pointing out the forms that are most important for Mozart and listing my proposed terminology.

A trill starting with the accented auxiliary on the beat will be called an appoggiatura trill; one starting with the main note a main-note trill; one starting with the unaccented (prebeat) auxiliary a grace-note trill. A miniature trill (which can start on either note) in which the auxiliary is sounded twice will be called a *Pralltriller* and, if reduced to a single alternation, a *Schneller* (often, but not here, referred to as an "inverted mordent"). If the starting note is extended we have either a supported appoggiatura trill or a supported main-note trill. A compound trill starting with a three-note prefix will be called a slide-trill and turn-trill respectively. The suffix is the ubiquitous two-note termination of many trills.

Conventional wisdom has it that the whole of the 18th century knew only the appoggiatura trill and, as some writers insist, in a form that carried the initial emphasis on the upper note throughout the length of the ornament. In a famous, much quoted formulation by Marpurg the trill is supposed to be a "series of descending appoggiaturas." The rule had its earliest sources in ornament tables of French keyboard players of the late 17th and early 18th centuries. From there the graphic pattern with the auxiliary on the beat found its way to J. S. Bach's brief *Explication* for his 10-year-old son, and later, most importantly, into C.P.E. Bach's enormously influential treatise of 1753. Following this last we find it in a host of—mainly German—treatises that were beholden to Philipp Emanuel and were published until well into the 19th century.

In *Ornamentation* I have adduced massive evidence, theoretical and musical, to show that the notion of a monolithic trill form is a myth; that the monopoly of the appoggiatura trill was limited to a few islands of doctrinaire rigidity; that even in France, the homeland of the upper-note start, the other trill forms played a substantial role during the whole of the 17th and 18th centuries. I have to refer the interested reader to that documentation (to be found in Chapters 24–34) which is too voluminous to be excerpted here. In the following I shall simply supplement it, as briefly as practical, by theoretical sources from Mozart's time that were *not* listed in *Ornamentation*.

Many of the theorists of Mozart's time give in their ornament tables the appoggiatura pattern as the chief trill model. Among them are J. C. Bach and Ricci, J. F. Schubert, and most orthodoxly, Türk. Türk explains the need to start with the upper note on the beat by reasoning that it results in an even division of two plus two, four plus four, and so on, without leaving an extra tone, which would be rhythmically disturbing, whereupon he quickly admits that the argument is too finicky ("auf eine zu grosse Subtilität hinausläuft") and therefore proves nothing.[1]

---

[1]*Klavierschule.* 1802 ed., p. 289n.

Unwittingly he reveals here the reason for the prevalence of the metrically orderly pattern  so often found in ornament tables: neatly and simply, as befits an abstraction, such a pattern shows the start of the trill with the upper note, as preferred by the French keyboard players, and its end on the main note, which is of the essence of the trill. It avoids such metrical untidiness as the surplus note that Couperin used in his model of the *tremblement continu* to indicate a prebeat start of the auxiliary, but has the disadvantage of conveying a sense of inevitability to those who fail to distinguish the stylized mathematical design of ornament tables from the facts of live music making. Out of this sense of inevitability then arose the canon of the obligatory upper-note-on-the-beat start, aggravated by the musically deplorable concept of a "series of descending appoggiaturas," and the frequent mannerism of playing trills with drill order precision.

In a longstanding Italian main-note tradition—tempered often at cadences and related spots by the insertion of long appoggiaturas—Giambattista Mancini may be the first important Italian author to ask for regular upper-note start of the trill, without, however, mentioning the rhythmic disposition of the start.[2]

Some theorists present the appoggiatura trill as the basic pattern but supplement it with other designs. One of these is Milchmeyer who writes: "There are trills that start with the main [*geschriebene*] note, but mostly they start with the note above the one written, except the compound [*verzierten*] trills many of which start with the written note." One of his main-note patterns is shown in Ex. 8.1. Other main-note patterns are given for long sustained trills against moving parts in other voices.[3]

Ex. 8.1. Milchmeyer

Muzio Clementi, whose basic pattern is the standard appoggiatura trill of Ex. 8.2*a*, nevertheless shows the main-note trill of Ex. *b* in stepwise ascent. When it is slurred to the preceding upper neighbor ("*tremblement lié*") he gives the two alternatives of Ex. *c*. His "transient shakes" are the *Schneller* of Ex. *d*, and so are the "short shakes" of Ex. *e*.[4]

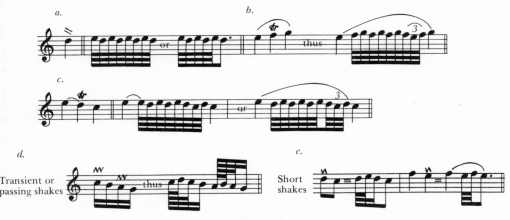

Ex. 8.2. Clementi

[2]*Riflessioni pratiche sul canto figurato*, p. 168.
[3]*Die wahre Art*, p. 42.

[4]*Introduction to the Art of Playing the Pianoforte*, p. 11.

Lasser adheres to the appoggiatura trill pattern but seems to make an exception (his wording is somewhat ambiguous) for trills after leaps of augmented or diminished intervals. These, he says, have to be "sharply attacked" ("bei solchen Betrügssprüngen muss der Triller scharf angeschlagen werden"), apparently so as not to water down the characteristic intervals.[5]

Pleyel's basic pattern is again the appoggiatura trill, but besides showing the *Schneller* in descending passages (Ex. 8.3*a*), he gives the interesting designs of what he calls *prallender Doppelschlag*, a turned trill starting with main-note support (Ex. *b*) and a *tremblement lié* starting with the slightly lengthened main note of Ex. *c*.[6]

Pralltriller or *Halbtriller*   *Prallender Doppelschlag*

Ex. 8.3. Pleyel

Some writers do not limit the options and leave the choice of trill design to individual judgment. Koch, for example, reports on the disagreement among theorists about whether to start the trill with the main or the upper note.[7] He himself expresses no preference. For the soloist, he says, this disagreement is of no special consequence, since both notes are played evenly and with equal strength, neither carrying greater weight. Thus, as soon as the first note is over, the difference between the two styles is unnoticeable. Only in ripieno or chamber music, where trills occur in thirds or sixths, do all involved have to agree on the way to start the trill and on its speed. In keeping with these ideas Koch shows his *Pralltriller* starting with either note (Ex. 8.4*a*). Interesting too is his comment on the compound trill, for which he still shows Bach's old symbols in addition to Mozart's little notes (Ex. *b*). "Occasionally," he says, "the trill is to be preceded by a few fast passing *Vorschlag* notes" ("Zuweilen sollen dem Triller einige geschwind durchgehende Vorschlagsnoten vorhergehen"). The term *"durchgehend,"* far more specifically an antonym of *anschlagend* than the English term "passing," points to their anticipation, and so does their graphic representation with the separation of the prefix from the trill proper.

Christoph Friedrich Wilhelm Nopitsch, music director in Nördlingen, gives in 1784 the main-note design for the cadential trill (Ex. 8.5*a*); in the text he says that the auxiliary has the "privilege" of starting the trill, meaning presumably an appoggiatura support. His *Pralltriller* is a *Schneller*, used on stepwise descent.[8] Nicolas Joseph Hüllmandel, a student of C.P.E. Bach's living in England and esteemed as a composer by Mozart, lists the three manners of executing trills shown in Ex. 8.5*b*. He explains: "The Shake begins indiscriminately with either of

[5]*Vollständige Anleitung*, pp. 135–137.
[6]*Klavierschule*, p. 7.
[7]*Musikalisches Lexicon, s.v. "Triller."*

[8]*Versuch eines Elementarbuchs der Singkunst*, p. 33.

Ex. 8.4. Koch

the two Shaken Notes, or sometimes by a note under those of the Shake, but it always finishes by the Note which bears the Shake."[9]

a. Nopitsch

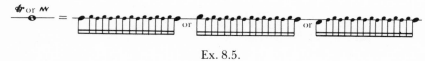

b. Hüllmandel

Ex. 8.5.

The opera conductor Carl Friedrich Ebers gives in his vocal treatise from the end of the 18th century mixed designs which are nevertheless predominantly of the main-note types.[10] For the cadential trill he shows the main-note *ribattuta* start of Ex. 8.6*a*. His trill on a fermata (Ex. *b*) starts with the sustained main note followed by an upper-note *ribattuta* introducing the trill proper. In chains (Ex. *c*) the trills also start with the sustained main note. In the pattern of Ex. *d* the auxiliary falls on the beat. The "brief" *(abgekürzte)* trill of Ex. *e* again has straight main-note character.

Justin Heinrich Knecht, in his time a "much esteemed music director" *(MGG)* illustrates first the "usual trill" ("gewöhnlicher Triller") in the standard appoggiatura form, but for the "long trill" at final cadences he gives the main-note design of Ex. 8.7, and for practicing the trill he proposes a slowly accelerating main-note pattern.[11]

In Italy, Luigi Antonio Sabbatini (1739–1809), "the last great Franciscan music theorist" *(MGG)*, a student of Padre Martini's, describes the trill exclusively in its main-note form: if there is a trill symbol over a G, he writes, "one must with greatest velocity sing G A G A G A etc. . . ."[12] Later (pp. 72–73) he returns to the trill, more specifically the trill on the final cadence or on a fermata. Again he

[9]*Principles of Music .. for the Piano Forte or Harpsichord.* pp. 16, 27.
[10]*Vollständige Singschule,* pp. 17-18.

[11]*Kleine theoretische Klavierschule,* p. 60.
[12]*Elementi teorici della musica,* p. 12.

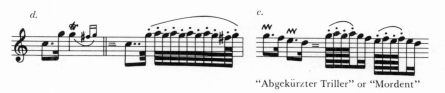

"Abgekürzter Triller" or "Mordent"

Ex. 8.6. Ebers

"Nachschlag"

Ex. 8.7. Knecht

explains its execution as first settling the voice on the (written) note, then quickly alternating with the auxiliary for the length of the note's value, or in case of a fermata for as long as one wishes. ("Fissata la voce su della *nota* che il Cantante vorrà trillare, passi immediatamente alla *nota* superiore . . . quindi dibbatta velocemente queste due *note* fin que duri il valore. . . .") He gives an illustration (Ex. 8.8*a*) of a trill that, he says, starts on the upper note and one (Ex. *b*) that starts on the main note. Yet, as both the cited verbal explanation ("Fissata la voce . . .") and the illustrations show, both of these trill types start with the sustained main note, their difference being simply that the alternations of the first type are upper-note, those of the second main-note anchored (provided the singer abides by the letter of the notation). The choice of one or the other style, he says, is solely a matter of taste ("dipende totalmente dal buon gusto").

Ex. 8.8. Sabbatini

Carlo Gervasoni (1762–1819), member of the Academy of Sciences and Arts and church music director in Borgo Taro, shows that the centuries-old Italian mirror-image dualism of (main-note) trill and (semitone) multiple mordent was still alive in 1800. "The trill," he writes, "quickly alternates the sound of the notated tone with its upper neighbor" ("Questo [trillo] consiste nel far alternare sollecitamente il suono della nota marcata con quella della superiore").[13] For the mordent the analogous alternations are with the half-tone below. His illustrations are shown in Ex. 8.9*a* for the trill, *b* for the mordent.

Ex. 8.9. Gervasoni

The same mirror-image dualism appears also in Giuseppe Liverziani's treatise of 1797 where the term *trillo* as well as the waggle symbol ⁓ can stand for either (main-note) trill or mordent.[14] ("Trillo . . . si dice, allore quando si vuole, che una Nota partecipe del suono della Nota anteriore, o posteriore, e si indica col segno ⁓.")

In France, Jean-Guillain Cardon (1732–1788), *maître de violon* of the conte de Provena, the future Louis XVIII, shows in a treatise only the main-note trill of Ex. 8.10*a*.[15] The eminent guitar virtuoso Joseph Bernard Merchi uses the same symbol of a cross for both the *Schneller (martellement)* and the trill which, as a main-note type, is defined as a "series of *martellements*" and given here in Ex. 8.10*b*.[16]

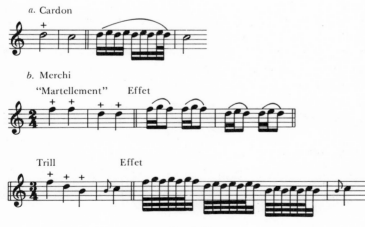

Ex. 8.10.

[13]*La scuola della musica*, vol. 1, p. 183.
[14]*Grammatica della musica*, p. 23.
[15]*Le rudiment de la musique*, p. 44.

[16]*Traité des agrémens de la musique, exécutés sur la guitarre*, art. IX and X.

In Austria, Johann Georg Albrechtsberger (Beethoven's teacher) shows the trill only in its main-note form, as given in Ex. 8.11.[17]

Ex. 8.11. Albrechtsberger

An analogous pattern for a cadential trill is offered by Jean Bisch, a German living in Paris (see Ex. 8.12).[18]

Ex. 8.12. Bisch

In a flute treatise of 1801, Andreas Dauscher at first describes and illustrates only the main-note trill: "The first tone sounds the main note and the next one the note a whole or half-step above" and illustrates it as in Ex. 8.13*a*. Later he offers the interesting model of Ex. *b*, showing a grace-note trill with a suffix which, he says, every trill has to have.[19]

Ex. 8.13. Dauscher

Far more important than all these documents is some direct evidence from Mozart himself. In *Così fan tutte,* Guglielmo in the aria "Rivolgete a lui lo sguardo" (later replaced by "Non siate ritrosi") demonstrates on the words *se cantano col trillo* the *ribattuta*-introduced main-note trill of Ex. 8.14.

Ex. 8.14.

The Mozart student Johann Nepomuk Hummel, speaking of trills in his piano treatise, writes: "I recommend the trill study that Mozart himself has shown me in which all five fingers alternate." This pattern, with its unmistakable main-note implications is reproduced in Ex. 8.15.[20]

[17]"Anfangsgründe zur Klavierkunst."
[18]*Explication des principes élémentaires de musique,* p. 68.

[19]*Kleines Handbuch der Musiklehre und vorzüglich der Querflöte,* pp. 107–109.
[20]*Ausführliche theoretisch-praktische Anweisung zum Piano-Forte-Spiel,* p. 385.

Ex. 8.15.

These theoretical preliminaries, supplemented by the documents compiled in *Ornamentation* (of which a great deal reaches well into Mozart's time), should suffice to dispel the belief that the "18th-century trill" had to be of the appoggiatura type and that consequently Mozart's trill must have followed the same model.[21]

Among modern writers who recognize the importance of the main-note types for Mozart is the eminent Hermann Abert who goes so far as to say that Mozart's trill "usually" starts with the main note.[22] Since Abert's monumental study of Mozart's life and works deals only peripherally with matters of performance practice, the opinion he expressed has had little influence on modern interpreters and scholars. It is fortunate that the Badura-Skodas in their study approach the question of Mozart's trills from a musical rather than an academic-dogmatic vantage point. They find that in "numerous" cases Mozart's trill ought to start with the main note, whereas in others either main-note or upper-note start is possible, and they also show examples of other trill types. They name the following circumstances that favor starting with the main note and illustrate them with convincing examples: 1) when in legato the trill is preceded by the next note above; 2) when the trill is preceded by three rising or falling notes like a "slide" (i.e. our "slide-trill" or "turn-trill"); 3) when the trill is on a dissonant note; 4) trills in the bass; 5) trills at the end of rising scales; 6) when the trill is preceded by the same note as a sharply attacked anacrusis; 7) in trill chains; 8) in the formula ♪♩, notably in allegro movements; 9) in "special cases" that clearly call for it (Badura-Skoda, pp. 111–116).

A single Badura-Skoda illustration, taken from the Two-Piano Concerto in E flat, and listed under the "special cases" category, should by the force of its evidence suffice to shatter the orthodox rule. To start the trill in the first piano other than with the main note is unthinkable (Ex. 8.16).

Ex. 8.16.

[21]The myth has a wide following among modern scholars. Typical is Rudolf Steglich's assertion that all Mozart trills have, as a matter of principle, the characteristics of a long appoggiatura ("Auszierungswesen," p. 224) or Nathan Broder's statement, when speaking of the piano, that Mozart's trill always starts with the auxiliary (on the beat) except when the auxiliary in appoggiatura function precedes the main note (preface to *Mozart Sonatas and Fantasias for the Piano*).

[22]*W. A. Mozart,* vol. 2, p. 189.

Heinz and Robert Scholz, in the preface to their edition of Mozart's piano sonatas (Universal, 1950) present the main-note style as the basic trill type. Much less to the point, however, is their further directive for strict rhythmic regularity of the alternations that sounds pedantic and stiff and contradicts the ornamental nature of the grace.

C. A. Martiensen and Wilhelm Weismann, in their Peters edition (1951) of the sonatas, make occasional main-note suggestions that are eminently sensible, and so does Otto von Irmer in his addenda to the Henle edition of the sonatas (ed. Lampe).

The old theorists, like all theorists who deal in abstractions, offered too narrow a picture of the world of performance; yet even they left us a picture, however incomplete, of the trill's multifaceted shape. To examine the various facets and their likely application to Mozart is the purpose of the next chapter.

The Trill: Practice 9

To mark the trill, Mozart from his earliest childhood almost always used the *tr* symbol. He often follows it with a wavy line,  indicating sustained alternations. If such a line is followed by the common two-note suffix, written in either regular notes or in small ornamental ones, the alternations are usually meant to continue uninterrupted to the end. A suffix written out in regular notes for the *soloist* need not be rendered with metrical precision: being an ornament it may be, and often should be, done faster, as if it had been written in little notes. When the suffix is not marked it should still be added when the circumstances favor it.[1]

On a few occasions Mozart uses the *chevron* ⌇ with two waggles only. Originally a French keyboard symbol for a trill of any length, in Germany it became after the mid-18th century the sign for a short trill, while three or more waggles denoted a trill of greater length. By the early 19th century the two-waggle symbol signified a *Schneller* in which sense it is occasionally used to this day. Whether this was already the case with Mozart is not entirely clear, but since he uses the symbol only on small note values, its possible range of meaning is limited. In Ex. 9.1*a* from the Piano Concerto in B flat K 456 it must mean a *Schneller* since the tempo hardly accommodates more notes. In the slow movement of the Piano and Woodwind Quintet the figure of Ex. *b* (or an analogous one) is marked with waggles in m. 22 for the oboe and in m. 24 for the horn, but with a *tr* sign in m. 26 for the bassoon. Here the tempo would, at least for the oboe, allow more than one alternation. In Ex. *c* from the Piano Concerto in E flat K 449 the symbols could stand for a short trill or perhaps for anticipated *Schneller*.

Ex. 9.1.

For Mozart as for other masters, the main subject of controversy is how to start the trill. A suggestion I made in *Ornamentation* concerning Bach's trills is, I believe, also applicable to Mozart because it is rooted in musical logic. The suggestion

[1]C. P. E. Bach tells us that "even the mediocre ear will always sense where the suffix may be made and where not" (*Versuch*, pt. 1, ch. 2, sec. 3, par. 17). Whereas Philipp Emanuel's rules are often dangerous, this nonrule has a wide applica- tion. A sensitive performer who knows that such additions are permissible will know where to ap- ply them; an insensitive one would not be helped by any rule one might formulate.

derives from the facts that 1) a trill starting with the upper note on the beat has the effect of a short appoggiatura; 2) a trill starting with a lengthened upper note has the effect of a long appoggiatura; 3) a trill starting with the upper note before the beat has the effect of a grace note. We find guidance by leaving out the trill and judging whether one of these ornaments would be a desirable addition to the bare melody; if so, the corresponding trill type is likely to be the proper or at least an acceptable choice. Where none of these ornaments seems to fit, the main-note trill is indicated. Where no clear-cut choice between one or more of the alternatives emerges, more than one trill design will be fitting. The test can also be extended to suggest compound trills whenever either a rising or a falling three-note prefix could be added to advantage. The short trill forms can also be tested by the same criteria except that for obvious reasons they cannot accommodate any kind of support. On the other hand they can on occasion be done in full anticipation.

THE APPOGGIATURA TRILL

When Mozart intended a supported appoggiatura trill (i.e. one starting with a lengthened upper note) he usually indicated his wish. He either wrote it out in regular notes as in Exx. 9.2*a* from the *Dissonance* Quartet, *b* from the Piano Sonata in A minor, and *c* from the Two-Piano Sonata (see also Ex. 9.1*b*), or, in his earlier years, indicated it with a *Vorschlag* symbol of a denomination suggesting a long appoggiatura. The notation of *any Vorschlag* symbol, long or short, preceding a trill, seems to have disappeared by circa 1780. Before that time, a symbol of a half-note, as in Ex. *d* from the Violin Sonata in G K 293a (301) or of a quarter-note as in Ex. *e* from the *Haffner* Serenade, indicates their approximate duration. That the value may only be approximate appears from a passage like that of Ex. *f* from the Missa brevis. Though an exact coordination of voice and violin is not necessary, the latter's line does suggest a shorter than quarter-note duration of the vocal appoggiatura. In many other cases, for which Exx. *g* from the Violin Sonata in E minor K 300c (304), and *h* from the Violin Concerto No. 2 in D are typical, it is safe to follow the denominations quite literally.

Without such notational indication, supported appoggiatura trills have a place mainly in certain spots from slow movements, such as the one in Ex. 9.3*a* from the Adagio for Violin in E. Here, according to our test, the inserting of a modest appoggiatura of about 16th- to 8th-note length seems fitting, as sketched in Ex. *b*. Fitting too and perhaps even more appropriate, would be the three-note prefix yielding the slide-trill of Ex. *c*. Another sample that can stand for many other similar ones is Ex. *d* from the Piano Concerto in G K 453. Here we can see three possibilities: the slightly supported appoggiatura trill of Ex. *e*; the slide-trill of *f* with the three-note prefix ad libitum on the beat, before the beat, or between the beats; or perhaps with no additions at all, a plain trill starting with an ever so slightly held main note.

A plain, nonsupported appoggiatura trill will often be fitting in an allegro movement on cadences, as in Ex. 9.4*a* from the C major *(Dissonance)* String Quartet. A similar appoggiatura trill or one with a modest support seems indicated in Ex. *b* from the E flat String Quartet K 421b (428) and in many analogous situations.

The short trills of Ex. 9.5 from the Piano sonata in D K 576 should, according to the Badura-Skoda list (see Chapter 8), be main-note trills, and certainly they could

Ex. 9.2.

Ex. 9.3.

be so played. Yet the appoggiatura type is perfectly fitting too as a quasi-embellished turn, and grace-note trills might well be the most elegant of the available options.

Ex. 9.4.

Ex. 9.5.

The conditions are different in Exx. 9.6*a* and *b* from the Piano Sonata in D *(Dürnitz)* where Irmer's appoggiatura trill solutions are questionable:[2] In Ex. *a* because the main note of the trill is itself an appoggiatura, hence a grace-note trill would be more fitting; in *b* because the appoggiatura start would obscure the melodic line. No appoggiatura would fit the "naked" melody; hence *Schneller* or brief main-note trills would be more proper. Two-alternation main-note trills, suggested in the Peters edition by Martiensen and Weismann, are a fitting solution. By contrast, for the brief upbeat trill of Ex. *c* from the Piano Sonata in D K 284c (311) Irmer's version of a turn as a miniature appoggiatura trill makes good sense.

a. K 205b (284)/1

b. Ibid./2

* Here the autograph has the most unusual (for Mozart) symbol ⑀. The first edition by Torricella has the ⚹ sign throughout.

c. K 284c (311)

Ex. 9.6.

[2]Otto von Irmer, preface and appendix to Mozart, *Klavier Sonaten.*

THE MAIN NOTE TRILL

Valuable as the Badura-Skoda list of contexts favoring the main-note trill is, my suggested test for identifying the best trill type is, I believe, more practical and more reliable. It is more practical because it does not require memorizing a list that must be passed in review in each case, more reliable because it takes all possible starting styles into consideration, including the grace note and compound trills. Each case grows out of the individual musical situation, and, as we have seen, the test also points up those circumstances that admit more than one solution. The use of the test will on the whole confirm the main points of the Badura-Skoda list but extend it to a wider spectrum of musical situations.

At the beginning of a piece or a section an appoggiatura is normally out of place and even a grace note rarely fitting; hence a trill on the first note should usually be of the main-note type. For illustrations see Exx. 9.7*a* from the Piano Sonata in B flat K 189f (281); *b* from the early Symphony in E flat (1772); and *c* from the Symphony in A of the same year.

Ex. 9.7.

The same considerations apply to a trill starting ex abrupto after a rest as in the case of Ex. 9.8*a* from the Piano Sonata in D *(Dürnitz)*. In Ex. *b* from the *Haffner* Serenade the main-note type is confirmed by the variant of *c* and further supported by the melodic logic of the scalewise ascent.

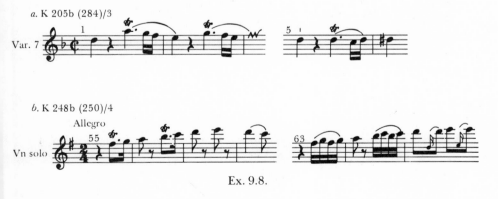

Ex. 9.8.

The just mentioned melodic logic will come to the fore when the trills are placed on a characteristic thematic formula whose profile would be impaired by an added appoggiatura. Clearly, the sequence of octave leaps in Ex. 9.9*a* from the tenor solo in *Litaniae Lauretanae* will suffer no intrusion. In the similar case of Ex. *b* from the Piano Sonata in G, Irmer suggests either a mordent or a turn. A mordent with a C sharp, on or before the beat, responding in the Italian tradition to the identical symbol, is a distinct possibility; a *Schneller,* possibly anticipated, is likelier than a turn, which, taken on the beat, would blur the sharp contour of the octave leap. An appoggiatura trill does not fit.

Ex. 9.9.

Whenever a triadic formula (or a similarly characteristic motive) forms part of the thematic essence, the notes that outlined the motive should enter clear and uncluttered. The festive triadic opening signal of the Sonata for Two Pianos of Ex. 9.10*a* would lose its cutting edge were an appoggiatura to intrude. The same can be said of spots like those of Exx. *b* from the *Hoffmeister* String Quartet; *c* from the Symphony in B flat K 319; *d* from the String Quintet in D K 593; and *e* from the late Violin Sonata in A with its diminished triads. The need to start on the main note is manifest also in the beginning of the Trio from the G major String Quartet K387 (Ex. *f*): here the ascending triad in octaves has trills in the upper strings but is unornamented in the cello where trills in the low register would be ineffectual. The unison and octave entrances must not be disturbed. In some of these cases, perhaps in Ex. *d* or *f*, a grace-note trill would be justifiable because it leaves the main note both accented and in place.

Any other sharply profiled theme will be equally inhospitable to an appoggiatura. Hence in Ex. 9.11*a* from the Piano Sonata in A minor the trills should be main-note types. In Ex. *b* from the String Quintet in D K 593 the lean laconic fugal theme is equally unreceptive; the pronounced linearity of any fugal theme will almost always resist interference by an appoggiatura.

Where pitch repetition is clearly thematic, as in Ex. 9.12*a* from the *Haffner* Symphony, there is no place for an appoggiatura and barely one for a much less obtrusive grace note. This passage also happens to fall in the Badura-Skoda category of sharply attacked anacruses on the same pitch. For Ex. *b* from the Piano Sonata in C K 300h (330), Irmer sensibly suggests the main-note solution of *c*. In Exx. *d* and *e* from the Piano Sonatas in D K 205b (284) and B flat K 189f (281) respectively, the persistent pulsating repeats of the upbeat note so obviously head for the main note of the following trill that any appoggiatura start would be

Ex. 9.10.

Ex. 9.11.

perceived as a disturbance. In Ex. *f* from the Piano Concerto in E flat K 482, the energy of the military, signallike theme would be senselessly softened by inserting an appoggiatura. For further specimens see the Piano Sonata in A minor, K 300d (310)/2, mm. 46 and 49; the String Quartet in D minor K 417b (421)/1, m. 2; the Violin Sonata in F K 374e (377)/3, mm. 170–175.

a. K 385/2

Andante

b. K 300h (330)/2

Andante cantabile

c.

d. K 205b (284) Rondeau en Polonaise

Andante

e. K 189f (281)/3

Allegro

f. K 482/1

Allegro

Ex. 9.12.

A scalewise moving melody carrying a trill or trills is similarly sensitive to interference. In Ex. 9.13*a* from the Sinfonia concertante the chromatic ascent with its breathtaking crescendo through nearly two octaves would have its line blurred by appoggiaturas, and the final approach to the climactic high C would be emasculated if both the trills on B flat and B natural were to start with an accented C. In the related chromatic passage of Ex. *b* from *Die Zauberflöte* appoggiaturas would weaken the sense of urgency conveyed by the chromatic ascent and further underlined by a steep crescendo.

A melody moving in a diatonic scale pattern will usually be equally resistant to linear disturbances. In Ex. 9.14*a* from the Piano Sonata in B flat K 189f (281), Irmer logically resolves the trill in the middle of a scale passage as given in *b,* and so do Martiensen and Weismann. Better still may be the solution without a suffix of Ex. *c.* The passage from the Chorus in *Figaro* of Ex. *d* would lose its linear drive: appoggiaturas would have a braking effect on the joyous ascent of the melody.

Another sharply etched theme that moves scalewise up and down and would favor main-note start is shown in Ex. 9.15*a* from the String Quintet in D K 593. For the downward-upward scalewise theme of Ex. *b* from the Piano Sonata in F

a. K 320d (364)

b. K 620, I, 1

Ex. 9.13.

a. K 189f (281)/3   *b.*   *c.*

d. K 492, I, 8

Ex. 9.14.

K 300k (332), the Artaria first edition has the notation of Ex. *c.* Though Mozart's consent is unprovable, the print shows a contemporary professional's endorsement of the supported main-note start, and *d* shows Irmer's concurrence. The scalewise line of Ex. *e* from the *Paris* Symphony, where trilled and plain notes alternate, will also benefit from main-note starts. So will the trills embedded in the chromatic sequence of Ex. *f* from the Violin Concerto No. 2 in D.

a. K 593/1

b. K 300k (332)/3   *c.*   *d.*

e. K 300a (297)/3

f. K 211/1

Ex. 9.15.

The shorter the trills that are part of a distinct melodic line, like the descending scale in Ex. 9.16*a* from the Terzetto of the three boys in *Die Zauberflöte,* the more important is their clean start with the main note, which otherwise would have no chance to be clearly perceived. Even grace notes would in such a narrow space obscure the line. For the same reasons of clarity the short trills within the characteristic sequence of "horn fifths" in Ex. *b* from the String Quintet in E flat K 614 require a main-note start. For another illustration see the Eight Variations for Piano, K 613, var. 6, mm. 1,2,5,6.

a. K 620, II, 16

b. K 641/1

Ex. 9.16.

A trill on the leading tone will usually have to start with the main note to bring out the tension inherent in its pull toward resolution. For a note of sufficient length a grace-note start might still permit such emphasis, but an accented appoggiatura would break the tension by obtrusively preempting the pitch of the resolution. In Ex. 9.17*a* from the late String Quartet in B flat the free entrance after a rest is an added factor favoring a main-note start. For short note values, such as those in Ex. 9.17*b* from the Piano sonata in F K 189e (280), a main-note start is as good as mandatory. In Zerlina's aria "Vedrai carino" of Ex. *c*, the characteristic interval of the augmented fourth—F-B—from trill to trill would be lost were appoggiaturas to be added, as would the sense of direction for the trill on the leading tone. Grace-note trills would be barely tolerable, but to start with an extended appoggiatura (Ex. *d*), as has been done, for example, by Richard Bonynge, a conductor whose concern for historical accuracy is well known, is an aberration.

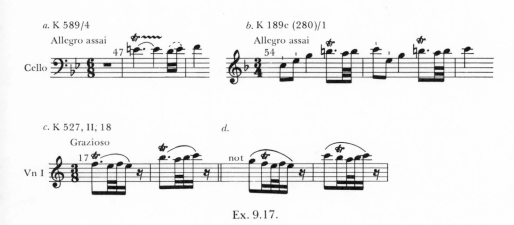

Ex. 9.17.

Trill chains are on the Badura-Skoda's main-note list. Their example (p. 115) is a chromatic trill ascent from the second movement of the E flat Concerto K 482/2, mm. 151–152 and 173–176, and they argue convincingly that appoggiatura starts "would obscure the chromatic progression, since in each case there would be two trills beginning on the same note."

Of all melodic figures the chromatic scale may be the most sensitive to the infiltration of foreign matter. A musical situation in which trills over a chromatic sequence are meant to enrich the harmony rather than reinforce the linearity is hard to imagine. In passages like those of Ex. 9.18*a* from the Piano Concerto in A K 385p (414), or *b* from the Violin Sonata in E flat K 481, even grace notes would disturb the line. In both cases the specification of the suffix after the last trilled note is sufficient to indicate that no suffixes are to be made within the chain itself.

Diatonic chains are less frequent, but they too would respond to the same melodic demands. In the descending chain of Ex. *c* from the early Piano Concerto in B flat, main-note starts are a technical, as well as a musical necessity: here the written-out suffixes lead spontaneously into the beginnings of the subsequent trills, the suffixes being in fact brief anticipations of the following main-note trills. The repetition of pitches involved in appoggiatura starts would be both unmusical and unidiomatic.

a. K 385p (414)/1

b. K 481/2

c. K 238/2

Ex. 9.18.

The widely held conviction that at least a cadential trill has to be of the appoggiatura type is contradicted by numerous items of musical evidence. In Mozart's autograph of the Capriccio for Piano we find the final cadence as given in Ex. 9.19a. We see a *Triller von unten* with the lower neighbor anticipated and the main note accented on the beat. Here we have also one of numerous cases where the addition of a suffix is obligatory. In other instances the final trill is reached as the culmination of a rising passage that can logically land only on the main note. Also on the Badura-Skoda list are trills at the end of rising scales, which the authors illustrate with the Two-Piano Concerto, third movement, m. 137. For further specimens see Ex. 9.19b for a dashing diatonic scale passage from the Concerto in E flat K 482, and for two chromatic ones Exx. *c* from the cadenza to the Concerto in A K 488, written in the autograph as an integral part of the movement, and *d* from the cadenza to the earlier Concerto in A K 385p (414). Had Mozart in any of these cases intended an appoggiatura trill he would have had to write the run up to the pitch of the trill. Failing this, the main-note start is imperative since an interruption of the élan by a sudden leap would be musically absurd.

There seems to be no instance of a scale leading up to the written pitch of *any* trill, evidence that would have suggested an upper-note start. If we add the frequent cases of turn or slide prefixes, we cannot help speculating that even Mozart's cadential trills were rarely of the appoggiatura type.

Related to the dashing scales leading up to a cadential trill are instances like Ex. 9.20 from the *Prague* Symphony where a sparkling scale passage first tumbles downward, then reverses course before landing on the trill. The case for the main note is, if possible, stronger still for Ex. *b* from the last of the Nine Variations on a Minuet by Duport where a long ascending run in broken thirds *has* to land on the g″.

A trill slurred to the preceding note one step above is another item on the Badura-Skoda list. Examples 9.21a from the Violin Sonata in C K 296 and b from the Piano Sonata in D K 284c (311) illustrate this principle. We can further extend

a. K 300g (395)

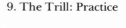

b. K 482/1

c. K 488/1 Cadenza

d. K 385p (414) Cadenza

Ex. 9.19.

a. K 504/3

b. K 573

Ex. 9.20.

it in that the slur need not be from the upper neighbor note. Even on an ascent, and on many a downward leap, the trill within a slur will tend to the main-note style. In such circumstances, as Rameau had wisely observed, the preceding note functions as preparation to any ornament that is slurred to it. That a main-note start of the trill was intended in Ex. *c* from the String Quartet in B flat *("The Hunt")* is confirmed in the fragment of an older version, given in *d.* In Ex. *e* from the

Piano Sonata in D *(Dürnitz)* Irmer gives the convincing solution of *f* with *Schneller* that, tempo and technique permitting, could be enriched by an added alternation. In Ex. *g* from the Eight Variations for Piano, K 613, only a main-note start of the trills in var. 3 can preserve the melodic line as revealed in the unornamented theme.

Ex. 9.21.

Quite frequently, Mozart writes out a main-note support. In these cases the trill represents an intensification that, particularly on the keyboard, should be introduced subtly and not with a sudden jolt. Obviously the alternations have to start with the upper note, but just as obviously a distinct accented appoggiatura start is inappropriate. In Ex. 9.22*a* from the *Jeunehomme* Concerto anticipation of the trill is a possibility (Ex. *b*), as is a grace-note start; the latter would serve well in Ex. *c* from the same work. In *d* from the *Litaniae Lauretanae* the trill was perhaps meant to be longer and could well start before the bar line; (a brief cadenza ought to follow the fermata).

Dynamic markings can suggest or demand a main-note start. In Ex. 9.23*a* from the Piano Sonata in B flat K 189f (281) the *fp* marks can refer only to the main notes, admitting not even a grace note. In Ex. *b* from an earlier passage of the same work Irmer concurs by giving the solution of *c*.

Where the trill in an accompanying part adds brilliance to a note played or sung without ornament in the principal part, an appoggiatura would make little musical sense. It certainly should not be used in Ex. 9.24 from *Don Giovanni* where its insistent repetition would be felt as an irritant.

a. K 271/1

b.

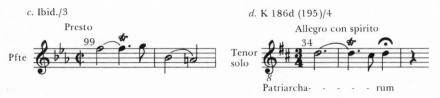

c. Ibid./3

d. K 186d (195)/4

Ex. 9.22.

a. K 189f (281)/3

b.

c.

Ex. 9.23.

K 527, I, 4

Ex. 9.24.

Still other situations favor a main-note start. In Ex. 9.25*a* from the overture to *Die Zauberflöte* an appoggiatura trill would efface the clearly intended contrast of this trill with the accented, written-out turn of the fugue theme. The same juxtaposition of the two characteristic motive fragments recurs in mm. 33–36.

Harmonic reasons favor the main-note trill in Ex. *b* from the Piano Sonata in F

K 300k (332) where the main note resolves the suspension, whereas in Ex. *c* from the *Hoffmeister* Quartet the first violin has to announce the main note on the beat in order to establish the suspension character of the tied-over a′ in the second violin.

a. K 620 Overture

b. K 300k (332)/1   *c.* K 499/1

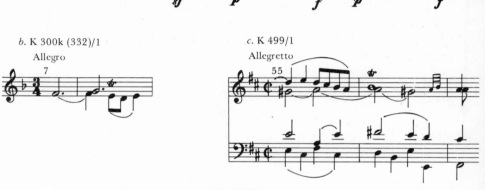

Ex. 9.25.

Two items on the Badura-Skoda list are also harmonic in nature: trills on a dissonance and trills in the bass, and for each they give the convincing illustrations of Ex. 9.26*a* from the Piano Concerto in E flat K 482 where "the friction of the A flat with the suspended G must, of course, be preserved," and Ex. *b* from the same movement with the voices reversed where, as in all such cases, "the function of the bass as root of the harmony might suffer if one began the trill on the upper auxiliary" (Badura-Skoda, p. 113). Related is Ex. *c* from the *Jeunehomme* Concerto, where the long organ point on the trill calls for main-note emphasis while the chromatic ascent to the trill requires a main-note start.

a. K 482/2

b.

c. K 271/3

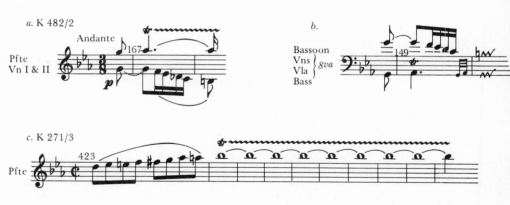

Ex. 9.26.

The Schneller

Where a main-note trill is indicated and the time is too short for multiple alternations, the answer is the *Schneller*. The line between *Schneller* and a brief (two-alternation) main-note trill is flexible: often it will depend on the technical skill of the performer which type is more fitting.

In Ex. 9.27*a* from the Serenade in D K 213a (204) technical instinct alone will keep violinists from inserting an extra note in the trill on top of the Lombard snap. Lack of time is a determining factor here, though main-note emphasis receives further support from the parallel spot in mm. 64–65 where the autograph has trill symbols only on the fourth beats, leaving the third ones plain. In such fairly fast scalewise passages as those from the Concertone (Ex. *b*) and the Serenade in D K 189b (203) (Ex. *c*), *Schneller* seem the sensible choice. Lack of time will again impose a *Schneller* solution on Ex. *d* from the *Coronation* Concerto; on Ex. *e* from the Symphony in A K 186a (201); and on Ex. *f* from the Piano Concerto in F K 387a (413) where the trills are marked with the two-waggle symbols that by this time *may* have already been associated with the *Schneller*.

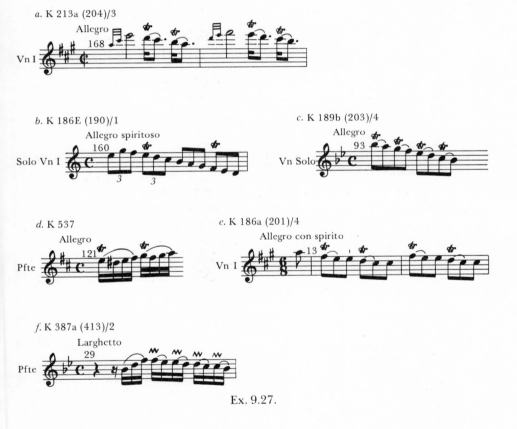

Ex. 9.27.

The Grace-Note Trill

As documented in *Ornamentation* the grace-note trill was in use long before Mozart. In view of its unobtrusive attractiveness in many musical situations where a start with the upper note is welcome but an appoggiatura out of place, its frequent presence in Mozart also should surprise no one. The grace-note trill was, as I was able to show (see *Ornamentation,* especially pp. 263–265), one of Couperin's favorite designs, and was doubtless used by many masters who clothed their trill models in deceptively rigid shapes that were not meant to be taken at their mathematical face value. Yet though textbook rules are always more rigid than the musical facts of life, I found and listed several theoretical descriptions of the grace-note trill and some convincing pieces of musical evidence in support of it. In this volume additional evidence was presented in Ex. 8.13*b.* A yet later document may have relevance simply by showing the idiomatic nature of this design for the voice. Manuel Garcia (son) in his famous vocal treatise of 1847 illustrates a trill chain from Donizetti's *Anna Bolena* (Ex. 9.28) where all trills start with the auxiliary and only the last has a suffix. The accents placed on the trilled notes clearly establish the grace-note character of the *Vorschläge.* (Also, the symbols used could by that date only mean grace notes.)

Ex. 9.28. Garcia (Donizetti)

Fortunately, some editors admit the occasional need for the grace-note trill, which has been used by many performers (by some perhaps unconsciously) but has been largely ignored by scholars. Wolfgang Plath and Wolfgang Rehm, in their edition of the piano trios (*NMA* VIII 22/2), speaking of the childhood works K 10–15 hold, as usual, that all trills have to start with the auxiliary. When Mozart writes ♩ they want it played ♩, but when he writes ♩ they give the grace-note solution of ♩. In the passage of Ex. 9.29*a* from *Litaniae Lauretanae* the *NMA* editors sensibly suggest the anticipation of the *Vorschlag* note. Martiensen and Weismann, in their Peters edition of the piano sonatas, give for the beginning of the C major Sonata K 300h (330) the grace-note solution of Ex. *b* as one of two alternatives.

a. K 186d (195)/5   *b.* K 300h (330)/1   Martiensen and Weismann

Ex. 9.29.

The Badura-Skodas point to the practice of fine string players who "do not accent the upper auxiliary note at the beginning of the trill, but play it as an anacrusis. This seems an inspired compromise; the accent can fall on the main note, but the preceding upper auxiliary allows the trill to begin easily and sweetly." They cite the strings of the Casals Festival Orchestra who play the trills of the Finale of the Sinfonia concertante given in Ex. 9.30*a* as shown in *b.* Applying the design to the piano, the Badura-Skodas show the rendition of *d* as one of their two preferred options for the cadential trill in the A major Piano Concerto K 488 (Ex. *d*) (Badura-Skoda, p. 118).

a. K 320d (364)/3

Ex. 9.30.

These may be rare cases, but they nevertheless represent a significant breach in the heretofore total silence of today's scholars and editors about this important trill design.

The grace-note type will be generally advisable where upper-note start is either prescribed by symbol, as in Ex. 9.31*a* from the Violin Sonata in B flat K 317d (378), or suggested by a context that favors the inserting of a grace, as in *b,* from the Violin Sonata in E flat K 374f (380), and where an appoggiatura is musically unwarranted or less desirable.

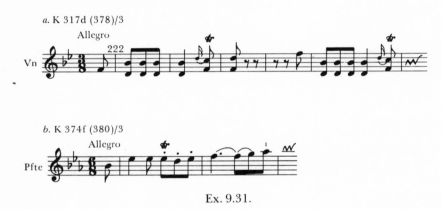

Ex. 9.31.

Even where appoggiatura or main-note trills are sensible solutions, a grace-note trill can often be a valid alternative that offers desirable variety.

Where the auxiliary is not specified in the notation, a grace-note trill will often be fitting when the trill is on the pitch of the preceding note; it will often be strongly suggested (with the main note the only possible, but often less desirable alternative) when the trilled note is itself an appoggiatura as in Exx. 9.32*a* and *b* from the Piano Sonatas in B flat, K 189f (281) and in D K 205b (284).

We find an interesting clue suggesting a grace-note trill in the third movement of the Serenade in D K 213a (204) where the passage of Ex. 9.33*a* had an inserted *Vorschlag,* for which the *NMA* with good reason suggests using a grace note. In the parallel spot in Ex. *b* a trill is placed on the same note: the grace note of the first passage will spontaneously transfer to the trill of Ex. *b.*

The trill in the theme of the G major Piano Concerto K 453 (Ex. *c*) is a distinct candidate for grace-note treatment which would have the smoothing effect of a

Ex. 9.32.

tierce coulée while leaving intact the rhythmically important dotted ratio. The Badura-Skodas go even further by suggesting the complete three-note anticipation of Ex. *d* which also makes a fine effect.

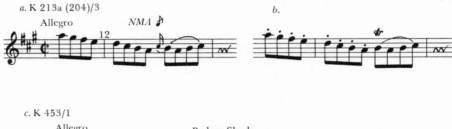

Ex. 9.33.

Where a symbol asks for a *Vorschlag* before the trill, a grace-note solution is usually indicated whenever the marked *Vorschlag* would have been anticipated without the trill. Such is the case in Ex. 9.34*a* from the Violin Concerto in B flat or in Ex. *b* from the Dixit und Magnificat. In Ex. *c* from the Violin Concerto No. 4 in D, 8th-note appoggiaturas in accord with the denominations would deprive the passage of its rhythmic vitality and the trills of their brilliance. Appoggiaturas would have to be very short in order not to brake the down-rushing melodic impetus. Grace-note treatment seems preferable here too.

Ex. 9.34.

c. K 218/1

Ex. 9.34 *cont.*

Once performers are aware of the legitimacy of the grace-note trill, they will find a wide range of contexts where our test will either suggest or allow its use.

THE COMPOUND TRILL

In its two forms of the "slide-trill"  and the "turn-trill" , the compound trill occurs (or at least is notated) more frequently in works for the piano than for other instruments or the voice. Türk, ever faithful to C.P.E. Bach's onbeat principle, tries to prove that even for Mozart these designs have to start on the beat by presenting the passage shown in Ex. 9.35 where, he says, lack of time forces the three-note prefix behind the bar line.[3]

Ex. 9.35. Türk (Mozart)

That occasionally the ornamented prefix had to be, or could be, placed on the beat, is certain, though lack of time does not necessarily force one's hand. We must not forget the soloistic freedom that would usually permit a slight rubato delay of the downbeat. There are unquestionably spots where, even without the pressure of time, an onbeat execution seems desirable, as in Ex. 9.36 from the Andante and Fugue in A for Violin and Piano where the preparation of the A sharp favors appoggiatura meaning for the first ornamental note. And Türk's example may well be justified on harmonic grounds rather than by lack of time. But such instances are rather rare, and to generalize from Türk's single passage is surely inadmissible.

K 385c (402)

Pfte

Ex. 9.36.

There are, by contrast, numerous cases where external evidence points to anticipation. In Ex. 9.37*a* from the cadenza to the B flat Concerto K 456, such anticipation is specified in regular notation for a slide-trill, in Ex. *b* from the

---

[3]*Klavierschule,* 1802 ed., p. 272.

cadenza to the third movement of the B flat Concerto K 450 for the turn-trill. Similarly we find at the end of the cadenza for the F major Concerto K 459 the written-out anticipation of the turn-trill, as given in Ex. *c*.

Ex. 9.37.

In the Piano Sonata in D K 205b (284) the unmistakable autograph alignment of the *f* sign with the trilled note in two successive measures, as given in Ex. 9.38*a*, signifies its placement on the beat, hence anticipation of the prefix. An analogous alignment in Ex. *b* from the autograph of the *Hunt* Quartet reveals the same dynamic-rhythmic disposition.

Ex. 9.38.

As is shown in the chapter on the turn, the rising or falling three-note grace is usually anticipated when it precedes an unornamented note, and this fact alone favors its frequent anticipation when it precedes a trill.

SUMMARIZING briefly, the chief question about Mozart's trill centers on its start. For the plain trill there are the three alternatives of starting 1) with the accented auxiliary on the beat (appoggiatura trill); 2) with the main note (main-note trill); and 3) with the unaccented auxiliary before the beat (grace-note trill). Variants derive from the possible lengthening of the first sounded note. The compound trill with its three-note rising or falling prefix can be done unaccented before the beat, more or less accented on the beat, or in any metric-dynamic transitional manner between beats.

Theoretical and musical evidence, distilled by musical common sense, points to the use of all these available trill types in Mozart. Among them the main-note trill appears to have the widest range of application, thereby vindicating Abert's perceptive judgment that Mozart's trills "usually" start with the main note. For choosing the most appropriate trill type in any given situation, the suggested test is to leave out the trill, then consider whether the addition of an appoggiatura or a grace note to the "naked" tone would be fitting or whether no addition should be made; the answer will then point to the related trill species. If the choice among alternatives is evenly balanced, more than one solution will be proper. A similar test can be made to probe the rhythmic-dynamic disposition of the three-note prefixes while keeping in mind that musical evidence, some of it still to be presented in the next chapter, points to Mozart's preference for the anticipated type.

Mozart never notated alterations of the auxiliary and relied on the performer's musicianship to do what was necessary. An unmarked two-note suffix can and often should be added whenever the trilled note can easily accommodate it. As with other masters, the speed of the trill should be adapted to the circumstances: fast for brilliance; less speedy for grace in slow movements; faster in higher than in lower registers; and faster in a locale with dry acoustics than in the opposite situation.

10

The Turn

CHARACTER AND NOTATION

The turn, as used by Mozart, consists mostly of three ornamental notes that either descend or ascend scalewise and straddle the pitch of the principal note. The descending type is more frequent and could be called the "standard," the ascending the "inverted" turn. The grace has two main forms: it either precedes the parent note ⌢•••• | ⌢•••• or is embedded in its middle ⌣•••⌣ (this latter form is generally limited to the "standard" design).

When preceding the principal note, the turn is an "intensifying" ornament that imparts to its parent grace or brilliance or accentuation or a combination of these. The embedded type will always serve as a "connective" ornament to grace the transition to the note that follows the parent, as in ⌣•••(•) . Occasionally, and maybe more often than we usually assume, the prenote standard turn has four instead of three ornamental notes starting with the pitch of the parent •⌢••• . This pitch, rendered at the speed of the other turn notes, is truly part of the ornament and is not perceived as an initial segment of the parent note. To be perceived as if it were part of an embedded turn, the first pitch would have to be held longer than the following ones. To make this distinction is not an exercise in splitting hairs; it is important to know, as we shall presently see, that four instead of three notes may on occasion be used in response to the turn symbol.

Unless Mozart writes the turn with regular notes, he signifies the prenote standard turn either by placing the symbol above the note ∾̃ or by writing the three little notes ⌢♫♪ or ⌢♫♪ . The inverted turn is exclusively marked by little notes, since Mozart never uses the inverted symbol ∾, introduced by C.P.E. Bach, to signify this grace. Mozart notates the embedded turn by placing the symbol between the parent note and the one that follows it: ♩ ∾ ♩ or by writing four little notes: ♪⌢♫♫(♪) . The notation with four little notes can be deceptive when used after a dotted note ♩·⌢♫♫(♪) , where the last of the four, as an extension of the parent, will often have to be held longer than the preceding three, thereby infelicitously belying the graphic suggestion of evenness. More about this later. Once in a while, Mozart uses the three-note pattern for the embedded turn when he writes out the continuation of the parent in a regular note such as ♪⌢♫♫♩♪ . When Mozart uses the symbol ∾ he usually, but not infallibly, indicates a required chromatic alteration.

A rare form of the inverted turn with the first ornamental note sustained (reminiscent of the dactylic slide) seems to occur only in the second movement of the *Jeunehomme* Piano Concerto, where in mm. 62 and 68 the autograph shows clearly the following notation: ⌢♫♪ (which might be done in a free straddling manner, ♩♫♫♫♪ , or perhaps, more simply on the beat, ♫♫♫♫♩ .

Before we examine the meaning of these various notational styles, it will be well to take a look at some contemporary theorists who will provide us with a helpful, if only approximate, frame of reference for Mozart's usage.

THE THEORISTS

For the antecedents of the classical era the reader is referred to *Ornamentation*, Chapter 41 as well as to pp. 453 and 460 on Tartini's and L. Mozart's *mordente*. From the many sources described there I mention here only two or three, and supplement them with reports on a few later writers.

C.P.E. Bach shows the "turn before the note" as given in Ex. 10.1*a*. We see that in an adagio he assigns the ornamental notes uneven values, starting fast and slowing down, presumably to achieve a snappy accentual effect on the beat. With increasing speed the pattern evens out. The notation of his Ex. *b* of what he calls the "geschnellter Doppelschlag" does not occur in Mozart, but Bach's remark that the four-note turn starting with the principal note may also be used when the little *Vorschlag* note is absent is significant. We should keep this important statement in mind. The "embedded turn" with the first note sustained and the symbol placed after the note is shown in Ex. *c*.[1] We see here an even more complex terraced pattern of lengthening pitches than the one for the adagio turn before the note. Bach demonstrates at the same time the *Zwischenraum* (space) between the turn and the following note, mentioned in his text as an element of the grace.

Other theorists accept these basic melodic designs but simplify the patterns by equalizing the ornamental notes, as shown in Ex. *d* from Albrechtsberger, *e* from Clementi, and, for the embedded turn, *f* from Tromlitz. Türk, as usual, follows Bach rather closely, except that he does not permit the four-note turn of Ex. *b* without the notated *Vorschlag* note.[2]

Ex. 10.1.

---

[1] *Versuch*, pt. 1, ch. 2, sec. 4; Table 5, figs. 50, 69, 70.

[2] Türk, *Klavierschule*, 1789 ed., pp. 283, 286; Albrechtsberger, "Anfangsgründe," p. 4; Clementi, *Introduction*, p. 11; Johann Georg Tromlitz, *Ausführlicher und gründlicher Unterricht, die Flöte zu spielen*, p. 254.

Very significant is the *full anticipation* of the three turn notes both descending and ascending, as described by Tartini and L. Mozart (see *Ornamentation*, pp. 453 and 460). Tartini makes the anticipation clear by stressing the great lightness and speed of the three ornamental pitches with the accent falling on the principal note: . Mozart, as so often, follows Tartini's description faithfully. (See also *Ornamentation*, p. 477, for a diminution model by Quantz showing the same design also quite certainly intended for anticipation.)

For the *turn after a dotted note,* which C.P.E. Bach did not show, Türk offers the design with the symbol of Ex. 10.2*a*, which, with rhythmic adjustments that do not affect the principle, is also given by Milchmeyer, Clementi, and J. F. Schubert. Türk gives the alternative notation with four even notes of Ex. *b*, which is clearly relevant to Mozart's usage, and adds significantly that the notation of *c* showing the lengthening of the fourth note is "clearer and more correct" ("noch bestimmter und richtiger").[3] Tromlitz agrees. First he indicates the synonymity of the two styles of notation in Exx. *d* and *e* in the meaning of *f*, showing the lengthening of the fourth of the evenly written notes, thereby clarifying its nature as an extension of the principal note.[4]

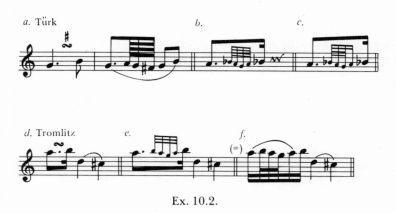

Ex. 10.2.

The models so far shown are the more common ones for the turn with the symbol both above and after the note, and are likely to have been widely used. There were, however, some interesting deviations.

Lasser, a singer and violinist of note, in 1798 uses the traditional model of 10.3*a* (albeit with the symbol placed vertically). He supplements it with new designs and terms: what he calls a *Zwicker* embodies the pitches of the turn but is in fact a mordent preceded by a grace note (its anticipation, already obvious from the notation, is spelled out in the text). In *Ornamentation* I called this design the "Italian mordent," and Lasser marks it with the traditional mordent symbol of Ex. *b*. Somewhat confusingly, he refers to the common, horizontal turn symbol above the note as a "mordent," which in "gay, sprightly" spots has, for the dotted note, the meaning of the four-note turn (C.P.E.'s "geschnellter Doppelschlag") of Ex. *c*, whereas in "expressive" spots, it takes the form of the embedded turn of Ex. *d*. The same applies to binary notes where Ex. *e* is "usually" the four-note turn of Ex. *f*, in "flattering" spots, the embedded one of Ex. *g*.

[3]*Klavierschule*, 1789 ed., p. 287.
[4]*Unterricht*, p. 254.

a. Lasser *Doppelschlag*   *b. Zwicker*

Fug-gia fi- nor   Ac-cel- le- rar- - - -

c.
Andantino
Mordent

bril- lar il cor mi sen- to

d.   *e.*   *f.*   *g.*

Die Lie- be

Ex. 10.3.

Lasser is not alone in treating the "Italian mordent" as a form of the turn. Significantly, J. F. Schubert shows, under the usual term of *Doppelschlag*, the same design (Ex. 10.4*a*) as an alternative solution for the turn symbol above the note. This illustration provides some possibly important theoretical support for a number of spots in Mozart, where this specific design appears to be eminently suited as the interpretation of the turn with the symbol above the note. Also interesting, on the part of this important theorist, is the further option "in slow tempo" of an embedded, after-the-note execution for the same symbol written above the note (Ex. *b*).

a. J.F. Schubert   *b.*
                                              Adagio

Ex. 10.4.

Mozart's Usage

The Wave Symbol

I address first the *turn before the note* ("prenote turn") that is marked with the symbol above the note head: $\widetilde{r}$. As we have seen, the great majority of theorists follow the general idea of C.P.E. Bach's solution (though simplifying it rhythmically) of starting the turn with the upper note on the beat. Of major theorists perhaps only Lasser endorsed Bach's option of starting the four-note figure of the *geschnellter Doppelschlag* on the main note. The usual three-note form, starting on the beat, will frequently be fitting for Mozart and should always be considered but not automatically applied, because often musical reasons call for other options. Among these are, besides the four-note design, rhythmic variants of the more common three-note type with full or partial anticipation of the turn notes within the scope of the following patterns, all of which, as we have seen, have found their reflection in various treatises:[5]

For this prenote turn the best rhythmic-melodic design can usually be determined by a test similar to that suggested for the trill. Since an onbeat three-note turn is closely related to a short appoggiatura, the former will be called for when an appoggiatura would be a fitting replacement. When a grace note seems more appropriate, either anticipation of the first turn note alone, or of the complete ornament should be considered. When neither appoggiatura or grace note will easily fit, a main-note start *(geschnellter Doppelschlag)* is likely to be the best solution.

Take, for example, the Allegro theme of the Violin Sonata in G K 373a (379) of Ex. 10.5*a*. Here the angry, almost violent expression calls for a sharply accented rendition. The standard solution of Ex. *b* is possible. But our test of substitution will hardly favor appoggiaturas; a snappy grace note, yes, or no *Vorschlag* at all. In keeping with that result, the version of Ex. *c* (Lasser's *Zwicker* or Schubert's option), by emphasizing the main note is more powerful: it is these threateningly hammered-out main notes that transmit the awesome energy of the theme. Another possibility would be the full anticipation of the turn with a sharp accent on the parent note (Ex. *d*): the turn will then appropriately sound like a whiplash. Conceivable, too, would be the solution of Ex. *e* with the *geschnellter Doppelschlag* on the beat. I would rank these options in the order *c, d, e, b.*

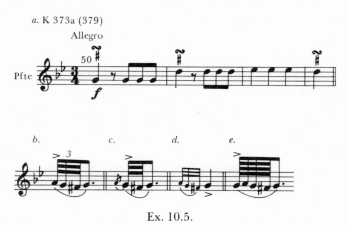

Ex. 10.5.

For another, contrasting expression, the joyful exuberance of the passage of Ex. 10.6*a* from the *Hoffmeister* String Quartet would seem to favor the snappy onbeat rendition of Ex. *b*, with *c* and *d* as possible alternatives that emphasize the tone repetition of E.

[5]Interestingly, and perhaps significantly, Haydn used the symbol above the note frequently, perhaps most of the time, in the sense of full anticipation. From an ample supply only one representative specimen can be shown here: in the slow movement of the late String Quartet Op. 77, No. 2 the principal motive is written in the autograph the first two times as in *a*, but from m. 5 on, and unquestionably with identical meaning, as in *b*. Melodically and rhythmically it is equivalent to an embedded turn after the 8th-note, the difference residing only in the interrupted slur.

a. K 499/1

Ex. 10.6.

The gracefulness of the theme from the Violin Sonata in B flat K 317d (378) of Ex. 10.7*a* will hardly call for more than a very subtle metrical accent (Ex. *b*). In fact, the thematic importance of the descending triad F-D-B♭ favors the solution of Ex. *c* which is no less graceful while preserving the audibility of the triadic progression. Our test might even suggest the option of the main-note turn of Ex. *d*.

a. K 317d (378)/3

Ex. 10.7.

Whenever rhythmic or melodic considerations favor emphasis on the main note of the turn, then full anticipation of either all three turn notes or the first note alone is indicated.

The Badura-Skodas give for Ex. 10.8*a* from the E flat Piano Concerto K 482 the solution of Ex. *b* to secure the rhythmic accent on the main note. Here any rendition other than full anticipation would also weaken the unity and with it the energy of the three-times-repeated motive.

a. K 482/3

Ex. 10.8.

In Ex. 10.9*a* from the G major Piano Trio K 496, the same authors consider full anticipation, as given in Ex. *b,* more appropriate. Their reason is presumably the thematic character of the pitch repetition, which would be obscured by an accented upper note. The solution makes good sense, but possible too are the alternative versions of Exx. *c* and *d*.

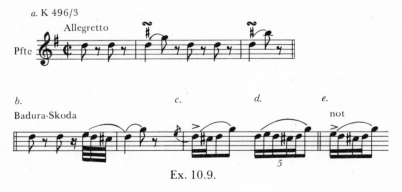

a. K 496/3

b.
Badura-Skoda

c.   *d.*   *e.*
not

Ex. 10.9.

The thematic importance of repeated pitches when the first note is an anacrusis will usually call for main-note emphasis, as in Ex. 10.10a from the Violin-Viola Duo in B flat. Here the sweet gentleness of the melody and the claim to integrity of the siciliano rhythm favor the anticipation of Ex. *b*.

Ex. 10.10.

Articulation can provide guidance. In analogy to a *Vorschlag*, a turn that precedes a short staccato note will best be anticipated to safeguard the latter's sharp delivery. The Badura-Skodas provide a good illustration from the Piano Concerto in B flat K 450 (Ex. 10.11)

Ex. 10.11.

Partial or total anticipation is generally only fitting when the turned note is placed on a principal beat, as was the case in the preceding examples. When placed off the beat, the ornament will normally be rendered in standard fashion within the time of the parent note, as shown in Ex. 10.12a from the Piano Concerto in G K 453; in Exx. *c* and *e* from the Piano Sonata in C minor; in Ex. *g* from the Piano Concerto in D minor, with performance suggestions given in Exx. *b*, *d*, *f*, and *h*, respectively. See also the Piano Concertos in B flat K 450/2, mm. 109–111, and in C major K 503/3, mm. 32–33.

The Badura-Skodas, guided by their artistic instinct, found several spots where starting with the main note seemed preferable, as in Ex. 10.13a from the Piano Concerto in E flat K 482 with their suggested solution of Ex. *b*. They find this design also "acceptable" for the pervasive motive of Ex. *c* from the Romance of *Eine kleine Nachtmusik* which they suggest should be played as in Ex. *d*. Their first illustration is thoroughly convincing with its thematic pitch repetition followed by scalewise ascent—a line better served by the main-note start. In the case of the Romance the standard solution with four notes (Ex. *e*) has the advantage of greater transparency, especially in the basses; five notes have the advantage of better motivic definition for the ascending half-step.

There are cases where starting with the main note is unavoidable, as in Ex. 10.14a from the Piano sonata in A minor, with the turned note slurred to its preceding neighbor, or where such a start is strongly suggested, as in Ex. *b* from the same movement, with the turn occurring in the middle of a slur. If, still in the same movement, we compare the passage of Ex. *c* with that of *d*, it is clear that the *fp* has to refer to the main note, not the upper one and that the passage should be played as given in Ex. *e*. See also the parallel spots in m. 80 with an equally clear

a. K 453/2

Andante

Pfte

b.

c. K 457/2

Adagio

d.

e.

f.

g. K 466/2

Vns

h.

Ex. 10.12.

a. K 482/2

Andante

Pfte

b.

Badura-Skoda

c. K 525/2

Andante

Vn I

d.

Badura-Skoda

e.

Ex. 10.13.

vertical alignment in the autograph of the symbols above the note. For a similar specimen see the first movement of the *Coronation* Concerto, m. 89 and parallel spots.

Examples like the foregoing make us wonder whether Mozart did not use the main-note start of the turn more widely than is generally assumed by scholars and historically oriented performers who rely—precariously—on the vastly predominant upper-note start in contemporary treatises. Even the Badura-Skodas see the main-note start only as an exception on musical grounds to what is supposedly

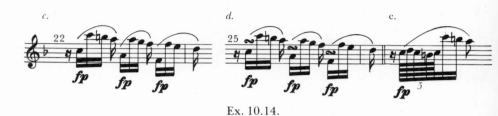

Ex. 10.14.

"historically correct." If, as I suspect, the main-note start did have a wider than exceptional use, we have to wonder why Mozart would place the turn symbol straight on top of the note and not to its right. The answer is that if he had placed the symbol after the note, the latter would be more or less sustained and become in fact the principal note, which is a different matter from the simple main-note start of the turn where the first note, as part of the ornament, is rendered as fast as its companions.

In the lyrical passage of Ex. 10.15*a* from the Piano Quartet in E flat the main-note turn of *b* is possible but could be crowded in the flowing tempo, in which case the textbook version of *c* might be preferable.

Ex. 10.15.

Mention should be made of a few cases where Mozart wrote a turn sign instead of a trill. A well-known instance occurs in the Finale of the *Jupiter* Symphony where the pervasive scale motive of Ex. 10.16*a* always has a trill symbol except in this one spot. Most likely this was an oversight which is understandable: since the main-note turn is simply a *Schneller* with suffix, the two graces are closely related.[6] In Ex. *b* from the Nine Variations on a Minuet by Duport, a brief trill or *Schneller* (elsewhere in this variation marked by ∿) was almost certainly intended, as is also suggested by the *NMA*.

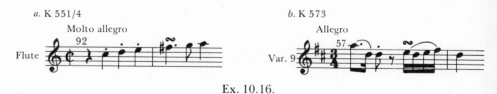

Ex. 10.16.

---

[6]H. C. Robbins Landon, in *NMA* IV/11/9, p. 64, concedes the possibility of trill meaning for this spot.

For the turn symbol placed *after the note,* which always signified an "embedded" turn, the most that can be said in a general way is that, time permitting, the first note should be more or less sustained. There are, however, important differences between a turn after a binary note and one after a dotted note.

The turn symbol *after a binary note* presents few problems. (In 6/8 meter, the dotted quarter-note as the metrical unit is equivalent to a binary note in a binary meter.) Generally, the three inserted notes plus the repeated principal note will lead directly without stopping, without C.P.E. Bach's *Zwischenraum,* into the following pitch. In so doing they give the impression of a single, four-note ornamental figure. Thus, the notated pattern of Ex. *a* will, depending on tempo, expression, and personal taste, be done approximately as in *b, c, d,* or *e,* with, of course, all possible gradation in between.[7]

For examples of spelled-out turns see Ex. 10.44*a* from the Piano Concerto in B flat K 595/1, m. 81, Ex. 13.17*a* from the Sextet of *Don Giovanni* and mm. 216 and 264 from its second Finale, or the String Quartet K 499/2, m. 2 and parallel spots (in these and many similar cases, the dot preceding the written-out turn must not delude us about the binary nature of the principal note). The many written-out turn figures in the first movement of the Clarinet Trio are in fact anticipated turns in that they are invariably slurred to the following, not the preceding, note.

For Mozart I would venture the suggestion that when in doubt, choose a faster rendition over a slower one, always keeping in mind both the character of the piece—a slower, more singing style is appropriate in an adagio, for example—and for soloistic playing the benefit of variety. Thus, the two turns of Ex. 10.17*a* from the Piano Concerto in D minor might be slightly varied as sketched in *b* and *c.*

Ex. 10.17.

The *turn symbol after a dotted note* ⌐•⁓⌐ permits a variety of solutions, and soloists will do well not to limit themselves to only one. What is blurred for the turn after a binary note—the "embedded" state of the three ornamental notes and the nature of the fourth note as continuation of the parent—is now made clear by the longer value of the main-note pitch that follows the turn proper. The most common solution, found in most treatises ⌐•⁓⌐ = ⌐⌐⌐⌐⌐ can probably be safely, if sometimes unimaginatively, used in all occurrences where the dotted note falls on the strong

[7]Because C. P. E. Bach specified for the turn in a slow tempo a *Zwischenraum* between the ornament and the following pitch (see the "adagio" and the "moderato" in Ex. 10.1*a*), Heinrich Schenker in his tract on ornamentation, asserts that Haydn's turns invariably call for such space. For this reason Schenker rules out (with often questionable results) the "trill-like" execution that leads without stopping into the next note. He overlooked the fact that even Philipp Emanuel used such an uninterrupted design for faster speeds (see in the same example the model for "presto") and besides does admit that this "space" rule often cannot apply to Mozart. (Heinrich Schenker, "A Contribution to the Study of Ornamentation," pp. 116–117, 127–129.)

beat. Fairly often Mozart spells out this design, as in Ex. 10.18a from the Piano Concerto in C K 503. This solution will be advisable in an ensemble where synchronization is important and in cases where the melodic-rhythmic design of the turn is essential to the thematic character. A fine illustration of both these conditions is the first movement of the E flat Piano Quartet. The first two measures of its subsidiary theme, first announced in m. 30, pervade as a motive the whole development section, which opens with its statement in all three strings in octaves (Ex. *b*). Within the next 43 measures this motive occurs 19 times in all instruments, sometimes alone, sometimes in partial unison, sometimes in stretto. Any deviation from the announced rhythmic design, as in Ex. *c,* would impair the sense of unity and compactness of the development. Should the four players prefer a different rhythmic interpretation, they would have to agree and be consistent.

Ex. 10.18.

The Badura-Skodas' rule that a turn after a dotted note is "played before the dot is reached" (Badura-Skoda, p. 105) is too confining. It does not apply when the dotted note falls on a weak beat, as in Ex. 10.19a (the fourth measure of the just mentioned subsidiary theme from the Clavier Quartet in E flat) where a solution close to that of Ex. *b* with the turn *after* the onset of the dot seems indicated.

Ex. 10.19.

Even some of the Badura-Skodas' examples do not conform with the rule, as in the second option they give for Ex. 10.20a from the Romance of the D minor Concerto. Their preferred solution of Ex. *b* sounds somewhat square against the regular pulse of the bass, and their second alternative *(c)* only slightly less so; the versions of *d* and *e* seem more graceful. The spot recurs in the solo part three times; since the orchestra does not imitate the turn, there is no danger of offering an unclear model, and hence the rendition can be varied from one time to the next. In such contexts a touch of rubato where the beats do not exactly coincide will often be desirable.

There are many other situations where the turn ought to be played *after* the onset of the dot. A good illustration is given in Ex. 10.21a from the Piano Concerto in E flat K 449. Here, in two measures, two turns on the strong beat follow one another. The difference in notation, consistently maintained for all recurrences of the phrase, indicates an intended difference in performance. A likely solution is sketched in Ex. 10.21b with the first turn starting after the onset of the dot. If we were to play the first turn before the dot was reached, as shown in Ex. *c,* we would

a. K 466/2 (Romance)

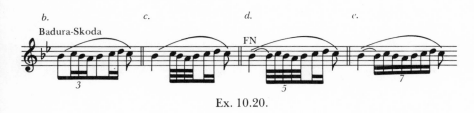

Ex. 10.20.

obliterate the intended difference between the turns and deprive the phrase of much of its attractiveness.

There are certainly contexts where the Badura-Skoda rule does apply, and Ex. *d* from the Quintet for Piano and Woodwinds is a case where the turn in the elegant oboe phrase might well be played as given in Ex. *e*.

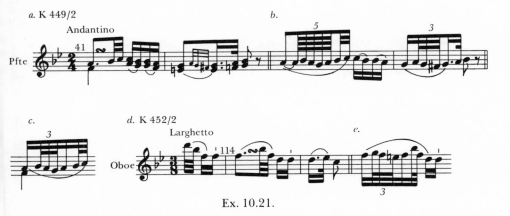

Ex. 10.21.

Turns after double dots are infrequent but do occur. There is a very interesting case later in the Andantino movement of the Piano Concerto in E flat K 449, given in Ex. 10.22*a* according to the autograph, where such a turn is followed by three prenote turns that grew motivically out of the first and where consequently no distinct rhythmic contrast was intended. (The first figure with the double dot was wrongly given in *W.A.M.* and all editions derived from it.) The three follow-up turns are written with four small notes, starting on the pitch of the principal note (main-note turns). This notation was dictated by the need to indicate both their main-note start and their anticipation (about the latter see the next section dealing with turns marked by small notes). The first turn being the matrix of the three following ones, the latter's unmistakable rhythmic disposition illuminates the desirable rendition of the first figures as shown in Ex. *b*. The main-note turns, incidentally, provide additional proof, if such is still needed, for the legitimacy of this design and of its anticipation.

Ex. 10.22.

Another specimen of a turn symbol after a double dot is given in Ex. 10.23*a* from the C minor Piano Sonata, where the likeliest solution is shown in *b*, which could be modified to *c* to preserve the dotted rhythm.

Ex. 10.23.

The Turn Marked by Small Notes

In addition to using the wave symbol, Mozart frequently wrote the turn with small notes: three for the turn before, four for the turn after the note. For the prenote turn we find both the design ⬚ or its inversion ⬚ . The postnote, "embedded" turn, written with four little notes (of which the fourth is the extension of the parent), occurs only in the standard design from above.

Addressing first the three-note figure, the use of this design was necessary for the inverted turn for which Mozart had no symbol. Its use for the standard design may at times have been haphazard and meaningless, but on occasion it *may* have been chosen to suggest prebeat execution. The latter is associated with little notes in theoretical sources and often favored by musical considerations.

As mentioned before, L. Mozart, following Tartini's lead, lists the turn as a subform of the *mordente,* written as shown in Ex. 10.24*a* by L. Mozart, in *b* by Tartini. Like Tartini, L. Mozart specifies that the three little notes are to be played very fast, very softly, and slurred to the principal note which receives the accent (see *Ornamentation,* pp. 453, 461). These rules clearly point to anticipation.

Ex. 10.24.

Only a few theorists who illustrate the prenote turn show little notes in addition to the usual wave symbol. Among the few is Tromlitz who gives for both the identical solution; but the ever perceptive Milchmeyer shows the spelling with little notes for the inverted turn only, which he significantly illustrates in anticipation (Exx. 10.25*a* and *b*).[8] Since he spells out anticipation for other related

[8]Tromlitz, *Unterricht,* p. 255; Milchmeyer, *Kleine Pianoforte-Schule für Kinder,* sec. 4, p. 4; Milchmeyer, *Die wahre Art,* p. 38.

ornaments, such as arpeggio-type figures or the *Schneller*, it is reasonable to assume that he would have done the same for the standard design from above.

Koch, also speaking of the turn and such related figures as the *Anschlag*, both given in Ex. 10.25*c*, says they should be "fleetingly and roundly *[flüchtig und rund]* slurred to the following notes" which suggests their unaccented nature, hence presumably anticipation.[9] J. C. Bach and Ricci illustrate the inverted turn in anticipation as given in Ex. *d*.[10]

Ex. 10.25.

For the singer, Domenico Corri, a student of Nicola Porpora, differentiates between the rising (i.e. inverted) and the descending turn. The former ♫, he says, starts softly, swells in the rise, then tapers into the principal note. The descending turn ♫ starts out strong, diminishes as it falls, then grows stronger after it has reached the principal note.[11] Such complex nuances imply a rather slow pace for the ornament. The descending one will tend to fall on the beat; the ascending one is more likely to anticipate it, at least partially, though the solo voice with its responsiveness to diction is freer than the instrumental soloist in fitting the ornaments into the meter.

Türk, the arch rigorist about ornamental onbeat starts, has a talent for ferreting out single instances where an ornament in Mozart seems unlikely to deviate from the textbook rules, and then naively formulating a general and binding rule from his one or two hand-picked examples. With such procedures he becomes the victim of the age-old fallacy of incomplete induction. In the 1802 edition of his treatise he gives an illustration (Ex. 10.26) from an unnamed Adagio (actually the eighth variation on "Lison dormait") where the ascending turn, if anticipated, would form octaves.[12] Quite apart from octaves which, by the way, are barely audible, a turn following the suffix to a trill—a rare occurrence—will spontaneously fall on the beat, since a trill's suffix normally serves as an anacrusis to the following beat. Also, the pitch repetition makes the most sense as a suspension-type preparation for an appoggiatura from below. Mozart gives a further clue by writing the turn with 16ths instead of his usual 32nd-notes. Here the turn is an ornamented appoggiatura, and its downbeat start is favored by several circumstances, among which the octaves are the least important ones. We shall find other contexts that suggest the downbeat, but there are many more that do not. There are cases where, as in Türk's example, the onbeat design is strongly

[9]*Journal der Tonkunst,* pt. 1, p. 188.
[10]*Méthode,* p. 17
[11]Domenico Corri, A *Select Collection of the Most*

Admired Songs, Duetts, etc. from Operas in the highest esteem, vol. 1, p. 8.
[12]*Klavierschule,* 1802 ed., p. 272.

suggested, others where it is a reasonable option, and others still where anticipation is the most fitting choice. Generally, slow movements will be more conducive to the onbeat style than fast and rhythmically incisive ones, and the soloist can often add a rubato touch by straddling the beat.

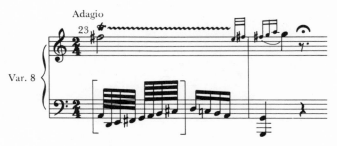

Ex. 10.26. Türk (Mozart)

Onbeat interpretation is clearly indicated in Ex. 10.27a from the Four-Hand Sonata in F where the turn could be played even a shade slower than the preceding 16th-notes (Ex. b).

Ex. 10.27.

In Ex. 10.28a from the *Hunt* String Quartet anticipation would not fit the expression. The turn is best done on the beat, unhurried, and, being in the middle of a crescendo, unaccented. Onbeat rendition, in conjunction with a subtle ritardando, is also favored for Ex. b from the slow movement of the B flat Piano Concerto K 450, as well as for Ex. c from the Violin Sonata in D K 300l (306). More options are available for the half-cadence with a fermata of Ex. d from the Finale of the *Hoffmeister* String Quartet. In the molto allegro tempo in pianissimo with a slight ritardando implied by the fermata, the turns should be rather fast but very gentle and unaccented. These characteristics matter more than the specific rhythmic disposition, which could range from anticipation (the main note being dissonant) through straddling to onbeat placement.

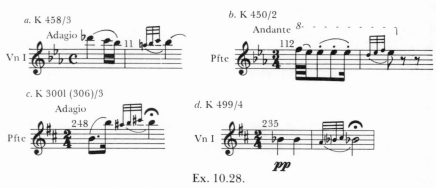

Ex. 10.28.

In slow movements we find options that lean to anticipation, particularly in cases where the turn occurs on a weak beat. In such placements a distinct appoggiatura function is less fitting or not fitting at all. A case in point is the Andante from the Two-Piano Sonata of Ex. 10.29*a*. The usually heard onbeat design sounds pedantic, particularly when burdened with a distinct accent. Unhurried, unaccented anticipation, or perhaps an imaginative, subtle straddling rhythm, seems much more to the point.

Similar is the case of Ex. *b* from the Violin-Viola Duo in B flat with a turn on the weakest beat, where the appoggiatura effect of the onbeat would create a singularly stilted impression. An unaccented, fluid style with either full or partial anticipation is recommended.

The same would seem to apply to the four turns of Ex. *c* from the C major *(Dissonance)* Quartet, though one of them happens to fall on the strong beat: appoggiaturalike accents would unseemingly obtrude on the melodic interplay of the other strings, disturb the linearity of the crescendo, and create unpleasant harmonic friction—particularly for the second and third turns. Besides, for the last turn Mozart unmistakably aligned the *f* with the main note.

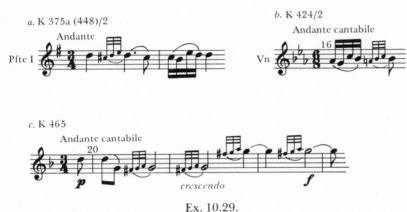

Ex. 10.29.

A turn that occurs in the middle of a beat can hardly ever have a claim to appoggiatura function; hence it will never be accented and will generally incline to anticipation. It seems that such turns are mostly, perhaps always, of the standard, descending type. When such turns connect, as they frequently do, notes of the same pitch, they closely approach the function of an "embedded" turn after a note, the only difference being an interruption of the legato. Their embedded function calls for anticipation. The passages of Ex. 10.30 offer good illustrations. In Ex. *a* from the String Quartet in C K 465 Mozart wrote the sudden piano clearly and logically under the first little note of the turn, not, as mistakenly given in the *NMA,* under the principal note in a manner that can lead to misinterpretation. Anticipation is also indicated in Ex. *b* from the Piano Trio in C, and in Ex. *c* from the Violin Sonata in A K 293d (305). Another turn in mid-beat that also happens to precede a dotted note pair, from the Piano Concerto in E flat K 449 (shown in Ex. *d*) offers proof of anticipation. A turn in the solo piano is answered by an echo in the violins. The three little notes in the piano part stand for an embedded turn; hence the echo of the violins has to be anticipated. The same pattern recurs two measures later, then twice more in parallel spots. This evidence further illuminates the needed anticipation of the main-note turns of the same movement, given in Ex. 10.22. For further illustrations see also the Two-Piano Sonata, K 375a (448)/2, mm. 66 and 69.

Ex. 10.30.

Different is the case of Ex. 10.31*a* from the Piano Sonata in F K 300k (332) with its flowing melody in allegro, where the solution of Ex. *b* may be preferable. Here too the turn between the two F's mimics the embedded species and could have been written as in *c* or *d* (the latter with a slight change of articulation but not of rhythm), either of which would have yielded our suggested solution. A similar treatment is suggested for Ex. *e* from the F major String Quartet K 590, given the tempo and the smooth legato link with the note following the turn. For suggested solutions see Ex. *f*.

Ex. 10.31.

If, on the other hand, the note preceded by the turn is part of an energetic angular theme, the integrity of this note must be preserved and the turn anticipated. Such need is clear in a passage like the one of Ex. 10.32*a* from the E flat Symphony K 543, where the clear autograph dashes over every note (not dots, as given in the *NMA*) carry accentual as well as articulative meaning. Only anticipation of the turn can secure such meaning and help project the full power of this dramatic theme.

The structural importance of such a first note is also indicated in Ex. *b* from the Introit of the Requiem, where the turn occurs only in the violins, not in the doubling violas, cellos, and basses. The turn should be anticipated, leading with a crescendo into the principal note (as sketched in Ex. *c*).

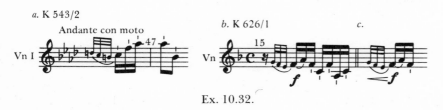

Ex. 10.32.

A similar dynamic-rhythmic treatment should be accorded to the pervasive figure of Ex. 10.33*a* in the last variation of the Andante from the E flat String Quintet K 614: clearly, the first note of the three-note motive is part of the thematic essence and must not be obscured; the anticipated turn serves to light up that important first note. If we were to play the turn on the beat, the three-note motive would become a two-note motive with an ornamented anacrusis. The structural nature of the main note is fully revealed when, a few measures later, the note stands alone, as in Ex. *b*, where onbeat execution would make the principal note practically disappear and leave an unattached ornamental curlicue suspended in a void.

In spite of the faster tempo, the same interpretation seems proper for the angular motive of Ex. *c* from the F major String Quartet K 590, where an onbeat turn would conceal the characteristic leap of a seventh that, again, is part of the motivic essence.

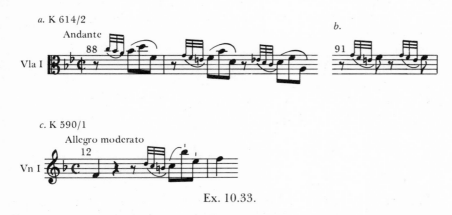

Ex. 10.33.

When the rhythmic profile is sharpened by staccato articulation, the turn, even when it occurs on the strong beat, has to be anticipated, as in Ex. 10.34*a* from the Piano Trio in C.

Even without such outward indication of sharpened profile, a characteristic rhythmic pattern will often resist ornamental interference with its starting points. Thus, in Ex. *b* from the Minuet of the *Hoffmeister* String Quartet the joyful energy of the theme would be weakened if an accented turn were to infringe on the precise entrance of the dotted note.

Ex. 10.34.

The sharpening by articulation has a counterpart in dynamic accents specified or implied. Often Mozart's autograph notation offers a graphic clue when he places an *fp* or similar sign clearly under the parent note. Such is the case in Ex. 10.35*a* from the *Jeunehomme* Concerto or in Ex. *b* from the Piano Sonata in C K 189d (279), which in the autograph has an *f* (in sforzando meaning) aligned each time with the principal note and again in the parallel spots of mm. 32–33. A similar, eloquent alignment occurs seven times, for both oboes and bassoons, in the autograph as well as in the original conducting score of *Die Entführung* (Ex. *c*).

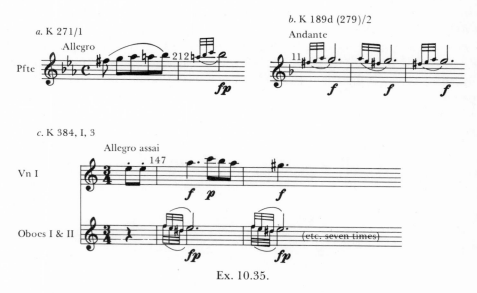

Ex. 10.35.

The same figure (without accentual signs) occurs many times in Figaro's Wedding March as a delightful woodwind interjection (Ex. 10.36). The prebeat placement of these figures in the spirit of Tartini's and L. Mozart's *mordente* seems unquestionable. They represent a delicate stylization of the rhythmic upbeat figures of ♪♪ | ♩ or ♪♪ | ♩ so typical of marches, especially those influenced by French military music (mentioned in note 4, Chapter 7, in connection with the bass slides in the Funeral March of the *Eroica*). These figures were invariably rendered before the beat, as, for example, in the solemn marchlike Introduction in *Idomeneo,* II, No. 23, with the upbeat slides in the strings, and, in m. 3, with the timpani rhythm: . See also the two-to-four-note upbeat figures in the March attending Sarastro's entrance in the first Finale, mm. 35 1ff., of *Die Zauberflöte.* Too often conductors of *Figaro,* trying to be "authentic," have these figures played on the beat with an accent and in so doing deface the enchanting grace and humor of the piece by a heavy-handed display of definitely unauthentic pedantry.

Ex. 10.36.

Also in *Figaro,* we have in the overture, mm. 14–15 and several parallel spots, the turns of Ex. 10.37. Ideally, they should be played before the beat, because of the rhythmic setting and the unison woodwinds without the turn. Such execution is difficult but feasible at MM♪ = 120, impracticable at the breakneck speed so frequently chosen by today's conductors (perhaps influenced by Richard Wagner's insensitive remark that Mozart's "naive" allegros should be played as fast as possible). Since what Mozart wrote was often difficult, but never impossible, these ornaments might give a clue to the maximum desirable speed of the overture of c. ♪ = 120. Even such speed might be viewed as an extreme in view of the fact that the Presto ("Allegro assai" in Mozart's own index) is tempered by a 4/4 meter. The alla breve meter, found in many editions, including that of Hermann Abert for Eulenburg, is unauthentic.

Ex. 10.37.

There are other passages where, as in the *Figaro* overture, the rhythmic-melodic context favors anticipation along the lines of the Tartini—L. Mozart *mordente,* but where the fastness of today's tempos makes such execution impracticable. Such is the case in the passage of Ex. 10.38*a* from the G major Piano Concerto K 453 where theoretically anticipation would be preferable. Practically, however, the *NMA* suggestion (by the Badura-Skodas) of Ex. *b* makes good sense, unless the tempo is eased to a point at which the three ornamental notes can be made to speak clearly before the beat. The same preference and the same practical solution would apply to Ex. *c* from the *Haffner* Serenade.

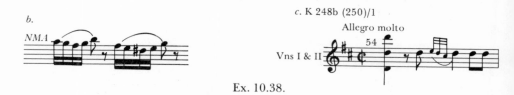

Ex. 10.38.

When the turn is inserted within repeated pitches that are thematically important, it will be better deemphasized by anticipation—tempo and technical skill
permitting—as would be the case for Ex. 10.39*a* from the G major Piano concerto
K 453 (as well as for the identical figures in the first movement of the F major
Piano Concerto K 459, mm. 168–170, 178–180). The same applies to Ex. *b* from
the B flat Piano Concerto K 456[13] and Ex. *c* from the overture to *Die Entführung*.

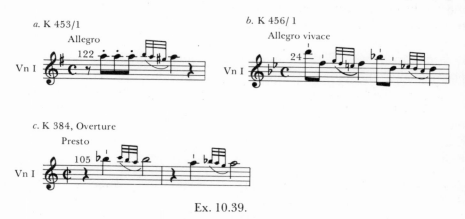

Ex. 10.39.

Such interpretation finds support from cases like the passage of Ex. 10.40*a*
from the Piano Sonata in D K 284c (311) where anticipation ensures the integrity
of the octave doubling. Similar is the case from the Variations on "Unser dummer
Pöbel meint" (Ex. *b*): the theme starts in octaves, which the first variation stresses in
the first two measures; in the second variation this doubling, thinly disguised by
the figuration in the left hand and turns in the right, is again part of the musical
essence and hence is best brought out by on-time entrance of the principal notes
on the strong beats—a need supported by the absence of all turns in the early
version of the piece (see *NMA* IX/26, p. 150).

Even in a slow tempo a characteristic design like the siciliano rhythm of the A
minor Rondo of Ex. 10.41*a* will be unreceptive to the intrusion of an onbeat turn.
The exact metrical placement of the ornament, which is repeated many times,
might occasionally be varied slightly, but basically it ought to have prebeat
character and always be unaccented. Beyschlag expressed this opinion in 1908

---

[13]The dashes over the first turn note in the Eulenburg edition by Hans Redlich are unauthentic.

a. K 284c (311)/3

b. K 455

Var. 2

Ex. 10.40.

and offered striking evidence from the A major section (Ex. *b*) where the friction created by onbeat rendition would make little sense.[14] Had Mozart wanted this turn started on the beat, surely he would have doubled the turn in thirds.

a. K 511
Andante

b.

Ex. 10.41.

Considerations of voice leading can influence the placement of the turn. In Ex. 10.42*a* from the Violin Sonata in B flat K 317d (378) a downbeat start with its hidden parallels, involving an empty octave, would in the slow tempo be unattractive. Complete anticipation, if done gently, is possible but not necessary: a rubato placement of the turn across the beat might be preferable.

Generally, in a slow movement in a passage without a sharply defined rhythmic design, the turn can often be rendered in a similar manner that adds grace by loosening the strict metrical bond between the two hands on the piano or between soloist and accompaniment. In Ex. *b* from the Piano Sonata in C K 189d (279) the Badura-Skodas have both the *Vorschlag* (in 16th-note value) and the turn start on the beat. The appoggiatura solution for the *Vorschlag* is advisable in view of the static harmony in the first measure. The turn could add some needed variety by shifting, to varying degrees, ahead of the beat.

For the *turn after the note,* the embedded species, Mozart often uses four little notes instead of the symbol. As mentioned before, this notation can be confusing by obscuring the fact that only the first three notes are ornamental, whereas the fourth is the tail end of the principal note, the "terminal principal tone" in Schenker's terminology; as such it is often, notably after dotted notes,

[14]Adolf Beyschlag, *Die Ornamentik der Musik*, p. 203.

a. K 317d (378)/2

b. K 189d (279)/2

Ex. 10.42.

held longer than the first three though the graphic design suggests even duration for all. Thus Schenker has a point when he says: "of all the ways of notating a turn, this is the very worst."[15] The notation is not all bad though: for binary notes such evenness is usually desirable, and there are even occasional cases, like that of Ex. 10.43, where four little notes are the only logical notation (since the wave symbol *after* the note implies a legato link with it, and such a link is not intended here).

K 589/2

Ex. 10.43.

For *binary* notes the four little notes will generally be played evenly at the end of the available space, leading without a stop into the following pitch. On various occasions Mozart wrote this out in regular notes, for example, at the start of the piano solo in the first movement of the B flat Concerto K 595, given in Ex. 10.44*a*, where the turns are added to the originally unornamented statement of the violins. See also *Don Giovanni*, Sextet, mm. 50, 52; the Piano Sonatas in D K 576/2, mm. 1, 5; in B flat K 570/1, mm. 23, 27; in C minor, K 457/1, mm. 23, 25; the above-mentioned slow movement of the *Hoffmeister* String Quartet, K 499, m. 2 and its many parallel spots; the A major String Quartet K 464, Trio, mm. 6, 26, 303; *Così fan tutte,* I, Finale, mm. 480, 482; II, No. 25, mm. 50, 52; No. 29, m. 98. Never does Mozart write out a turn even remotely resembling the rhythmic complexity of C.P.E. Bach's "adagio" pattern.

Similarly, Ex. *b* from the Piano Sonata in B flat K 315c (333) is best done as in *c*; Ex. *d* from the late String Quartet in B flat as in *e,* or perhaps as in *f,* since the slower tempo permits a slight metric contraction without sacrificing songfulness. Example *g* from the Violin Sonata in F K 374e (377), on the other hand, might need the slight metrical expansion of Ex. *h* to do justice to the tender affection of the theme. In Ex. *i* from the Violin Sonata in E flat K 374f (380) the turn, in the

[15]"A Contribution," p. 127.

gentle andante con moto, must not be too fast, lest it sound perfunctory and uncongenial to the prevailing mood. The principal note should be slightly sustained to clarify its thematic role. A solution close to Ex. *j* seems better than *k*.

Ex. 10.44.

In 6/8 meter the dotted quarter-note, as mentioned before, is a close equivalent of a binary note because it leads not into an unstressed short complementary companion but into a stressed beat. In Ex. 10.45 from the last Piano Concerto in B flat we have a rare case where Mozart first writes a turn in little notes a few times, as in Ex. *a,* then writes the same turn in regular notes a few times, as in *b* and *c,* providing a clear translation of the little notes as suggested above: played late and leading without interruption into the next note.

By the same token, a quarter-note in 6/8 meter, followed by a turn, has a kinship to a dotted note in binary meter, because it is followed by a short, unstressed companion. In a slow tempo, beaten in six, this fact is likely to influence the shape of the turn by lengthening its last note. But in an allegro, as in Ex. 10.46*a* from the Oboe Quartet, it is difficult to find a solution different from Ex. *b* or *c* that does not sound contrived.

Ex. 10.45.

In the 6/8 Rondo of the Piano Sonata in D K 284c (311) we encounter interesting turns that are written in three different styles. First, as in Ex. *d,* they are crammed in so little space that, were we to take the notation literally, the turn would have to be dashed off with great speed as in *e.* Later we find the unique notation of Ex. *f,* where the turn starts *before* rather than *after* the first 16th-note and where the nature of the fourth note as extension of the parent is graphically acknowledged and with it its longer duration. Its approximate rendition is sketched in Ex. *g.* Shortly thereafter, Mozart writes as in Ex. *h* what is undoubtedly rhythmically synonymous with Ex. *f* but not with *d.*

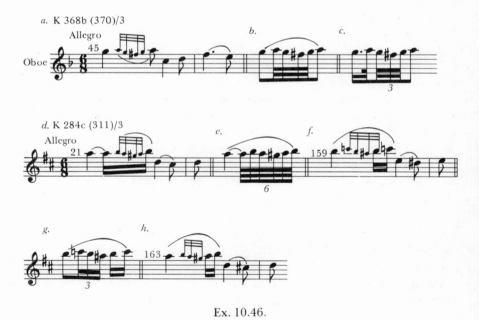

Ex. 10.46.

In binary meters the usual problem of *dotted notes* is complicated by the above-mentioned frequent graphic deceptiveness when the fourth of the evenly written notes needed to be lengthened. We have also gathered from Türk's and Tromlitz's models (Exx. 10.2*b, c,* and *e,*) that Mozart was not alone in using this misleading even notation for uneven rendition. The practice of others, reflected in these models, may explain Mozart's puzzling habit. It may also be that because the even notation is rational for binary notes it became to him a formula that he mechanically transferred to the dotted note. Always counting on the performer's musicality, he may have been either unaware of, or unconcerned about, the potential for misunderstandings.

Whatever the explanation, Mozart's little notes, written after a dot, seem to have the same meaning as the wave symbol, and consequently the appearance of equal duration is usually deceptive. There are, however, some cases where a solution consonant with the graphic design either is indicated or is a possible alternative. This applies particularly to a dot followed by two regular notes, rather than one, that fill the balance of the beat, as in Ex. 10.47a from the String Quartet in D K 575, with the suggested solution of Ex. b. Schenker's solution is given in c, but I believe Ex. b is preferable because it maintains the thematically important identity of the two 32nd-notes from the motive announced in the preceding measure, now simply repeated with an added turn.

For a specimen in 6/8 meter see Ex. d from the Violin-Viola Duo in B flat, with the suggested solution of e. Evenness is almost mandatory where lack of space does not permit an extension of the fourth note, as in Ex. f from the Violin Sonata in A K 293d (305) with the suggested solutions of g.

These are cases, though, that would be rendered in the same manner if notated with the wave symbol, as we have already seen (e.g. in Ex. 10.20 or 10.21). These cases cannot therefore be considered as evidence that the two styles of notation, when used after a dotted note, represented a different musical intent.

In some instances the choice between an equal or unequal fourth note is open. The passage of Ex. h from the Piano Sonata in F K 300k (332) was probably meant to be played as in Ex. i, but could conceivably be done as in j. In Ex. k from the Violin Sonata in F K 374e (377) the version of Ex. l seems preferable, though m is possible.

In the great majority of cases, however, an attempt to match the evenness of the four-note figure does not fit the situation. In Ex. 10.48a from Tamino's and Pamina's solemn walk through fire and water the first turn should, I believe, be played as in b. Some would favor the performance of c, where rhythmic contraction brings out the dotted rhythm which is obscured by the turn, and besides achieves assimilation with the dotted 16th-note at the end of the measure. It is possible but not too likely that this was Mozart's intention. The mature Mozart was on the whole very precise in his rhythmic notation and frequently used either the double dot or rests to signal sharpened rhythms. Only five measures later in this solo of the magic flute we find a sharpened dot spelled out, and we have seen before Mozart's use of the turn after a double-dotted note. I do not believe that we have to do with a casual notation that calls for adjustment, the less so since the spacious rhythm of Ex. b as opening of the march reflects its solemn dignity. Observe also the spelled-out main-note turn at the end of the measure, a further proof that this design was at home in Mozart's ornamental vocabulary.

Mozart probably intended the spot from the Queen of the Night's first aria shown in Ex. 10.49a to be sung according to the common design of b, with c far less likely, because it would obscure the underlying rhythm. Similarly, for the siciliano rhythm of Ex. d from *Idomeneo* there is hardly any reasonable alternative to the approximate solution of Ex. e. For the phrase of Ex. f from the String Quartet in G K 387, the solution recommended in g is usually followed, though the version of h is conceivable as it does not interfere with the rhythm.

Ex. 10.47.

Ex. 10.48.

Ex. 10.49.

Ex. 10.49 *cont.*

Whereas rhythmic sharpening to maintain the sense of a dotted relationship, as advocated by some 18th-century theorists, may occasionally be permissible or even desirable within a phrase having a sharp rhythmic contour, it would be inappropriate in a lyrical passage like that of Ex. 10.50a from the late String Quartet in B flat K 589, which is best rendered approximately as in Ex. *b*.

Ex. 10.50.

To SUMMARIZE, Mozart's turn is a complex ornament which, like other ornaments, cannot be handled by recourse to textbook formulas. Most of the time his turn consists of three ornamental notes that move scalewise either down or up with the pitch of the principal note in their middle. Moving downward they form the standard turn, moving upward the inverted one. The turn either precedes its principal note (prenote turn) or follows it (embedded turn). Unless Mozart writes out the turn in regular notes, which he does fairly often, he indicates it either with the wave symbol ∿ or with three or four little notes. The wave symbol always stands for the standard turn from above and occurs almost exclusively in instrumental music. We find it placed either above the note, usually specifying a prenote turn, or after the note, always signifying the embedded one.

Mozart uses little notes for all media and almost always writes them in 32nd denominations. For the prenote turn he usually writes three notes, either rising or falling. When falling, they are once in a while preceded by the pitch of the principal note, forming what C.P.E. Bach called *geschnellter Doppelschlag* (snapped turn), a miniature main-note trill, more precisely a *Schneller* with a suffix. For the embedded type Mozart uses either the wave symbol, placed to the right of the principal note, or four little notes—always from above—of which the fourth is functionally the extension of the parent note. This notation can be graphically deceptive when, after a dotted note in a binary meter, this fourth note needs to be extended because of its function as the final segment of the principal note.

There is reason to believe that for the prenote turn little notes generally tend to full anticipation whereas the wave symbol can accommodate the full range of available designs, from full anticipation over the "Italian mordent" to accented onbeat style, further including the option of a main-note start and, for the soloist, occasional rubato-style shifting of the ornamental notes across the beat.

The Arpeggio

Mozart uses two main types of arpeggios. The first, for all instruments, is perhaps the more frequent one. It is written with small notes that are not held 🎵 . The second, for keyboard only, is marked by oblique dashes 🎵 for which modern editions substitute the vertical wavy line ⁞ . Here the notes of the chord are struck in close succession from the bottom up and are held. On occasion we find a graphic design that seems to call for a kind of arpeggio that falls between the two main types, where the chordal notes under the melody are, if at all, only partially sustained. Specimens are shown in Ex. 11.1*a* from the Variations on "Unser dummer Pöbel" and Ex. *b* from the Eight Variations in F.[1] For other examples see the Piano Concertos in E flat K 449/3, mm. 152, 154, and in D K 451/1, mm. 261–263, and Ex. 11.7*a*.

Ex. 11.1.

Modern scholars and historically oriented performers subject Mozart's arpeggio of both principal types to the downbeat rule, though they have only very tenuous theoretical and hardly any musical evidence for so doing. Except for one presently to be cited rule by the formalistic Türk, no explicit verbal directive about the onbeat start of the arpeggio seems to have come to light. The only authority for such treatment derives from a number of ornament tables from Chambonnières and d'Anglebert to Clementi which have been far too literally interpreted. They are of the kind 🎵 .

It is ill considered to derive binding rules from these patterns. They simply show the principle of breaking the chord and do so, as all ornament tables do, in the *abstract* with no reference to any concrete musical situation. The simplest way to give such abstract, graphic equation is always within the metrical value of the principal note, because any infringement on the space outside of its value can prove incompatible with a specific musical situation. Besides there are always cases where an ornament, including the Arpeggio, ought to be rendered within the value of the principal note. Geoffroy-Dechaume's previously quoted saying about the "inanity of ornament tables" is perhaps nowhere, not even for the trill, more fitting than it is for the arpeggio. Probably aware of how easily the usual arpeggio models can be misunderstood, such eminent theorists as Saint Lambert and Couperin presented ingenious patterns that are rhythmically noncommittal (see *Ornamentation*, pp. 495–96). In Mozart's time, Milchmeyer defied the routine of staying within the metrical space by spelling out the anticipation of the arpeggio as shown in Ex. 11.2.

[1]See Kurt von Fischer, preface to *NMA* IX/26, p. XI.

Ex. 11.2. Milchmeyer

Türk, ever eager to defend the case of the downbeat against such unorthodoxy, lists in the 1802 edition of his *Klavierschule* two spots from Mozart's violin sonatas where, he argues, the arpeggio has to fall on the beat (p. 272). His first example, from the G major Sonata K 373a (379) is given by him in the form of Ex. 11.3*a*. How, he asks, can the arpeggio be played in Milchmeyer's anticipation, when the notes immediately preceding do not leave enough time for such an interpretation? The forte under the first note reinforces his case for the downbeat solution. Unfortunately, Türk fell victim to a corrupt edition. The passage, without a forte under the arpeggio, is written in the autograph as shown in Ex. *b*. There is in fact no dynamic marking at all for the whole first section of the Adagio introduction; in the absence of any marking, forte is, as usual, understood as the basic dynamic, as further evidenced by the piano marked in m. 34 and a forte again in the parallel spot of m. 37. The argument of the forte is therefore invalid. Regarding the contention of insufficient space, certainly with a mechanical beat the five-note arpeggio could not be accommodated, but the point is that the beat need not and should not be mechanical. The downbeat must in fact be delayed, because the ascending triadic melody in the bass has to wait for the top a″ to be struck and must not become enmeshed in the right-hand arpeggio whose function is that of a stylized portamento that bridges quickly and lightly the leap of a 12th. Such delays, often done as *Luftpausen* (in modern notation marked with a comma or the ∥ sign), are commonplace in artistic performances by soloists, chamber music players, and even well-trained orchestras. Here in an Adagio 2/4, the delay need only be minimal but is vital: unless the a″ is perceived as the brilliant downbeat that gives a send-off to the bass melody, not only will the interplay of the voices be disturbed, but the characteristic four-measure rhythm of the right hand will be crippled the very first time it occurs. Ex. *c* gives a rough idea of how such rhythmic nuance might be indicated in modern notation. In the parallel spot of m. 38 the violin will have to delay the downbeat subtly by ever so slightly lengthening the preceding 16th-note.

In Türk's second illustration, given in Ex. 11.4*a*, anticipation is said to produce "harshness" *(Härten)*. The passage, from the Violin Sonata in B flat K 454, is shown in a longer excerpt in Ex. *b*. What sounds "harsh" and what not is, of course, a matter of individual taste. To me the onbeat rendition, which would have to involve all the arpeggios in these two measures, sounds harsher and more stilted than the smoother anticipation. The latter can and ought to be done very fast, actually after the last 32nd on f′ has been touched. (On the piano, any arpeggio within the scope of an octave can be done with lightning speed.) The arpeggios, as is so frequently the case, are here, in the truest ornamental sense, only surface adornment that helps to put the melody in pleasing, plastic relief, adding elegance, not substance. That they are not part of the melodic essence is made clear when the theme is immediately taken up by the violin: of the four arpeggios only the second is left, revealing the pure state of the melody and the expendable nature of the arpeggios.

a. Türk (Mozart) *b.* K 373a (379)

c.

Ex. 11.3.

a. Türk *b.* K 454/2

Ex. 11.4.

Now when the arpeggio on the keyboard spans an octave, as it so often does for idiomatic reasons—in our example in the bass—then at least the pitch denomination of the first arpeggio note is identical with that of the main note. Consequently its appearance on the beat will have a clear rhythmic, but less decisive melodic effect, and often no greater harm is done than the sound of pedantry: "Listen how authentic I am." But when the span is smaller or larger than an octave, then a wrong pitch gets a musically unwarranted emphasis. Such would be the case in the right hand: were we to play as in Ex. 11.5*a* we would distort both rhythm and melody. By contrast, the solution of Ex. *b*—which is much easier than it looks on paper—restores the correct musical priorities.

a.   *b.*

Ex. 11.5.

The arpeggio, unlike the *Vorschlag*, cannot enrich the harmony or invigorate the rhythm, and therefore it ought not to receive the metric-dynamic emphasis. True, there are cases where an onbeat start of the arpeggio is either called for or a reasonable option. In Mozart most of these cases are probably limited to an arpeggiated recitative accompaniment where the bass note matters more than whatever top note of the chord the player chooses. Yet in recitative the beat is usually so flexible that the idea of playing on or off the beat can be meaningless. Continuo realization in piano concertos is with good reason rarely practiced any more (see Chapter 16), and the organ in sacred music does not arpeggiate its chords. Also, the notation of Türk's arpeggio, as shown in Ex. 11.6a, had become obsolete and does not seem to occur in Mozart. Where he desires the kind of rhythmically defined sequence of nonsustained arpeggiated figurations, he does not leave them to the performer's fancy, but writes them out as in Ex. *b* from the fragment of a violin sonata (better known in Abbé Stadler's completed version for the piano alone). Here in this improvisatory opening, the arpeggio is not an embellishment of the g″ but an integral part of a grand sweeping melodic line whose thematic importance is confirmed by its sixfold return in mm. 7, 8, 9, 11, 12, and 13.

a. Türk *b.* K 385f (396)

Ex. 11.6.

In the overwhelming majority of cases, however, Mozart uses the arpeggio like the anapestic slide, to add brilliance to the principal note by a preparation previously likened to a well-aimed stroke headed for a target. Like the slide and the upward leaping *Vorschlag,* the arpeggio that lands on a melody note is an instrumental descendant of the vocal portamento, and when serving a similar musical purpose should, like the portamento, always be placed before the beat. It stands to reason that when subservient to the melody, the arpeggio should behave accordingly and not elbow its master, the melody note, out of its rightful place in the measure.

Let us look at two characteristic passages. The Coda from the *Alla Turca* has, as shown in Ex. 11.7a, a "chordal," at least partially sustained arpeggio in the right hand, a nonsustained one in the left. That the top note has the melodic emphasis is clear from the following measures as well as from its half-note denomination as against the quarter-notes of the chord. In the left hand the percussive rhythm of relentless 8th-notes is part of the rhythmic essence (we can hear a triangle beat for the 8ths and maybe a brief tambourine shake for the arpeggio). To distort their evenness by entering late on every downbeat would be illogical. Both left-hand and right-hand arpeggios should be done with great speed and hit their target exactly on the beat.

A striking contrast is presented by Ex. *b* from the G major Violin Sonata K 373a

(379) (just encountered in Türk's illustration of Ex. 11.3). Its introductory slow, solemn Adagio has the melody accompanied by majestic chords, arpeggiated as on a big lute. Though melody and harmony are more in the foreground than rhythm, the very preeminence of the melody does not allow an infringement on its rhythm. The melody would be impaired to the point of sputtering, if instead of sounding like Ex. *c,* it were to sound like *d.* Therefore at least the right-hand arpeggio has to precede the beat. Though the left-hand arpeggio starts on the foundation of the harmony, the fact that this foundation keeps ringing, that the bass pitch is duplicated as the end note of the arpeggiated chord, that the bass does not have a vested interest in rhythmic integrity as it would in a genuine polyphonic thorough bass or even in a speedy secco recitative, makes anticipation here too not only possible but preferable. Both hands, by the way, ought to move together, not in sequence.

When the violin enters in m. 9 to take up the theme, the arpeggio stops except for the downbeat of the left hand in m. 10, where Mozart writes a nonsustaining arpeggio that is quite certainly anticipated and is a likely guide for the earlier left-hand arpeggios.

a. K 300i (331)/3

b. K 373a (379)

Ex. 11.7.

Anticipation of the bass arpeggios is obvious in Ex. 11.8*a* from the Two-Piano Concerto, where the regularity of the written-out broken chord figuration, divided between the right hand and the top note of the left, requires that the latter enter exactly on time. In Ex. *b* from the Concerto for Flute and Harp the synchronization of the top notes of the harp with the flute melody an octave above would seem to be desirable, which in turn suggests anticipated arpeggiation.

The Badura-Skodas devote only a short section to the arpeggio. They quote, with apparent approval, the two previously mentioned passages from Türk that were meant to prove the onbeat start of Mozart's arpeggios. An arpeggio in the right hand, they say, that is set against a chord or note in the left, should start on the beat, and they give Ex. 11.9*a* from the Piano Sonata in A which is to be played as in Ex. *b* (p. 98). I find this solution unconvincing. The very unison is so

a. K 316a (365)/2

b. K 297c (299)

Ex. 11.8.

characteristic that its integrity has to be respected by anticipation of the arpeggio. The Badura-Skodas' delayed accent is an acceptable solution and often attractive as an *improvised* rhythmic nuance, but not, I think desirable as a routine solution.

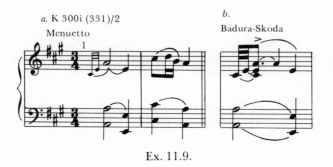

a. K 300i (331)/2
Menuetto

b.
Badura-Skoda

Ex. 11.9.

The same objection applies to the Badura-Skodas' suggestion to play the wide arpeggio of Ex. 11.10 from the Finale of the C minor Concerto on the beat. I believe the authors here pay too large a tribute to the downbeat dogma. If we see this passage in the context shown, it becomes clear that not only is there plenty of time for anticipation, but also that after the insistently pressing chromatic ascent to the high F, a continuation after the dramatic pause on that very same F is imperative to safeguard the musical line and maintain the built-up tension. This high F crowns the build-up and has to sound assertively, triumphantly, on the beat, while the preceding arpeggio adds to its brilliance by its preparatory gesture. In emphasizing instead the b' of the arpeggio's start, we break the tension, break the melodic line, and weaken the power and luster of the high F by displacing it from its prominent metrical place and substituting a much lower note of melodic irrelevance.

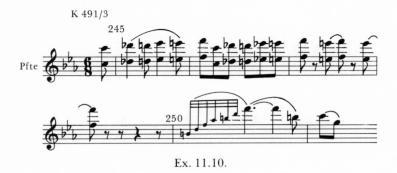

Ex. 11.10.

In Ex. 11.11 from the last Piano Concerto in B flat K 595, the characteristic dotted motive, announced by the violins, answered first by the lower strings, then (not shown here) by the winds, returns two measures later in the solo piano, introduced by an arpeggio, first analogously answered by the violins, then by the lower strings. Clearly, the rhythmic integrity of the motive has to be preserved by anticipation of the arpeggio. See also the parallel spot of m. 256.

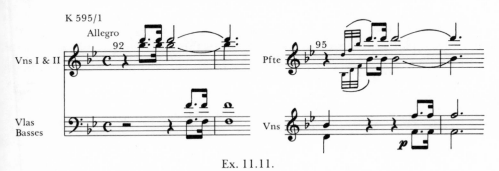

Ex. 11.11.

Also in bondage to the downbeat dogma, the editor of *NMA* volume III/8 gives for the accompaniment figure of Ex. 11.12*a* from the song "Oiseaux si tous les ans" the solution of Ex. *b*. The gently rocking motive disappears, the wrong notes receive the accent, and the graceful arpeggio figures, portraying, so it seems, the fluttering of birds' wings, are pegged to the ground in what amounts to a complete misrepresentation.

Ex. 11.12.

String instruments give us an interesting clue: three-note chords can only briefly and in forte be played together; four-note chords never can and thus have to be "broken." In the strongly rhythmical passage of Ex. 11.13*a* from the String

Quartet in C *(Dissonance)*, the top note carries the melody and, as the solitary dot indicates, has to be sustained. The chord has to be broken in one of several ways that are sketched in *b, c,* and *d,* depending on the style, taste, and skill of the performer. It must not be played as in Ex. *e* or a related manner, since this would deprive the melody of its vigor and rhythmic integrity as well as of its logic by sacrificing the essential to the accessory.

Ex. 11.13.

The same is the case with countless three- and four-note chords for string instruments, even if their top note does not continue in a melodic line, such as we find in cadential chords of the kind

The string arpeggio has its counterpart in the right-hand arpeggio on the piano. As noted before, its onbeat start will always affect the rhythm of the melody, and in those cases where such an arpeggio starts on a scale pitch different from the principal note, it also affects the melody itself. In Ex. 11.14 the C sharp would acquire an unjustified prominence by being placed on the beat. An attempt to make amends by playing it softly and accentuating the top note (B flat) would only sound artificial and precious when the obvious answer is anticipation. Four measures later in a parallel spot, Mozart, by writing the full chord without arpeggio, makes it clear that the top note belongs on the beat. The same point is illustrated in Ex. 11.5*a.*

Ex. 11.14.

Impairment of the harmony is shown in Ex. 11.15 from the Violin Sonata in E flat K 374f (380), where the strongly dissonant high C would be replaced by the consonant D if the arpeggio were played on the beat. See also the Piano Quartet in G minor, K 478/2, m. 139 and the Piano Sonata in C K 284b (309)/1, mm. 27, 28.

Ex. 11.15.

An arpeggio is often used to achieve smoother voice leading when a leap is involved, especially, though not exclusively, with strings. In Ex. 11.16*a* from the String Quartet in E flat K 421b (428), the double stop at the end of m. 30, A♭-D in the second violin, resolves smoothly into the G-E♭ of the arpeggio which, acting as lubricant, bridges the leap in the same manner we have previously encountered (e.g. in Exx. 4.32 *a-c*) for the upward leaping *Vorschlag*.

In Ex. *b*, from the opening of the *Haffner* Symphony, the arpeggio, for the violins alone, bridging the two-octave upward leap, adds a touch of flamboyance to the powerful unison of the whole orchestra. The accent has to hit the high D along with all the other instruments. To do otherwise would disturb the unison and soften the steel-edged contour of this heroic theme.

Similar is the case of Ex. *c* from the *Posthorn* Serenade where the arpeggio, here, too, limited to the violins, adds a flourish to the majestic opening. Again, the arpeggio must not infringe on the rhythmic design of the unison, signallike opening statement.

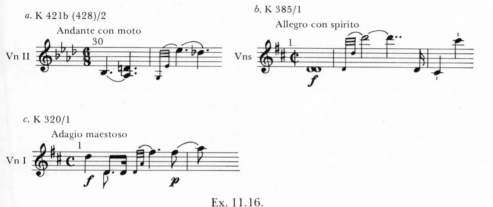

Ex. 11.16.

In numerous cases parallel parts for different instruments require the exact coordination of the main notes, but one part has an arpeggio while the other has either nothing or a simple *Vorschlag*. In all such cases the desired coordination requires prebeat style for all ornaments. Particularly interesting is the spot from the A major Violin Sonata K 293d (305) where the passage of Ex. 11.17*a* from the autograph is editorially changed in both the *NMA* and Henle editions by converting the piano arpeggios into *Vorschläge* (Ex. *b*), thus achieving a neater ensemble. Though the *NMA* acknowledges the—obvious—need for anticipation of the graces, anticipation of the arpeggios along with the *Vorschläge* solves the problem of coordination.

Equally eloquent, and correctly reproduced in the *NMA,* is the combination of *Vorschlag* and arpeggio of Ex. *c* from the Violin Sonata in F K 374e (377). Clearly, violin and piano have to hit the half-note D simultaneously and can do so only by anticipation.

Among other musical evidence for anticipation, onbeat style for the arpeggio of Ex. 11.18 from the violin-Viola Duo in B flat would create hidden, but unpleasant, octaves in the adagio two-part setting.

Very frequently we find such musical evidence reinforced by external evidence. Whenever the main note of an arpeggio carries a forte or sforzando mark, the signs are usually placed in the autograph under the main note. Even though

a. K 293d (305)/2
aut. version

Andante grazioso

b.
NMA version

c. K 374e (377)/3

Tempo di Menuetto

Ex. 11.17.

K 424/1
Adagio

Ex. 11.18.

Mozart, as mentioned before, habitually places the dynamic marks somewhat to the left of the note to which they belong, in the case of arpeggios their reference to the main note is hardly ever in doubt. Whenever Mozart's notation is faithfully reproduced, the pictorial suggestion of placing the accent on the main note and the arpeggio before the beat is inescapable to all but blindly loyal downbeat devotees.

In Exx. 11.19a and b from the Violin Sonatas in F K 374d (376) and D K 300l (306), such graphic evidence is reinforced by musical necessity, since here again the need to coordinate the start of the main notes in the piano with the unornamented notes in the violin is obvious. In Ex. a, moreover, the high D in the piano, being the ninth of the bass, has to fall on the beat.

The Badura-Skodas record (p. 99) a spot from the Piano Sonata in A minor where Mozart wrote out in regular notes the design of an anticipated arpeggio and accented principal note, as shown in Ex. c.

For the violin arpeggio of Ex. 11.20a from *Don Giovanni* the graphic evidence is again strengthened by the musical need for coordination with the voice. The same applies to Ex. b from *Thamos*.

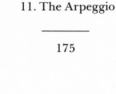

Ex. 11.19.

Ex. 11.20.

Summing up it can be said that of all ornaments the arpeggio may be the one for which an encompassing downbeat rule makes the least musical sense. The orthodox Türk may be the only theorist who postulates the rule verbally. For the rest its roots stem from ornament tables that show the principle of breaking a chord in purest abstraction, detached from any concrete musical situation. Yet it is precisely the concrete musical situation that in the vast majority of cases calls for modification.

A mass of external and musical evidence supports the proposition that Mozart's nonsustaining arpeggio, written with small notes, is almost always anticipated; that the sustained arpeggio, written with a symbol, will also tend to prebeat style when it ends in a melody note because in such a context anticipation alone can ensure the rhythmic and thematic integrity of the melody. Such arpeggios are only surface ornaments which can be omitted with little loss to the musical substance. It stands to reason that what is expendable as an accessory should not be given precedence over what is part of the musical essence. Whenever arpeggio-style figurations *are* integral to the melody, Mozart writes them out in regular notes.

A left-hand arpeggio can reasonably start on the beat when the bass note with which it starts could profitably do so, but not when the end note of such an arpeggio is rhythmically sensitive.

Anticipation can on occasion be modified within a rubato intent. When done with an impromptu flair that is artistically convincing, such a rhythmic nuance can be attractive, but it can also become intolerable when it turns into a mechanical formula.

PART II
IMPROVISATION

Introduction

———◆◆———

Mozart lived at a time when composers still gave the performer license to make certain improvisatory additions to the written text. A child of his time, Mozart was no exception. (The term "improvisation" will be used hereafter to designate any pitches sung or played that were not written in the score, whether done in impromptu spontaneity or prepared in advance.)

For Mozart such improvisations ranged from single pitches, especially appoggiaturas, or the insertion of other "small" ornaments—grace notes, slides, turns, trills, and the like—to larger additions of two distinct kinds: one, the florid elaboration of a written melody, the other, the filling in of empty spaces with transitional passages. Such filling in usually occurs at a fermata and takes the form of a brief embellishment, a preparatory passage (an *Eingang*, i.e. a lead-in), or a cadenza of varying length.

All these types have their individual problems which will be discussed at their proper places. One problem, though, is basic to all, namely the need to identify what could be called the "white spots" in Mozart's music, spots left unfinished to be finished by the performer, where the latter's failure to do so leaves an undesirable void. This problem of identification looms large in all the discussions yet to follow in this study.

In dealing with Mozart's improvisation we must stay clear of the dual dangers of too little and too much. We do too little if we ignore needs that have largely passed from the consciousness of performers into the limbo of what Riemann called "vergessene Selbstverständlichkeiten" (forgotten matters of course). Among them are certain appoggiaturas in recitatives and arias, fermata embellishments both vocal and instrumental, and *Eingänge* preparing the entrance of a theme. The peril of *too much* harbors an actual and a potential danger. Actual is the bane of listeners: overblown concerto cadenzas that are stylistic misfits. Potential is the danger of an infection that could spread from extravagant vocal and instrumental embellishments that were practiced in Mozart's time by Italians and Italianate Germans.[1] Because excesses hit eye, ear, and memory more forcefully than moderation, the belief could easily spread that such improvisatory luxuriance was a common procedure, maybe another *Selbstverständlichkeit* of Mozart's time. In view of the many false leads that today's performance-practice theorists have given us through misplaced faith in "common practices," in view also of Mozart's indebtedness to the Italian style, and in view of some contemporary documents of embroidery in Mozart's mature operas, there is a danger that soon we shall be asked to believe that such ornamental exuberance is a requisite of "authentic" Mozart performance. This matter is serious enough to warrant closer inspection.

[1]See e.g. Luigi Marchesi embellishing a Cherubini Rondo, as reproduced from a Vienna MS in Robert Haas, *Aufführungspraxis der Musik, Handbuch der Musikwissenschaft*, pp. 225-230; 48 versions of a Tartini Adagio; and a decorated version of a Nardini sonata, the last two reproduced from Cartier's *L'art du violon* (Paris, 1798) in Hans-Peter Schmitz, *die Kunst der Verzierung im 18. Jahrhundert*, pp. 131–39.

Reviewing the matter we find that even in Italy such extravagances represented an extreme and not the norm; important composers and theorists objected to them, and many eminent performers did not indulge in such practices. Above all we know that Mozart was opposed to them, as is documented in later chapters. Even a contemporary theorist had the wit to say that "the compositions of Mozart, Haydn, Cherubini, and Winter suffer fewer embellishments than those of Salieri, Cimarosa, Martin [y Soler], and Paesiello."[2]

Unquestionably, the last named composers and many others of their artistic persuasion either welcomed or at least tolerated a fair amount of improvised embellishments, yet the excesses must have gone well beyond the range of what even these masters had in mind. For a more balanced view it is enlightening to scan the opinions of authorities who endorsed restraint.

Early in the century Tosi, in his famous treatise, made a fervent appeal for moderation and ridiculed the extravagant embellishment antics of contemporary singers (for details see *Ornamentation*, pp. 551–552). Agostino Steffani, reports John Hawkins, "would never admit any divisions, or graces, even on the most plain and simple passages, except what he wrote himself . . ."[3] J.A.P. Schulz confirms this revealing report: "Concerning the added coloraturas of the singers, each conductor ought to adopt the principle of the famous Hannoverian Capellmeister Steffani who would not permit a singer to add a note that was not written down. . . . The rage of the arbitrary *passaggi* has veritably led to the ruin of the vocal art. . . ."[4]

The great reserve practiced by some of the most famous singers is illustrated in the manner, recorded in notation, in which Faustina Bordoni performed an aria by Giuseppe Vignati,[5] as well as in her rendition of an aria from Hasse's opera *Cleofide* that is the more striking, first, because she was the composer's wife and second, because we see it juxtaposed to the extravagant embellishments for the same aria by Frederick the Great.[6]

In Corri's collection of Italian arias and ensembles, notated as performed by celebrated singers, we find many embellishments but no extravagance.[7]

Mancini's famous and influential vocal treatise from the latter part of the 18th century discourages ornamental extravagance. He only deals with free ornamentation in his chapter on the cadenza, more specifically focusing on the final cadenza in an aria. Whereas Tosi had discouraged cadenzas, in Mancini's time, at least the final cadenza has become so firmly established that he considers it a necessity ("la cadenza è necessaria in ogni appropriata finale . . "), without which the piece remains incomplete and dull ("resta il tutto imperfetto e languido").[8] Mancini lists two contrasting approaches to the cadenza, one of restraint and one of excess, and makes it clear that restraint "is doubtless more correct and rational" (pp. 179–180). According to this "correct" approach the cadenza should form an epilogue to the aria, should preferably use motives from the ritornello or the aria proper, and should be *contained within a single breath*. The contrasting approach, which Mancini rejects, uses the cadenza as an arbitrary occasion to dazzle with the

[2]Schubert, *Neue Singe-Schule*, p. 138.
[3]Quoted by Robert Donington, *The Interpretation of Early Music*, p. 156.
[4]Schulz, writing in J. G. Sulzer, *Allgemeine Theorie der schönen Künste*. s.v. "Passagen."

[5]George Buelow, "A Lesson in Operatic Performance Practice," pp. 79–96.
[6]H. C. Wolff, *Original Vocal Improvisations: from the 16th-18th Centuries, pp. 143ff*.
[7]*Corri, A Select Collection*.
[8]Mancini, *Riflessioni pratiche*, p. 185.

splendor of *passaggi* and vocal acrobatics (p. 179). Such singers drag out the cadenza to undue length and abandon proper expression for the sake of a multitude of notes (p. 183).

The important theorist Arteaga praises Mancini's book and supports his attitude toward improvisation.[9] Later in his extensive work, Arteaga discusses free ornamentation in some detail (vol. 3, pp. 41ff.). Such embellishments, he writes, should be neither always admitted nor always prohibited. He welcomes them when they cover up defects of a composition, but issues a long list of prohibitions. Embellishments, he writes, should be avoided when they are superfluous or too contrived ("palesan di troppo l'artifizio"); when they weaken through trifles the vivacity of feeling; divert attention from the main subject; destroy the effect of other musical parts; impart a coloring to the theme that does not fit its character; alter the passion or the nature of a personality. Ornaments, he continues, are improper in recitative, at the start of an aria, for the warmth of great passion, for sentiments of candor and simplicity, for bucolic moods, for lively airs, for duos, trios, finales, and choruses. They are allowed, he says, where there is no action: in festive airs, hymns, invocations, and the like. Even where admitted, they must be done with great reserve and appropriateness ("con parsimonia e con opportunità"), must be *limited to a single breath,* and must not be done in bravura style. A man of taste, he adds, does not go to the theater to find out how many coloraturas and how many trills can roll out within 15 minutes from the facile throat of a Gabrieli or a Marchesi (vol. 3, p. 46).

Agricola, Tosi's translator and annotator, admits the need for cadenzas despite Tosi's aversion, and lists eight rules for their proper invention. The eighth one establishes the same one-breath principle that was to be later confirmed by Mancini and Arteaga: "A singer must not breathe during a cadenza; hence it must not be longer than a single breath, while still leaving time for an incisive trill."[10]

The preceding documentation strongly suggests that the often reproduced samples of vocal excentricities may have been something of a marginal phenomenon, deplored by composers and theorists, and avoided by some of the finest singers themselves; and that they did not represent the mainstream of Italian operatic usage, let alone its presumed "common practice."

The same is probably true of instrumental extravagances like the ones listed in note 1 of this chapter, which do not seem to have been considered models of good style by thoughtful critics of the time. All theoretical documents of any consequence repeat the warning against such exaggerations, against embellishing to a point where the underlying melody gets buried under the mass of ornamental overgrowth, and where, as Quantz put it, every Adagio by the sheer mass of inserted notes turns into an Allegro (see *Ornamentation,* pp. 563–564).

In his autobiography, Dittersdorf castigates the embellishment mania of keyboard players. He speaks of "a new custom which I gladly accept from men like Mozart, Clementi, and other great creative geniuses who display their ready creativity in so-called improvisation by playing a simple theme which they then vary several times according to all the rules of the art. But before long there appeared a host of little manikins who imitate everything like monkeys; now the vogue of variation and improvisation has spread to a point that whenever a

[9]Stefano Arteaga, *Le rivoluzioni del teatro musicale italiano,* vol. 2, p. 42.

[10]Agricola, *Anleitung zur Singkunst,* p. 204.

fortepiano is played in a concert, one can be sure to be regaled with overwrought [verkräuselte] themes."[11]

From sources like the ones cited and mentioned we gain a picture of improvisation of Italian and Italianate performers that ranged from the necessary minimum over opulence to excess. It is unlikely that any composer of note would have gladly suffered excess. But many probably either welcomed or at least tolerated opulence. The simple *galant* texture of their music was receptive to rich embellishments and often genuinely enhanced by it. Salieri, Cimarosa, Paesiello, Martin y Soler, listed by J. F. Schubert as being more admissive of improvised embellishments than Mozart or Haydn, were probably rather typical of the masters in this category.

The case was very different for the mature Mozart. His complex harmony, intricate part writing, and eloquent opera orchestra were highly vulnerable to ill-fitting arbitrary additions. Not that Mozart was averse to florid passage work or the display of virtuosity, but like Bach before him, he chose to write out the desired ornamental figurations with ever greater specificity, to protect himself against the intrusion of incompetence and bad taste. These facts have to be kept in mind whenever the question of improvisation arises in Mozart's music.

For the basic problem of identifying the "white spots" in his music of all types and forms we must be alert to the possibility that what looks white might be an intentionally simple passage, meant to be rendered as written, or that an empty space may have been meant to remain empty; after all, not every fermata calls for embellishment, and silences can be powerful means of musical expression.

Concerning simple passages, Koch puts it well when he speaks of the problematic question of whether the composer has left certain places not fully finished ("nicht völlig ausgemahlt") to give performers the chance to complete them in their fashion; or kept them simple, "in the shade," to put into stronger relief the "light" of neighboring passages. We have, he continues, to ask whether a musical idea, expressed in noble simplicity, needs embellishment and whether it would not be more advantageous to try to execute it in its elevated simplicity ("in seiner hohen Simplizität") rather than to smudge it with idle glitter ("mit Flittergold zu beklexen").[12]

The piano concertos are a case sui generis. Those Mozart wrote for his own use contain passages that are clearly unfinished, but not with a view to giving performers a chance to shine and display their improvisatory skill. They were fragmentary not by intent but by duress: Mozart was often under great pressure to finish the score in time for a performance, and whereas he always took all the necessary pains with the orchestral parts, he could afford to leave the solo part in less final form by relying on his extraordinary ability to improvise what he did not have time to finish in the score. In his performance, Mozart *may* have given free rein to this genius for improvisation in embroidering ("gently," as an earwitness reports) even passages that were not necessarily unfinished and where it is questionable whether he would have wanted others to try the same. (Chapter 16 deals with these matters in more detail.)

Of the many issues connected with Mozart's improvisation, I shall in the rest of the book deal one by one with the most important ones. Starting with vocal music,

---

[11]Karl von Dittersdorf, *Karl von Dittersdorfs Lebensbeschreibung*, p. 47.

[12]Koch, *Musikalisches Lexikon*, s.v. "Manieren."

I address the question of the appoggiatura in recitative, the appoggiatura in arias and other closed numbers, the important fermata embellishments, and the florid elaboration of arias. In the instrumental realm I deal with the special problems of the piano concerto, with cadenzas and *Eingänge,* then here, too, with fermata embellishments and other occasions for filling in possible white spots, such as ornamentation on repeats.

Except for briefly touching on it in connection with the piano concerto, I do not discuss thorough-bass accompaniment. It does not, for Mozart, partake of genuine improvisation, unless it were to be done fancifully, which would be out of place. Used in his music, apart from the piano concertos, principally in recitative and in church music, it hardly calls for imagination, only for problem solving on the level of "keyboard harmony." Concerning church music, we find only in youthful works spots that depend on the organ for the fullness of harmony. In works of his maturity the organ is desirable mainly for adding with its coloring the aura of sanctity, but the harmonization rarely depends on it.

Finally, a reminder: improvisation is strictly the province of the soloist. It has no place in orchestral or choral performance, and hardly any in chamber music.

The Appoggiatura in Recitative

One of the problems in performing Mozart's recitatives concerns the addition of appoggiaturas. This chapter addresses the question of when appoggiaturas could or should be added and what kind they ought to be.[1] The inquiry focuses on those appoggiaturas that take the place of the first of two notes written on the same pitch on feminine endings, as given in Ex. 12.1a. We can exclude from consideration such endings following the fall of a fourth (Ex. b), because Mozart, along with most of his contemporaries, invariably wrote out this formula the way it was intended to be sung (Ex. c). Appoggiaturas on masculine endings, such as those in Ex. d, will be considered only marginally. They are rare because they introduce a melisma into the typically syllabic setting of recitative and are fitting only for occasional words with a strong emotional tone, such as *amor* or *pietà*.

Ex. 12.1.

In the case of feminine endings, we are dealing with a convention, still fully alive for Mozart, whereby the insertion of a stepwise falling appoggiatura was often necessary and sometimes optional, but also from time to time undesirable. The main purpose of the following discussion is to provide approximate guidelines for identifying the three categories of the obligatory, the optional, and the undesirable in Mozart's recitatives.

The convention of adding appoggiaturas had long been forgotten, and until recently most recitative formulas were sung as written. With the rising interest in historically accurate performance, however, awareness of this convention was revived; but now a new problem arose, marked by an exaggerated swing in the opposite direction, coupled with a misunderstanding of the underlying principles. We can observe this happening in several volumes of the *NMA*, where editors suggest not only too many appoggiaturas, but appoggiaturas of the wrong kind.

By the mid-18th century, earlier differences between church, chamber, and theater recitative had lost their meaning. For Mozart we have to be concerned

---

[1]This chapter appeared, in slightly modified form, as "The Appoggiatura in Mozart's Recitative," *JAMS*, vol. 35 (1982), pp. 115–137. An enlarged German version came out in *MJb 1980-83*, pp. 363–384.

mainly with the difference between *recitativo semplice,* better known by the 19th-century term secco (which I shall use hereafter), and the *recitativo accompagnato.* The secco is accompanied by cello, bass, and cembalo or fortepiano, whereas the *accompagnato* involves the whole orchestra. The two types serve different purposes. The secco often comprises very fast exchanges that carry the action forward like the spoken dialogue in *Singspiel* or *opéra comique.* The *accompagnato* is often a monologue that sets the stage for a following aria. As such it is also used in *Singspiele* (e.g. in *Die Entführung* or *Die Zauberflöte*). As a dialogue, it usually occurs at moments of dramatic gravity or tension.

Concerning both types of recitative, theorists of the period agree on several general points: that recitative represents musical prose declamation which often approaches everyday speech ("halfway between speech and song" as some put it); that as such it is syllabic, not melismatic; that it is rhythmically and metrically free, and not bound by a specific key or key scheme. They also agree that a stepwise descending appoggiatura is often necessary to do justice to the prosodic accent on the penultimate syllable of a feminine ending; and that the function of such an appoggiatura is not primarily one of expression, but of musical diction. This is the crux of the matter. In Italian, in German, and in English, the speech accent is rendered by a combination of greater loudness and higher pitch. Both loudness and pitch elevation can range from almost imperceptible to considerable, depending on the emphasis placed on the word. But never will either loudness or speech melody be *lowered* for the accented syllable. For these reasons a recitative appoggiatura on a feminine ending has to be applied from above, not from below; moreover, since Mozart writes out those syllabic appoggiaturas that fall a fourth (and are extremely frequent at phrase endings), as well as those involving larger intervals, the appoggiatura that is to be, or may be, freely inserted, can only be the stepwise descending one.

If recitative is to approximate speech, then the prosodic accent on a word will vary with the weight of that word within a sentence as well as with the overall degree of emphasis on a particular passage; it will be stronger in an oratorical delivery that might be proper for certain accompanied recitatives, weaker in the fast give and take of daily conversation as so often encountered in the secco style (notably in buffo settings). Thus often in the middle of sentences rendered in fast parlando fashion the accents are minimized to near or total disappearance, obviating the need for and often the desirability of added appoggiaturas. Their proliferation in such contexts would be unnatural and impart a theatrically unjustified singsong quality to a fast dialogue. In the *accompagnato,* by contrast, the words are generally rendered with more deliberation; in addition, the participation of the orchestra will tend to limit the speed of delivery and with it the range of rhythmic freedom for the singer. But those are differences of degree, not of kind.

The need for an inserted appoggiatura will normally be greatest for the falling third at the cadence, because there a stepwise descent, along with the prosodic accent, would reflect the gradual tapering of a falling speech melody better than a downward leap to the accented syllable. The need is less obvious for the falling second, because there is no angular leap to be bridged. The need will be smallest when the repeated pitches are approached from below because the upward step or leap can often by itself be sufficient to mirror the tonic accent. That is most evident with such characteristic intervals as, say, the augmented fourth. The need will also be small for words so casually spoken that they call for no accentuation. At the other end of the spectrum, an appoggiatura will be improper for words of such forcefulness that they would be weakened by the smoothing effect of the grace.

To gain a better perspective on the problems of Mozart's recitative I first examine the historical sources for the appoggiatura convention.

Georg Philipp Telemann is among the authors most frequently cited on the question of the recitative appoggiatura. He offers an illustration that shows how singers do not always sing the note as written but "occasionally" ("hin and wieder") use an appoggiatura ("Akzent").[2] Since his illustration served a pedagogical purpose, the fact that he added appoggiaturas to all masculine and feminine endings does not undermine the reservation of "occasionally." His example shows 11 descending appoggiaturas and one that, ascending chromatically, fills in the interval of a whole step. Several factors disqualify the transfer of this rising appoggiatura to Mozart: its date, solemn religious tone, and generally poor diction, which was later to be devastatingly criticized by J. A. P. Schulz in his study of the recitative.

Johann Friedrich Agricola in 1757 joins in the widespread agreement that on feminine endings the falling fourth preceding two identical pitches should always be delayed by an inserted appoggiatura, as illustrated in Exx. 12.1b and c; for the falling third, however, a connecting, stepwise appoggiatura should be inserted only "occasionally" ("zuweilen").[3]

In a lengthy serialized essay on recitative, Friedrich Wilhelm Marpurg criticizes the notation of the feminine cadence with the falling fourth on the beat: "This notation is unquestionably reprehensible because one ought not naturally and without good cause write differently from the way one sings" since by so doing one confuses the singers.[4] From this principle alone we can infer that when Marpurg writes repeated pitches, he means it, and his many examples contain numerous pitch repetitions. He is even more explicit on the matter when, in speaking of half-cadences ("schwebenden Absätzen"), he lists as one of their alternatives an execution with repeated pitch ("mit dem wiederholten Einklange"). A few of his illustrations are given in Ex. 12.2, where we see a fall of a fifth in *a*, of a fourth in *d*, and pitch repetition in *b, c,* and *e*. The remarkable fact that among his many illustrations, including those for full cadences, he shows not a single appoggiatura filling in a descending third, would seem to indicate that he found tone repetition preferable.

Ex. 12.2. Marpurg

[2]*Der harmonische Gottesdienst.*
[3]*Anleitung zur Singkunst,* p. 154.

[4]*Kritische Briefe über die Tonkunst,* vol. 2, pt. 3.

Like many other writers, Hiller warns against the use in recitative of ornaments other than the appoggiatura; trills and mordents, he says, may be applied only once in a while.[5] Appoggiaturas *may* be used for all falling thirds; also, after three or four stepwise ascending notes, the last one may receive an appoggiatura from above. Interestingly, these appoggiaturas ("Vorschläge") do not replace the written note but are of the very short species ("unveränderliche") that resolve in Lombard rhythm into the written note. Even if such a *Vorschlag* is indicated by a symbol, as in Ex. 12.3a, it is to be sung as in *b*, not as in *c*.

Ex. 12.3. Hiller

Schulz offers a long and thoughtful disquisition on recitative,[6] which was later admiringly cited by Koch. Schulz reconfirms for recitative the lack of an exact meter and key scheme and its nonlyrical, syllabic nature that should allow no melismatic ornaments. For full cadences he gives the models of Ex. 12.4 without indicating a rendition differing from the notation.

Ex. 12.4. Schulz

For feminine endings he restates the principle that the formula of the falling fourth to the repeated note should be written as sung, that is, as a downward leaping appoggiatura. Since Schulz, like Marpurg, obviously wants the cadences written as sung, we must assume that in his numerous examples the many repeated notes that follow the fall of a third or other melodic progressions were intended to be rendered literally. In the same vein he objects to altering a masculine fall of a fourth, as shown in Ex. 12.5, which would sound "dragging and unpleasant" ("höchst schleppend und widrig").

Ex. 12.5. Schulz

Schulz admits such appoggiaturas that result in melismas only exceptionally in spots of unusual expression and then only when sung by first-class artists. He makes an exception only for masculine endings on a falling third where in the passage of Ex. 12.6a the last note receives an appoggiatura as if it had been written like Ex. *b*.

[5]*Anweisung zum musikalisch-richtigen Gesange*, p. 202.

[6]Schulz, writing in J. G. Sulzer's *Allgemeine Theorie der schönen Künste*, s.v. "Recitativ."

Ex. 12.6. Schulz

Very interesting and logical is his rule that cadences expressing questions, violent exclamations, or strong injunctions must emphasize not the final syllable of the sentence but the principal word ("Hauptwort") carrying the meaning. For questions he lists the formulas of Exx. 12.7a and b, then sensibly corrects the solution of Ex. c, with the upward leaping third, to Ex. d, with the repeated pitch.

Ex. 12.7. Schulz

In Germany we find more theoretical mention of appoggiatura inserts as the 18th century nears its close. Johann Carl Friedrich Rellstab points out that in recitative the appoggiaturas are not written out but left to the judgment of the singers.[7] Significantly he adds that "in the theater, a singer who knows what action means will add few if any appoggiaturas, and even in church or chamber . . . I prefer the plain rendition [platte Ausführung]" (Ex. 12.8a as opposed to b). As a good compromise he suggests the notation of Ex. c, which the singer "obviously" sings as in Ex. d.

Ex. 12.8. Rellstab

Lasser shows the descending appoggiatura inserted on the fall of the third in feminine endings (Ex. 12.9a) and on the last of several ascending pitches (Ex. b). J.F. Schubert limits the use of the appoggiatura to "every so often" ("öfters") in order to bring out a declamatory emphasis as shown in Ex. c. Neither he nor Lasser mentions any rising appoggiaturas.[8]

Koch, in two partly overlapping articles, stresses the declamatory, syllabic nature of recitative and its freedom from meter and key. He largely follows Schulz, mentions no appoggiaturas, and gives no examples.[9]

All these German theorists took the Italian vocal art as their model and offer Italian as well as German texts for their examples. Though the degree of

[7]*Versuch über die Vereinigung der musikalischen und oratorischen Declamation*, pp. 47–48.

[8]Lasser, *Vollständige Anleitung zur Singkunst*, p. 160; Schubert, *Neue Singe-Schule*, p. 145.

[9]*Versuch einer Anleitung zur Composition*, vol. 3, pp. 233–240; *Musikalisches Lexikon*, s.v. "Recitativ."

a. Lasser   b.

mei- ne   See-le   See- le   Die mit er-hab-ner Tu-gend Tu-gend

c. J.F. Schubert

Die Welt mit ih- rer   Herr-lich-keit hat für mich kei- ne   Rei- ze

Ex. 12.9.

relevance to Mozart of these or any other theorists is uncertain, we can ignore neither the large role that many of them assign to pitch repetition on feminine endings, nor, excepting the solitary model of Telemann, their total disregard of the rising appoggiatura.

We have few Italian documents on 18th-century recitative. In Tosi's famous treatise, *Opinioni de' cantori antichi e moderni* (Bologna, 1723), the chapter on recitative is disappointingly lacking in specifics. For the latter part of the century, however, we find some interesting accounts in Mancini, Manfredini, and Corri. Mancini, like the German theorists, stresses the declamatory character of recitative which, he says, is at its best when the notes imitate natural speech ("perfettamente imitano un discorso naturale"). He emphasizes the importance of the "valuable appoggiatura" ("accento prezioso") performed *one tone higher* than written and used primarily when two syllables of the same word are written on the same pitch. Such a stepwise falling appoggiatura is characterized as a prosodic accent that underlines the declamatory nature of recitative.[10] Important too is Mancini's precept that even in an aria, where melody is far more independent from declamatory intonation patterns, exclamations of invective, great fervor of action, or the passion invested in words like *tiranno, crudele,* or *spietato,* would be denatured by an added appoggiatura. A fortiori this principle has to apply to recitative. The same idea is expressed by Türk who, speaking of instrumental music, lists defiant ("trotzige") and sharply articulated passages among the contexts in which appoggiaturas do not fit well. In a footnote he adds: "when an idea is to be rendered defiantly . . . appoggiaturas would be totally improper because they impart a certain smoothness to the melody that is unfitting for such occasions."[11]

For the first of two notes of equal pitch and value, Vincenzo Manfredini stipulates the need to sing an appoggiatura stepwise *from above.* By contrast, he writes, an instrumentalist is under no clear obligation to insert such an appoggiatura unless it is prescribed by the composer. Manfredini considers other ornaments undesirable for both secco ("semplice") and *accompagnato* ("obbligato") recitative and admits some very brief embellishments only for uninteresting and indifferent words, but never for an animated, tender, or expressive text.[12]

In his collection of arias and duets from operas, Corri shows how specific Italian

[10]*Riflessioni pratiche,* pp. 237–239, 143.

[11]*Klavierschule,* 1789 ed., pp. 205–206, and p. 206, n. 2.

[12]*Regole armoniche,* pp. 65 and 71.

singers render the musical text.[13] As is to be expected, these virtuoso singers take considerable liberties even with, say, Gluck, who would hardly have welcomed their embroidery and their altered melodies (e.g. in "Che farò senza Euridice"). In recitatives, both secco and accompanied, Corri almost always replaces feminine endings on the same pitch with a stepwise descending appoggiatura, never with an ascending one, as shown in Ex. 12.10*a*. (See also the recitatives to Giordani's *Artaserse,* pp. 1–2, and Sacchini's *Perseo,* pp. 48–49.)

We have significant proof for Gluck's disagreement with Corri in the first-act recitative from *Orfeo.* We see in Ex. 12.10*b* a written-out appoggiatura on *cara,* but the exclamation "Euridice!," the question *dove sei?,* and the phrase *di mano tremolante* are each followed by an instrumental "echo" that unmistakably indicates the absence of vocal appoggiaturas.

Ex. 12.10. Gluck

Because of the scarcity of Italian theoretical sources on recitative, several editors of the *NMA* had recourse to a vocal treatise by Manuel Garcia (son), written

———

[13]*A Select Collection, vol. 1.*

in French 50 years after Mozart's death.[14] The editors attach great importance to a sentence in which Garcia, speaking of the *accompagnato* only, admits the use of a stepwise rising appoggiatura, which he characterizes as being more "moving" ("plus pathétique"). This is an elaboration of a previous statement concerning recitative in general, in which he defined the appoggiatura as a "raising of the voice for the tonic accent." Garcia's testimony has to be viewed with reservations. Even if his father, who was Rossini's first Almaviva, had bequeathed Rossinian principles to his son, they are not a reliable guide for Mozart. Rossini, born a year after Mozart's death, was heir to a tradition of liberal improvised embellishment from which the mature Mozart had thoroughly emancipated himself. We need only look at Garcia's interpretation of Donna Anna's great opening recitative (Ex. 12.11) to realize that he should be dismissed, not summoned, as an expert witness for Mozart's recitative. The same conclusion is inevitable when, in the dialogue between Don Giovanni and Zerlina in Act I, scene 9, Garcia has the impertinence to recompose Mozart's text. Apparently bothered by Don Giovanni's threefold repetition of the triadic formula on the words, "quegli occhi bricconcelli, quei labbretti sì belli, quelle dituccie candide e odorose," Garcia tried to "correct" an imagined monotony. He was unaware of the psychological masterstroke with which Mozart revealed Don Giovanni's insincerity by the very mechanical way in which he rattles off his flatteries. Garcia is further disqualified when he authorizes the singers to change the melody of the secco recitative (the "récitatif parlant," as he calls it), on the grounds that it is "only a platitude" to begin with.

Ex. 12.11. Garcia (Mozart)

Considerable inconsistency characterizes the approach of the various editors of the *NMA* to the recitative appoggiatura. Nearly all of them underplay the role of pitch repetition, but they do so to different degrees: some admit no such repetitions at all, others only a carefully limited number. They diverge more strongly in their treatment of the appoggiatura from below. Some editors limit this type to the stepwise ascending formula and use it sparingly. Others use it more generously and extend it to upward leaps by thirds and fourths.[15]

In the remaining part of this chapter I apply the criteria of diction, speech melody, word meaning, and affect to some characteristic passages of recitative from Mozart's operas, in order to arrive at some working principles about advisable, questionable, and inadvisable procedures.

IN MOZART's recitatives masculine endings rarely pose a problem: in general we ought to leave them alone to avoid melismas unwarranted by diction. Once in a while, however, when word meaning and length of syllable combine, an appoggiatura will be advisable, as in Exx. 12.12*a* and *b*; whereas *c* and *d* will best be sung as written.

[14]*A Complete Treatise on the Art of Singing*, pt. 2.
[15]For an evaluation of the appoggiatura treatment by various editors of the *NMA* see the German version of this chapter in *MJb 1980–83*, pp. 363–384.

Ex. 12.12.

For a feminine ending, the *locus classicus* is of course pitch repetition after a falling third. Here the tendency to fill the gap will be strongest when the speech contour is one of gradual descent, as in Exx. 12.13*a* and *b*.

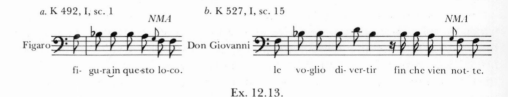

Ex. 12.13.

The humble, pleading tone of Ex. 12.14*a* calls for a gentle articulation pattern, hence for an appoggiatura on *ubbidisco,* and probably also on *Signore.* (The *NMA* omits an appoggiatura on *Signore,* certainly a reasonable option.) In German, the urgency of the plea in Ex. 12.14*b* requires an appoggiatura.

Ex. 12.14.

In a stepwise fall, or when a note is preceded by one of the same pitch, the need for an appoggiatura is lessened because there is no disturbing break in the speech contour. When the repeated pitch is approached from below the need for an appoggiatura fades still more, as mentioned before, because the melodic rise will often be sufficient to take account of the tonic accent. In all of these cases an appoggiatura will be suggested either by a need for distinct emphasis or, particularly in an *accompagnato,* by a sense of warmth or tenderness. Thus, in Ex. 12.15 no appoggiatura is needed for *momento* after the stepwise rise; for *affanno* the decision could go either way, but for *idol mio,* where warmth of feeling coincides with a falling third, an appoggiatura is obligatory.

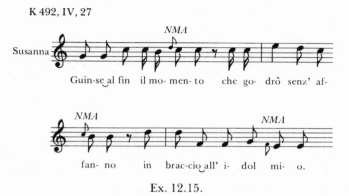

Ex. 12.15.

In the stepwise descent of Ex. 12.16*a* the word *bella* pronounced by Don Giovanni calls for emphasis. In Ex. *b* the stepwise rise alone is sufficient for the weak speech accent on *vestirlo,* and an appoggiatura would be pointless for the two *E poi.* In Ex. *c questo* is not important enough to require extra emphasis, and in *d* the leap of a fourth is sufficient to render the speech accent and obviates the need for an appoggiatura.

Ex. 12.16.

The need for caution in adding appoggiaturas after upward leaps is underscored by numerous instances in which Mozart, in cases where they are clearly called for, specifically writes them out, as shown in Exx. 12.17*a-c*. (See also Ex. 12.29*b*.)

a. K 527, I, 10

b. Ibid.   *c.* Ibid., II, 12

Ex. 12.17.

Such examples suggest reserve, not prohibition. Where the meaning of a word calls for special emphasis, appoggiaturas sometimes may, sometimes should, be added. The pleading of Zerlina in Ex. 12.18*a,* of Donna Elvira in Ex. *b,* would be pale without an appoggiatura, and so would Susanna's flirtatious *Figaretto* in Ex. *c* or her joyous anticipation *il mio diletto* of Ex. *d.* In Ex. *e, loco* is too neutral a word to require an appoggiatura though one would be defensible, whereas Rudolf Steglich's solution  has barely a justification;[16] *terra* should have a linking grace; *risponda* on the rise is ambiguous, leaning to addition; *la notte* will best be sung as written to reflect the descent into darkness; at the end a linking appoggiatura on *seconda* is indicated.

a. K 527, I, sc. 16   *b.* Ibid., II, sc. 7

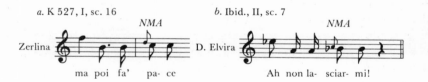

c. K 492, I, sc. 1

d. Ibid., IV, 27

e.

Ex. 12.18.

[16]"Auszierungswesen," p. 217.

Ex. 12.18 *cont.*

The meaning of the words is not always the main criterion, however. What often matters more is the way they are rendered: whether spoken soft or loud, fast or slow, casually or with authority, legato or staccato. Phrases and sentences will often give a clue, and occasionally so will the composer, by tempo markings or by specifying the character of the declamation. The *sotto voce sempre* in Ex. 12.19 suggests a minimum of inflections; hence the *NMA* with good reason omits appoggiaturas on *sei* and *voi*; the one on *disgrazia* follows the natural speech flow. See also below (in Ex. 12.30) the directive *con risolutezza* and its presumable implications.

Ex. 12.19.

Although an appoggiatura from below contradicts the prosodic accent, once in a while it can be harmless when introduced discreetly as in the *NMA* interpretation of Ex. 12.20a. Here the rising appoggiatura on *rivedi* is unnecessary, but unobtrusive, being prepared and rising only a half-step. The infraction of prosodic principles is small, and the result in the frame of the whole phrase is pleasing. The appoggiatura on *felice* is unobjectionable, the one on *Mitridate* necessary.

Though melodically similar, the case of Ex. 12.20b is not comparable.

Ex. 12.20.

Occurring at the end of the recitative, Susanna's exclamation: "Cherubino, you are crazy!" calls for emphasis on the key word *pazzo*—which has to have an appoggiatura from above, not from below; the word does not call for a gentle ingratiating inflection but a musical exclamation point.

More serious still are appoggiaturas that leap upward a fourth or more, because here the infraction of proper declamation is so drastic as to subvert the basic principle of the recitative. This is true of cases like those shown in Exx. 12.21*a* and *b*. Even more objectionable are related specimens like those of Ex. *c*, where the rising appoggiatura is approached by an upward leap for words that should have no appoggiaturas to begin with, because their expression of contempt and fury must not be softened by a "pathetic" ornament.

Ex. 12.21.

Another frequent application of the rising appoggiatura that has crept into several volumes of the *NMA* involves questions. It is true that in Italian, as well as in German and English, a question will more often than not involve a rising inflection of the voice. Such a rise is clearest in masculine endings where it will be more evident the more pointed the question, and less evident—occasionally to the point of disappearance—the more casual and timid the question. Such shadings are reflected in Exx. 12.22*a-c*.

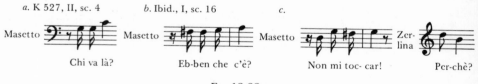

Ex. 12.22.

By contrast, in feminine endings of questions, the voice contour will generally rise to the accented first, then fall to the unaccented second syllable. In a monotonous delivery the voice may not rise at all, and may even fall to the accented syllable, but it will hardly ever rise from the accented to the unaccented one. Mozart himself confirmed the tonal descent from the penultimate to the final syllable in countless instances for which the three illustrations of Exx. 12.23*a-c* are typical. The third of these, Ex. *c*, shows both the descent for the feminine and the rise for the masculine ending.

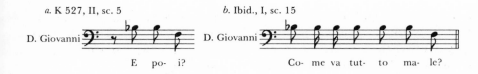

a. K 527, II, sc. 5

D. Giovanni

E po- i?

b. Ibid., I, sc. 15

D. Giovanni

Co- me va tut- to ma- le?

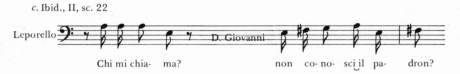

c. Ibid., II, sc. 22

Leporello

Chi mi chia- ma?

D. Giovanni

non co- no- sci il pa- dron?

Ex. 12.23.

Given this characteristic of Italian and German diction, the introduction of a rising appoggiatura for questions is a misunderstanding. Nevertheless we find it being suggested on many occasions in the *NMA,* notably in *Idomeneo, Le nozze di Figaro,* and *Die Zauberflöte,* as shown in a few instances in Ex. 12.24. (See also Exx. 12.21*a* and *b.*)

a. K 492, I, sc. 2

Figaro

che c'è di nuo- vo?

b. Ibid., I, sc. 1

Susanna

E in que- sta stan- za?

c. Ibid., sc. 5

Susanna

Se- cre- ta- men- te il vo- stro cor so- spi- ra?

d. K 620, I, Finale

Priester

Ist das, was du ge- sagt, er- wie- sen?

e. K 384, III, sc. 1

Ilia

o m'a- scon- do?

Ex. 12.24.

Tamino's famous recitative, from which Ex. 12.25 is taken, merits closer scrutiny for the overuse of both types of appoggiaturas. Whereas the appoggiatura on *Knaben* in Ex. *a* is appropriate, the one on *Pforten* in *b* is unnecessary and disturbs the musical line, whose ascent to *Säulen* portrays Tamino's growing astonishment at the grandeur of the temple. Next, the *NMA* has falling appoggiaturas on *Klugheit* and *Arbeit,* and a rising one on *weilen.* All three had far better be left out. Tamino's wondrous awe is better reflected by the simple, dignified, unornamented line with its striking ascent by thirds, than through the appoggiatura clichés, while the idea of *weilen* (to endure, to reign) finds a far better pictorial reflection in the persistence, the *Weilen* on the pitch, than in a would-be "expressive" appoggiatura.

a. K 620, I, Finale

Tamino

Die Weis- heits- leh- re die- ser Kna- ben

b.

Doch zei- gen die Pfor- ten, es zei- gen die Säu- len,

Dass Klug- heit, und Ar- beit, und Kün- ste hier wei- len.

Ex. 12.25.

In Donna Anna's narrative of Don Giovanni's intrusion into her room at night (see Ex. 12.26), it seems that the slow stepwise ascent from *quando nelle mie stanze* builds up its tension to the climax of *istante* far more stirringly if its linearity is not interrupted by appoggiaturas on *stanze, sventura,* and *avvolto,* as suggested by the *NMA.* The only advisable appoggiatura is that on *alquanto* in the first measure of the example.

K 257, I, 10

D. Anna

E- ra già al- quan- to a- van- za- ta- la not- te, quan- do nal- le mie

stan- ze, o- ve so- let- ta mi tro- vai per sven- tu- ra,

en- trar io vi- di in un· man- tel- lo av- vol- to

un uom che al pri- mo i- stan- te a- vea pre- so per voi:

Ex. 12.26.

In Ex. 12.27 from the same recitative, the *NMA* suggests, with good reason, appoggiaturas for the three falling thirds in mm. 64–65. In m. 66 an appoggiatura on the falling second is even more necessary to do justice to *più forte*, but I would suggest eliminating the appoggiatura on *suo* in the following measure. By repeating the words *compie il misfatto suo*—a rare occurrence in recitative—Mozart achieves an extraordinary dramatic effect; yet the intensification inherent in the repetition on a higher pitch level is weakened by the suggested appoggiatura.

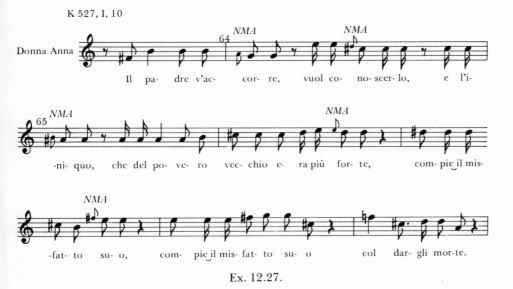

Ex. 12.27.

In another passage from *Don Giovanni*, given in Ex. 12.28, the appoggiatura in m. 2 on *vuoi* is unnecessary, and the one in m. 3 is optional; if the latter is left out, then the obligatory one in m. 4 will more effectively bring out the augmentation from *importante* to *importantissimo*. In m. 5, Don Giovanni's *finiscila*, as a cool command, could normally do without an appoggiatura, but the Don mimics Leporello's inflection, hence the appoggiatura is needed; so is the one on *collera*; in m. 9 one is unnecessary on *soli*, optional on *vedo*; and in m. 10 *sente* can do without one.

Whenever the rounding, softening effect of an appoggiatura is unfitting, we should avoid inserting one. Generally, words expressing authority, decisiveness, threats, violence, terror, stubbornness, finality, and similar affects will be more fittingly rendered by pitch repetition.

A striking example is the first accompanied recitative in *Don Giovanni*, where Donna Anna comes upon the body of her slain father. Her anguished terror is poignantly rendered by the upward rushing triadic figure of Ex. 12.29*a*. The two appoggiaturas suggested by the *NMA* in the first measure weaken the dramatic impact of the outcry—its force underlined by the powerful interjections of the orchestra. That Mozart did not have appoggiaturas in mind becomes clear four measures later when terror yields to compassion at the sight of the wound and Mozart writes out the appoggiaturas of Ex. 12.29*b* accompanied by tender woodwind figures. To bring this contrast into still clearer focus, the recurring feeling of terror brings forth a similar triadic outcry (Ex. *c*), again punctuated by dramatic orchestral interjections, followed, above a soothing chord in the strings,

K 527, I, sc. 4

Ex. 12.28.

by *padre amato,* which should have an appoggiatura from above, not from below, as suggested by the *NMA* (presumably to provide a change from their proposed appoggiaturas on *mio* and *padre,* which again would be better left unsung).

Ex. 12.29.

In the preceding brief secco that starts scene 3 (Ex. 12.30), Mozart's directive *con risolutezza* strengthens the case for pitch repetition on *periglio*; an appoggiatura would weaken the force of this word.

Ex. 12.30.

Although on a less pathetic level, the words *ingrato* and *crudele* in Ex. 12.31a are better not softened by appoggiaturas from above and below. Similarly, in Ex. *b* *perfidia* is stronger when sung as written, and in Ex. *c* the tone of command can dispense with an appoggiatura.

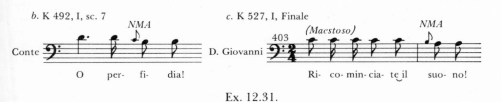

Ex. 12.31.

There is a revealing passage in Mozart's insert for Gluck's *Alceste*, "Popoli di Tessaglia" (Ex. 12.32a), where, in addition to the grimness of the word *funesto*, the orthography of A sharp and A natural, following closely the high B flat, definitely precludes an appoggiatura. The latter would even theoretically be feasible only if Mozart had written a B flat instead of an A sharp, since the solution given in Ex. *b* is irrational.

Ex. 12.32.

In Ex. 12.33a the word *resto* (like the word *weilen* at the end of Ex. 12.25b) is more congenial to literalness than to the rising appoggiatura in the *NMA*. Similarly, the solemn authority of the old priest in Ex. *b* is better served by omitting an appoggiatura on *Gründe* (and none is suggested here by the *NMA*).

Ex. 12.33.

As a final illustration of the three options open for notated pitch repetitions, an appoggiatura on *Susanna* in Ex. 12.34 is possible, but unnecessary; one on *l'istoria* is necessary, whereas *finita* should be sung as written, since pitch repetition better conveys a sense of finality.

Ex. 12.34.

Summing up the insights gained from theoretical and musical evidence, I can tentatively formulate the following principles for Mozart's recitatives:

1. Appoggiaturas on repeated pitches range from necessary to undesirable with a gray area of ambiguity between the two.

2. The appoggiaturas should descend stepwise from above. They mirror the prosodic accent and should be used whenever a distinct accentuation is warranted by the situation.

3. Ascending appoggiaturas on questions should be avoided. They involve a misunderstanding of Italian and German diction.

4. Appoggiaturas leaping from below are never appropriate because they conflict too sharply with proper declamation.

5. In rare cases, in an *accompagnato,* a chromatically rising appoggiatura may be admissible if fitted smoothly into the melodic line, but it is never necessary and is better avoided.

6. For the fall of a third, even where the speech accent is very weak, an appoggiatura is often used as a lubricant to avoid an unwarranted break in the speech melody.

7. An appoggiatura is undesirable:

    a. when it infringes on a characteristic melodic design

    b. for words expressing firmness, finality, resolution, hatred, terror, or any other state of mind that should not be subjected to the softening effect of the grace

    c. for commonplace utterances in fast parlando style and for unimportant words.

8. An appoggiatura is optional when approached from below by either step or leap, where the melodic rise alone may be sufficient to render the prosodic accent.

In general, I see wisdom in moderation. Excess is always tiresome. Good speakers, always cited by 17th- and 18th-century writers as models for proper musical interpretation, do not give equal emphasis to every word accent. By the same token, the appoggiatura will be more effective, the more discriminatingly it is used, and the more its use is attuned to word meaning and speech melody. In the last analysis, the singer's intelligence has to decide in each case whether an appoggiatura will add or detract.

The Appoggiatura in
Closed Numbers

Since many Italians ornamented their arias with florid embellishments it stands to reason that they added small graces as well, notably the appoggiatura.

When Mancini, speaking of arias, lists the cases where appoggiaturas are inappropriate because they would soften words expressing sternness or violent passion (see chapter 12), he implies their use on other occasions. His appoggiatura in arias either descends one step or rises a half-step. He calls it the appoggiatura *semplice,* as given in Ex. 13.1a. Under the term of appoggiatura *doppia* or *gruppetto* he also lists the rising or falling turn, shown in Ex. *b.*[1]

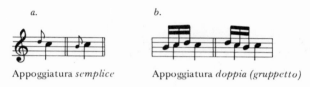

Appoggiatura *semplice*   Appoggiatura *doppia (gruppetto)*

Ex. 13.1. Mancini

Just as the florid Italian embellishments do not apply to the mature Mozart (as is further discussed in Chapter 15), so is the Italian proliferation of appoggiaturas not directly applicable to him. A lucky piece of external evidence (see the preceding chapter) shows that even in recitative Gluck forwent appoggiaturas that no Italian would have left out. Though Mozart was presumably less austere than Gluck, Wolfgang Plath and Wolfgang Rehm (in the preface to their *NMA* edition of *Don Giovanni*) say that in Mozart's closed numbers appoggiaturas play only a minor role. Regarding Mozart's last great Italian operas they speak of a "transitional style" ("Zwischenstil") in which the improvised ornamentation of the opera seria is largely eclipsed, as shown for instance in the absence of cadential fermatas, and in which even the more recent forms of *Eingänge* and transitional fermatas are rare "in their pure form."

The question of Mozart's appoggiaturas is complicated by the fact that we do find many spots in arias or ensembles that seem to demand their impromptu insertion, yet there are countless instances where Mozart writes them out with either symbol or regular notation.

A striking illustration for the many cases of specified appoggiaturas is Cherubino's aria "non sò più cosa son," of which the beginning is given in Ex. 13.2. In the first 64 measures alone, there are no less than 22 written-out specimens, of which 19 fall, three rise.

For further illustration, Ex. 13.3 gives a random sampling: Exx. *a* and *b* from *Figaro* for masculine, *c-h* from *Don Giovanni* and *i* from *Die Zauberflöte* for feminine endings. See also Ex. 2.16. The very frequency of spelled-out appoggia-

[1]*Riflessioni pratiche,* p. 142 and fig. 10-11.

K 492, I, 6

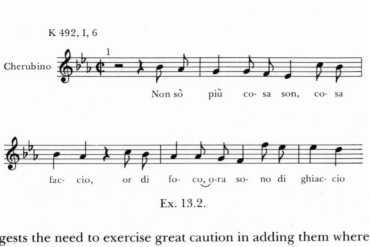

Ex. 13.2.

turas suggests the need to exercise great caution in adding them where they are
not specified.

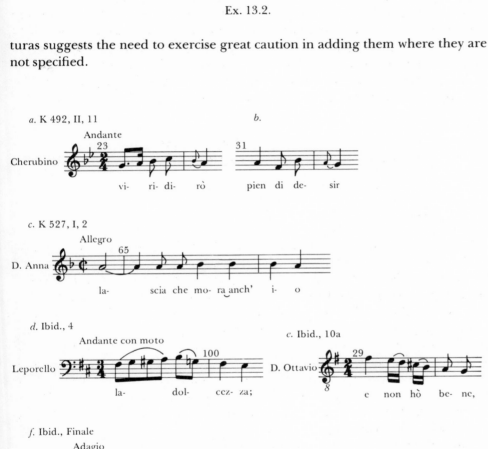

Ex. 13.3.

Ex. 13.3 cont.

Intriguing is Don Giovanni's Canzonetta. At the beginning of the song, given in Ex. 13.4a, we have pitch repetition on *finestra*. Steglich holds that the word must have an appoggiatura.[2] Yet if we add one, we lose the wonderful gradation from the neutral word *finestra* (window) over *consolar,* with a symbolized appoggiatura of circa 8th-note length (Ex. *b*), to the written-out appoggiatura of a quarter-note on *dolce* (Ex. *c*), referring to a mouth sweeter than honey. *Finestra* does not call for an affective emphasis and is better sung as written.

Ex. 13.4.

Example 13.5 shows a few characteristic cases where the addition of a falling appoggiatura was probably intended. In Don Giovanni's remarkable, perhaps intentional anticipation of the Canzonetta (Ex. *a*), the flattery of *bella* calls for an appoggiatura (as suggested by the *NMA*). In *b*, Donna Elvira's emotional state justifies the appoggiatura (as in the *NMA*); so does Donna Anna's affect-laden word *pena* in Ex. *c*. The Countess's depth of feeling poured into the recurring word *tesoro* (Ex. *d*) needs the intensification of an appoggiatura every time the word appears (in mm. 30, 40, 47). In m. 30 the *NMA*'s suggestion of an appoggiatura from below (Ex. *e*) is musically defensible as being prepared and rising a half-tone, but one from above would seem to be preferable.

[2]"Auszierungswesen," p. 214.

a. K 527, II, 15

b. Ibid., I, 3

c. Ibid., II, 19

d. K 492, II, 10

e.

Ex. 13.5.

As in recitative, we have reasons to assume that the added appoggiaturas in arias were predominantly from above, not from below. First, Mozart wrote out those from below with a frequency that suggests a greater care in specifying them than he exercised for the descending one, for which the element of expression was powerfully supported by the strong pull of diction. Second, the rising appoggiatura has a much stronger expressive coloring and is therefore less likely to have been left by the mature Mozart to the discretion of the singers whom he kept on a shorter leash than did his Italian contemporaries. Third, in view of the strong musical flavor of the rising appoggiatura, its insertion involves deeper inroads into the musical fabric and for that reason it should not be lightly used. Fourth, it is unnecessary: I have yet to find a single instance where an appoggiatura seems fitting that a descending one did not fully take care of the musical need with less obtrusiveness. Nor have I found a single instance where a rising appoggiatura, not marked for the voice, is marked for a shadowing instrument, whereas, as will presently be shown, such instances do occur for the descending one. For these combined reasons modern editors, conductors, and singers will be well advised to exercise extreme reserve in applying the rising type.

Example 13.6 offers a brief sampling of written-out rising appoggiaturas: Ex. *a* from *Don Giovanni* (see also mm. 54, 55, 56, 57); *b* from *Così fan tutte; c* from *Figaro; d* and *e* from *Die Zauberflöte*. See also the illustrations shown in Ex. 2.17.

Ex. 13.6.

Occasionally the accompaniment can offer guidance as to the desirability and design of an appoggiatura. In Ex. 13.7 from *Così fan tutte* the unison violin part is a cue for an appoggiatura on *fede*.

Ex. 13.7.

Often such unison or octave doubling gives an indication of how a symbol-indicated appoggiatura, particularly on masculine endings, was meant to be sung. Two such spots from *Don Giovanni* are shown in Ex. 13.8.

Ex. 13.8.

In other instances, the clue given by the accompaniment can be deceptive: first because vocal parts are often simpler in melody and rhythm than the more agile attending instruments; second, because the singer had to be given greater leeway with regard to ornaments.

In Ex. 13.9 the adjustment of Figaro's part to the violin appoggiatura, as suggested by the *NMA,* is unnecessary and probably a misunderstanding. Two octaves apart there is no disturbing friction to speak of; as mentioned before, Figaro's part is written throughout in a straightforward style with a minimum of melismas (in contrast to the sophistication of the Count). After all, Figaro does not match the violins in articulation and trill on *notte ti* nor on the phrase ending on *chiama.* The quarter-note on *madama* will best be sung as written.

Ex. 13.9.

A striking illustration of the danger in reading too much into the orchestral parts was shown in Ex. 2.14 from *Così fan tutte* where reasons were given why the two voice parts ought to be sung as written and not be assimilated to the orchestra's downward leaping appoggiaturas.

For masculine endings Mozart often writes appoggiaturas with little notes (as in Ex. 13.8). We see in Ex. 13.10*a* two symbolized masculine, and one spelled-out feminine, appoggiaturas, in *b* another masculine one. The many written-out or symbolized masculine appoggiaturas should, as was the case with the feminine ones, suggest great reserve about adding them when not indicated.

Whereas in Ex. 13.11*a* from *Idomeneo* the appoggiatura suggested by the *NMA* is justified by the affective word, in Ex. *b* from *Die Zauberflöte* such addition is possible but not necessary. And whenever there is room for doubt, especially in late works, it seems wiser to abstain.

a. K 620, II, 17

b. Ibid., I, Finale

Ex. 13.10.

a. K 366, III, sc. 2   b. K 620, I, 4

Ex. 13.11.

In Ex. 13.12 the rising appoggiatura on *istante*, as suggested by the *NMA,* seems inappropriate, and even one from above seems uncalled for. The word is neutral and the appoggiatura would upstage the written-out one on *amante* and the symbolized masculine one on *parlar* (which might well be taken as an approximate 8th-note, rather than the suggested quarter-note, since the latter would give disproportionate emphasis to this word).

K 527, I, 2

Ex. 13.12.

Though there is no need for exact coordination of the voice with the accompaniment, and though a vocal appoggiatura can on occasion effectively clash with an instrument, there is a line beyond which the clashes become unreasonable and provide a cue for abstention. Roughly, a clash with a unison or quasi-unison instrumental part can be pleasing, or at least acceptable, when the vocal appoggiatura resolves to the unison before the instrument has moved. For this reason, in Ex. 13.13a from *Figaro* an appoggiatura on *so-spi-ro* would be possible; in Ex. *b* the clash with the appoggiatura on *pene* (suggested by the *NMA*) is less welcome, since the violins have moved on; more disturbing still are the clashes in *c* and *d* with the unjustified rising appoggiaturas. Granted, the friction passes quickly, but the point is that here the violins nestle tenderly around the words, and nothing is gained by disturbing this intimate interplay.

a. K 492, III, 17

b. K 527, I, 2   *c.*

d.

Ex. 13.13.

In Ex. 13.14*a* from the bass aria "Aspri rimorsi atroci" the word *atroci* does not invite a softening appoggiatura, and besides, its metrical accent is underlined by the *fp* entrance of the full orchestra on an F minor chord. The clash of the appoggiatura, as suggested by the *NMA,* would detract from the dramatic effect of the sudden orchestral punctuation. The same holds for the clash in Ex. *b* of a suggested appoggiatura after the thematic scalewise descent along with flute and oboe to the *fp* E. In a passage from the very young Mozart from *Betulia liberata,* given in Ex. *c,* the appoggiatura proposed by the *NMA* would produce an unpleasant sequence of parallel seconds.

Generally, caution about adding appoggiaturas should intensify in ensembles, since such additions are eminently individual. This applies to two voices and even more so to three and more. Thus in Ex. 13.15*a* from *Idomeneo,* Mozart carefully wrote out the appoggiaturas for two voices on *irato,* and when, two measures later, he has a pitch repetition for three voices on *divide* he almost certainly intended it to be taken literally, without the complicated combination of falling and rising appoggiaturas suggested by the *NMA.* See also the parallel spot in mm. 96ff. where the corresponding appoggiatura is again written out for two voices, and followed by the phrase with the pitch repetition repeated three times in a breathtaking rising sequence.

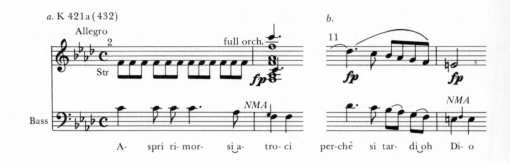

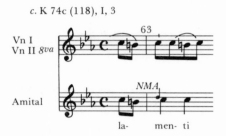

Ex. 13.14.

Ex. 13.15.

The severity of the words *atroci* in Ex. 13.14*a* or *spada* in Ex. 2.14 are only two samples out of a multitude illustrating Mancini's previously cited principle that words expressing violent emotions, invective, or by extension, determination, strong injunctions, and the like must not be softened by an appoggiatura. A few further examples will illustrate this important point.

After recognizing Don Giovanni as the killer of her father, Donna Anna enjoins Don Ottavio to avenge her in the majestic aria "Or sai chi l'onore." Her imperious tone must not be softened by appoggiaturas, not even on the repeat of her injunction in m. 101 where the *NMA* makes the suggestions indicated in the small notes of Ex. 13.16*a*. Literally repeating the powerful pitch repetitions reinforces the power of the summons by its sense of insistence. The proposed variant is anticlimactic.

The Queen of the Night's curse and invocation of the gods of revenge pack greater force when sung without the appoggiatura of the *NMA*, shown in Ex. *b*. Fiordiligi's proclamation of rocklike steadfastness (Ex. *c*) would be weakened by the intrusion of an appoggiatura. A similar mood of determination on the part of Donna Elvira is more suggestively rendered by respecting the pitches on *l'empio* and *scempio* (Ex. *d*) than by evading them through appoggiaturas as proposed by the *NMA*.

Similarly in Ex. *e* from *Zaide* there is no reason for the 8th-note resolving appoggiaturas of the *NMA*. They blunt Gomatz's defiance of fate which is made more convincing by the threefold insistent tone repetition.

a. K 527, I, 10

b. K 620, II, 14

c. K 588, I, 14

d. K 527, I, 3

e. K 336b (344) I, 4

Ex. 13.16.

Donna Anna's invocation of death in Ex. 13.17*a* is more gripping without the suggested appoggiaturas. Don Ottavio is more credible as a messenger of death and destruction with the stern pitch repetitions on *torti* and *morti* in Ex. *b* against the martial rhythms in the orchestra. In a less heroic vein, the Countess's fidelity is well mirrored in the pitch repetition on *costanza* in Ex. *c*.

a. K 527, II, 19

b. Ibid., 22

c. 492, II, 19

Ex. 13.17.

SUMMING UP, it is well to remember the thought of Plath and Rehm that inserted appoggiaturas should play only a minor role in closed numbers, where Mozart is much more specific in indicating them than in recitative. Yet many editors and writers seem to abhor pitch repetition and are overzealous in their crusade to eliminate it. If this fashion continues to spread it will not be long before we hear Leporello inserting appoggiaturas in his catalogue figures of Ex. 13.18a, and Basilio inserting them in his hypocritical apologies of Ex. b, where the pitch repetition is confirmed by the accompanying strings.

a. K 527, I, 4

b. K 492, I, 7

Ex. 13.18.

Appoggiaturas in closed numbers are necessary where a feeling of warmth, longing, tenderness, or similar emotions will spontaneously summon them, or where in songful passages the logic of melodic continuity suggests their insertion. The need for them will practically always be fulfilled by the stepwise descending type. Because of the stronger flavor of the ascending one and its correspondingly stronger musical repercussions, the probability is great that Mozart did not leave them to the singers' discretion but marked all those he wanted sung. Here, too, as in recitative, they are never needed, and here, too, it will be best to defer to the descending type.

As in recitative, appoggiaturas are improper for any words, emotions, or thoughts that are better represented by angularity than roundness: heroism, imperiousness, terror, defiance, steadfastness, and the like.

As was to be expected, we meet again with a gray area of ambiguity, but where there is room for reasonable doubt it will generally be advisable to opt for restraint.

Vocal Cadenzas
(Fermata Embellishments)

The need for vocal cadenzas is thoroughly documented. We have part-autograph specimens that Mozart wrote in Mannheim for arias by J.C. Bach of which three samples are given in Ex. 14.1.

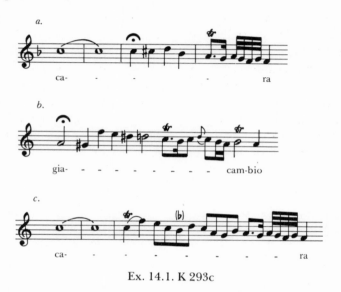

Ex. 14.1. K 293c

More important, we have autograph fermata embellishments separately written for the Rondo "L'amerò" from *Il rè pastore,* shown in Ex. 14.2.

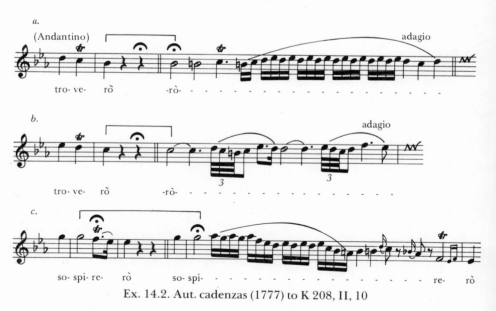

Ex. 14.2. Aut. cadenzas (1777) to K 208, II, 10

Furthermore, for the revival of *Figaro* in 1789, Mozart wrote a brilliant aria for Adriana Ferrarese del Bene who was the new Susanna and who apparently found "Deh vieni" not challenging enough. An autograph fermata embellishment for that aria has been preserved and is shown in Ex. 14.3.

cen- to

Ex. 14.3. Aut. cadenza to K 577

Mozart's letters provide further evidence. From Munich, where he prepared the performance of *Idomeneo,* he writes his father on November 15, 1780: "But to my molto amato castrato Dal Prato I shall have to teach the whole opera. He has no notion how to sing a cadenza effectively . . .!" (E. Anderson's translation).

Once in a while Mozart writes out the embellishment, either when he may have had reason to mistrust the singer, as perhaps in Ex. 14.4*a* from Don Ottavio's "Dalla sua pace" (written for the Vienna performance) and Ex. *b* from *Zaide*; or when he may have wished to limit the embellishment to a small figure, as in Ex. *c* from *Così fan tutte*.

a. K 527, I, 10a

b. K 336b (344)/3

c. K 588, I, 2

Ex. 14.4.

The vocal cadenzas have two distinct functions. One is to extend a phrase ending that is followed by a rest. The other both extends the held note and as an *Eingang,* prepares the next phrase. Specimens of the first kind (referred to in the following interchangeably as "end" or "terminal" embellishment) can be seen in Exx. 14.2*c* and 14.3; those of the connective type in Exx. 14.2*a* and *b* and 14.4*a, b,* and *c*.

The main problems that concern us here are obviously when and how to embellish. The second problem, the *how*, is at least theoretically the easier one and I shall address it first.

The principle of the previously cited theorists Agricola, Mancini, and Arteaga, that vocal cadenzas should not exceed the extent of one breath, is fully confirmed by the above examples of Mozart's own specimens. Cadenzas can be shorter, as we have seen in the scored Ex. 14.4, but they must not be longer. Furthermore, the ornament should fit the character of the piece and if possible that of the specific passage in which it occurs; one should also consider the words and the dramatic situation.

The question of *when* to ornament is even hard to decide theoretically. The answer is fairly clear-cut only for fermatas at the end of an aria where a cadenza was generally required. Such cadenzas had become a fixture of the opera seria, but Mozart used them last in *Idomeneo*. After that, that is, after 1781, he did not use them in any of his operas, not even in *Tito*. Hence for the great operas and arias of Mozart's last decade the problem focuses on fermatas in mid-aria.

For this problem we have to evaluate in each instance whether the context seems to admit or demand an embellishment. This effort will involve considering whether a grand pause in the case of a terminal fermata, or an abrupt transition in the case of a transitional one, is unjustified musically, dramatically, or textually.

At the other pole are fermatas that ought not to be ornamented, when stopping the pulse on a note or a rest does have dramatic meaning. In between is the unavoidable area where a decision either way could be justified.

Where autographs are extant, Mozart often gives us an important graphic clue in the way he notates the fermata symbol. When it contains a wide arc that covers more than a single note or single rest, it could conceivably have the meaning of a ritenuto, yet there are many cases where such a wide arc is more suggestive of an embellishment. In the spot shown in Ex. 14.5a from the second-act duet of Guglielmo and Dorabella Mozart at first wrote only small fermatas over the quarter-note for both voice parts, then for Dorabella replaced the small arc with a large one reaching over two of the following 8th-note rests. Had he wanted a simple fermata, the change of notation would have been superfluous since a ritenuto involving the following rests makes no sense. The only rational explanation for the correction is a desire to suggest an embellishment, certainly for Dorabella, but probably for both singers, since in the previous 10 measures, as well as in the eight to follow, the two voices move in close linkage of thirds and sixths. A suggestion is offered in Ex. *b*. (On this occasion I want to emphasize that all my performance suggestions for cadenzas and related ornaments aim to show form rather than content: to indicate the approximate length and character of the embellishment in the hope that others with more inventive talent will improve on their musical substance.)

An analogous case occurs in the first-act duet of Fiordiligi and Dorabella where Mozart, as shown in Ex. *c*, replaced a small fermata symbol he had written for Fiordiligi slightly to the right of the quarter-note with a large symbol, spanning the whole measure. Here again, the original notation would have fully expressed the wish for a hold on the note alone or even for the whole measure; hence Mozart's notational change can best be explained by his wish for an embellishment. The latter should be shared by both singers, perhaps in the manner intimated in Ex. *d*.

Mozart used the extended symbol from his earliest years. Though it could be read, as pointed out before, as a ritenuto spanning two or more beats, it should

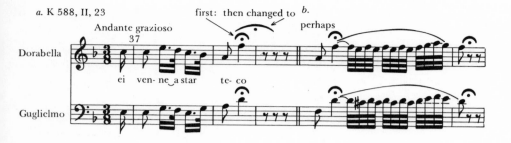

a. K 588, II, 23

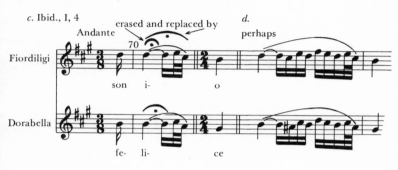

Ex. 14.5.

always alert us to the possibility of a desired embellishment. The decision between these alternatives will depend on the musical situation. Interesting and problematic in this respect is Fiordiligi's aria "Come scoglio" where Mozart wrote in its first two sections no less than seven such broad fermatas. In spite of this unusual density of occurrence it is likely that some embellishment is called for in each case, not the least because the part was written for Ferrarese del Bene who, as mentioned earlier in this chapter, prevailed upon Mozart to replace Susanna's "Deh vieni" with a dazzling virtuoso aria (completely out of character for Susanna). Though Mozart did not esteem her artistry highly, he may have deferred, once again, to a singer's wishes. She apparently was not only eager to display the enormous range of her voice, but also desired occasions to show off her proficiency in singing cadenzas. In view of this circumstance and in view of Mozart's clearly purposive use of the broadly written fermata, it will be advisable to consider some embellishment for the seven cases shown in Exx. 14.6a-d, perhaps in the manner suggested in each case following the original notation. It is probable that an eighth case, that of m. 64, should be similarly treated, since Mozart wrote fermatas over the rest of the orchestra and may have omitted a corresponding symbol for the voice.

For Exx. a, b, and d, the case for embellishment is strong. In a and b a simple broadening intent would have been more simply and clearly indicated by small fermatas on the respective downbeats. Example d is a cadential fermata that is prepared in the orchestra by a crescendo leading to an *sfp* on the downbeat. The sense of expectation thus engendered would be disappointed by the plain unadorned figure, when the words *nell'amor* alone are conducive to embellishment.

I realize that for the two first fermatas of Ex. *c* one could argue that the words *come scoglio immoto resta* (to remain immovable as a rock) favor the stark simplicity of the unadorned notes written under the fermata, sung quasi andante, in sharp contrast to the excited orchestral figures that precede and follow. But because the contrast is strong enough when sung in time, its ritenuto broadening, which would break the tension, is dramatically unwarranted. For that reason embellishment rather than a ritenuto interpretation of these wide fermatas seems indicated.

Ex. 14.6.

In the duet with Dorabella we find for Fiordiligi another specimen of a broad fermata, given in Ex. 14.7*a*, where the suggestion of an embellishment is strengthened by Mozart's directive *a piacere* in the preceding measure. This term, calling for improvisatory freedom, is clearly meant to inform the whole phrase and is therefore more suggestive of a small cadenza than of a simple ritenuto broadening. Example *b* offers a suggestion.

In Despina's aria "In uomini, in soldati" a traditional one-note fermata in m. 19

on *fedeltà* (Ex. *c*) could have, but does not need, a brief embellishment. By contrast, the broad fermata in m. 56 (Ex. *d*) does call for a small cadenza, possibly as sketched in Ex. *e*.

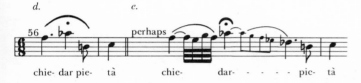

Ex. 14.7.

Although a broad fermata is often a cue for a desired cadenza, a narrow, traditional symbol by no means implies abstention from embellishment, as will presently be shown in several examples. But I would venture the suggestion that the graphic design affects the burden of proof. For a broad fermata one should give reasons why *not* to embellish, for a narrow one reasons why an embellishment is desirable.

In Don Ferrando's aria "Un aura amorosa" the first, small fermata in m. 41 (Ex. 14.8*a*) does call for a connective embellishment to lead into the repeat of the opening theme. Example *b* offers a suggestion. The second fermata on *porge-rà* in m. 67 of Ex. *c* should remain unadorned, since it is followed two measures later by a broad fermata on *ristoro,* a clue for embellishment that is strengthened by a crescendo and decrescendo in the woodwinds: against this background a simple ritenuto on the descending triad would sound unconvincingly thin. A solution is suggested in Ex. *d*. No embellishment is needed for the fermata at the end of the phrase.

In Ex. *e* from Dorabella's aria "Smanie implacabile" there must be no cadenza in m. 89. Not only is the note following the fermata its logical continuation, picking up its thread, as it were, but a cadenza would break up the relentless drive of the impassioned aria and break, too, the dramatic tension created by the sudden interruption, for the four mm. 90–93, of the agitated violin figures that pervade the rest of the piece.

Often the answer about the *when* is in doubt. In Despina's second aria, "Una donna a quindici anni," I would suggest a *yes* for mm. 36 and 66, a *no* for m. 51, a *perhaps* for m. 79. The fermatas in mm. 36 and 66 are in parallel spots where a short cadenza for the first, a longer one for the second occurrence seems

a. K 588, I, 17

b.

c.

d.

e. Ibid., 11

Ex. 14.8.

indicated, as suggested in Exx. 14.9a and b. For the fermata of Ex. c all that seems desirable is a subtle ritardando on the three preceding 8th-notes. In Ex. d, on the downward leap of a seventh a small embellishment as shown in Ex. e is possible, but not necessary, and perhaps not even welcome in view of the mock-imperious tone of the downward octave leaps on *voglio* and *passo* in the two preceding measures.

So far the examples in this chapter have been taken from *Così fan tutte* which at the time of writing had not yet come out in the *NMA*. In the following I discuss cadenzas in other works with reference to the suggestions made by its various editors.

It is one of the many great merits of the *NMA* to have brought the requirement of vocal cadenzas to the attention of conductors, singers, and teachers. As was to be expected, its various editors have different opinions about where to apply embellishments and how to design them. As to their placement, there is hardly a case of an undesirable location, though there are a number of instances where a cadenza was passed over that I would consider desirable.

In a rough evaluation of the *NMA* volumes that have so far appeared, I would rank Luigi Ferdinand Tagliavini and Walter Giegling high in placement, design, and the musicality of their suggested embellishments (though Tagliavini's are sometimes perhaps a little long).

Stefan Kunze, the editor of the four volumes of arias, has longer cadenzas in the first two volumes from the young Mozart than in the third and fourth from his full maturity. Though the distinction makes sense and the cadenzas are all very

a. K 588, II, 19

sa- per men- ti- re, e qual re- gi- na men- ti - - - - re

b.

sa- per men- ti- re, e qual re- gi- na men- ti - - - - re

c.

vi- va De- spi- na che sa ser- vir, che sa ser- vir

d.   *e.*

col pos-so e vo- glio, col pos- so e vo- glio   e vo- glio

Ex. 14.9.

musical, a few are too long even for the boy Mozart: for example, those in "Misero pargoletto," K 73e (77), m. 66; "Sol nascente," K 61c (70), m. 113; "Fra cento affanni," K 73c (88), m. 137. Even though it is a final one, the cadenza for "Il cor dolente," K 295 of 1778, still seems too long; it resorts to word repetition and far exceeds a single breath. In the aria "Sperai vicino," K 368, a very long final cadenza may find some justification in the bravura character of the piece with its unusually long and brilliant virtuoso passages. In volumes 3 and 4, covering the years 1782–1791, there are a number of very fine brief cadenzas and *Eingänge,* and here Kunze may have occasionally shown too much restraint in leaving some spots unembellished where a brief cadenza seems indicated, for instance in "Vado, ma dove?," K 583, mm. 7 and 22; in "Resta, o cara," K 528, m. 38 for the broad fermata on *cara;* in "Alma grande e nobil core," K 578, m. 85 on *sono,* with its preceding directive *a piacere.*

Daniel Heartz suggests in *Idomeneo* a number of fermata embellishments that are too long, even considering that some are final cadenzas in the obsolescent tradition of the opera seria. On the other hand he fails to suggest ornaments that would seem to be proper. In Act I, Idamente's aria "Non ho colpa" should probably have *brief* embellishments in mm. 46, 48, 56, 119, and 143, whereas the proposed final cadenza in that aria is disproportionately long with its requirement of several breaths.

That some singers of the time may have sung such long cadenzas is likely, but irrelevant, since we have no reason to assume that Mozart wanted such extensive fantasies, and good reason to assume that he preferred moderation. The one-breath type is generally sufficient to fill in where he left a musical cue. The longer the non-Mozartian implants, the more they are likely to contrast unfavorably with the genuine material. In fact one of the more difficult tasks in inventing embellishments is to find the proper mean between too much and too little.

Ludwig Finscher in *Figaro* has a few very fine cadenzas of just the right length and character, among them two brief ones for Figaro's "Non più andrai." Wisely, he has no cadenzas for Cherubino's "Non so più cosa son." In the final section of that aria, shown in Ex. 14.10, the many fermatas, sudden starts and stops, tempo changes, and sharp dynamic contrasts picture with uncanny psychological acuity the emotional turmoil of awakening sexuality. The fermatas ought therefore to be left alone lest their dramatic effect be impaired. They are, incidentally, all of the small type, with the possible exception of the very last one (the second in m. 98), which might, no doubt by inadvertence, cover the quarter-note along with the rest. For the unison violins, Mozart wrote the (small) fermata above the rest only, which is more logical. A cadenza here would disturb the musical line from Bb-Bb-C-D-Eb-F and obliterate the dramatic effect of the sudden forte in the last measure after the sudden piano in the preceding one.

Ex. 14.10.

If Finscher had excellent reasons for his abstinence from cadenzas in this aria, there are one or two cases where a similar reserve seems less justified. In the Countess's aria "Dove sono" (Ex. 14.11*a*) there ought to be a transitional embellishment on *trapassò* in m. 61. Alternative suggestions are given in Ex. *b*.

a. K 492, III, 19

Andantino

Contessa

non tra- pas- sò? Do- ve so- no trapas-sò- - - - - Do-ve

b.

perhaps

or at least

-sò- - - Do-

Ex. 14.11.

In Susanna's "Deh vieni" a small end embellishment seems proper on *coronar* in m. 70, as shown in Ex. 14.12*a*. In m. 62 the fermata on *vieni* is a borderline case: a small transitional embellishment, perhaps of the kind sketched in Ex. *b*, is possible, but would not be missed.

a. K 492, IV, 27

[Andante]

Susanna

in co- ro- nar di ro- se coro-nar- - - - -

perhaps

b.

perhaps

vie- ni! ti vò la fron- te vie- ni!- - - ti

Ex. 14.12.

Wolfgang Plath and Wolfgang Rehm's embellishments for *Don Giovanni* are always in impeccable taste but seem to be overly cautious. These two eminent editors leave out some embellishments that were probably intended, and those they do suggest are invariably very sparse. In several cases their shortness is adequate, for instance in Leporello's "Notte e giorno faticar" in m. 19 on *mal dormir* and in mm. 43–44 on *sentinella;* or in Donna Anna's second-act aria, "Non mi dir," m. 48 on *moro.*

Other spots, however, seem to call for a more characteristic embellishment, and in the following I list some samples that I consider too perfunctory.

In Ex. 14.13*a* from the duet "Fuggi, crudele, fuggi!," Donna Anna's impassioned plea to Don Ottavio, *Giura!,* calls for a formula of greater urgency than those offered as alternative solutions in the *NMA* (Ex. *b*). Something on the order of Ex. *c* is probably more fitting.

At the end of Donna Elvira's aria "Ah chi mi dice mai" Don Giovanni's seductive interjections at the sight of a distressed lady end in the broad fermata of Ex. *d*. The *NMA* suggestion of Ex. *e* could be somewhat extended, perhaps in the manner of *f*.

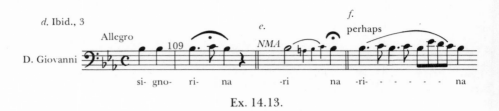

Ex. 14.13.

In Leporello's "Madamina" of Ex. 14.14*a*, the *NMA* has for the climax of the catalogue—*mà in Ispagna*—the discreet embellishment of Ex. *b*; an ironic trill-like hum (Ex. *c*) might be considered here instead. For the fermata on *maestoso* in the same aria, shown in Ex. *d*, the *NMA* suggests the embellishment of *e*. Yet perhaps Leporello's histrionics could use a touch of swagger, as intimated in Ex. *f*.

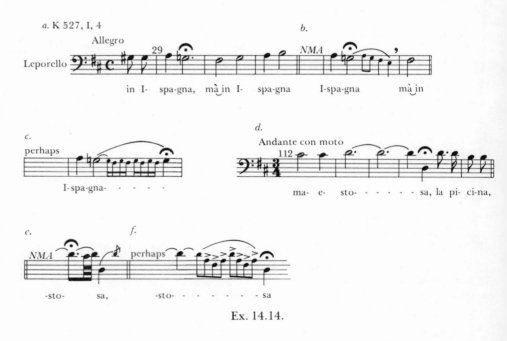

Ex. 14.14.

Donna Anna in her aria "Or sai chi l'onore" imperiously enjoins Don Ottavio to avenge her. Her feverish emotion would seem to call for a stronger outlet for the words *d'un giusto furor* set under a broad fermata (Ex. 14.15*a*), than that provided by the *NMA* in Ex. *b*. Perhaps formulas like those of Ex. *c* or *d* might serve here.

For contrasting emotions, consider Zerlina's coquettish pleading in her aria "Batti, batti." Here, too, a stronger release on *hai core* (Ex. 14.16*a*) than that granted in *b* should be possible. A design in the vein of Ex. *c* might be considered. In Zerlina's second aria, "Vedrai carino" (Ex. *d*), the *NMA* suggestion for the fermata on *stà* might perhaps be slightly expanded, as shown in Ex. *f*.

Ex. 14.15.

Ex. 14.16.

For the end of the heroic section of Don Ottavio's "Il mio tesoro" (Ex. 14.17a) a more virtuoso cadenza than the one given in Ex. *b* seems fitting. Examples *c* and *d* offer a suggestion.

In Donna Anna's aria "Non mi dir" there is a spot at the end of the slow section (Ex. *e*) where the broad fermata strongly suggests the wish for a cadenza, since the intent to prolong the long C could have been more clearly marked by a small symbol over the dotted 8th-note alone. The *NMA* offers no suggestion here; one possibility is sketched in Ex. *f*.

In Mozart's German operas the need for cadenzas occurs much less frequently, but from time to time we find spots that call for them. A few such spots from *Die Entführung* are shown in Ex. 14.18.

In Belmonte's aria "O wie ängstlich" (Ex. *a*) a transitional embellishment is needed; and a suggestion is made in Ex. *b*. Similarly, a transition to the repeat of the opening phrase is indicated in his aria "Wenn der Freuden Tränen fliessen" (Ex. *c*), with a suggestion in Ex. *d*. Later, in m. 46 (Ex. *e*) an end embellishment connecting the two fermatas is advisable, as sketched in Ex. *f*.

In *Die Zauberflöte* Mozart at first wrote out, then rejected, a cadenza for the three ladies in the first scene. Elsewhere there is hardly a spot that genuinely requires added embellishment. Conceivable candidates are the two fermatas in Papageno's

a. K 527, II, 21

c. perhaps   *d.*

e. Ibid., II, 23

Ex. 14.17.

aria "Ein Mädchen oder Weibchen" in m. 35. In view, however, of Papageno's childlike naiveté a cadenza can either be omitted or, to stay in character, should be extremely simple, perhaps like the one shown in Ex. *g.*

a. K 384, I, 4

c. Ibid., II, 15

e.

g. K 620, II, 20

Ex. 14.18.

To SUMMARIZE, vocal fermatas often require a measure of embellishment. The need for such embellishments is truly one of the "forgotten matters of course," and it will take a while to recondition performers and audiences to their appropriateness, indeed their necessity.

There are two basic kinds of such embellishments: those that occur at or near the end of a phrase, extending it and characteristically ending in a rest (terminal or end embellishments) and those that combine an extension of the preceding phrase with the preparation of the next one (transitional embellishments).

Where such embellishment is necessary, where acceptable, where undesirable, is largely a matter of musical-dramatic judgment, though the following circumstances need to be considered. An embellishment is undesirable when the rest following the fermata has dramatic meaning; it is required when it occurs at the end of an aria, but after *Idomeneo* Mozart discarded this opera seria tradition; an embellishment is usually desirable as a transition to the principal theme in ABA or rondo form; a terminal cadenza is often desirable when the words climaxed by the fermata appear to reach for a more expansive musical treatment than the naked text provides and the place can be identified as one of the "white spots" that Mozart left to the singer to fill with needed color.

An external clue is Mozart's "comprehensive" symbol of a broadly drawn fermata that covers more than one note or rest. It is almost always found in spots that favor the introduction of a cadenza. Unfortunately, so far only the *NMA* has been reasonably consistent in reproducing this important graphic variant. Sometimes the configuration of a passage kept Mozart from using this extended sign in which case the need for a cadenza has to be judged on the merits of the situation.

The cadenza, whether terminal or transitional, should be short, not exceeding one breath; preferably it should not repeat words and it definitely should not introduce new ones; and it should be in character. Too short is better than too long, and where there is reasonable doubt whether a fermata calls for an embellishment, it is better either to forgo it or to make it inconspicuous.

15   Diminutions in Arias

The need for fermata embellishments is uncontested. More difficult is the question of ornaments in the main body of an aria. In his youth, Mozart was still influenced by older vocal practices inherited from the late baroque where incomplete notation in slow arias gave ornamental leeway to the singer and where *da capo* arias in particular called for added embellishment on the repeat. Also, as an adolescent and a young man, Mozart could not have asserted himself with famous singers who would have balked at any attempt to keep them on a tight rein. The mature Mozart still tried to please his singers, and to the very end there were probably few, if any, arias he did not write with special regard for the nature of the voice and the abilities of the singer who created the role—hence the changes he made for the Vienna performances of *Idomeneo* and *Don Giovanni* or for the 1789 revival of *Figaro*. In a letter to his father of September 26, 1781, about *Die Entführung* Mozart admits, "I have sacrificed Constanze's aria a little to the flexible throat of Mlle. Cavalieri," but adds significantly, "I have tried to express her feelings as far as an Italian bravura aria will allow it." He is speaking of the first-act aria "Ach, ich liebte" and the virtuoso passages that recur three times on the word *meinem (Schoos)*, each time growing more elaborate. At the time he had not yet composed No. 11, "Martern aller Arten," in which the concessions to Mlle. Cavalieri reach a point where the link to Constanze's feelings seems almost lost. We might find such concessions later in a few concert arias but hardly ever in his late operas. The coloraturas in Donna Anna's last aria may have been intended to please the singer, but as an expression of the hope that heaven will yet take pity on her, they are in no way dramatically incongruous. Neither are the glittering bravura passages of the Queen of the Night out of keeping with the cold, demonic character of the part, though they were written for the voice of his sister-in-law Josepha Hofer. These examples show how Mozart could satisfy his singers while remaining true to his artistic aims.

We must realize that it is one thing for Mozart to write virtuoso passages or whole bravura arias for a singer and another thing altogether to expect or permit the singer to superimpose such passage work on Mozart's text.

As said before, we shall probably find situations in which ornamental additions are legitimate only in the young Mozart, when he was still writing *da capo* arias which vanish from his later works. Here, as Eduard Melkus has justly pointed out, some variants for the *da capo* section are in order, and they do not have to be strictly of ornamental nature.[1] Luckily, Mozart left us fine examples of both a semi–*da capo* aria with ornaments, variants, and cadenzas, and an ornamented version of one at least partially skeletal aria.

The first of these is from the early opera *Lucio Silla*, K 135, of 1772. Its embellishments are preserved in a copyist's hand, tentatively ascribed by Wolfgang Plath to Mozart's sister, in the Mozarteum in Salzburg (which graciously lent me the microfilm). This version was presumably written around 1778 for

---

[1]"Zur Auszierung der Da-capo-Arien in Mozarts Werken," especially p. 165.

Aloysia Weber. Mozart referred to it as an "Arie mit ausgesetztem gusto" that is, with spelled-out variants and embellishments. The aria is in ABA′ form, and the alterations concern only the first and third sections. Example 15.1*a* presents those changes in the first section that are noteworthy, Example *b* gives the complete third section (with the correction, without comment, of obvious scribal errors). In both cases the original is juxtaposed with the emendations.

a.

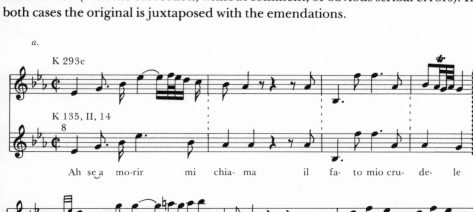

Ex. 15.1. K 135, II, 14 and 293e

II. Improvisation

232

Ah se a mo-rir mi chia-ma il fa- to mio cru- de- le, il

fa- - - - - - - - - - to mio cru- de- le se- gua-ce om- bra fe-

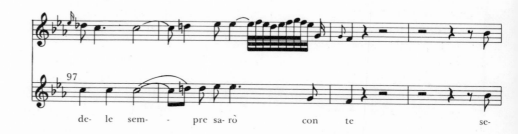

de- le sem- - pre sa- rò con te se-

gua- ce om- bra fe- de- le, om- bra, om- bra fe- del - - se-

gua- ce _____ sem- pre sa- rò con te. sem- - - - -

Ex. 15.1 *cont.*

(b.)

112

- - - - - - - - - - pre sa- rò _____ con te sa-

rò _____ con te

Ex. 15.1 *cont.*

The document has many interesting features. Most arresting are the two cadenzas, one semifinal one in m. 57 at the end of the first section and a final one, in m. 114, possibly the only such authentic specimens extant. Both of these cadenzas, in spite of their location and would-be opera seria traditions, are simple, brief, and of the one-breath variety. They offer powerful support to the arguments made about this point in the preceding chapter.

Viewing the main body of the first and third sections, we find a comparable restraint, with most of the ornaments made up of simple formulas. There are brief melismas of the *circolo mezzo* type in mm. 8, 18, 34, 41, 89, 91; a full *circolo* in m. 106, winding playfully around the E flat; a similar melisma, consisting of turns and scale fragments in m. 21; only the coloratura on the full cadence in m. 112 takes a somewhat freer flight; there are several appoggiaturas whose resolution is occasionally (in mm. 11 and 92) embellished by a trill; in mm. 93 and 101, where the original melody was left intact in the first section, we find genuine melodic variants rather than ornaments. Interesting are rubatolike rhythmic shifts to syncopation in mm. 37, 104, and 105, and interesting too, as a further sign of restraint, is the lack of animation in mm. 102–103 in spite of their skeletal look. All in all, it is a far cry from the lavish decorations so often associated with Italian bravura arias in opera seria.

A perhaps still more important document is the aria "Non sò, d'onde viene," K 294, the only Mozart aria for which autograph embellishments are extant. It is similar in form, consisting of three parts of which the third, though not a *da capo*, uses themes of the first. All the significant additions are shown in Ex. 15.2. The changes are all genuine ornaments that add new pitches; we find no variants, no rhythmic shifts.

The embellishments of the first part were probably written soon after the original aria and are preserved in the Stadtarchiv Braunschweig. The two versions of the first part are superimposed in the *NMA* II/7/2, No. 19. For the third part of the aria the BN has autograph embellishments (Cons. MS 234) that must have been written at a later date (possibly for Aloysia Weber's performance in Vienna in 1783) because they reflect a revision of the aria that has not been preserved.

The *NMA,* in an annex to volume II/7/2, prints a reconstruction of this revision with the embellished version given alone. Since the revision consists basically of a rearrangement, mm. 141–154 having changed places with mm. 131–144, it is possible to present here (see Ex. 15.2) a juxtaposition of the revised original with the embellished parts. (The measure numbers show the concordances after reconstruction of the revised sections.) Mozart wrote the *gusto* specifically for his beloved Aloysia Weber and asked his father not to let anybody else have it. Since Weber was a virtuoso singer whom he desperately wanted to please, the extraordinary restraint we find in the ornamented versions is doubly significant. To give Weber a chance to shine, Mozart had already written out florid passages toward the end of both the first and third sections of the original version, for which additions were neither needed nor made. Intriguing is the absence, in the ornamented version, of fermata embellishments that seem to be called for occasionally (e.g. in m. 45). Whether Mozart entrusted them to Weber's inventiveness or whether he felt that his written-out coloraturas sufficiently animated the simple, warm emotions expressed in the slow parts, is impossible to know.

Here again the ornaments are almost entirely limited to the standard small designs of appoggiaturas, turns, slides, *anticipazioni della nota,* and related graces. Nonstandard embellishments (like those of mm. 19, 23, or 27) are extremely restrained, simply circumscribing the chord. Characteristic of the reserve are mm. 38–42 where the near-monotonous threefold repetition of a simple motive would seem to invite a greater measure of variety than the authentic embellishment provided.

On the whole, the original version, except for the florid endings of both sections, is written in the kind of simple, semiskeletal melodic line that is in need of animation and that is not found in Mozart's later works.

Stephan Kunze with good reason warns us against using this sole example of a Mozart embellishment, written for an aria of his own, as a model for other arias.[2]

These revealing documents of ornamental restraint establish Mozart's aversion to the kind of embellishment excesses that certain Italian singers and instrumentalists indulged in. That these documents stem from Mozart's youthful years adds emphasis to their evidence.

That Mozart's aversion to excess developed at a very young age is apparent in a fascinating report from a letter of Leopold to Wolfgang of December 7, 1780. The father writes of a visit that morning from Herr Esser (a famous violinist), "whom we met in Mainz eighteen years ago and whose playing you criticized by telling him *that he played well, but that he added too many notes and that he ought to play music as it was written.*" The meeting occurred in August 1763 when Mozart was seven years old! He remained true to this aversion throughout his life; we have both musical and literary evidence that in his mature years he strongly opposed willful embroidery by performers.

The musical evidence is the ever greater richness of the spelled-out inflections of his vocal melody. From the *Entführung* on, we look in vain for the kind of austere line that seems to demand ornamental animation.

Papageno's two strophic songs are no exception. They could not be further

[2]Preface to *NMA* II/7/2, p. XIV.

Ex. 15.2. K 294.

Ex. 15.2 *cont.*

Ex. 15.2 *cont.*

na- sce nel pet- to, quel gel- che le — ve — ne scor- ren- do — mi

va, quel gel, che le ve- ne scor- ren- do mi va.

ve- ne scor-

* The B♭ is unmistakable in the autograph. The *NMA* changed it to an A♭, presumably to avoid a clash with the A♭ in the violins that, an octave below, double the unembellished voice part. At the pitch of the voice such a clash may have been harsh, but not in the lower octave. The correction is quite certainly a misunderstanding.

† In this version mm. 141-154 changed places with mm. 131-144.

Ex. 15.2 *cont.*

removed from the Italian manner with their folk-song-like character so fitting for a child of nature. In the second of these, "Ein Mädchen oder Weibchen," variety is achieved by the changing accompaniment of the magic bells, and the written-out variants for the second and third strophes are again remarkably modest. Although the arias of his last great operas are, on musical grounds, never in need of ornamental "enrichment"—except of course for the already discussed fermata embellishments—we also have important witnesses testifying to the same point.

Franz Niemetschek, who was on friendly terms with Mozart and witnessed the Prague performances of *Entführung* and *Figaro*, writes: "He dared to defy the Italian singers and to banish all those unnecessary and pointless garglings, squiggles, and *passaggi*; hence his vocal writing is always simple, natural, forceful, the pure expression of the feeling and the individuality of a person and his situation. The sense of the text is always so justly and precisely captured that one is led to exclaim: 'truly, the music speaks.' "[3] Niemetschek points out that Mozart had to make concessions to the singers: "Wasn't he forced to be obliging to singers if he wished them not to spoil his pieces?"

Ignaz Mosel writes: "One could not offend the sublime [*verklärten*] Mozart more deeply than by adding ornaments to his compositions. Incensed, he always said, 'Had I wanted it, I would have written it.' "[4] This quote is a footnote to a lengthy disquisition on the excessive embellishment of arias which deserves to be cited at least in part:

Considering that arias that are the most masterfully composed, where in other words, the composer observes the most correct declamation and brings

[3]*Leben des k. k. Kapellmeisters Wolfgang Gottlieb Mozart*, pp. 260–262.

[4]*Versuch einer Aesthetik des dramatischen Tonsatzes*, pp. 74–78. Mosel was vice-director of the Vienna Imperial Theaters, then director of the Imperial Library (the present Nationalbibliothek). He was an active composer and arranger, and the author of several treatises on music and musicians.

the feelings expressed therein to the highest degree of truthfulness, suffer the most from such disfigurement . . .; that furthermore most of the embroidery-mad singers, for lack of sufficient knowledge of harmony, introduce pitches in their coloraturas that are at odds with both the original melody line and the orchestral accompaniment . . ., we see this habit . . . in its full incongruousness and its full noxiousness. There is a small number of singers who combine knowledge with taste, elegance with nature, to a degree that permits them to judge with fine discernment and complete assurance where a small ornament (which, however, has to remain within the character of the melody) could enhance the expression, and who are modest enough to rein in their imagination. This small number of singers should be permitted to add here and there, with clever reserve a few notes more than the composer has put down. But since for one such singer there are at least 10 who only repeat a hundred times tasteless routines which ruin all that they believe to embellish, it is always dangerous to stipulate such freedom."

Many singers, he says, indulge in tasteless antics to please the crowd. One should not insult a talented nation, he continues, by referring to these extravagances as "Italian" vocal method since they are rejected by enlightened Italians, as they are by educated Germans and Frenchmen.

It is from such a perspective that we must view certain documents that offer embellishments to arias of *Le nozze di Figaro, Don Giovanni,* and *Die Zauberflöte,* some, as Eva Badura-Skoda writes, tasteless, some acceptable or even good, but none necessary.[5] That none is necessary is the heart of the matter, and in fact they should be strongly discouraged for all operas starting with *Idomeneo,* and all arias after approximately 1780.

It is regrettable that even singers who had been associated with Mozart could not, when freed from his strictures, refrain from playing to the galleries with their coloraturas. Stefan Kunze reports that the bass Ignaz Ludwig Fischer, Mozart's first Osmin, was criticized at least twice in the *Allgemeine Musikalische Zeitung* (1802–1803, col. 174, and 1809–1810, cols. 810ff.) for his added embellishments in *Figaro* and *Die Zauberflöte* (e.g. in Sarastro's "In diesen heil'gen Hallen").[6]

Still more distressing is the thought that early in the 20th century a fabled primadonna recorded both arias of the Queen of the Night and inserted in both extended cadenzas whose grotesqueness is beyond description. The first of these arias has no fermata at all that could conceivably serve as a pretext, and the one fermata in the second aria is over a dramatic pause, hence not of the kind that could be seen as a cue for embellishment.

It is hoped that such abuses have died out. But ironically the present concern with historically correct performance carries new dangers. Some scholars and historically conscious performers are inclined to confuse what was being done in Mozart's time (and shortly thereafter) with what Mozart wished to see done, and it is only the latter that we ought to be concerned about. Since some singers *did* superimpose coloraturas on the written text in Mozart's late operas, such practice might be resurrected under the aegis of "historical authenticity." Therefore it bears repeating emphatically that other than the above-discussed appoggiaturas and (one-breath) fermata embellishments, arbitrary ornamentation should not be added to arias of Mozart's maturity.

[5]*The New Grove,* s.v. "Improvisation, sec. I, no. 3, The Classical Period," vol. 9, p. 47.

[6]Preface to *NMA* II/7/3, p. XVIII.

16

The Special Case of the
Piano Concertos

The special status of the piano concertos has already been mentioned. There are two main aspects to the role of improvisation in these works. One is that because of haste, Mozart's notation was sometimes fragmentary and needs to be completed, the other that Mozart's genius for improvisation occasionally prompted him in a performance to elaborate on a text that was self-sufficient as written. Then we find borderline cases where the question of whether or not a melody is self-sufficient can be decided either way.

Mozart wrote many of his piano concertos for his own use, particularly in the years 1784–1786 when he was the acclaimed favorite of the Viennese public and was able to give a large number of subscription concerts, called "Academies." Some of these concertos were written in a great hurry. Thus the scores of the D minor and C major Concertos K 466 and 467 were not finished until the day before the performance, and as Mozart's father reports to his sister, Mozart had no time to rehearse the Finale of the D minor Concerto because he had to supervise the copying of the parts. The score of the C minor Concerto shows many indications of haste. Even when pressed for time, however, Mozart was always very careful in writing for the orchestra, but he resorted to shorthand notation for the solo part.

We find different types of shorthand devices. One involves virtuoso figurations in fast movements, like the well-known passage from the C minor Concerto, shown in Ex. 16.1, where the intention of continuing a preceding pattern of arpeggiated figurations within the range indicated by the long held notes seems clear.

Ex. 16.1.

A similar passage occurs in the E flat concerto K 482/3, mm. 164-172. For both of these spots we find very good performance suggestions in both the *NMA* edition of these works and in Badura-Skoda (pp. 186-187 and 194-95). Nowhere is the fragmentary nature of concerto notation more obvious than in the *Coronation* concerto, K 537, where, notably in the second movement, the better part of the left hand is missing altogether.

Another problem is that of skeletal notation, where in a slow movement a theme is given only in austere outline that served Mozart as an *aide-mémoire,* to be enriched in performance with ornamental figuration. Such cases, like the previously listed ones, occur almost exclusively in works written for himself. They are very rare in works readied for publication, like K 385p (414), 387a (413), 387b (415), or 595, and in those written for other performers, like K 271, 449, 453, and 456.

For the Concerto in D K 451, written for himself (performed on March 31, 1784), we are fortunate in possessing a document showing an eight-measure phrase in the Andante (mm. 56–63) in skeletal notation with the ornamentation Mozart supplied for the benefit of his sister, the only known document of this type. On June 9, 1784, he writes his father about this concerto: ". . .in the Andante of the Concerto in D there is no question that in the solo in C something needs to be added. I shall send it to her [his sister] as soon as possible along with the cadenza." These eight measures have been published in the sixth edition of Köchel, in Badura-Skoda (p. 178), in the *NMA* edition (V/15/5, p. 208), and in the *New Grove* (s.v. "Improvisation, sec. I, no. 3, The Classical Period"). Because of their importance for this chapter they are shown again in Ex. 16.2.

Ex. 16.2.

From this episode the Badura-Skodas infer with good reason that if Mozart trusted neither his sister, who was an accomplished performer, nor even his father, to prepare the embellishments and the cadenzas, he was hardly likely to leave to others the embellishment of his works.

What is significant about this ornamented passage is the simplicity of the elegant embroidery, which leaves all the key notes of the "skeleton" in place. The octave leap in m. 58, which replaces the original leap of a sixth remains within the chord, and is a probable allusion to the passage of mm. 33–35, shown in Ex. 16.3

Mozart's ornamental reserve, exhibited in this document, condemns implicitly the extravagant embellishments (presently to be sampled) of some of Mozart's contemporaries and students. Also very revealing is the fact that this passage "where something is missing" is followed by another one, shown in Ex. 16.4, not

K 451/2

Ex. 16.3.

quite as skeletal, but still very simple, which Mozart seems to have considered in no need of added embellishments, or else he would have continued with the elaboration.

Ex. 16.4.

Here the woodwinds add some animation and help make the piano melody self-sufficient. This is an important point, overlooked by Carl Reinecke:[1] *We must not compare the piano parts in concertos with solo piano works.* It is more to the point to compare them with piano parts in chamber music, where empty looking passages are filled out by other instruments: see, for example, the phrase of Ex. 16.5 from the G minor Piano Quartet, where lively figuration in the strings supplements the leanness of the piano writing.

Ex. 16.5.

In concertos the eloquence and textural richness of the orchestra will often provide the perfect foil for a piano melody that *by itself* would be too austere to dispense with added embellishments. Take, for example, the passage of Ex. 16.6 from the G major concerto K 458. It looks skeletal, but the ascending staccato figures in the strings give it life, sufficiently so, I believe, to obviate the need or even the desirability of added embellishments. (This passage is discussed again shortly.)

[1]*Zur Wiederbelebung der Mozart'schen Clavier-Concerte,* p. 16. Reinecke postulated the need for embellishing the slow movements and based his claim on the comparison of the solo parts with the piano sonatas.

K 453/2

Ex. 16.6.

By contrast, there are spots where such melodic austerity is set against the background of a static, uneventful orchestral accompaniment. It is then that "something needs to be added." A good illustration is the passage of mm. 44–45, (Ex. 16.7) from the second movement of the D minor Concerto. The "something" may be of the kind shown in the upper staff. Beautiful and noble as the original is, it is unlikely that Mozart would have performed it in its bareness or that he would not have rewritten it had he prepared the work for publication.

K 466/2

Possible execution

Original notation

Ex. 16.7.

The same movement presents a problem of a different kind, also clearly caused by the great haste with which Mozart was forced to complete the score. The Badura-Skodas point out (p. 191) that the principal theme occurs 13 times; that, whereas the orchestral repetitions of the theme show slight variations in orchestration and rhythm, there is not a single ornament in the piano part. The authors refer to the need for careful additions and suggest (p. 192) some tasteful and discreet variants for mm. 119, 125, and 133.

In view of the sketchy nature of the piano part I would further suggest that in mm. 127–130 (Ex. 16.8) the repeat of the melody of mm. 17–20 with its fourfold sequential ascent of the motive (and only small changes in the left hand) might be varied, perhaps as in the upper staff, even though the orchestra takes it up again in its original form, or maybe just because of its imminent fourth repetition.

Embedded in the Finale of the E flat Concerto K 482 is an Andantino cantabile section (mm. 218–264) where a woodwind melody of exquisite tenderness is taken up by the piano. The latter's two separate phrases are given in Ex. 16.9. The piano

Ex. 16.8.

right hand is doubled by the first violins and the left by the cellos and basses. The harmony, filled in by the middle strings, is very simple, the texture thin and somewhat static—an impression increased by the straight doubling of both melody and bass. A modest embellishment would seem to be called for. Paul Badura-Skoda proposes a sensitive and tasteful solution involving an enriched accompaniment.[2] Perhaps the simpler version suggested here in the upper staff would be adequate for the purpose.

What justifies such additions is the previously mentioned fact that we find neither obvious shorthand notation nor numerous literal repetitions in works either prepared for print or written for other performers; in all of these the piano part is fully written out and in no need of any textual revision. One exception is two measures in the B flat Concerto K 595 where the piano has, against a slow moving half cadence in the winds, the notation of Ex. 16.10, which, for the performers of the time, was an obvious cue for a connective passage, made more obvious still by the absence of rests in the right hand. Wolfgang Rehm in the *NMA* sensibly suggests a chromatic scale. The main reason for this shorthand device may have been the enormous pressure under which Mozart labored at the time of the piece's publication by Artaria in August 1791.

If we take a look at the three earlier concertos prepared for publication, we find the Andante in the A major Concerto K 385p (414) well ornamented. Only the first four measures, taken from a symphony by J. C. Bach, who had just died, retain throughout their hymnlike simple dignity. They may have been, as the sixth edition of Köchel suggests, a memorial for the admired friend and mentor of his childhood. (Christoph Wolff disputes this idea in the preface to the *NMA* edition of this concerto, pointing out that Mozart had used this theme before. Yet it may have been that Mozart held the melody in high esteem and reused it on this occasion in the French manner of a *"tombeau."*) In the F major Concerto K 387a (413) the Larghetto theme of mm. 9–15 is ornamented on its return in m. 35. In

---

[2] *Kadenzen, Eingänge und Auszierungen zu Klavierkonzerten von Wolfgang Amadeus Mozart*, pp. 32–33.

K 482/3

Original
notation

Ex. 16.9.

K 595/1

Ex. 16.10.

the Andante of the C major Concerto K 387b (415) the theme, introduced by the orchestra, is ever so slightly enriched in its solo entrance in m. 17, then further gently ornamented on its return in m. 51.

Concerning the concertos destined for other performers, in the one in E flat K 449, written for Barbara Ployer, the slow movement is fully ornamented throughout. The numerous turns and trills alone, not to mention the profusion of 32nd-notes whose blackness hits the eye on first sight, make it clear that Mozart left no room for further embroidery.

The same can be said of the G major Concerto K 453, also written for Ployer. The Badura-Skodas in the preface to the *NMA* volume V/15/5 (p. XIV), consider, with good reason, added embellishments unnecessary for this work. (A borderline case is discussed in Chapter 18.) They make a possible exception for the above-cited mm. 39–40 of the second movement (Ex. 16.6) and give a tentative solution, but add that Girdlestone's statement that "it is nonsense to play those bars as written" notwithstanding,[3] it is perfectly justified to do so. They refer to Mozart's predilection for large leaps in works where embellishment could not conceivably have been intended. They mention the Violin Sonata K 454, the Piano Concerto in A K 488. Other pieces that come to mind are the Andante of the C Major concerto K 467, where the huge leaps of the right over the left hand in mm. 30, 32, 94, and 96 preclude any ornament; the Divertimento in E flat, K 563/2, mm. 30–33 and 97–100; the beginning of the *Haffner* Symphony; Donna Elvira's "Ah chi mi dice mai"; and many, many more.

In the B flat Concerto K 456, written for the blind pianist Maria Theresia Paradis, the slow movement is in variation form. For this reason alone the shape of the theme is constantly changing, and the movement is rich in florid figurations that interweave with the melody.

Mozart gave us an important caveat against excessive embellishment in the B flat Concerto K 450. Its autograph shows an extensive rewriting of the piano part in the Andante, without increasing its floridity. On the contrary, for the mm. 99–100 we see a striking simplification when Mozart changed the version of Ex. 16.11a to that of b.

A difficult issue is that of ornamenting slow movements when neither a patently skeletal character nor the frequent unchanged repetition of a theme points to incomplete notation. Carl Reinecke was the first relatively modern pianist to point out that Mozart in the performance of his piano concertos deviated from the written text and added improvised embellishments. As mentioned before, Reinecke based his theories on a comparison of lean passages in the concertos with florid ones in the solo piano works. The argument, as pointed out, can be

[3]*Mozart and His Piano Concertos*, p. 250, m. 1.

a. K 450/2

b.

Ex. 16.11.

deceptive, and for this reason, Reinecke's performance suggestions are often too ornate.

To give an idea of Reinecke's elaborations, Ex. 16.12 shows two specimens, both from the *Coronation* Concerto, K 537. In Ex. *a* some embellishment is needed, since the theme is literally repeated and set against a static accompaniment with the simplest of harmonies. Reinecke's version on the repeat of the motive is all right, though it could be simpler. But Ex. *b* seems more Chopinesque than Mozartian and is too fussy. Often a subtle touch of change is all that is needed, and I believe something on the order of Ex. *c* for m. 64 would suffice to break the monotony.

Reinecke, writing in the 1890s, deserves great credit for his campaign to revive Mozart's piano concertos, which the 19th century had almost totally neglected—with the exception of the D minor, because it was "Beethovenesque," and the *Coronation* Concerto for reasons less clear. He deserves credit too for having alerted pianists to the occasional need for added embellishments, even if his enthusiasm sometimes carried him beyond the legitimate needs.

Adam Gottron has reported one item of literary evidence for Mozart's habit of embellishing in performance.[4] He writes that Mozart met the brothers Hoffmann—Heinrich Anton, violinist, and Philipp Carl, pianist—on the occasion of his unsuccessful concert in Frankfurt on October 15, 1790, when he played the *Coronation* Concerto, K 537, and the F major Concerto K 459. He then visited them in their parents' home in Mainz, where he went on October 25 to give a concert in the Elector's palace. Mozart played with Heinrich Anton his Violin Sonata in A (probably K 526) and with Philipp Carl a Four-Hand Sonata in F (probably K 497). The Swiss composer and music teacher Xaver Schnyder von Wartensee wrote a biographical article about the two brothers and in it reports that Philipp Carl told him that Mozart did not play the adagios of his piano concertos as simply as they were written but that he embellished them "tenderly and tastefully once one way, once differently following the momentary inspiration of his genius."[5]

It was apparently a very brief acquaintance with Mozart and his playing style that prompted Philipp Carl Hoffmann to publish overloaded embellishments, often of questionable taste, for slow movements of several Mozart concertos, as well as overly massive cadenzas.[6]

---

[4]"Wie spielte Mozart die Adagios seiner Klavierkonzerte?."

[5]In Gustav Schilling, *Enzyklopädie der gesamten musikalischen Wissenschaften*, vol. 3, p. 606.

[6]His embellishments to Mozart's last six concertos, originally published in 1801 and 1802, are available in a modern edition by Hinrichsen (Peters). Those for K 503 are also in the Norton Critical Scores edition.

a. K 537/2

b.

c.

Ex. 16.12.

More regrettable still than Hoffmann's lavishness are the excesses of Hummel which Reinecke castigated for their "banality" and the "empty virtuosic grandiloquence" that "deforms more than ornaments."[7] Hummel, a talented composer, flamboyant piano virtuoso, and Mozart's student, made arrangements of several of his teacher's concertos in which he combined, often quite cleverly, orchestra and solo part in two hands. Unfortunately, he indulged in Lisztian paraphrases which are not even limited to slow movements. For a characteristic illustration see in Ex. 16.13 a few measures (220–227) from the first movement of the C minor Concerto. Example *a* gives Mozart's original (without the purely harmonic string accompaniment), Ex. *b* Hummel's transcription. Mozart would have certainly used the higher register, had it been available on his instrument, but hardly in this particular spot where the piano part is perfectly integrated with the solo flute. Mozart once wrote his father that he was "no friend of difficulties" (meaning virtuosic challenges). Hummel delighted in them, and in using Mozartian material to satisfy these ambitions he sinned against Mozart's spirit.

[7]*Zur Wiederbelebung*, p. 38.

Ex. 16.13.

Ex. 16.13 *cont.*

Distressing, too, is the way in which he corrupts the deeply moving, tender epilogue of the slow movement, converting it into a passage of flashy technical display, as shown by the brief excerpt of Ex. 16.14 (Mozart's melody in Ex. *a*, Hummel's version in *b*). True, the same phrase had been announced four measures earlier, and a case could be made for a slight embellishment on its repeat. Yet, Mozart's subtle change of harmony on the last 8th-note of the first measure might well be all that is needed here. Any embellishment would have to be very modest, maybe on the order of Ex. *c*, but no more. There is a further reason for great reserve. The sovereign calm of the theme in both appearances contrasts with the inner agitation of two and one-half measures of woodwind interchanges that precede the first appearance of the theme and again separate it from its repeat. Any obtrusive embellishment would destroy the spell cast by the juxtaposition of Elysian tranquillity with the flurry of restlessness.

a. K 491/2

b. Hummel

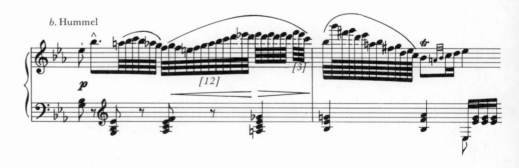

c.

Ex. 16.14.

A serious matter, too, is a version of the embellished Adagio from the Concerto in A K 488. The document is reproduced in the *Kritische Bericht* to *NMA* volume V/15/7. There no attempt is made to assign authorship, but Wolfgang Plath told me that he considers it to have been written by Barbara Ployer and he therefore attaches great importance to it. Although I accept his judgement about the author, the musical content of the document belies any spiritual connection with Mozart.

The Ployer manuscript derived from the estate of Mozart's son and its date is unknown. If it contained the slightest entry from Mozart's pen that would indicate his approval, it would be important. But such is not the case. Worse yet, the embellishments are often tasteless and redundant. Eleven long chromatic scales (in addition to a few shorter ones) and two long diatonic scales create a tedium of repetitiousness when avoidance of repetition is one of the main functions of ornament.

Granted, there are in this movement a few measures that have a skeletal look, say, mm. 80–83, shown in Ex. 16.15*a*, but the look may be deceptive if we consider the interaction with the orchestra. The duet of the left hand with the first bassoon, combined with the striking chromatic harmony provided in these measures by the other woodwinds, would seem to offer enough movement by itself to obviate the need for further animation.

Also, if Mozart had used here a skeletal notation, would he not have written m. 83 as in Ex. *b?* The very intensification provided by the melisma of m. 83 before the cadence would be weakened by anticipating it with similar figuration. If anything is added, it will have to be extremely modest so as not to upstage Mozart's line in m. 83—perhaps something on the order of the few notes suggested in Ex. *c*.

Ex. 16.15.

The Badura-Skodas suggest for these measures two versions (p. 191). The first is in excellent taste, but unnecessarily florid, and it deprives Mozart's figuration in m. 83 of its sense of climax. The second version, with a new voice added, is too complex, especially inasmuch as the harmony is fully provided by the winds, horns, and basses. The authors themselves have reservations about it.

Girdlestone, like Reinecke before him, and of course Ployer, sees the need for embellishment in mm. 85–92 (Ex. 16.16). Girdlestone's suggestion, starting in two-part writing and in siciliano rhythm, almost totally obscures the melody and should be disqualified on that count alone, not to speak of the ensuing erratic rhythmic restlessness.[8] Ployer, as was to be expected, has a long diatonic scale in m. 86, a still longer chromatic one in m. 90.

[8]*Mozart and His Piano Concertos,* p. 383.

The melody as it stands (Ex. 16.16), set against the eerie backdrop of the unison strings moving like fleeting shadows, the lower ones in pizzicato, the violins, arco, in afterbeats, is a gripping utterance of resignation. Only Mozart could have invented ornaments without impairing its indescribable poignancy. The Badura-Skodas agree that with its pathos and earnestness, the phrase should be left undecorated (p. 191).

Ex. 16.16.

In the final eight measures the flute repeats three times the plaintive second theme of the movement, on each repeat enriched, the second time joined by the clarinet, the third time further underscored by the bassoon, while the piano sounds a note of hope, in a brief motive, built on a reiterated staccato pitch, then enchantingly extended, ringing like silvery bells. Nothing should be allowed to interfere with the magic of this peroration. Ployer's stock device of a dashing chromatic scale (Ex. 16.17), wiping out the silver bells as with a wide sweep of a mop, is an abomination.

There is no doubt that Mozart added embellishments to fill out any incomplete notation and that he did so "tenderly and gracefully." It is also possible, indeed

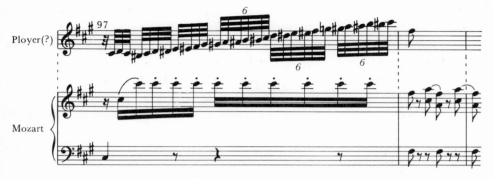

Ex. 16.17.

probable, that when the spirit moved him, his embellishments exceeded what was needed. He had, to his father's sorrow, a playful disposition, and when in a mood to do so must have derived pleasure from his inexhaustible facility at improvising. That does not mean that he wished for others to follow his example, for the simple reason that they would not have been able to do so.

It is possible that such occasional flights of fancy may have served as cues for the excesses of the epigones. There is an inveterate tendency of students and followers of the great to exaggerate when they try to emulate their model. Unable to match the essence, they compensate by overdoing the outer trappings.

The Hoffmanns, Ployers, and Hummels fit the picture painted in the previously quoted passage from Dittersdorf's autobiography (see the introduction to Part II) of the manikins who sail in the wake of the very great, imitate everything like monkeys, and regale us with embellishments so overwrought that they "nauseate instead of delight."

These early documents are all interesting in showing what was being done by some performers of that time. They are also potentially dangerous if they are erroneously taken as descriptive of a genuine Mozartian tradition. Modern performers could see in them a license to take extraordinary freedoms with Mozart's text that far exceed the range of legitimate embellishments.

Frederick Gulda, in his Pearl recording of the C major Concerto K 467, resorts in the slow movement to drastic rhythmic distortions that cannot by any stretch of the imagination be related to either embellishments or artistic rubato. He does the most astonishing things in the first movement as well. In the very first tutti, attempting, I suppose, to realize imaginatively the continuo, he invents a whole new solo and with this legerdemain manages to destroy the whole structure of the movement with its tutti-solo alternations, not to speak of the massive interference with Mozart's musical texture. What he did is at best a gross misunderstanding of the role of Mozart's continuo. Since his is by no means the only case of such misunderstanding, a brief digression is necessary to discuss the controversial question of the continuo part in Mozart's concertos.

In the frame of this study there is no need to go into much detail on this question since for Mozart, particularly in the concertos, the continuo had severed its link with any improvisation worthy of that name and had at best become no more than the transcription of a bass into simple chords for the right hand of the keyboard player.

In the two hundred years of thorough bass from Viadana to Mozart the role of improvisation, presumably large at first, steadily diminished until by the end of the 18th century it was practically nil. We don't know much about the realization of the thorough bass in the monodies and operas of the early baroque, but the likelihood is great that in scores that notated only the melody and the bass, the empty spaces between the two invited improvisatory enrichment by the continuo instruments. With the return of polyphony, independent voices began to occupy the empty space. Now the role of the continuo became secondary and limited to reinforcing the written-out parts and holding the ensemble together. With Bach and his contemporaries, however, we still find next to highly complex textures many arias or instrumental solos written on two staves as of old, for solo and continuo. Though many of these accompaniments were quite simple, as we know from many cases (even in Bach) where the realization is written out, such pieces provided improvisatory opportunities and occasionally necessities, as, for example, when the soloist fell silent and an awkward gap had to be bridged. We also know from treatises and other literary documents that more elaborate realizations were often practiced. In the time of the classical masters the two-staff solo-continuo writing had become obsolete, and whereas the bass lost its continuity and generally also its melodic nature, the middle voices were specified in varying degrees of melodic independence. Empty spaces became the exception rather than the rule. In Mozart's early church music we find occasional spots that are not fully harmonized and obviously count on organ chords. Such spots seem to disappear in his mature sacred works.

In the tuttis of his piano concertos he provided for the doubling of the bass line by the soloist with the indication *col basso.* In the early concertos, up to K 271, the bass is figured (probably by Leopold) in the autographs, but it is not in the later ones where only the *col basso* entry indicates the continuing participation of the piano. Several early editions, but by no means all, also had figures entered for some of the later concertos; some of these editions seemed to provide for the right hand too, mostly by printing the first violin part or another instrument that carries the melody. Obviously such arrangements were meant to serve as a substitute score to permit the soloist-conductor to see approximately what was happening in the orchestra.[9] Surely the pianist did not double the violins or the oboe!

Most important, we have Mozart's autograph realization of the *Lützow* Concerto, K 246. It is now easily accessible in the *NMA* (V/15/2), and we can see that the realization is of extreme simplicity: purely chordal in three or four parts, no frills, not even passing notes, often remaining silent, often *tasto solo.* The document clearly shows that the piano had to stay in the background, simply providing support for the ensemble. In the preface to the *NMA* edition Christoph Wolff tries to downgrade this evidence by saying that Mozart "obviously" wrote the realization for an amateur (p. XIII) and that he himself would have infused a greater dose of improvisation. The argument is not convincing. Suppose it was written for an amateur (which is no more than a guess); this would be only the more reason to write out any richer elaboration that Mozart might have had in mind; and anyone who could handle the solos and the cadenzas would not have been limited to a beginner's technique. We have good reason to take this document at face value as a guide to the piano's usual thorough-bass playing. It is likely that Mozart may have done more at times, when a shaky ensemble called for

[9]For details on the early concerto editions and their treatment of the bass line see Henry G. Mishkin, "Incomplete Notation in Mozart's Piano Concertos," pp. 349–350.

momentarily stronger support, or less when he needed the right hand for conducting or where its intervention was either not fitting or not necessary.

No doubt the soloist participated in the tuttis but the degree to which soloists participated then and should participate now is controversial. Perhaps the most sensible and balanced discussion of the matter is to be found in chapter 9 of Badura-Skoda. The authors give examples where a—purely chordal—realization is desirable, others where the piano will best remain silent, others where it should be limited to doubling the bass line; where chords are played they should be given as bright and slender a sound as possible, and as a general rule, "Too little is better than too much" (p. 204). Very important and very much to the point is their stipulation that the continuo "should never be decorated or quote thematic material" (p. 207).

Concerning today's usage we find a fair agreement that continuo playing in the concertos calls for a Mozartian fortepiano whose tone blends well with the orchestra, particularly the strings; that a modern concert grand has too brittle and thick a sound which fails to adapt to its musical environment. The contrast in timbre, tolerable and even acceptable in those solo passages where the piano takes on the role of antagonist, is unacceptable in the supporting part of the continuo.[10] Marius Flothuis points to the fact that Mozart conducted from the keyboard and that, in contrast to the role of the organ in church music, the continuo in the piano concertos served only as a technical performance help that we can do without today.[11] Charles Rosen is in full agreement: "As the size of the orchestra for concertos increased, the continuo became not only unnecessary but absurd as well." He gives good reasons to support the claim that the autograph continuo part for K 246 was prepared for a performance without winds, that is for string quintet alone. Hence, "this unique piece of evidence in Mozart's hand has no bearing on public performances of the concerto."[12]

Both of these writers make a good point, yet a *discreet* participation of a Mozartian fortepiano is an acceptable alternative. The emphasis is on discretion in order not to blur the structurally important solo-tutti polarity. For this reason the above mentioned solo-type improvisations over the continuo line are a stylistic aberration so grave that they amount to a distortion.

IN SUMMARY, the piano parts in Mozart's concertos contain "white spots" that were left unfinished. Where we can identify such spots with a degree of assurance we need to make additions and should do so with great care and modesty and without any aspirations to flamboyance. Simplicity of line is not necessarily a sign of "whiteness" when the passage is enlivened by the orchestra. The fact that in performance Mozart may well have embellished even beyond an otherwise self-sufficient text is not a valid defense for similar attempts by anybody who lacks Mozart's genius—which means of course everybody. The embellishments of Hoffmann, Hummel, and Ployer must not be taken as a model. When in doubt about the appropriateness of additions it will generally be best to refrain: even a Mozartian skeleton or sketch will be preferable to an attempt at completion that

[10]Among others, Hans Engel and Horst Heussner, in the preface to *NMA* V/15/6, p. XI, consider continuo playing on today's concert grands as inappropriate. They see occasional exceptions, such as the final measures in the last movements of both K 466 and 467, where the piano is to play the chords along with the orchestra.

[11]Preface to *NMA* V/15/1, p. X.

[12]*The Classical Style; Haydn, Mozart, Beethoven,* pp. 192–193.

carries the danger, demonstrated by Ployer's clumsy use of stock formulas, that one is destroying rather than reconstructing.

Clearly I have to disagree with Robert D. Levin where he writes: ". . .if modern performers tried to adopt the posture of performers as *composer* [meaning Mozart-like improvisation] Mozart's music would be played more profoundly, more expressively and above all more spontaneously—for spontaneity is an essential element of his art."[13] The Hoffmanns, Hummels, and Ployers, who were far closer to Mozart than we are, have shown that such sentiments are utopian.

I am far more in sympathy with Charles Rosen who, speaking of the slow movement of K 503, sees in it a beautiful combination of simplicity and lavish decoration "which it would be a pity to spoil by decorating the leaner phrases. I have myself added ornaments to a few measures when playing this work, and am very sorry for it now."[14]

[13]"Improvisation and Embellishment in Mozart's Piano Concertos," p. 3.

[14]*The Classical Style*, p. 258.

Instrumental Cadenzas

In Mozart's piano concertos cadenzas are a standard feature of every first, many third, and, until K 453, several second movements. Mozart uses as his cue for the placement of a cadenza in a movement the formula that was apparently already established for preclassical concertos: two fermatas, the first on the 6/4 chord of the tonic (or its bass alone) for the beginning of the cadenza, the second on the dominant seventh for its end. The spot usually occurs at the start of the coda. The cadenza proper is a free fantasia of undetermined length. It can consist of pure florid, usually virtuoso, figuration with no organic relationship to the movement, but will more commonly combine such passage work with the citation and elaboration of one or more themes from the movement.

Luckily, we have a goodly number of original Mozart cadenzas for the piano which offer us an insight into Mozart's style of improvisation and all-important models for what he did and did not want of a cadenza. We have specimens that range from his first independent concerto, K 175, to the last one, K 595. For some concertos we have two, for some even three, sets of cadenzas. But then, unfortunately, for a number of his greatest ones (among them the C minor, the D minor, the two C major ones, K 467 and 503, and a few others) we have none. Neither do we have any for concertos for any other instruments nor for solos in serenades, divertimentos, and the like.

Roughly, but only roughly, there is, for the piano, a trend toward growing thematic integration into the movement. Some of the early cadenzas (such as the first versions for K 238 or the first two versions for the *Lützow* Concerto, K 246) are very brief and nonthematic. The third version of K 246 does elaborate thematic material, but it may have been written at a later date. It is of interest that the cadenza to the first movement of K 175 already works with themes. The magnificent *Jeunehomme* Concerto, K 271, of early 1777 has two sets of cadenzas of which the second is a considerably improved reworking of the first. The second version for the first movement is already a sample of the Mozartian cadenza at its matchless best, achieving a degree of integration and unification that later cadenzas could hardly surpass. Besides the themes that are common to both the piano and the orchestra, this cadenza also elaborates with striking effect on the energetic bass fanfare that in the movement proper belongs to the orchestra alone.[1]

Mozart wrote many of his cadenzas for his students, or his sister, or other pianists who may have commissioned the concertos. Christoph Wolff speculates that Mozart wrote them mostly for his own use and guarded them jealously.[2] This is of course possible but hardly provable. In view of his fabled gift for improvisation they may be records, edited perhaps, of what he had done impromptu in performance. They could also have been shown to several students

[1] In view of this cadenza alone it is difficult to agree with Christoph Wolff that the cadenzas for the three first Viennese concertos, K387a (413), 385p (414), and 387b (415), represent a watershed in Mozart's stylistic evolution between pure figuration and thematic integration.

[2] "Zur Chronologie der Klavierkonzert-Kadenzen Mozarts," pp. 244–245.

Original Cadenzas

use or NOT ?

to study or copy, which could more easily explain why they were found among his papers than would the desire to withhold them for his exclusive use. Those found in Salzburg were probably written for the benefit of his sister. Mozart's letter of January 22, 1783, which Wolff quotes, says: "I have not yet changed the *Eingänge* in the Rondo [of K 271] because when I play the concerto I always do what comes to my mind." This is clear proof of improvisation which, as Marius Flothuis has pointed out in a personal communication, was hardly limited to this concerto alone.

The important question has been raised whether an original cadenza by Mozart has to be used by today's performers; whether, in the words of Robert D. Levin, they are "sacrosanct" or whether others can or even should be substituted.[3] Such substitution is hard to defend. Quite apart from our present-day concern for stylistic congruence, the fact remains that Mozart's cadenzas, whether written for himself or for others, whether based on his improvisation or independently invented, are often the product of a carefully planned compositional process, as witnessed by a few surviving sketches and by second revised versions. In the case of the great A major Concerto K 488, the first-movement cadenza is written into the autograph score as an integral part of the work. Strangely, it is the one that sounds most like a spur-of-the-moment improvisation: none of the major themes is cited and the only thematic link occurs at the beginning with a brief quote of a two-measure subordinated motive, the rest being pure passage work. But the fact that it was written into the score proves that the cadenza was conceived as part of the movement. Girdlestone's schoolmasterly suggestion to omit it and replace it cannot be taken seriously.[4] It may not be one of Mozart's most arresting cadenzas, but the passage work, charmingly interrupted in mm. 11-14 by a gentle phrase, is as good and effective as any. *All* of Mozart's cadenzas, beginning with the second version for K 271, are masterfully written, fitting structurally and of course stylistically as perfectly into the frame of the movement as if they had been conceived as part of it. Often they achieve the ultimate unification by functioning as a second development that shows some of the themes in a new light through their harmonic and melodic elaboration; thereby they intensify the dramatic tension that finds its resolution in the coda.

For such reasons I do believe that where we have an original cadenza it should be considered "sacrosanct" and not be replaced by a transplant that is bound to be inferior in invention, style and form. And that is exactly the problem with Robert D. Levin's thesis that improvisation and the concomitant uncertainty that promises surprises are of the cadenza's essence. That may have been true for audiences exposed to the excitement of witnessing a genuine, unprepared improvisation by an artist famous for such skill. Today such artists and the display of such skills have disappeared from the concert stage. Cadenzas we hear nowadays are all prepared or bought in the stores, and the "surprise" with which the audience can be expected to be regaled is more likely than not going to be an unpleasant one.

There are still other flaws in this train of thought. The usual and sensible goal of historical performance is to render a piece in the spirit of the composer. In an authentic Mozartian cadenza we have the manifestation of the composer's spirit bequeathed to us as clearly as notation permits. Are we to throw it away in the hope

___

[3]"Improvisation and Embellishment in Mozart's Piano Concertos," p. 11.

[4]*Mozart and His Piano Concertos*, p. 374, n. 1.

of finding more originality or more spontaneity? Who among today's pianists can presume to match his or her compositional or even improvisatory skill with a thought-out composition by Mozart? And every written work, by the mere fact of being written, was thought out with more judiciousness than any living act of improvisation. The process of notation by its mechanics alone slows the process of musical thought and turns improvisation into a deliberate creation. And those of today's pianists who can neither compose nor improvise—and they are the vast majority—turn normally to printed cadenzas by others, most of which are too long, too complex, too flashy, too wrong in style, and all too often too unmusical.

There are enough problems with the proper performance of Mozart's concertos that it is unreasonable to add to them by preparing or improvising cadenzas or *Eingänge* for which we have authentic Mozartian materials. Instead we have to turn to the question of how to prepare or, for one who has the gift of true improvisation, how to improvise cadenzas and *Eingänge* for which we do *not* have any authentic specimens.

Turning for guidance to the surviving original specimens we find that in all their variety they have several important traits in common, which give us a framework within which to work.

They are all relatively short, averaging for the first movements of the mature works between 25 and 35 measures. They quote one or more themes—not necessarily the most important ones—and show them in a different light either by melodic development (spinning out or fragmentation), or by *brief* harmonic digressions, but they never modulate into distant keys nor engage in fanciful polyphonic elaborations. In other words, they use on a moderate scale some of the procedures associated with a development section. Roughly half of their content is filled with nonthematic brilliant figurations, and they always end in a trill on the dominant seventh chord leading into the coda.[5]

These characteristic traits show that such cadenzas as Hummel's of more than 100 measures for the C minor, or Hoffmann's 110-measure piece for the C major Concerto K 503 are, simply by the fact of their excessive length, objectionable in form, not to speak of their overcharged figuration which is technically incompatible with the main body of the work. The style exemplified by the bloated specimens of the post-Mozartian generation persisted throughout the 19th and well into the 20th century and can even be found in the cadenzas of famous composers and performers. Beethoven's cadenzas to the D minor Concerto are fine compositions and technically reasonable, but they do not fit the work either; they are too long, and they modulate too soon and much too far afield; also the endless trill chains in the cadenza to the Rondo are a stylistic misfit.

Only rather recently, with the awakened concern for historical correctness, have a number of artists felt the need to return to the basic outline, the conciseness, and the relative simplicity of Mozart's own models. Among the finest specimens of such cadenzas are those by Paul Badura-Skoda[6] in which the author makes occasional, clever use of ideas by Hummel, Edwin Fischer, Lipatti, and for some *Eingänge,* by Mozart himself. Musically and stylistically admirable too are the cadenzas by the Dutch composer-musicologist Marius Flothuis who deserves special credit for having also written badly needed cadenzas for the violin, flute, bassoon, and horn concertos as well as for the Double Concerto for Flute and Harp.

[5]For greater detail in this matter see the chapter on cadenzas and *Eingänge* in Badura-Skoda.

[6]Published by Bärenreiter, Kassel, No. BA 4461

As a rule of thumb one should shy away from any cadenza that is more than 50 measures long, that has technical demands that are strikingly out of line with the main body of the movement, that modulates to, and dwells for any length of time in far-off keys, or that looks like a counterpoint exercise.

Since Mozart has written for one or another of the early concertos cadenzas that, even for the first movement, are only a few measures long, it would be easy to argue that cadenzas we have to supply should be as brief as possible to minimize the extent of non-Mozartian inserts. The argument is seductive but fallacious. A cadenza of more than a handful of measures is necessary to establish the planned formal balance of the great mature concerto movements. The cadenza must satisfy the expectation engendered by the fermata on the 6/4 harmony as well as the need to build up enough tension to secure a sufficiently dramatic impact to the tension's release when the cadential trill resolves into the orchestral coda. We have, after all, Mozartian thematic material to work with, and if we do so with restraint and taste we can achieve the length necessary for the architectural function of the cadenza without upsetting listeners with what they could feel is too much foreign matter. The main need is a true sense of proportion: we must do what is necessary to support the design, to keep the 6/4 chord from toppling too precipitously into the coda, while on the other hand being wary of long-windedness.

Whenever more than one solo instrument is involved, be it in double concertos, serenades, or chamber music, Mozart almost always wrote out any cadenza he wished to insert. (No cadenza survives for the Flute and Harp Concerto. Most likely he wrote one, as usual, on a separate sheet, and it was lost.) Where, incidentally, original cadenzas are as ideal in form, beauty, and of course, style, as those for the Sinfonia concertante or for the Two-Piano Concerto, it takes a heavy dose of presumption to try (like Lionel Tertis or Soulima Stravinsky) to replace them with one of one's own manufacture.

The Quintet for Piano and Winds has in its Finale a "Cadenza in tempo" of 46 measures: a free fantasia (with, perhaps, a brief allusion in the piano to the theme of mm. 150–154) worthy of its magnificent parent movement. The violin Sonata in D K 300l (306), too, has in its third movement a long cadenza that is thoroughly nonthematic throughout its 45 measures. The "Concertante" movement of the *Posthorn* Serenade has a cadenza of 15 measures, almost entirely given to the winds, that is thematically closely linked to the movement. For works of this type we might need an occasional *Eingang*, but by and large we do not have to worry about cadenzas.

For many pieces with solo melody instruments—the five violin concertos, the many violin solo movements in serenades and divertimentos, the concertos for clarinet, oboe, flute, horn, and bassoon, and several single concerto-style movements—the problem is far greater. We do not have a single original cadenza to serve as a model.[7] The cadenzas that come closest to serving as a model are the beautiful ones for the Sinfonia concertante for Violin and Viola: the first, 25 measures in 4/4; the second, for the slow movement, 18 measures in 3/4; in the final Presto rondo movement in lieu of a cadenza each instrument plays in turn a brief virtuoso run ending in a cadential trill. In this work, the combination of two

---

[7] Only in *Ein musikalischer Spass*, a spoof on incompetent composers and performers, do we find a violin cadenza that is uproariously funny; there is more humor in its single pizzicato note and its whole-tone scale than in the whole of some comic operas.

string instruments adds a new dimension by permitting easy harmonization (up to three parts) and even polyphony (see the beginning of the second cadenza). This heightened sonorous range increases the length to which the cadenza can be effectively extended. A violin solo cadenza, in view of the instrument's natural limitations, should be rather shorter. All the 19th- and many 20th-century cadenzas are far too long and resort to technical complexities to achieve harmonic depth or even polyphony or to startle the audience with acrobatic feats. The combination of anachronistic technical difficulties, stylistic incongruousness, and inordinate length makes such cadenzas a plague of recordings and the concert stage. Violin cadenzas should be relatively brief and simple; they can have some brilliant passage work but should be sparing with double and triple stops. Here again, we have some good examples by Paul Badura-Skoda and Marius Flothuis that, it is hoped, will set a new standard for the future.

Whereas the violin can, even within the Mozartian technical range, provide some harmonic support in double stops and occasional full chords, for the wind instruments the possibilities of sustaining interest and of thematic elaboration are smaller still. Here the cadenza for the first movement will best limit itself to quoting, after an *Eingang*-like introduction, one of the themes or a fragment thereof, then modifying it slightly, following it up with some brilliant passage work, and coming to the cadential trill without undue delay. Fifteen to 20 measures ought to suffice to accomplish this task and provide the necessary structural support to the movement. For the slow movement a few measures should be enough; they may start with a thematic quote leading into passage work whose speed must not be at odds with the prevailing mood. For the last movement the cadenza should be very brief; there need be no thematic recollection, and in the manner of the Sinfonia concertante the cadenza could consist mainly of a brilliant passage leading to the trill.

To the extent to which any general guidelines for cadenzas can be formulated, it can be said that one should keep them short and simple and not compound the unavoidable break in inspiration with an avoidable one in incongruence of style, of mood, of technique.

For a fitting close of this chapter Ex. 17.1 offers, with kind permission of the publishers Broekmans & Van Poppel, Amsterdam, Marius Flothuis's fine cadenza for the first movement of the C minor Piano Concerto.[8]

MARIUS FLOTHUIS, 1937

Ex. 17.1. Cadenza for the C minor Concerto, K 491/1

[8]Available at the same publishing house are Flothuis's cadenzas to the Piano Concertos in D minor, in E flat K 482, in D K 537, in C K 467 and 503; to the Concerto for Flute and Harp; and to the Flute Concertos in G and D. His cadenzas to the Violin Concertos Nos. 2, 3, 4, and 5 are published by Albersen & Co., Den Haag.

Ex. 17.1 *cont.*

Ex. 17.1 *cont.*

18 *Eingänge*

Eingang (plural *Eingänge*) is Mozart's own term for an ornamental passage that leads into a theme. An *Eingang* is always spelled out in orchestral music, usually spelled out in chamber music, and sometimes spelled out in soloistic music. Every so often, however, especially in concertos and related solos, it is left to the performer's initiative, to be inserted at a fermata sign. Its problems are different from those of a cadenza. It can occur anywhere in a movement; it serves as an introduction to an important theme, highlighting the latter by its preparatory thrust. It can start freely, that is, without link to what precedes, but more commonly it serves to connect the end of one phrase to the beginning of another.

Related to the *Eingang*, but serving a different function, in analogy to the vocal "end embellishments," are ornamental passages following a fermata, which extend a preceding phrase rather than prepare the following one.

The *Eingang*, in its proper sense as transitional embellishment, most frequently leads from dominant to tonic; as a rule it is fairly brief and nonthematic, consisting mostly of passage work, but we find exceptions to both of these characteristics. The two main problems are obviously determining where it is needed and how to design it. The answer to the desirable location is often fairly clear, but usually not as obvious as for a cadenza. A fermata on a note or a rest or on both is a necessary but not a sufficient signal that an *Eingang* is needed. Its most frequent and typical use occurs in rondo movements as a link between the end of a section and the reentry of the principal theme. Whenever we find in such a situation a fermata followed by the direct, that is unprepared, refrain the likelihood of an expected *Eingang* is so strong that the burden of proof is reversed: unless we can summon good reasons for avoiding it we can assume that the insertion of an *Eingang* is desirable.

For just a few illustrations see the Rondo of the D minor Concerto in mm. 166–167 where the wide fermata over the bar line is itself a strong indication that an insertion was expected. The spot is shown in Ex. 18.1a with a suggested solution in *b*. In cases like these the *NMA* either proposes a design or indicates in a footnote that an *Eingang* needs to be played. See for other characteristic locations the Rondo of the C major Concerto K 467, mm. 20 and 177, the first of which is shown in Ex. *c*, or that of the E flat Concerto K 482, m. 264, shown in Ex. *e*, with suggestions sketched in *d* and *f*, respectively.

a. K 466/3

Ex. 18.1.

b. perhaps

c. K 467/3 *d.* perhaps

Allegro vivace assai
Pfte

e. K 482/3

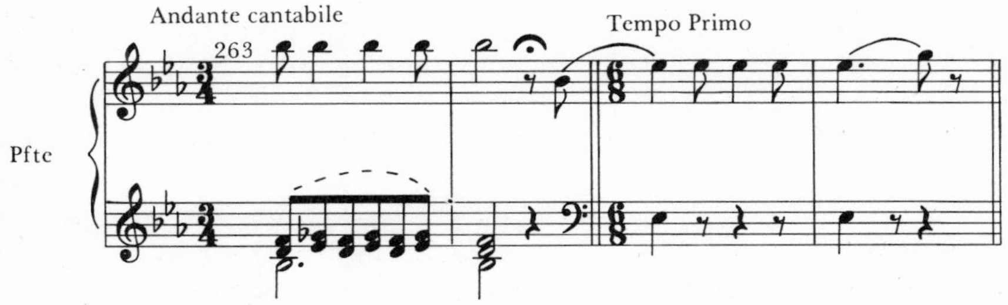
Andante cantabile
Tempo Primo
Pfte

f. perhaps

Ex. 18.1 *cont.*

There are other contexts besides the refrains of a rondo that call for an *Eingang*. It should be considered when a fermata leads to a theme that appears to enter too abruptly. Yet we also find spots that answer this description where such abruptness may have been intended and where consequently an *Eingang* would be undesirable. Then there are the unavoidable borderline cases where the decision to add or not can go either way. Intriguing in this connection is the case of the Andante of the G major Piano Concerto K 453. There are three spots, mm. 34, 68, and 94, where fermatas and brusqueness combine to make for a difficult decision. The spots are given in Exx. 18.2*a, c,* and *d.*

The first and third of these are close parallels. In both the break occurs between two phrases played by the solo piano; in both the first phrase is identical to the principal theme of the movement. It ends on a quarter-note, followed by a broad fermata that extends over the second and third quarter-note rests. By contrast, in the second *(c)* the same first phrase is played by the flute and comes to an end, on a half note (the other winds also stop at this point), followed by just a quarter-note rest with a fermata. The piano now reenters with an entirely new musical idea. Here it appears that the relatively small break is integral to the musical thought which involves a change of tone color and the surprise entrance of a new melody of different mood. Here we seem to have to do with a truly dramatic caesura that would be disturbed by an *Eingang*-like insertion. The problem cases are therefore limited to the twin spots of *a* and *d.*

The Badura-Skodas, who edited the work for the *NMA,* give no hint that insertions might be desirable. Charles Rosen specifically and very pointedly rejects any *Eingänge* for this movement. A case can certainly be made here for abstinence, and the strongest argument is probably the passage from the original cadenza, shown in Ex. *f,* where an *Eingang*-type figuration would have been spelled out. But there is no fermata here, whereas the three mentioned spots in the movement proper all have fermatas of which the two problematic ones, *a* and *d,* are of the broad design that, extending over two rests, usually signals the wish for embellishment. Also, had Mozart intended a brusque surprise entrance of the new themes there would have been no need for fermatas that, taken literally, open gaps so wide as to threaten the melodic continuity. With its pros and cons this is a borderline case. If *Eingänge* are introduced, they must be very modest, perhaps of the kind sketched in Exx. *b* and *e.*

Ex. 18.2.

The need for *Eingänge* is as frequent, if not more so, in concertos for melody instruments, and here again they are most likely to occur in the rondos.

In the Rondo Finale of the G major Violin Concerto there is in mm. 121–124 the written-out *Eingang* of Ex. 18.3*a* with the usual dominant-tonic harmony. In m. 217 before the next entrance of the refrain there is a telltale fermata (Ex. *b*), but also an unusual harmonic leap from the dominant of the parallel minor to the tonic. An *Eingang* is probably in order, but it has to traverse a larger harmonic distance. The Badura-Skodas make the good suggestion of Ex. *c*. The fermata of m. 251 leads to a section in andante alla breve, so drastically different that the very break in character, tempo, and meter is, as a dramatist's stroke, an integral part of the musical thought, and an attempt to smooth the brusqueness of the transition would be a mistake. At the end of this section the fermata rest on m. 290 should not be tampered with, the less so since the first eight measures of the Tempo I are a

Ex. 18.3.

bridge passage that takes the place of an *Eingang*. The final fermata of Ex. *d* in m. 377 is definitely in need of a transitional passage which can be somewhat longer since at the meeting place with the coda it can assume some cadenzalike features. A suggestion is essayed in Ex. *e*.

The Rondo of the D major Violin Concerto K 218 with its multitude of fermatas offers interesting challenges. The problem here is to avoid a sense of fragmentation without blurring intended contrasts. The first entrance of the Allegro theme after the fermata in m. 14 should probably be a surprise and therefore start unprepared. In m. 70, for the fermata preceding the return of the slow opening theme (Ex. 18.4*a*) a brief *Eingang* seems indicated, perhaps as sketched in *b*. When after the fermata in m. 84 the Allegro theme returns (Ex. *c*), the surprise effect is gone and a preparatory insertion, possibly as in *d*, seems desirable. For the new alla breve section starting after the fermata of m. 126, any addition would detract from the sudden change of meter, mood, and character. In m. 178, for the third appearance of the opening theme (Ex. *e*) an embellishment seems called for, if only as in the brief formula of Ex. *f*. At the fourth and final entrance of the opening theme in m. 210 (Ex. *g*) Mozart deleted an originally drafted virtuoso passage, then wrote at the end of the deletion across the double bar at mm. 209–210 one of his broad fermatas. By following the fermata with a single 8th-note d'''' he indicated in *a*—for him—unusual way his wish for an *Eingang* ending on that high note. For a suggestion see Ex. *h*.

A related case occurs in the Rondo of the E flat Piano Concerto K 482. In m. 217 piano and orchestra end on a fermata on the dominant seventh of A flat major, the tonality of the next section, followed by another fermata on a rest. The new section is a total contrast in tempo (andantino cantabile), in meter (3/4), and in mood. It is introduced by the orchestra alone, and probably for that reason the *NMA* does not suggest an *Eingang*. Yet some kind of insertion is possible and perhaps desirable, but again as in the preceding example it had better be of the end-embellishment type that extends what precedes rather than linking to what follows. A suggestion is given in Ex. *i*. In the flute Concerto in G, K 285c (313), m. 154 of the Rondo calls for an *Eingang*, and Ex. *j* gives a rough idea of what might be done.

Ex. 18.4.

Ex. 18.4 *cont.*

As said before, in chamber music the *Eingänge* are usually written into the score, but here and there we find spots where context plus fermata suggest an improvised insertion. Such a case is shown in Ex. 18.5*a* from the G minor Piano Quartet in the Rondo Finale connecting the end of a section with the reentry of the refrain. A possible solution is given in Ex. *b*. In the Rondo of the Four-Hand Sonata in C the fermata in m. 203 before the last reentry of the refrain (Ex. *c*) is a likely cue for an *Eingang,* possibly of the kind shown in *d*.

By contrast we find analogous transitions where no *Eingang* was intended. In the Finale of the C major String Quintet we find written-out brief *Eingänge* in mm.

Ex. 18.5.

38–41 and 249–252, but in mm. 210–211, shown in Ex. 18.6, the absence of a fermata and continuation of the regular beat indicate that the refrain was meant to enter unprepared.

Ex. 18.6.

Unusual is the case in the Finale of the Violin Sonata in F K 374d (376), mm. 60–65, and still more in its extension in mm. 139–149, which has the unmistakable character of an *Eingang,* its improvisatory nature underlined by the hold on the dominant ninth chord and an implied ritardando on the quarter-notes. It therefore seems that the fermata on the following rests means simply an unmeasured silence and is not a cue for extending the *Eingang.* A similar rest and not an *Eingang* is most likely intended in the Finale of the E flat Violin Sonata K 374f (380) in mm. 152 and 177. The very few spots in the violin sonatas that call for an improvised *Eingang* are noted in the *NMA* with fine suggestions for their execution by the editor Eduard Reeser. We find them among other places in the slow movement of the Sonata in B flat K 317d (378), mm. 30 and 44; in the last movement of the F major Sonata K 374e (377), m. 108; in the last movement of the Sonata in E flat K 481 bridging the transition from the fifth to the sixth variation. The Finale of the A major Sonata K 526 has a written-out *Eingang,* consisting of a—for the most part—chromatic rising scale in mm. 164–167.

Concerning the *design* of an *Eingang* it stands to reason that we should look to the many written-out specimens for models. But we must do so with a caveat. Mozart's *Eingänge* are very much more diverse in both length and character than the cadenzas and do not offer us a common denominator as a guide for a stylistically proper design. Whereas the cadenza is an indispensable structural pillar in the architecture of the movement, the *Eingang* has only the ornamental function of providing a smoother link between sections. Such a link need not be as long as some of Mozart's were when he gave free rein to his imagination. When we have to provide one it would be better to model it on Mozart's short, not his long specimens. Here truly we should be guided by the thought that, as long as the ornamental needs are satisfied, the smaller the un-Mozartian implant the better. There is hardly a gap that cannot be bridged by, say, a transition of three to four measures (or their equivalent in nonmeasured passage work).

Among Mozart's original *Eingänge* we find three interesting specimens in the Rondo Finale of the *Jeunehomme* Concerto. The first in m. 149 preparing the first reentry of the principal theme is very long. Actually called "cadenza" by Mozart, it is of cadenza length, but in its placement and corresponding function, its harmonic setting as well as its nonthematic nature, it is a genuine *Eingang*. The second specimen, shown in Ex. 18.7*a*, which leads to the Menuetto insert in the unusual design of this movement, is relatively short and a useful model for emulation. The third one, again rather substantial, prepares the final statement of the Rondo theme. For short, instructive specimens of an *Eingang* leading to the refrain of a Rondo see Ex. 18.7*b* from the Piano concerto in A K 385p (414) and Ex. *c* from the *Lützow* Concerto.

3 Types of Eingang

← leads to Menuetto insert

← prepared for Final statement of Rondo Theme

a. K 271/3

b. K 385p (414)/3

c. K 246/3

Ex. 18.7.

For a few other short *Eingänge* that deserve study see Ex. 18.8*a* from the Violin Sonata in E minor K 300c (304); Ex. *b* from the piano Rondo in D K 485; Ex. *c* from the Sonata for Two Pianos; Ex. *d* from the Piano Sonata in C K 284b (309); Ex. *e* from the Piano Sonata in B flat K 315c (333); and Ex. *f* from the Sonata in B flat K 189f (281). A somewhat longer specimen from the Sonata in D K 284c (311) is shown in Ex. *g*.

Ex. 18.8.

In the variations on the French children's song "La Bergère Célimène," K 374a (359), which are set in the simplest ABA form, there is a fermata in m. 8 at the transition from B to A in both the theme and all the variations. Since every time an *Eingang* is written out, the fermata is to be taken at face value; the fermata presumably implies a slight retard preceding it and adds an improvisatory touch to the *Eingang*. The *Eingänge* offer a rich Mozartian vocabulary and are given in Ex. 18.9 as a useful source of ideas where brevity is welcome (only variation 8 is omitted because its exchange of held-out notes between violin and piano is too specific to that particular spot to be transferable). A similar set of generally longer *Eingänge* from the variations on "Ein Weib ist das herrlichste Ding," K 613, can be found in Badura-Skoda (pp. 237–238).

Ex. 18.9.

SUMMING UP, *Eingänge* are a problem mainly in concertos and only occasionally in sonatas and chamber works where Mozart wrote out practically all the *Eingänge* he wished inserted. In concertos we find by far the highest incidence in rondo finales where the *locus classicus* is the transition to the refrain. Generally, the clue that an *Eingang* is desirable is a fermata on the dominant and what seems like an unjustified gap preceding a new phrase or section in the (prevailing) tonic. But the clue has to be interpreted with caution. When the new section is dramatically different, the very brusqueness of a sudden unprepared entrance can form part of the musical essence. There are no rules to guide us in such circumstances; only musical intelligence can make the decision whether linking or breaking is fitting in a specific situation. And where the decision goes for linking, brevity patterned on Mozart's *short* specimens will be the better part of wisdom.

Embellishments in Repeats

———————•◦•———————

In the Italian *da capo* arias of baroque opera seria it was expected that the singers would add embellishments to the *da capo*. Instrumental soloists who repeated a section generally did the same. An adagio written in skeletal notation even called for a measure of added embellishment the first time, with more florid embroidery in the repeat. In fast movements that offered little scope for added ornaments the soloist often varied the melody in the repeat without necessarily adding to the number of pitches, in which case we have to do not with embellishment but with nonornamental variants. Of the available documentation of such practices the best known is C.P.E. Bach's *Sonaten mit veränderten Reprisen*. There are many others. Geminiani, in a performance version of a Corelli sonata, offers embellishments for the slow movements and variants for the repeats of the fast ones,[1] and so do Franz Benda and many others (see *Ornamentation*, Ch. 49).

There is, however, no reason to assume that these procedures had any bearing on Mozart's instrumental music, in which we hardly ever encounter skeletal notation outside the piano concertos. As always there are exceptions. In piano solo works, but practically never in chamber music, here and there we find a spot that seems to call for some ornamental animation. Obviously such added embellishments apply only to soloistic music.

A much quoted case is a spot from the Piano Sonata in F K 300k (332) where the text of the autograph is ornamented in the first edition, as shown in Ex. 19.1. As explained before, changes in first editions can never be securely traced to Mozart (since the editors of the Viennese publishing houses were willful and Mozart may not have proofread). But here the change rings true. Considering that the movement, an Adagio in 4/4, is very slow, the 16th-notes of the first two measures gain by diminution, the passing notes on the syncopations have great charm, and in the fourth measure the exact repeat, a fourth higher, of the third measure is delightfully varied by the chromatic scale. Here Mozart's hand was unmistakably at work. The example, however, is dangerous because it can encourage players to diagnose as too plain passages that are best left alone. Extreme caution, tact, and humility are in order before we apply plastic surgery to an authentic Mozartian line.

Added ornaments or variations are believed by some to be called for in the repeats of a theme in the spirit of, say, Quantz's directives on how to play an adagio in the Italian style, where each repeat of a theme calls for a greater degree of embellishment.

Now it is perfectly possible that in performance Mozart playfully varied a theme in the repeat, though other than for slow movements in concertos we can, in the absence of any documentary evidence, only resort to speculation.

Looking for theoretical guidance, we find Quantz or C.P.E. Bach far out of touch with Mozart's style. Leopold's added embellishments are limited to a few standard formulas such as the *groppo* (the turn), the *Halbzirkel* (inverted turn), and

---

[1]Printed in John Hawkins, *A General History of the Science and Practice of Music*, pp. 904–907.

K. 300k (332)/2

1st ed. (Artaria 1784)

Adagio

Aut.

Ex. 19.1.

the *tirata* (the connection of two-notes by a scale or a scale in broken thirds).[2] They are a far cry from the fanciful coloraturas of many Italians and even of Quantz, Leopold then adds that even these very modest embellishments are to be used only for a solo and then only "very moderately, at the proper time, and only to bring variety to passages repeated in close succession."[3]

[2]*Violinschule*, 1756 ed., ch. 11, pars. 18–21.
[3]"Alle diese Auszierungen brauche man nur, wenn man ein Solo spielet; und dort sehr mässig, zur rechten Zeit, und nur zur Abwechslung einiger oft nach einander kommenden Passagen."

We have seen before that already at age seven Mozart objected to improvised embellishments, and we have no reason to assume that he changed his mind in his maturity; that outside of the special cases discussed in previous chapters, he never approved of, let alone expected, elaboration on his music by others.

Even the generally old-fashioned Türk allows only a narrow range for free embellishments. They are, he says, only permissible for spots that would otherwise be dull and tiresome and then only in the repeats. Though on occasion ("hin und wieder") one might change an allegro passage in the repeat, fairly sizable additions are made mostly in an adagio. He throws together ornamental additions (the examples are very modest), variants with changed pitches and the same or a smaller number of notes, and rhythmic alterations such as syncopation or dotting. Changes, he adds, must not be made for passages that are by themselves beautiful or lively enough, nor for works marked by sadness, seriousness, noble simplicity, pride, solemn grandeur, and similar character.[4]

Türk then presents in par. 25, in what appears to be meant as a deterrent example, a sizable fragment of a lavishly embroidered simple Adagio and adds that a clavier player of taste would not overload a melody "of some value" with the kinds of additions he has shown here. He rightly criticizes Hiller's ornamented Italian arias for overloading beautiful simple melodies and for overusing certain small ornaments.

Rare indeed are the cases where Mozart's melodies are in need of a helping hand. With melodic poverty eliminated as a pretext for added embellishments there remains the problem of literally repeated statements, the alleged site of desirable, if not required, ornamental additions.

Before we form the idea that literal repetition is aesthetically objectionable it behooves us to remember that repetition is the most important element of formal design in music (and architecture as well) and that a need for variety arises only when repetition breeds monotony. Mozart and other great masters avoid this danger by subtle alterations of various sorts: in rhythm, dynamics, tempo, color, orchestration, or written-out ornamental additions or thematic elaboration. For an illustration of a lovely variant by ornamental means see Ex. 19.2 from the duet of Pamina and Papageno.

Ex. 19.2.

[4]*Klavierschule*, 1789 ed., ch. 5, sec. 3, pars. 22–23.

There are, however, many instances where an exact repeat was probably intended. The most important circumstances suggesting literal repeats are 1) repeat marks; 2) the recapitulation in sonata form; 3) the *da capo*; 4) the refrain of a rondo. The question is whether the literalness implied by the notation was truly intended or meant to be modified by improvisation. The following pages essay some answers, which, by the nature of the matter, can only be tentative.

Repeat Marks

It is possible, perhaps even likely, that in performance Mozart made small additions in the repeat of a passage or a section, and a soloist who very discreetly adds here and there a *Vorschlag,* a trill, a slide, or a turn need not be condemned in principle. But such additions are hardly ever necessary. After all, we have repeats in orchestral music where impromptu embellishments are out of place, and the same is true of genuine chamber music (Türk sensibly prohibits embellishments whenever one or more of the other voices exceeds the role of pure accompaniment). Hence it cannot be argued that a literal repeat of a section is stylistically wrong.

These considerations indicate that even if we knew, rather than speculated, that Mozart as soloist embellished a repeat, we would not need to feel obligated to try to emulate him since there is a danger that instead of embellishing we might be defacing. One of Türk's principles sensibly demands that an embellishment must be significant and at least as good as the notated melody. "In the opposite case it would be better to leave the piece unaltered."[5] For a soloist, some change in tone production, in dynamics, in phrasing (such as a subtle rubato) in the execution of prescribed small ornaments will usually provide a sufficient measure of variety where such seems desirable.

Recapitulation

For the recapitulation in sonata form we can again find important clues in orchestral works and in chamber music. Mozart often resorts to the labor-saving device of not writing out that part of the first theme group that is to be exactly repeated but referring the copyist to a sign and the number of measures involved. Thus, in the first movement of the *Haffner* Symphony, he writes "Da Capo 12 Tackt" repeating only a small section of the group in the tonic key. In the second movement a *"da capo"* of 16 measures includes the whole first theme group. In the Presto Finale 10 *da capo* measures are just sufficient to recall the first theme after which Mozart turns to structural changes. If, given the orchestral setting, the wish for an exact repeat is implicit in these instructions, the same wish is made even more manifest in numerous other instances where Mozart spelled out such exact repetition in the autographs of orchestral works.

In the first movement of the B flat Symphony K 319 the first 24 measures of the exposition are written out in the autograph in the recapitulation without the smallest change in any instrument. In the last movement, beginning with m. 17, 32 measures are exactly repeated in the recapitulation and fully written out.

In the three last great symphonies all recapitulations are written out in the

---

[5]Ibid., par. 24.

autographs. In the first movement of the E flat Symphony the notes in the recapitulation are identical with no less than 39 measures of the exposition; there are, though, a few changes in the slurring patterns which are more likely due to oversight or unconcern for the niceties of consistency than to an intention of providing diversity.[6] For such an intention they are not noticeable enough, and besides they are reminiscent of similar discrepancies between the text of a composition and the *incipit* put down by Mozart in the catalogue of his works. In the Finale of the symphony Mozart adds a delightful touch of color to the beginning of the recapitulation by tracing the violin melody first an octave higher in the flute (mm. 153–156), then an octave lower in the bassoon, and by harmonically supporting the cadence in mm. 159–160 by woodwinds and horns: color, not ornament. The next 21 measures are identical to their counterpart in the exposition.

In the G minor Symphony the entrance of the recapitulation miraculously sneaks in before the end of the bridge passage; in mm. 168–172 a bassoon adds a countermelody, but mm. 173–84 are unchanged. In the second movement the first eight measures of the recapitulation are identical in substance, whereas in mm. 78 and 79 violas and basses enliven the accompaniment with no change in harmony. In the last movement the exposition starts with an eight-measure phrase that is exactly repeated, followed by another eight-measure phrase, also repeated. In the recapitulation these two repeats are omitted.

In the first movement of the *Jupiter* Symphony Mozart writes out for the recapitulation the repeat of the first 23 measures, literal in every detail. In the slow movement the recapitulation of the first theme is totally irregular—a rarity for Mozart—in that after the first measure is sounded he proceeds to develop it further; regularity returns with the second theme which, except for its usual return from dominant to tonic, is quite literal. In the extraordinary fugal-sonata movement, too, recapitulation of the first theme, beginning in m. 225, is enriched structurally by a contrapuntal line in the lower strings and coloristically by woodwinds and brass harmonic support.

The important lesson we can derive from these examples of symphonic movements (which could easily be multiplied) is that recapitulations are often exact repetitions and that any changes Mozart wished to make were either structural or coloristic, *not ornamental.* Coming from some of his most mature and sublime works the examples tell us that we are under no stylistic obligation to ornament any recapitulation.

THE DA CAPO

Da capo arias are rare in Mozart and the few he wrote date mostly from before 1771. We do find a number of *dal segno* arias as early as *Mitridate* and *Il sogno di Scipione* where the repeat starts in the middle of the A section. Often, as in *Mitridate,* No. 2, or *Il sogno,* No. 3, this section already contains such brilliant coloratura passages that any further embellishment would be senseless. In the early genuine da capo arias, as Eduard Melkus has pointed out,[7] a measure of extra embellishment in the *da capo* is indicated, if only to conform to a longstanding

---

[6]Editors whose sense of propriety is disturbed by such untidiness usually restore order "per analogiam."

[7]"Die Auszierung der Da-capo-Arien in Mozarts Werken."

tradition that had become a singer's uncontested franchise and quasi obligation. We may wonder whether Mozart turned to through-composed arias in part because he did not wish to be victimized by tasteless embellishers.

Among the strophic arias of *Die Zauberflöte,* the solemn grandeur of Sarastro's "In diesen heil'gen Hallen" should discourage any embroidery.[8] Papageno's songs reflect so perfectly his childlike simplicity that they too must be left alone: ornamental sophistication would denature the part. And in the three strophes of his "Ein Mädchen oder Weibchen" the written-out variants of the glockenspiel, and for the third time, the added woodwinds, take care of any need for change. In Monostato's song the musical essence resides in the orchestra; this fact alone, combined with the speed and nature of the vocal line, forbids any ornamentation. In the duet of Pamina and Papageno Mozart gently ornamented the second stanza, as shown in Ex. 19.2, and fittingly did so almost entirely in Pamina's part. Clearly, where Mozart wanted a variant he spelled it out.

THE RONDO

The rondo is another controversial matter. Several writers point to the great A minor Rondo, K 511, in which Mozart specified a number of ornamental variants on the many repeats of the theme. This example is then used as evidence of the desirability of introducing ornamental additions in other rondos where the written repeats are literal. Such an argument is dangerous because the A minor Rondo is not typical. Mozart's rondos are mostly vivacious and lighthearted, whereas the A minor one is slow (andante) and deeply personal, and its dominant mood is melancholic with tragic overtones. It is no coincidence that for another rondo in andante, (albeit in alle breve), K 494, Mozart also introduces small variants for each entry of the refrain. A slow melody is less able than a fast one to hold up under several literal repeats and therefore in greater need of gentle ornamental or rhythmic variants, and Mozart characteristically spelled them out. Also, a slow melody can be more readily ornamented in a manner that leaves its structural features in clear view.

By contrast, a lively theme is more likely to have its identity disguised by ornamentation, and in a rondo the basic identity of the refrain is the essence of the form. For that reason we find in the allegro rondos either no changes at all or only such minor ones as add a touch of variety without perceptibly altering the profile of the theme. We find such to be the case in the rondos written for orchestra—mainly in serenades and divertimentos; in the sonata-rondos of the great String Quintets in C, G minor, D, and E flat; in the piano quartets; in the Divertimento for String Trio; in violin sonatas, piano trios, and numerous other works where ornamental additions are either impracticable or out of place. In the piano concertos the rondo theme occurs more often because most of the time the orchestra echoes the soloist, but by the same token the differences in color and dynamics offer variety. The theme itself remains mostly unchanged and what changes are made are usually minor. In the Rondo of the A major Concerto K 488, we find such subtle variants as the change in the second part of the theme, shown

---

[8]I reported in Chapter 15 how Mozart's first Osmin, Ignaz Ludwig Fischer, who should have known better, was severely castigated by the *Allgemeine Musikalische Zeitung* for his bad taste and his arrogance in embellishing this very aria.

in Ex. 19.3a, to the form of Ex. *b* eight measures later when the orchestra takes up the refrain. The same syncopated idea recurs on the second statement of the theme in mm. 206–207, whereas on its third appearance woodwind harmonies add color to the second theme-half in mm. 445–448.

Ex. 19.3.

In the Rondo of the E flat Piano Concerto K 482 we find an unusual case: the theme is ornamented by three written-out turns that are left out in all its later appearances for both piano and orchestra. We do not have to do with an understood *simile* transfer of the ornament to all later appearances: first, the turns occur in part in the orchestra and section violinists were not meant to add ornaments not written in their parts; second, the ornamented version, because of its floridity, bears repeating less well than the simple theme that Mozart used in all subsequent appearances. Here variety is achieved by discarding rather than adding ornaments. On the other hand, Mozart brings in a few subtle rhythmic variants: the pattern of m. 3, shown in Ex. 19.4a, becomes that of *b* in m. 36 and again in m. 267, and that of *c* in m. 364, whereas the original rhythm returns in mm. 184 and 389.

Ex. 19.4.

The lesson to be learned from the study of the many allegro rondos, notably those written for media not admitting impromptu ornamental additions, is that the variants in the refrain of the two mentioned andante rondos must not be interpreted as models for the elaboration of rondo refrains that appear in literal repeats. In a rondo more than anywhere else the repeat itself lies at the heart of the musical structure.

SUMMING UP, it seems reasonable to say that ornamental additions on certain repeats may be proper but are rarely required; that only those who combine musical imagination, fine musicianship, and a thorough familiarity with Mozart's style should attempt to make them; that before making such alterations it will be well to consider whether a change of color or dynamics, or, say, in the *da capo* of a minuet, a slight change of tempo might not be sufficient to fill a strongly felt need for variety; that any addition deemed desirable be as discreet as possible, best limited to simple ornamental formulas: *Vorschläge,* slides, trills, passing notes, *cambiate* (the latter two delightfully illustrated in Ex. 19.2 from *Die Zauberflöte*). In most cases, though, it will be found that the repeat of a Mozart melody, however simple, is preferable to an ornamented version by Messrs. or Mesdames X, Y, or Z.

Appendix
List of Köchel Numbers and
Dates for Works Cited

———◆•◆———

The appendix is intended to serve as a cross-reference for the index, which lists Mozart's works by categories rather than dates. It should also help orient readers bewildered by the duplication of old and new numbers by systematically listing the correspondences.

The old numbers are those of the first edition of the catalogue of 1862; they are for most performers and listeners still far more familiar than the composite new ones. The new ones are those of the sixth edition of 1965 as are the dates listed in this appendix. Whenever there is a new number, it is listed first, followed in parentheses by the old one.

The Köchel numbers were meant to reflect the chronology of the works, but in the hundred years since their original listing, Mozart research has shown that many of the dates, and hence the numbers, needed revising. The first major adjustment was made by Alfred Einstein in the third edition of 1937. Then new insights growing out of the intensified research of the following decades called for the further large-scale revision that is embodied in the sixth edition of the catalogue.

The Piano Concerto K 449, completed on February 9, 1784, is the first work entered in Mozart's own catalogue, in which he listed and dated all his subsequent works until his death. Except for fragments and a few minor works we are therefore on firm ground for the chronology of the last seven years.

The numbers added in parentheses to the symphonies are the familiar ones and as such a concession to practicability. They derive from the *W.A.M.* and will serve our purpose, though they are not accurate.

23		Aria for soprano "Conservati fedele"	1765
33i	(36)	Recit. and Aria for tenor "Or che il dover" and "Tali e cotanti sono"	1766
36	see 33i		
46a	(51)	*La finta semplice*. Opera buffa in three acts	1768
47a	(139)	Missa [solemnis]	1768
51	see 46a		
61c	(70)	Recit. and Aria for soprano "A Berenice" and "Sol nascente"	1769
66		Missa in C (*Dominicus* Mass)	1769
70	see 61c		
73a	(143)	Recit. and Aria for soprano "Ergo interest" and "Quaere superna"	1770
73c	(88)	Aria for soprano "Fra cento affanni"	1770
73e	(77)	Recit. and Aria for soprano "Misero me" and "Misero pargoletto"	1770
74a	(87)	*Mitridate, Rè di Ponto*. Opera seria in 3 acts	1770
74c	(118)	*Le Betulia liberata*. Azione sacra in two parts	1771

77	see 73e		
87	see 74a		
88	see 73c		
118	see 74c		
126		*Il sogno di Scipione*. Serenata drammatica	1772
130		Symphony in F (No. 18)	1772
132		Symphony in E flat (No. 19)	1772
133		Symphony in D (No. 20)	1772
134		Symphony in A (No. 21)	1772
135		*Lucio Silla*. Dramma per musica in three acts	1772
139	see 47a		
143	see 73a		
167A	(205)	Divertimento in D for violin, viola, bassoon, bass, and 2 horns	1773
167a	(185)	Serenade in D for 2 violins, violas, bass, 2 oboes (flutes), 2 horns, and 2 trumpets	1773
173dB	(183)	Symphony in g (No. 25)	1773
174		String Quintet in B flat	1773
175		Piano Concerto in D (Mozart's first piano concerto; seven preceding ones, listed in Köchel under the five numbers 37, 39, 40, 41, and 107, and assigned numbers 1-5 by *W.A.M.* are adaptations from other composers; the ensuing confusion made it seem advisable not to number the piano concertos)	1773
179	see 189a		
183	see 173dB		
185	see 167a		
186a	(201)	Symphony in A (No. 29)	1774
186b	(202)	Symphony in D (No. 30)	1774
186c	(358)	Four-Hand Sonata in B flat	1774
186d	(195)	*Litaniae Lauretanae*	1774
186E	(190)	Concertone for two solo violins	1774
186f	(192)	Missa brevis in F	1774
186g	(193)	Dixit and Magnificat	1774
186h	(194)	Missa brevis in D	1774
189a	(179)	Twelve Variations for Piano on a Minuet by J.C. Fischer	1774
189b	(203)	Serenade in D for 2 violins, violas, bass, 2 oboes (flutes), bassoon, 2 horns, and 2 trumpets	1774
189d	(279)	Piano Sonata in C	1774
189e	(280)	Piano Sonata in F	1774
189f	(281)	Piano Sonata in B flat	1774
189g	(282)	Piano Sonata in E flat	1774
189h	(283)	Piano Sonata in G	1774
189k	(200)	Symphony in C (No. 21)	1774
190	see 186E		
192	see 186f		
193	see 186g		
194	see 186h		
195	see 186d		
196		*La finta giardiniera*. Opera buffa in 3 acts	1774-1775
200	see 189k		
201	see 186a		
202	see 186b		
203	see 189b		
204	see 213a		
205	see 167A		
205b	(284)	Piano Sonata in D *(Dürnitz)*	1775
207		Violin Concerto in B flat (No. 1)	1775

300g	(395)	Capriccio for Piano	1778
300h	(330)	Piano Sonata in C	1778
300i	(331)	Piano Sonata in A	1778
300k	(332)	Piano Sonata in F	1778
300l	(306)	Violin and Piano Sonata in D	1778
301	see 293a		
302	see 293b		
303	see 293c		
304	see 300c		
305	see 293d		
306	see 300l		
307	see 284d		
309	see 284b		
310	see 300d		
311	see 284c		
313	see 285c		
315c	(333)	Piano Sonata in B flat	1778
315d	(264)	Piano Variations on "Lison dormait" by Nicolas Dezède	1778
316	see 300b		
316a	(365)	Concerto for Two Pianos in E flat	1779
317d	(378)	Violin and Piano Sonata in B flat	1779
318		Symphony in G (Overture) (No. 32)	1779
319		Symphony in B flat (No. 33)	1779
320		Serenade in D *(Posthorn)*	1779
320d	(364)	Sinfonia concertante for violin and viola in E flat	1779
330	see 300h		
331	see 300i		
332	see 300k		
333	see 315c		
336a	(345)	Choruses and entr'actes to *Thamos, König in Ägypten*	1779
336b	(344)	*Zaide.* Singspiel in two acts	1779-1780
337		Missa solemnis	1780
338		Symphony in C (No. 34)	1780
344	see 336b		
345	see 336a		
353	see 300f		
354	see 299a		
358	see 186c		
359	see 374a		
360	see 374b		
361	see 370a		
364	see 320d		
365	see 316a		
366		*Idomeneo, Rè di Creta.* Opera seria in three acts	1781
367		Ballet music to *Idomeneo*	1781
368		Recit. and Aria for soprano "Ma, che vi fece, o stelle" and "Sperai vicino"	1781
368b	(370)	Oboe Quartet in F	1781
369		Recit. and Aria for soprano "Misera, dove son!" and "Ah non son' io che parlo"	1781
370	see 368b		
370a	(361)	Serenade for 13 Instruments in B flat	1781
373a	(379)	Violin and Piano Sonata in G	1781
374a	(359)	Violin and Piano Variations on "La Bergère Célimène"	1781
374b	(360)	Violin and Piano Variations on "Hélas, j'ai perdu mon amant"	1781
374d	(376)	Violin and Piano Sonata in F	1781

Appendix
———
285

Appendix

———

286

Bibliography of Works Cited

Abert, Hermann. W. A. Mozart. Reworked and enl. ed. of Otto Jahn's Mozart. 2 vols. 7th ed., Leipzig, 1955 (1st ed. 1919). Index, Leipzig, 1966.

Agricola, Johann Friedrich. Anleitung zur Singkunst, trans. from P. Tosi's Opinioni de' cantori, with extensive additions in different print. Berlin, 1757; facs. (ed. Erwin R. Jacobi) Celle, 1966.

Albrechtsberger, Johann Georg. "Anfangsgründe zur Klavierkunst." Aut. MS., GMF (XIV 1952).

Anderson, Emily, trans. and ed. The Letters of Mozart and His Family. 3 vols. London, 1938.

Arteaga, Stefano. Le rivoluzioni del teatro musicale italiano dalla sua origine fino al presente. 3 vols. 2nd ed. enl., varied, and corr., Venice, 1785.

Bach, Carl Philipp Emanuel. Versuch über die wahre Art das Clavier zu spielen.... Part 1, Berlin, 1753; 2nd ed., 1759; 3rd enl. ed., Leipzig, 1787. Part 2, Berlin, 1762; 2nd ed., Leipzig, 1797, Facs. Leipzig, 1957; English trans. and ed. William J. Mitchell, New York, 1949.

Bach, Johann Christian and F. Pasquale Ricci. Méthode ... pour le forte-piano ou clavecin. Paris [1786].

Badura-Skoda, Eva. "Improvisation, sec. I, no. 3, The Classical Period." The New Grove, vol. 9, pp. 43–48.

Badura-Skoda, Eva and Paul Badura-Skoda. Interpreting Mozart on the Keyboard. London, 1962. Trans. Leo Black from German ed., Mozart-Interpretation, Vienna, 1957.

————, eds. NMA V/15/5 (piano concertos).

Badura-Skoda, Paul. Kadenzen, Eingänge und Auszierungen zu Klavierkonzerten von Wolfgang Amadeus Mozart. Kassel, 1967.

Ballin, Ernst August, ed. NMA III/8 (songs).

Beyschlag, Adolf. Die Ornamentik der Musik. Leipzig, 1908; reprints Leipzig, 1953 and 1970.

Bisch, Jean. Explication des principes élémentaires de musique. [Paris, 1802].

Broder, Nathan, ed. Mozart, Sonatas and Fantasias for the Piano. Bryn Mawr, 1960.

Buelow, George. "A Lesson in Operatic Performance Practice by Madame Faustina Bordoni." In A Musical Offering: Essays in Honor of Martin Bernstein, ed. Edward H. Clinkscale and Claire Brook, New York, 1977.

Cajani, Giuseppe. Nuovi elementi di musica.... [Milan] n.d.

Cardon, Jean-Guillain. Le rudiment de la musique.... Versailles and Paris [c. 1786].

Clementi, Muzio. Introduction to the Art of playing the Pianoforte. Facs. reprint of 1st ed., 2nd issue (London, 1801), New York, 1974. Introduction by Sandra Rosenblum with reports on all later editions and changes therein.

Corri, Domenico. A Select Collection of the Most Admired Songs, Duetts, etc. from Operas in the highest Esteem. 3 vols. Edinburgh [vol. 1, c. 1777].

Dannreuther, Edward. Musical Ornamentation. 2 vols. London [1893–1895].

Dauscher, Andreas. Kleines Handbuch der Musiklehre und vorzüglich der Querflöte. Ulm, 1801.

Dittersdorf, Karl von. Karl von Dittersdorfs Lebensbeschreibung. Leipzig, 1801.

Döbereiner, Christian. Zur Renaissance alter Musik. Berlin, 1950.

Doles, Johann Friedrich. "Anfangsgründe zum Singen." MS, n.d., GMF 547/16.

Donington, Robert. The Interpretation of Early Music. New Version, New York, 1974.

Ebers, Carl Friedrich. Vollständige Singschule. Mainz [c. 1800].

Engel, Hans and Horst Heussner, eds. NMA V/15/6 (piano concertos).

Finscher, Ludwig, ed. NMA II/5/16 (Le nozze di Figaro).

Fischer, Kurt von, ed. NMA IX/24/26 (variations for piano).

Flothuis, Marius, ed. NMA V/15/1 and 4 (piano concertos).

Galeazzi, Francesco. Elementi teorico-pratici di musica.... 2 vols. Rome, 1791–1796.

Garcia, Manuel. A Complete Treatise on the Art of Singing. Part 2. Editions of 1847 and 1872, ed. and trans. Donald V. Paschke, New York, 1975.

Geminiani, Francesco. *The Art of Playing on the Violin*. . . . London, 1751; facs. ed. D. Boyden, Oxford, n.d.

Geoffroy-Dechaume, Antoine. "L'appoggiature ancienne." In *L'interprétation de la musique française aux XVIIème et XVIIIème siècles*. Paris, 1974.

Georgii, Walter. *Die Verzierungen in der Musik: Theorie und Praxis*. Zurich, 1957.

Gervasoni, Carlo. *La scuola della musica*. 2 vols. Piacenza, 1800.

Giegling, Walter, ed. *NMA* I/4/1 (*Die Schuldigkeit des ersten Gebots*); I/4/4 (cantatas); II/5/20 (*La clemenza di Tito*).

Girdlestone, Cuthbert. *Mozart and His Piano Concertos*. New York, 1964; repr. and corr. from 2nd (1958) ed. (First publ. London, 1948, under title *Mozart's Piano Concertos*.)

Gottron, Adam. "Wie spielte Mozart die Adagios seiner Klavierkonzerte?" *Musikforschung*, vol. 13 (1960), p. 334.

Haas, Robert M. *Aufführungspraxis der Musik, Handbuch der Musikwissenschaft*, Wildpark-Potsdam, 1931.

Hawkins, Sir John. *A General History of the Science and Practice of Music*, 5 vols. London 1776. Reprint of 2nd ed. (1853) New York 1961 in 2 vols.

Heartz, Daniel, ed. *NMA* II/5/11 (*Idomeneo*).

Hiller, Johann Adam. *Anweisung zum musikalisch-richtigen Gesange*. . . . Leipzig, 1774.

———. *Anweisung zum musikalisch-zierlichen Gesange* . . . . Leipzig, 1780. Facs. Leipzig, 1976.

Hüllmandel, Nicolas Joseph. *Principles of Music, chiefly calculated for the Piano Forte or Harpsichord*. . . . London [c. 1795].

Hummel, Johann Nepomuk. *Ausführliche theoretisch-praktische Anweisung zum Piano-Forte-Spiel*. Vienna, 1828.

Irmer, Otto von. "Preface" and "Appendix." Mozart, *Klavier Sonaten*. Cologne (Henle ed.), 1955.

Kalkbrenner, Christian. *Theorie der Tonkunst*. Berlin [1789].

Klein, Johann Joseph. *Versuch eines Lehrbuchs der praktischen Musik*. . . . Gera, 1783.

Knecht, Justin Heinrich. *Allgemeiner musikalischer Katechismus*. . . . Biberach, 1803.

———. *Kleine theoretische Klavierschule*. . . . Munich [1800].

Koch, Heinrich Christoph. *Journal der Tonkunst: Erstes Stück*, Erfurt, 1795.

———. *Musikalisches Lexikon*. . . Frankfurt am Main, 1802; facs Hilldesheim, 1969.

———. *Versuch einer Anleitung zur Composition*. 3 vols. Leipzig, 1782, 1787, 1793.

Köchel, Ludwig Ritter von. *Chronologisch-thematisches Verzeichnis sämtlicher Tonwerke Wolfgang Amadé Mozarts*. 6th ed., rev. Franz Giegling, Alexander Weinmann, and Gerd Sievers, Wiesbaden, 1964 (1st ed. Leipzig, 1862).

Kunze, Stefan, ed. *NMA* II/7/1-4 (arias, scenes).

Landon, H. C. Robbins, ed. *NMA* IV/11/9 (symphonies).

Lasser, Johann Baptist. *Vollständige Anleitung zur Singkunst*. Munich, 1798. (2nd ed. 1805 is identical.)

Leroy, P. *Flötenschule für die ersten Anfänger*. Berlin, n.d. Trans. from French *Petite méthode da flûte*.

Levin, Robert D. "Improvisation and Embellishment in Mozart's Piano Concertos." *Musical Newsletter*, vol. 5, no. 2 (Spring 1975), pp. 3–14.

Löhlein, Georg Simon. *Anweisung zum Violinspielen*. . . . Leipzig and Züllichau, 1774.

Liverziani, Giuseppe. *Grammatica della musica*. . . . Rome, 1797.

Mancini, Giambattista. *Riflessioni pratiche sul canto figurato*. 3rd ed., Milan, 1777.

Manfredini, Vincenzo. *Regole armoniche*. 2nd corr. and enl. ed. Venice, 1797.

Marpurg, Friedrich Wilhelm. *Anleitung zum Clavierspielen*. . . . Berlin, 1755; facs. New York, 1966.

———. *Kritische Briefe über die Tonkunst*. . . . Vol. 2, part 3. Berlin, 1762.

Martiensen, C. A. and Wilhelm Weismann, eds. Mozart, *Sonaten für Klavier zu zwei Händen*. Frankfurt am Main (Peters), 1951.

Melkus, Eduard. "Zur Auszierung der Da-capo-Arien in Mozarts Werken." *MJb 1968-70*, pp. 159–185.

Merchi, Joseph Bernard, *Traité des agrémens de la musique, exécutés sur la guitarre*. Paris [1777].

Milchmeyer, Johann Peter. *Kleine Pianoforte-Schule für Kinder, Anfänger und Liebhaber*. . . . Dresden, 1801.

———. *Die wahre Art das Pianoforte zu spielen.* Dresden, 1797.

Mishkin, Henry G. "Incomplete Notation in Mozart's Piano Concertos." *Musical Quarterly,* vol. 61 (July 1975), pp. 345–359.

Mosel, Ignaz Franz. *Versuch einer Aesthetik des dramatischen Tonsatzes.* Vienna, 1813.

Mozart, Leopold. *Versuch einer gründlichen Violinschule.* . . . Augsburg, 1756; 2nd ed., 1769 and 1770; 3rd enl. ed., 1787; facs. (1st ed.) Vienna, 1922; facs. (3rd ed.) Leipzig, 1956.

Mozart, Wolfgang Amadeus. *Letters.* See Anderson, Emily and Schiedermair, Ludwig.

———. *Verzeichnüss aller meiner Werke vom Monath Febrario 1784 bis Monath.* . . [November 1791]. Aut. MS at Library of Congress. Facs. Vienna, 1938; New York, 1956.

Müller, August Eberhard. *Elementarbuch für Flötenspieler.* Leipzig, n.d.

Die Musik in Geschichte und Gegenwart ("MGG"). 16 vols. Edited by Friedrich Blume. Kassel, 1949–1979.

Neue Mozart Ausgabe. Kassel, 1955–.

Neumann, Frederick. "Appoggiatur und Vorschlag in Mozarts Rezitativ." (Enl. German version of Ch. 12 in this book.) *MJb 1980-83,* pp. 363–384.

———. *Essays in Performance Practice.* Ann Arbor, 1982.

———. *Ornamentation in Baroque and Post-Baroque Music: With Special emphasis on J. S. Bach.* Princeton, 1978.

Neumann, Hans and Carl Schachter. "The Two Versions of Mozart's Rondo K. 494." *Music Forum,* vol. 1 (1967), pp. 1–34.

Niemetschek, Franz Xaver. *Leben des k. k. Kapellmeisters Wolfgang Gottlieb Mozart.* Prague, 1798.

Nopitsch, Christoph Friedrich Wilhelm. *Versuch eines Elementarbuchs der Singkunst.* Nördlingen, 1784.

Petri, Johann Samuel. *Anleitung zur praktischen Musik.* 2nd. ed. Leipzig, 1782; facs. Giebing über Prien am Chiemsee, 1969.

Plath, Wolfgang and Wolfgang Rehm, eds. *NMA* II/5/17 *(Don Giovanni);* VIII/22/2 (piano trios).

Pleyel, Ignaz Joseph. *Klavierschule.* 3rd improved and enl. ed. Vienna, n.d.

Quantz, Johann Joachim. *Versuch einer Anweisung, die Flöte traversiere zu spielen.* . . . Berlin, 1752; facs. of 3rd ed. (Breslau, 1789), which is identical with the first except for some modernized spelling, Kassel, 1953; English ed. and trans. Edward R. Reilly, *On Playing the Flute,* London, 1966.

Reeser, Eduard, ed. *NMA* VIII/23/1-2 (sonatas and variations for piano and violin).

Rehm, Wolfgang, ed. *NMA* V/15/8 (piano concertos); IX/24/2 (piano works for four hands); see also Plath, Wolfgang and Wolfgang Rehm.

Reichardt, Johann Friedrich. *Über die Pflichten des Ripien-Violinisten.* Berlin und Leipzig, 1776.

Reinecke, Carl. *Zur Wiederbelebung der Mozart'schen Clavier-Concerte.* Leipzig, 1891.

Rellstab, Johann Carl Friedrich. *Versuch über die Vereinigung der musikalischen und oratorischen Declamation.* . . . Berlin [1786 or 1787].

Rosen, Charles. *The Classical Style: Haydn, Mozart, Beethoven.* New York, 1972.

Sabbatini, Luigi Antonio. *Elementi teorici della musica.* . . . Rome, 1789.

Schenker, Heinrich. "A Contribution to the Study of Ornamentation." Rev. and enl. ed. *Music Forum,* vol. 4 (1976), pp. 11–139. Trans. Hedi Siegel from German *Ein Beitrag zur Ornamentik,* Vienna, 1904; rev. ed. 1908.

Schiedermair, Ludwig. *Die Briefe W. A. Mozarts und seiner Familie.* 5 vols. Munich, 1914.

Schilling, Gustav. *Enzyklopädie der gesamten musikalischen Wissenschaften.* With various collaborators. 6 vols. Stuttgart, 1835–1838.

Schmitz, Hans-Peter. *Die Kunst der Verzierung im 18. Jahrhundert.* Kassel, 1955.

Scholz, Heinz and Robert Scholz, eds. Mozart, *Klaviersonaten.* Vienna (Universal ed.), 1950.

Schubert, Johann Friedrich. *Neue Singe-Schule.* Leipzig [1804].

Schulz, Johann Abraham Peter, in J. G. Sulzer's *Allgemeine Theorie der schönen Künste.* Berlin, 1771–1774; facs. Hildesheim, 1967–70.

Senn, Walter, ed. *NMA* IV/12/4-5 (serenades for orchestra).

Steglich, Rudolf. "Das Auszierungswesen in der Musik W. A. Mozarts." *MJb 1955,* pp. 181–237.

Tagliavini, Luigi Ferdinando, ed. *NMA* II/5/4 *(Mitridate, Rè di Ponto).*

Tartini, Giuseppe. "Regole per arrivare a saper ben sonare il violino. . . ." MS Bologna; facs. as supplement to German-French-Italian publication *Traité des agréments,* ed. Erwin R. Jacobi, Celle and New York, 1961. French trans. P. Denis, Paris, 1771; German and English translations based on Denis's partially unreliable French version, before the original was discovered c. 1960 in a MS by Tartini's student G. F. Nicolai.

Telemann, Georg Philipp. *Der harmonische Gottesdienst.* Hamburg, 1725–1726.

Tosi, Pier Francesco. *Opinioni de' cantori antichi e moderni, o sieno osservazioni sopra il canto figurato.* Bologna, 1723; facs. as supp. to J. F. Agricola, *Anleitung,* facs. ed. E. R. Jacobi, Celle, 1966.

Tromlitz, Johann Georg. *Ausführlicher und gründlicher Unterricht, die Flöte zu spielen.* Leipzig, 1791.

Türk, Daniel Gottlob. *Klavierschule.* . . . Leipzig and Halle, 1789; facs. Kassel, 1962. 2nd enl. and corr. ed. Leipzig and Halle, 1802.

W. A. Mozarts Werke. Complete, crit. reviewed ed. in 24 series. Leipzig, 1876–1905.

Wolff, Christoph. "Zur Chronologie der Klavierkonzert-Kadenzen Mozarts." *MJb 1978–79,* pp. 235–246.

————, ed. *NMA* V/15/2-3 (piano concertos).

Wolff, Hellmuth Christian. *Original Vocal Improvisations: From the 16th-18th Centuries.* Trans. A. C. Howie. from German. Cologne, 1972.

For further references see *Mozart-Bibliographie (bis 1970),* compiled by Rudolph Angermüller and Otto Schneider, *MJb 1975* (whole issue), and its supplement (same compilers), *Mozart-Bibliographie 1971–75,* Kassel, 1978.

Index

Page numbers in italics indicate musical examples. "Mozart" without initials refers to Wolfgang Amadeus.

ABBREVIATIONS

acc.	accompaniment	interp.	interpretation
appogg(s).	appoggiatura(s)	*N'g*	*Nachschlag*
arpg.	arpeggio	orn(s).	ornament(s)
emb.(s)	embellishment(s)	perf.	performance
ferm. emb(s).	fermata embellishment(s)	rec.	recitative
impr.	improvisation	*V'g*	*Vorschlag*
instr(s).	instrument(s)	*Zw'g*	*Zwischenschlag*
instr'l	instrumental		

I. WORKS

Works are given in the order of the *NMA*, which follows the Thematic Overview of the Köchel catalogue.

SACRED VOCAL WORKS

Masses and requiem
  Mass in C, K 47a (139), 44–*45*
  Mass in C, K 66 ("Dominicusmesse"), 44, *90*
  Missa brevis in F, K 186f (192), *68,* 114–115
  Missa longa, K 246, 98
  Credo Mass, K 257, 29–*30*
  Mass in C, K 317 ("Coronation"), 82
  Missa solemnis, K 337, 28–*29, 43,* 49–*50,* 90–*91*
  C minor mass, K 417a (427), 7, *20,* 25
  Requiem, K 626, *18,* 90–91, *153*
Litanies and vespers
  'Dixit' et 'magnificat,' K 186g (193), *132*
  Litaniae Lauretanae, 91, *118,* 126–*127,* 130
Minor sacred works
  Sancta Maria, K 273, 57, 90–91
Oratorios, cantatas, etc.
  La Betulia liberata, K 74c (118), *35, 58, 60,* 65, 211–*212*
  Freimaurerkantate, K 623, 20–21

STAGE WORKS

Operas
  La finta semplice, K 46a (51), *18*
  Mitridate, K 87, 25, *195,* 279
  Il sogno di Scipione, K 126, 279
  Lucio Silla, K 135, 230–*233*
  La finta giardiniera, K 196, 28–*29, 54*
  Il rè pastore, K 208, 216–217
  Zaide, K 336e (344), 28–*29, 43,* 91, *213*
  Idomeneo, K 366: appogg., *20,* 209–*210,* 211–*212;* aria embs., 230, 239; coordination of vocal with instr'l line, *20,* 80; ferm. embs., 217–218, 223, 229; grace note, 66, *68;* rec. appogg., 191–*192,* 196–*197,* 201–*202;* slide, 99; turn, 154–*155,* 161, *163; Zw'g,* 93–94
  Die Entführung aus dem Serail, K 384: appogg., 16–*17, 19,* 23–*24,* 26, *52;* aria embs., 230, 234; coordination of vocal

with instr'l line, *80;* ferm. embs., 227–*228;* grace note, 47–*48,* 52; slide, 98, *100*–*103;* turn, *135, 156; Zw'g,* 91–92, 94–*95*
  Der Schauspieldirektor, K 486, 21–*22,* 80, 98
  Le nozze di Figaro, K 492: appogg., *16,* 20–*21,* 26–*27,* 204–*211,* 213–*214;* aria embs., 230, 239; coordination of vocal with instr'l line, *25,* 209–210; ferm embs., *217, 224*–*225;* grace note, 58, 87–*88;* mordent, *58;* rec. appogg., *192*–*197,201*–*202;* slide, 98, *101*–*102;* trill, 120–*121;* turn, 154–*155*
  Don Giovanni, K 527: appogg., 16–*17,* 21–22, 26–*27, 39, 52,* 204–*214;* aria embs., 230, 239, 246; arpg., 174–*175;* coordination of vocal with instr'l line, 24, 174. 209–210; ferm. embs., *217,* 225–*228;* grace note, 44, *46–48,* 53–*54, 59,* 87–*88;* Lombard rhythm, 39n; mordent, *59;* rec. appogg., *191*–201; slide, 98, *100*–*102;* trill, *123,* 126–*127;* turn, 145, 158
  Così fan tutte, K 588: appogg., *19, 25, 39,* 208–209, 212–*213;* coordination of vocal with instr'l line, *25,* 209; ferm. embs., *217*–*223;* grace note, 47, 53–*54;* Lombard rhythm, 39n; rec. appogg., *191*–*192;* trill, *110;* turn, 158; *Zw'g,* 91
  Die Zauberflöte, K 620: appogg., 16–*17, 19,* 23–*24,* 25–*26,* 204–*205,* 208–*210,* 212–*213;* aria embs., 230, 234–239, 280; coordination of vocal with instr'l line, *19,* 24–25; ferm. embs., *217,* 227–*228;* grace note, 44–*45;* rec. appogg., *192,* 197–*198,* 201; repeated passages, embs. of, 277, 280–281; slide, *99*–*102;* trill, 120–*122,* 127–*128;* turn, 85n, 155, 161–*163; Zw'g,* 90, 93–*94*
  Le clemenza di Tito, K 621, 99, 101–*102,* 218
Music for plays, ballet, etc.
  Thamos, König in Ägypten, K 336a (345), 174–*175*
  Idomeneo, ballet music, K 367, 92–*93*

turn formula: definition, 81
turn-trill, 104, 106, 111, 124, 133–134

Verdi, Giuseppe: drum rhythms in *Il trovatore* and *Les Vêpres siciliennes*, 103n
Vignati, Giuseppe: improvised emb., 180
Vorschlag, ch. 1; beat placement of, 8–10, 14, 37, 42; in cadential formula, 76; coordinated with arpg. in parallel lines, 173; denomination of, 16, 18–20, 30–38, 40, 46, 50–51, 53, 55, 57–58, 62, 64–70, 75, 77–78, 80; downward leaping, 35–36, 62–63; equalization applied to turn and scale formulas, 81–89; guidance of: articulation, 60, 65, 75, context, 18, 36, diction, 18–19, 23–24, 28, 30, 42, 53–54, 65, dynamics, 8–10, 14, 42, 47, 54–55, 65, 87, expression, 18–19, 23, 31, 35, 40, 42, 63–64, 77–78, 80, 87, harmony, 20, 40, 42–43, 73, 87–88, melody, 42, 47, 62–63, 65, 73, 74–75, 78, 87, rhythm, 42, 44, 47, 55–62, 65, tempo, 46, 60, 62, 65, 70, 77–78, 87, 89, word meaning, 20, 23–25, 28, 30, 52; metric value, 11, 14, 18–19, 32–38, 40; in scale and turn formulas, 81–89; before staccato notes, 42, 44, 47, 49, 72, 75, 78, 82; symbolized, 16, 31–34, 53, 63, 66–69, 71, 74, 78; in *tierces coulées* context, 39, 76–81; vs. *Zw'g*, 90; upward leaping, 36, 73, 75; written out, 52–53, 66, 71, 85. See also *acciaccatura;* Agricola; appoggiatura;

Bach, C. P. E.; Bach, J. C.; Bisch; Dannreuther; Doles; Dussek; Gervasoni; grace note; Haydn; Hiller; Klein; Knecht; Lasser; Milchmeyer; Petri, Pleyel; Quantz; Ricci; slide; Steglich; Türk; *Zwischenschlag*

W. A. Mozart's Werke (W. A. M.); coordination of vocal and instr'l lines., 24–25; Lombard rhythm, 38; as source, ix; turns, 147; *Zw'g,* 92
Wagner, Richard: on Mozart's tempos, 155
Wartensee, Xaver Schnyder von, 247
Weber, Aloysia, 231, 234
Weinmann, Alexander, 4
Weismann, Wilhelm: interp. of Mozart's trill, 112, 116, 120, *130*
Winter, Peter: improvised emb., 180
Wolff, Christoph, 244, 254, 257–258

Zwischenschlag, ch. 6, 76; guidance of: context, 91–93, 96, diction, 90, dynamics, 92, 94, expression, 92, 95, melody, 91, 94–95, rhythm, 91–93, 95, tempo, 92–93, 95; *NMA,* 90, 92–93; before nonharmonic notes, 93, 96; notation, 91–92, 94–95; repeated within even notes, 93, 96; before single notes, 95–96; before staccato notes, 92, 96; before syncopation, 91, 93; before thematic rhythm, 92, 96; before triplets, 92, 96; *W. A. M. 92*

Library of Congress Cataloging in Publication Data

Neumann, Frederick.
Ornamentation and improvisation in Mozart.

Bibliography: p.
Includes index.
1. Mozart, Wolfgang Amadeus, 1756–1791—
Criticism and interpretation.   2. Embellishment
(Music)   3. Improvisation(Music)   I. Title.
ML410.49N26   1985   780′.92′4   85-42694
ISBN 0-691-09130-7 (alk. paper)